A GATEWAY TO HOPE

Also by E. C. Jackson

A Living Hope
Pajama Party: The Story

A GATEWAY TO HOPE

a novel

E. C. Jackson

ISBN: 978-0-9961812-2-8

Editing: jenichappelle.com
Proofreading: amberbarryeditor.com
Cover design: indiecoverdesign.blogspot.com
Typesetting: FormattingExperts.com
Book Blurb: standoutbooks.com

The Write Way – A Real Slice of Life: ecjacksonauthor.wordpress.com
Author Page: facebook.com/ecjacksonauthor
Designed by Standoutbooks

Acknowledgments

God's love, mercy, and grace fostered my dream of writing this book until full grown.

Throughout the journey, cheerleaders kept me focused, beginning with Mom, and also Dad, who passed away two weeks after my fourteenth birthday. Thanks also goes to three sisters, one at home with the Lord, and nieces and nephews, especially the nephew who admonished me to write. A beloved aunt and many cousins constantly pray for my success. And friends and co-workers have blessed me beyond measure.

Many individuals I have never met sharpened the presentation along the way.

Thank you, one and all, for believing that God might do a good work through me.

List of Main Characters

The Laceys
Nikhol "Neka" Lacey

Parents:
Karen and Lawrence

Sisters:
Kelly, married to Michael Smith
Tammy, engaged to Kenny Latham

The Copleys
James Copley

Parents:
Fran and Gene

Sister:
Brandie, married to David McKinley

Brothers:
Ryan, married to Sandi
Matt, married to Celia

Friends and Non-Immediate Family Members
Teri Campbell: James's ex-fiancée and Kelly's friend
Maureen and Charles McKinley: James's godparents and David's parents
Hazelle Singleton: Neka's cousin

"But now I am going to woo her — I will bring her out to the desert and I will speak to her heart. I will give her her vineyards from there and the Akhor Valley as a gateway to hope. She will respond there as she did when young, as she did when she came up from Egypt."

Hosea 2:16(14)-17(15)
The Complete Jewish Bible

Chapter One

Nikhol Lacey stepped into the muted glow from the wall sconce above the door, grabbed her luggage from the porch, and hurried down the stairs. The path lights cast a shining arc across the yard. Pine scented the air, and fresh-cut grass clung to her sandals.

She sidestepped debris along the footpath to avoid snapping any twigs. To anyone looking, the maneuverings would have resembled a child's game of hopscotch. It seemed like ages had passed, but at last she reached her destination. Lips curving into a fleeting smile, she placed her cases at the cab driver's feet.

After shaking her hand, he lifted the bags. His raspy voice broke the silence. "Good morning ..."

"Call me Neka."

She scooted into the car and eased the door shut behind her. But she froze in place when the noisy driver stomped every twig she had missed and slammed the trunk. Her gaze swept over the second-floor windows. The house remained dark inside.

Good. No signs of movement.

Neka lay back on the cushion but bolted upright when the driver sped away, crunching loose twigs scattered across the road.

She brushed her fingers over her neck and chest and then clung to the front of her T-shirt. Familiar landmarks silhouetted against the dusky morning. She sighed, touching the window as her home faded into the receding darkness.

Regret surfaced. Would her family understand her leaving home without notice? Massaging her right earlobe, she laid her head against the seat.

James needed her. She was the only person able to help him. Finally, someone she cared about required assistance that only she could provide. Tears blurred her vision at the admission that she often felt unneeded. Self-

1

revelation came at a price. Closing her eyes, Neka laid her face into the palms of her hand.

She was committed. It was too late to turn back now.

Lord, help me.

* * *

James Copley stood half hidden in the shadows outside the Tulsa airport terminal. He contemplated the disruption to his plans, sighing as he shoved the cell phone into his pocket. Through the window, he watched a stooped man swishing a mop over the lobby floor.

He jerked around and frowned when a car pulled up to the curb behind him. The taxi dropped off an older man in plaid shorts, who hurried into the building without noticing James's six-foot frame standing to the side.

The stillness shifted. Red and orange lights streaked a pattern across the eastern sky. Dawn hovered on the horizon as the night subsided into a brand-new day.

The quiet June morning sprang alive. Steady streams of cars carrying a bevy of people rolled down the street. A white four-wheel-drive SUV pulled to a stop in the no-park zone. A gray-haired lady dropped off a family of five, and they hugged their farewells. When the SUV drove away, it was replaced by a black sedan. A jean-clad man exited the passenger's seat, laughing as he waved good-bye. Vehicles continued replacing each other in fast succession.

The touching scenarios highlighted his fiancée's absence. Did Teri over-sleep or have a car accident on the way to meet him? He rejected those ideas, struggling to remember her travel plans. Had she mentioned who would bring her to the airport? Or had he assumed she'd order a cab as he'd done?

Leaving the milling people, he searched for a secluded corner. The spot he chose placed him closer to the curb, though he remained a great length away from the cars. James was a master planner and detested surprises he didn't spring. Not that he willfully devised sneak attacks behind anyone's back. He just worked overtime to ensure no one else affected him with their unpredictability.

A no-show Teri Campbell dealt a harsh blow to plans he'd thought he'd carved in stone. His mind replayed the strategy he'd conceived four weeks ago. Jaw muscles pulsated as he clenched his teeth and bit down hard. An old sinking feeling rose at an alarming rate and failed to retreat when ordered.

Get a grip, man. You can do this. James was no longer the thirteen-year-old boy with lofty ideas.

He glanced at the clock in the lobby and shook his head. Six o'clock. Their flight would depart in ninety minutes. The cell phone had made it halfway out of his pocket before he realized and pushed it back into place. Knowledge of Teri's scheming nature stopped him from calling her.

Why now? Like most people, he hated fighting a hidden foe. No one could adequately prepare for an unknown assault. Without sufficient warning he was just an unarmed soldier in the midst of battle.

As he forced his back against a pillar, James cringed at the thought of abandoning his plan. A sudden chill struck him, as if a northern wind swirled around him. He willed his mind to focus and weigh the situation. The unfurling trouble begged a response, but the wishy-washy brigade held no sway over him. Once he reached a decision, he stayed the course.

Frowning, he stepped forward to reaffirm his resolve. In spite of Teri's absence, his plans would proceed without another hitch. Snags to his plans didn't matter. After living six years on the periphery of his family, James craved their acceptance more than ever. His life was spartan and geared to obtain his primary goal—running the family company. He closed his eyes but failed to block out the memory: days and nights occupied with endless planning, strenuous labor, and not enough rest in between.

But those times were gone forever. Years of hard work with minimal play had paid off. It was time to return home and prove to his folks that life existed after mistakes and bad decisions.

He relaxed his knotted shoulders. He hadn't spent half a decade spinning a web to see it dissipate without ensnaring its prey because of one little snag. This trip was crucial. A lifetime of professional achievements depended on its outcome. He narrowed his eyes as he considered Teri's inflexibility when they'd spoken yesterday. She'd refused to share a cab with him this morning.

The laughter in her voice when he'd tried to change her mind had riled him. "Believe me, James. Nothing could stop me from meeting you tomorrow. Count on me showing up. I'm coming."

Those words hadn't sounded ominous when spoken last night, but now ...

He ran his hand over the concrete pillar. "Not today, Lord. Not after I gave in to Father's demands."

A maroon sedan swept up to the curb. Teri alighted from the vehicle—sans luggage.

3

James steeled himself. The woman who'd accepted his proposal four weeks ago glanced around as if admiring the scenery. Her slow gait indicated she expected him to meet her halfway.

Forget that idea. That contradicted the way he'd play her game.

His tensions diminished as she approached. Many years battling his older brothers had taught him that remaining calm despite provocation usually won the victory. She hoped to toy with his emotions. Stiffening, he widened his stance, holding his position until she reached him.

Teri's lips curved into a welcoming grin. "Hello, handsome."

When James remained silent, her ready smile vanished. It seemed she'd lost composure after he failed to respond to her tease. Her glance flickered over to people yelling good-bye a few feet away, and keys jangled in her hand.

Eyebrow raised, he centered in on the restless movements. Teri brushed a bright-copper hair from her face. Nodding, she studied his features as if seeking out weaknesses.

A slight smile touched his lips at the war of wills.

Her tenacity amazed him. She read him well. Instead of being icy, her blue eyes flashed fire.

"When does your flight leave?" Teri pursed her lips whenever she wanted to drive home a particular point. It removed any thought of convincing her of the immediacy of the situation. "You can lower that one eyebrow. I'm not going with you to St. Louis."

Though Teri appeared to brace for an angry outburst, she couldn't keep the smirk off her face. She rubbed her chin, peeking over her shoulder to where the sedan had once idled at the curb.

In one smooth movement, James gently gripped her arm, pulling the unresisting Teri closer. His gaze never left her face.

"So this is the real James Copley." Locking gazes with him, a thin bead of sweat dotted the skin above her lips. "I thought this engagement secured our future. Yet you refuse to talk to me."

"Why should that matter when you disrupted our arrangement at the last moment?"

"I agreed to marry you in good faith. It would be good for both of us." Tossing her curly hair over her shoulders, she laughed. "But you sabotaged our engagement from the start. Twice my friends spotted you around town with Cynthia Ward."

The jealous act caught him off guard. She was acting like a scorned woman instead of someone who'd traded herself for personal gain. He knew her real motive for agreeing to marry him. At another time, her Oscar-winning performance might've entertained him. But he didn't have time to be amused. The clock in the lobby showed he had less than ninety minutes before the flight left.

Teri tossed her hair again, gathering steam.

"We shared two wonderful years together. But Cynthia Ward? For four weeks you claimed you needed me to secure your place in the family business. You should've concentrated on me. Okay, I get it. Women fall all over themselves to please you." She jerked her hand from his grasp. Sneering, she leaned closer. "Where's that winsome smile now?"

James shook his head, looking at the cabs dropping off passengers. "So, unfounded rumors made you destroy our arrangement. You just brushed me off without notice. What about those two wonderful years you just raved about? Your response to your friends' accusations says it all."

"Why did you take her out?"

He laughed. "That question's a little late. I promised to escort her to three events *before* we got engaged."

Moving nearer, her perfume saturated the air. Her quiet appeal might have weakened a lesser man.

"You could have told me about the previous arrangements. Instead, you allowed me to stew in everyone else's version."

James stepped backward. "I can only fix problems I know exist."

Teri's body went limp until she plastered herself against him.

"I blew it, huh? I guess my emotions went into overdrive." She glanced away, shaking her head. "I let a job promotion replace my desire for us to marry. At the time, it seemed simple—career increased, so James Copley must decrease."

She fingered his collar, letting her thumb brush along his neck.

Chapter Two

Neka slumped against the seat as the cab queued in line for curb space. She sighed, glancing out the window at the couple glued to one another. Instead of being at odds with James, Teri was stroking his cheek in a loving caress. Neka wondered if she'd made the right decision to come. Closing her eyes, she buried her face into her hands for the second time since leaving home.

She'd only decided last night to accompany James to St. Louis. Before she could change her mind, she'd packed her luggage, ordered a cab, and then fallen into a peaceful sleep. Sweet dreams about rescuing him built up her confidence that morning. At four o'clock, she sprang out of bed and dressed in the dark. She tiptoed through the house and placed a note on her mother's desk. Finally, she crept outside to wait for the cab to arrive.

Like a mirage, the future she'd imagined was crumbling before her eyes. The exchange between Teri and James baffled her. There was no friction. In fact, they looked quite cozy. They behaved like an engaged couple.

But if all was well, they would be checking in luggage instead of talking. Squinting her eyes, Neka looked more closely. James's cases leaned on the column next to him, while Teri seemed to be baggage-free.

Clapping her hands, she sat upright. It was much too early to give up.

This trip was indeed a godsend. She determined to leave her doomsday imaginings aside. Teri had broken off the engagement. Today Neka would show James the same kindness he'd always shown her. She wouldn't shy away from the moment. A brand-new world waited in the wings. Grinning, she repeated her mom's promise from two months ago, a week after her twenty-first birthday.

"A sea of change will overtake me."

Since those precious words were spoken, she'd vowed to seek out new experiences. She would live instead of waft around on autopilot. In the past, days slid into one another without her noticing the prospects each one held.

After a conversation with her mom yesterday, the doubt door closed forever. Today she would step outside a humdrum existence into a marvelous adventure.

While the cab driver removed her luggage from the trunk, she leaped from the vehicle. Holding the money above his hand, she smiled. "Thank you for letting me linger in your cab."

Taking in the scene with a suitcase in each hand, she glanced at the men checking baggage. Destination: skycaps.

Neka waited beside a group of travelers standing in line, just outside Teri's and James's line of sight. Hidden behind a cart piled high with duffel bags, she encouraged herself when Teri sashayed away while talking into her cell phone.

Luggage in hand, James headed toward the place where she stood trembling.

"Here we go." The words almost stuck in her throat.

Scanning the area in an offhand manner, he recognized her. His alert gaze froze her to her spot.

Neka and James made a striking pair. He was six feet tall, reserved, and oozed confidence. Vigilant and steady, he commanded attention but ignored glances thrown his way. Washed jeans and a thin-striped designer shirt revealed a man who spared no expense on clothing.

Neka knew that the way she squinted her eyes revealed her pensive nature. Five-foot-two and comfortable in her black jeans, Oklahoma City Thunder T-shirt, and sandals, she smiled at everyone she met but preferred others to take the limelight.

"Hi, James." She relaxed.

His mouth curved into the grin she adored. Though this time, it failed to warm his eyes. Those hazel eyes, golden flecks shimmering.

"Neka, sweetie, you always turn up when I need a friend." He noted her carry-on bag and one suitcase. "You're traveling today. Alone? Where're you headed?"

"Am I a friend, James?" She walked beside him with jerky movements as the line crept forward. She lowered her cases to the ground whenever the people stopped moving. Elation at his remark didn't blind her to one fact: Other ears listened in on their conversation. "You're the one who told me not to bandy the word around."

8

His smile widened as he stretched his hand toward her shoulder, but then he dropped it to his side.

She took a deep breath and forged ahead. "I ... do hope ... I ... hope we share a relationship."

Though James remained silent, his countenance softened at her stumbling speech. She felt like he was making this conversation harder than necessary. Couldn't he just talk to her? "I want to travel to St. Louis with you this morning," she said.

Amazement flared across his face and then vanished just as quickly. "Did you buy a ticket?"

Neka paused, shaking her head. Last night she'd practiced a lengthy explanation. Set to tick off the many reasons for leaving with him today. Perhaps he considered her request reasonable. It seemed no further clarification was required.

Still, she stiffened her body for his refusal. "I didn't want to spend money on a ticket I might not use."

Once those words passed her lips, James's alert expression returned full force. He unwound like a rocky road that had been smoothed or a winding path made straight. When he stepped aside, relinquishing his position in line, relief flooded her. Though Neka believed that James was going to accept her help, the severe expression on his face alarmed her.

James had always seemed like a laidback man in charge. The main argument his detractors leveled against him was lack of transparency. But he was just a planner, examining every angle of a situation before acting. She liked that about him. His averted eyes examined the skycap's techniques.

What was he thinking?

Retrieving his cases, he added her largest suitcase to his load and stepped aside.

"We'll get your ticket inside the terminal and check our bags at the counter." Smiling, he winked at her. "Ladies first."

Neka took a deep breath, courage refreshed. She knew she'd just passed a major milestone in her life.

While waiting in line, they chatted comfortably. His agreement validated the decision she'd made last night. New purpose fed her hopes and allayed her fears.

After leaving the counter, his demeanor changed. Slowing down his pace, he paused just before reaching the escalator. He turned to her with out-

9

stretched hands, though he didn't touch her. "When did you find out Teri would dump me this morning?"

Neka almost tripped over her feet but made a fast recovery. "Last week."

"You tried to warn me at the restaurant Sunday."

She nipped at her bottom lip and nodded. "Yeah, I did."

James's eyes softened. "After your visit I should have anticipated a problem was brewing."

"Why would you?"

His lips curved into a smile. "I'm the one who always initiates our meetings. Sunday, you came to me after my construction manager left the table."

She recalled her embarrassment. In full work mode, he didn't seem to see her. Failing to capture his attention, she'd rejoined her cousins on the opposite side of the room. "Did I interrupt you somehow?"

"Forgive me, sweets. My mind had wandered to an earlier one-sided talk with the senior Copley."

Finally, her week-long burden lifted. "Oh. I hope everything's okay."

He ran his fingertip down her nose. "It is now."

A shudder flooded her body, even though he'd performed the ritual many times before. The morning's adventure was already getting to her. She needed a moment alone.

Spotting a restroom just ahead, she veered in that direction, calling over her shoulder, "I'll only be a minute."

Inside the stall, she inspected the neutral nail polish on her toes, squeezed her eyelids tight, and wrapped her arms around herself, shivering. In a soft voice, she counted to ten. Perspiration dotted her skin. *Ohhh ... Lord, I need You.*

Suddenly, she felt awkward with James. Or maybe with herself. These emotions had never come up before.

Welcome to the real world. Surprises lurk outside your normal safety net.

One ten-count didn't suffice before facing him again. The lack of questions outside the terminal had offered her a false sense of security. Whatever the reason, her body still trembled from his touch. A sigh flowed from the pit of her stomach. Her fingers tapped on the door, like an S.O.S.

Being alone with him wasn't the issue. More people roamed inside this building than at any event they'd attended. Her heart raced while she sorted out her feelings.

Was she having a panic attack?

No way. The new journey had just skewed her reactions. What had she gotten herself into?

"One, two, three ..."

* * *

James ignored the stares women threw at him. A plan unfolded while he watched her walk away. Was she offering to hold his hand or replace Teri?

Being with Neka was always a delight. He approved of everything about her. Except her propensity to hide in shadows. It bothered him to distraction. People with far less to show promoted themselves daily. Meanwhile, one of the smartest women in the room minimized her best qualities.

Well, she'd certainly popped out of the box this morning. And he was determined to keep her from going back in.

Twenty-twenty hindsight illuminated his mistakes. His proposal to Teri was a mischance at best. At worst ... well, forget that idea.

He never overreached. The Teri debacle represented blunders he hated making. James bit down hard, accepting the verdict. Abandoning his policy not to let another person's agenda affect him is what had created this predicament. Why hadn't he found a way around his father's marriage mandate?

James had proposed to Teri a week after receiving an urgent message from home. After cancelling an important meeting, he'd returned the call before reaching the elevator, only to hear his father outline immediate plans to restructure the family business. Without any fanfare, Gene Copley delivered his youngest son an ultimatum—get married, or lose your seat at the table. Usually, someone else's demands pushed him into the opposite direction, but this time there was too much at stake.

He clenched, then reopened his fist. Without a doubt, his brothers had manipulated events in an attempt to block his return to the company their father had founded thirty years ago. If he didn't comply with the peculiar requirement, they would reorganize without his input. And James would be left owning a fourth of a company that someone else designed.

The pressure had mounted as his father restated his position daily. He either had to give in to demands or suffer the consequences. Instead of walking away, he questioned private channels for inside information.

11

Independent sources painted a dismal picture of a business in decay. The company no longer bid on construction projects. James capitulated, unwilling to allow his inheritance to deteriorate further into the abyss. Thus, his proposal to Teri.

Grimacing, he shook his head. Nothing good came from hasty decisions.

Several motions entered his peripheral vision, drawing him back to his surroundings. Neka headed toward him but swung aside when earsplitting shrieks pierced the lobby.

A frazzled teenager lugged a screaming baby in one arm and dragged a resistant toddler yelling, "No!" in the other hand. All three were unkempt, like they'd slept overnight in their clothes. The crew trudged their way.

Stealing a quick glance at him, Neka waited for the disgruntled travelers to come closer. James knew the exact moment she decided to intervene on their behalf—her finger and thumb rubbed her earlobe just before the party drew up at her side.

"Please, let me help you." She reached for the baby as the girl backed away.

Then the child's screams developed into high-pitched squeals. The pair spoke in low voices until Neka turned, pointing to James. She lifted the writhing baby from the girl's now limp arm. Apparently resigned to needing help, the unencumbered young mother scooped up the thrashing toddler and fell in line behind Neka. Although the foursome disappeared from James's sight, the ruckus never diminished.

Once again, Neka had refused to ignore another person's troubles. Teri would never do that.

A lack of foresight had forced him to pick a wife from three women he never expected to marry. The unfortunate incident reinforced what he already knew. He'd always limited mistakes by restraining his emotions. Feelings only wreaked havoc during vulnerable periods. His unchecked emotions had forced him to choose between bad alternatives.

Squeezing his left shoulder blade, he reassessed his original position. In the end, Teri's flair and strong family convictions won out over his other dates. Cynthia didn't care about family, and Teri's finesse and sophistication tipped the scale in her favor over Peggy. His future wife would need it. His sisters-in-law often joined forces to rout unsuspecting victims—that is, whenever they called a truce between themselves.

James glanced at his watch. He couldn't help but admire Neka's good deed, but it disrupted their timetable. She needed to learn to choose her projects. She couldn't support everyone she met.

He chuckled, relaxing his stance. Despite the wife nonsense, his family's scheming fit his plans to perfection. It was the ideal season for James to resume the life he'd discarded on a whim. Not really on a whim, since he'd planned it carefully. And his reasons for relocating to Oklahoma had proved sound enough. He'd produced an abundant crop with little watering.

High stakes had caused the Teri gamble. Nikhol Lacey had just changed that loss into a win. The folks—especially his mother—prayed he would acquire a godly spouse, a woman who'd curb his willingness to separate himself from his family.

James felt a tug on his sleeve, and he studied the woman filling his thoughts. Returned from her hiatus in the restroom, Neka surveyed him with hopeful eyes. For a moment he couldn't breathe.

She was adorable. Her skin glowed with vibrant health. Extra-long lashes adorned beautiful light-brown eyes. She had a perfect nose and the deepest dimples he'd ever seen. Shortening the gap between them, he caught a whiff of her perfume. The fresh scent suited her personality to perfection.

Usually, beautiful women flaunted their attributes. Her humbleness only added to her appeal. James tilted his head, studying her petite frame. A haircut, stylish clothing, and distance from her family would boost her self-assurance beyond measure. He wanted her confidence level to rise before their vacation ended.

Of course, she must be traveling to St. Louis without her parents' blessing. If she left a letter, the Laceys would rush to the airport. They needed to move away from the common area, pronto.

He picked up her carry-on bag while surveying the entranceway. They must pass the security check-in without meeting her parents on the upper level. Hand brushing her upper arm, he pointed to the escalator.

"We may miss our flight if we don't hurry. Our plane won't be crowded. We'll discuss our plans once we're on board."

Chapter Three

Neka gazed at the flight attendant without seeing or hearing the safety presentation. The conversation last Saturday between her eldest sister, Kelly, and Teri dominated her thoughts. They'd talked on the deck while she lay on the chaise in the upstairs sunroom. Half listening as they discussed Teri's promotion, she hastened to the window once the topic changed to James. That discussion had catapulted her life into a different direction.

Teri had plotted to destroy James—Neka's only friend.

She wasn't sure how to handle the unsolicited information that dropped into her lap. Doing nothing wasn't an option. Did God allow her to overhear to thwart Teri's revenge?

Neka revisited her warm encounters with James, those numerous occasions he'd rescued her from uncomfortable situations. His easy banter and strong hugs always distracted and comforted her. At her sister Tammy's birthday party, his kindness lessened the impact of being ignored.

She glanced at him, smiling. A pattern had developed that evening that had lasted four years. At social functions, James drew her into every discussion, asked her to dance, or conversed with her for hours. It didn't matter where they were or who he'd come with. His personal interest meant everything to her. A highly sought-after man was drawn to her, even if it wasn't romantic.

Since helping him was the top priority, Neka had spent the previous Saturday evening coming up with a plan. Catching him at lunch the next day had nose-dived, so the missed opportunity had forced her to revise the plan.

But how would she contact him? Asking family members for his phone number might raise speculations.

Yet she had to protect this man who'd always shielded her. James had singlehandedly made socializing worthwhile. Others viewed his actions as a thoughtful gesture.

But to Neka, his care validated her life. One day others would also appreciate the vibrant woman he saw, if she could only figure out how to relax with her peers. Only he and her family knew the real Nikhol Lacey.

Overhearing Teri's schemes invigorated her. New purpose permeated every step she took, and boundless energy propelled her through each day. Even her mom's promise that change was coming spurred her on. Routine activities gave joy as she prepared to vindicate James.

Feeling a light breeze on her skin, Neka looked up as a flight attendant pulled up beside their row.

"May I get you something to drink?"

"Ginger ale?"

Making small talk, he handed her a glass filled with ice cubes plus a full can. "I believe you have the prettiest dimples ever."

James regarded the steward. "I thank you for us both."

Turning to Neka, James spoke in a low voice, forcing her to lean closer.

The man didn't budge but inquired if he could assist her further.

Smiling, she shook her head, but her gaze shifted when James touched her arm. Hostility radiated from both men. She popped the top on her can, looking from one to the other. The brief exchange ended when the man pushed his cart down the aisle.

Neka looked at James, hoping they could discuss meeting his parents. Instead of sharing their itinerary, he averted his gaze back out the window.

While bubbles fizzed against her tongue, several essential elements sprang to mind. How would her mom respond to the hastily written letter? Her heart sank, envisioning her reading it multiple times trying to comprehend the impulsive act. She refused to consider her father's and sisters' reactions.

She frowned. Not even her faithful cousin Hazelle could downplay the curious behavior.

What about James's parents? Both families played pivotal roles for a successful trip. Until now, she'd centered her energy on boarding the flight. But now she couldn't help but worry how their relatives would respond.

Once her mom weighed the situation beside her own encouraging words, she'd applaud the display of courage. But even her mom's approval wouldn't satisfy her dad. He knew that James acted as her self-appointed social savior. Her father always reciprocated acts of kindness and would understand her drive to do the same.

Swiping the back of her hand across her forehead, she smiled. That took care of the Laceys.

She glanced at James, tapping a finger against her lips as she considered his parents. The knowledge that some woman dumped their son at the airport could break their hearts.

Of course, he probably didn't tell them he and Teri weren't in love.

Would they tolerate a friend's presence when they expected to meet his fiancée? Neka squeezed her forehead between her fingers. What had she hoped to gain by showing up that morning?

James proved a fountain of strength when she'd needed him. But his assistance had always come without a cost. There were no consequences in his spending time with her.

Her fingers applied pressure to the rising discomfort above her right eyebrow. He needed a fiancée to visit his parents. If getting married was important, why hadn't James and Teri set a wedding date? Who was Cynthia Ward? Did she attend his church? If they dated, why choose Teri over her? Why did he seek a wife? She had never entertained any of those questions before this moment.

A voice inside warned her. There were consequences to foolish behavior.

Don't get cold feet. She squeezed the cup between clenched fingers and silently prayed. *Father, I need you. Please guide me through this obstacle course of my own design. I believe I'm obeying You but feel so alone. Lord, help me make the right decisions going forward.*

Her gaze darted to James as she willed herself to relax.

Leaning over, she peered up and down the aisle. He had called it. The first-class section contained only a smattering of travelers.

James still looked out the window, probably consumed with thoughts about meeting his family without Teri by his side. Nevertheless, as a guest in his parents' home, the decisions he made would affect her as well.

These circumstances were proving to be too dramatic. She counted to ten underneath her breath, bolstering her courage. After the second go-round, she tapped his arm.

"Psst."

He surveyed her through narrowed eyes, and she withdrew. Somehow he seemed distant. Did he truly see her?

She massaged her right earlobe in tugging motions. "So what's the plan?"

17

* * *

James plunged into small talk about their flight until Neka excused herself. His fingers dug deep into shoulder muscles, concentrating on the spots just below his neckline. He'd spent too much time weighing pros and cons against endless tasks looming ahead, neglecting her and almost blowing his chance.

The bottom line was, without a fiancée, he may as well return to Tulsa. Now his only choice was to convince Neka to risk a lifetime with him in less than six hours.

How would he delay their arrival to his parent's home after reaching St. Louis?

Next he faced the bait-and-switch fiancée scene. His mother equated marriage with genuine happiness, while his father considered stability and matrimony as interchangeable. Timing held the key to each challenge, though the how eluded him.

Where was that fast course on altering directions midstream?

After her return from the restroom, James gazed at the graceful way Neka nibbled her lower lip. He wanted her stress-free, not overwhelmed and dreading their time together.

"Forgive my rudeness. I'm reeling from getting jilted." He chuckled. The little joke hit close to home. "We'll pick up a rental car at the off-site location. My folks live in the Central West End, about thirty minutes from the airport."

Before he finished speaking, the flight attendant appeared again, giving Neka a slow wink. His gaze never left her face.

James squelched the rebuke the blatant show deserved. On another day, he would've responded with a direct challenge.

But Neka shied away from confrontations. She never noticed the men queuing up for her attention. This newcomer's interest would prove no different. James dropped her trash into the bag, barely concealing his contempt. He didn't speak until the man moved away.

Grinning, he pointed to the window. "Let's switch places."

Neka stood to one side. After James had passed her, she settled into his seat and shifted to face him. Her engaging smile hooked him. He grinned at her resiliency. "We'll reach Lambert Field in twenty minutes. I'm open to any questions."

"I do have several serious ones." She hesitated, looking down.

James studied her discomposure. Her eyes sparkled with uncertainty. He'd met the lovely teenaged Neka years ago at Lacey Corp's Christmas celebration. Amazed at her antics, he'd watched her animated visits whenever someone stopped to talk. Yet she'd flitted away to a quiet spot if they overstayed their welcome. Intrigued, he'd introduced himself, and they'd spent the last hour conversing about the Bible. Scriptures topped her chat list then and now.

Three weeks later at Tammy's birthday party, he'd encountered a lonely girl hiding in the shadows, wishing she were somewhere else. At the Christmas party everyone had chatted with her. But at the birthday party that night, only family members had sat down to talk.

Then he'd understood. Her stock had lost value among her peers. The desire to protect her had ensnared him from that night onward. What caused her angst today? Sometimes they talked for hours in a single evening.

"I don't want to pry, but I'm worried about meeting your family." She shifted her position in her seat. "They're expecting a fiancée. How do you explain Teri's no-show?"

"I'll give the folks a heads up. I love my mother as much as she loves me. She'll inform Father. Now may I ask something of you?"

She nodded slowly.

James leaned closer. "What are your intentions for traveling with me?"

She dropped her head.

He knew Neka didn't appreciate having the tables turned and didn't know if she would voice her reservations.

"In answer to the earlier question," he said. "I value our friendship. Let's build on trust." While he talked, James slid a finger across her cheek. She trembled at his touch. How odd. "I'm curious. Why are you flying to visit people not expecting you to come?"

Neka exhaled, smiling. "To help you. Like you've always helped me."

Unlike his earlier conversation with Teri, James wanted to cushion Neka against any harshness. He liked her too much to see her uneasy. "Your quick response tells me you've covered the bases. So how will you help me?"

She remained silent, like she was searching for an appropriate answer. Finally she shrugged her shoulders. "I confess. I'm clueless about that part. I'll lend support wherever needed."

"And this backing includes?"

Neka leaned away from him. "I guess we play everything by ear. You know, see how it pans out."

She reclined against the seat, her closed eyes and hands folded in her lap signaled an end to the discussion.

Frowning, James considered his options. They'd reached the point of no return. He was sorry but couldn't let her off the hook. "Do Karen and Lawrence know you're traveling with me?"

She shook her head. "I didn't tell them."

He wished she would open those pretty light-brown eyes and reveal what she was attempting to hide. "I've seen the close relationship you have with your mother." James waited for a response. "Neka?"

"They would've disagreed with my decision to help you." She stared at him without blinking. "I respect my parents' guidance. They're seldom wrong. But in this case, they would be."

He stared at a point just above her head. "Were you afraid to disagree with their opinion?"

"No."

James studied her bowed shoulders. Neka turned her head to one side. "Of course I disagree with their opinions when I think they're wrong. But sometimes I defer to them if I can't change their minds. I didn't want to give up my quest. I wanted to help you."

James glanced down the aisle and smiled. "I'm surprised you used the word quest."

She pointed a finger toward his chest. "You're my knight in shining armor."

"I can't champion you this time. There's no way to protect you from myself." He grabbed her hand and smiled at her innocence. "You're traveling to an unfamiliar city with a man you don't know."

"You just said we were friends. We've spent the last four years talking about every imaginable topic. So now you're a stranger?" She squirmed in her seat. "You're a kind man. You've assisted me lots of times."

"At parties, my motives were purely selfish. You deserved better treatment than you were receiving." James hesitated. "You're probably one of the few guileless people left in the world."

Neka's mouth hung open. "Only my family treats me like you do."

"Next you'll designate me Saint James." He closed his eyes, envisioning life without her. Legitimizing their relationship obligated him to protect her.

He touched her cheek and allowed his finger to linger. *As if being sweet wasn't enough, add beauty and a gentle spirit ...* "You can't compare social functions to a two-week trip to another state."

Sighing, Neka lay her face against the cushion. "Do I need shielding from you?"

James brushed hair from her face. "Like most people, you need protection from yourself. I'm surprised your mother hasn't called."

"I left a note on her desk at home, but she doesn't go into her office in the mornings. She works half days on Fridays and gets home around eleven."

* * *

"Then what happens?"

Neka pulled her hair away from her neck and closed her eyes. Inhaling deeply, she modulated her tone. "I explain why I left."

"And if they don't understand your rationale?"

She squinted at him. Perhaps he grasped her parents' personalities better than she did. "They'll support my decision despite their disappointment. Several good reasons could sway their opinion my way."

"Wishful thinking." Doubt filled his eyes, and he lifted her face toward his. "Trust me through difficult times. Our relationship is secure."

Even reaffirming their friendship failed to revive her good mood. She didn't know how to answer these questions. Each one felt like a weight being laid upon her body one stone at a time. Perspiration beaded on her back. She couldn't just dish out platitudes that rang hollow even to her ears.

Why *had* she come on this trip? What seemed like a wise decision last night shattered before reaching her destination. Lightheaded, Neka blinked to balance herself. She closed her eyes, unable to move.

Somehow she'd fallen into the same habits that had tripped her up since middle school. Setting her focus on life after eighth grade hadn't worked. High school had failed to produce the friends she coveted. Who needed friends and dates? Thank God for accelerated classes and college courses in the evenings. Sometimes she'd even forgotten real life passed her by.

It wasn't that no one had asked her out. The men who did just didn't appeal to her. Working as an interior designer at her parents' company brought plenty of men across her path. But most of them spent all their time talking about her dad, expecting a career boost at her expense. Her dream man was kind and considerate almost to a fault.

One day, it hit her that she practically lived in obscurity. The same empty pattern repeated itself. Gloom had overwhelmed her trust barometer while watering flower beds one Saturday afternoon, and hopelessness covered her like a shroud. Uncertainty had overcome her as she pondered God's purpose for her life. Her mom had removed her gloves and sat beside her. Underneath the weeping willow tree, Neka had confessed fears that true happiness would always elude her.

Head tilted to the side, Karen had sighed.

"Honey, your days are crammed with works that produce lasting effects for every person you bless. Each of my girls has a different path to follow. God allows you to touch others in unique ways." She grasped Neka's chin. Smiling, Karen gazed into her eyes. "Take your mind off everyone else and focus on Jesus as the only example to follow. God speaks these words to my heart concerning you, dear one: change is coming. Embrace His special will for your life. Count on Him to fulfill your destiny for His own good pleasure."

Neka's eyes had opened wide, and her pulse rate increased. Every sense she possessed had intensified. Later that night in her room, she'd renewed the promise to welcome each day God blessed her to live. Her mother's belief that new prospects awaited her had revived expectancy to its fullest. She'd wasted too many years wishing for life to dazzle.

And now, without a word to anyone, she'd left her home. The magnitude of the plan made her speechless. Thank God she'd already planned to take off work today. But James deserved an explanation. He never asked her to go to St. Louis with him. The Copleys didn't invite her into their home. The space swayed in front of her.

Oh my God.

She was always the daughter who obeyed her parents. Yet this morning she'd slipped away like a thief in the night. Rebuffing all their sound teaching, this blew her sister's disobedient acts right out of the water.

"Oh Lord."

She'd always fled chaotic situations but now sat beside James on a flight to St. Louis.

Neka had weathered her parents' disappointment before. Their disagreement with her decisions didn't matter when she was standing on principle, but actions founded on misconceptions crumbled once the truth came out.

22

What was she thinking? Who traveled out of town with another woman's fiancé? But James was a free man the moment Teri decided not to marry him. Still the thought worried her conscience.

Of course, she'd slunk away from the house. It was easier to pretend they'd back her if they knew the truth rather than face the reality of their opposition.

Love had driven her to board the plane. Love emboldened her to dismiss her family. Love enabled her to disregard the job she loved.

She loved James Copley.

Instead of bouncing out of her seat, Neka's spirit sunk lower. He didn't love her. The realization doomed her inside a trap of despair. In one misguided act, she'd handed another person the power to ruin her.

Oh Lord, please help me. I'm on a plane to St. Louis with the man I love. A man who doesn't love me.

Chapter Four

Sympathizing with Neka's anguish, James peered into the aisle to give her privacy. Today she'd blindsided him. In the next two hours, he had to figure out how to blend two lives into one. What a dilemma. This was proving harder than he thought, because she was among the few people he respected. He'd never considered his words might hurt her.

No, it was just that love disarmed intelligent people.

He drew her into his arms, displaying the compassion he seldom acknowledged. "Hey ... calm down. You don't go around throwing caution to the wind. Usually your problem is being too cautious. What distressed you?"

Averting her face, she pushed against his embrace.

He placed his mouth close to her ear. "You risked a lot to help me. I'm betting you had good intentions. Instead of shutting me out, let's help each other through these difficult times."

Closing his eyes, James stroked her back. He had to shift the direction their day was taking. Teri had known what she was getting into, whereas Neka was in uncharted waters. And unlike with Teri, he had a vested interest in Neka's struggles.

At last she rested her head on his chest and recounted the two conversations with her mother. A path out of this emotional turmoil peeped through every word. James pressed his cheek to her forehead when she finished speaking.

"Thank you for trusting me. Now do me a big favor. Turn around and look out the window." Neka studied him in silence. His heart softened, remembering the countless evenings she'd charmed away the problems of his day. "Please trust me."

Her teary eyes gazed at him for a moment before she turned to look. An involuntary shiver ran down his spine, and he pulled her closer until her back rested against his chest, although their seat belts hampered them a bit. "Look at the peace and tranquility formed when the sun, clouds, and sky work together in perfect harmony. Like an orchestra blends notes, reverberating throughout the theater."

New to calming fears on a personal level, he tread slowly. He wondered what Lawrence would really make of his youngest daughter's actions, and an invisible band tightened around his chest, remembering that first whirlwind meeting with her father. He'd met Lawrence Lacey while attempting to get permits at city hall to renovate his first house. After being unable to put together a team that was efficient but inexpensive, the inspection regulations tied him into knots. The blond man everyone seemed to know happily offered his assistance. Thus began the sponsorship that eventually boosted James to the top of his field.

"A wise woman once told me there is life after mistakes and bad decisions because we're not a product of our past but of God's grace." He methodically stroked her upper arm. "At another gathering, she said that each day is one of new beginnings, bright tomorrows, and endless promises in Christ. Her wisdom is part of what strengthens me to repair the severed bonds with my family on this trip."

Neka studied the traffic on the ground. "My mom?"

"Karen is a godsend. Just like her daughter." He grinned, and it showed in his voice. "Both show up at the right moment."

"Mom's a special lady. She hears from God and doesn't make stupid mistakes."

"Like traveling with me to St. Louis?" James rested his chin on her head, disliking the despair in her voice. Discussions with Karen enriched his life. The similarities in Karen's and Neka's desire to help others inspired him. "I wonder how she fared at your age. The two of you bless everyone you touch."

"Mom enjoys people."

"Like her, you strive to improve individual lives. You quote the scripture— *we walk by faith, and not by sight*—along with *Jesus is the same yesterday, today, and forever*."

She wiped her hand over her eyes and leaned back against the seat cushion. Although she didn't float off of the plane when it landed, she seemed perkier than before. She was still quiet but smiled as they claimed their luggage.

They stood together outside the terminal, and she jumped a little when the shuttle pulled up to the curb, off in her own world. James spent the shuttle ride on the phone with his mother. She always worked off of her own agenda and wasn't pleased with his change of plans. She'd prepared a big breakfast to welcome him home, and now she and Brandie had to eat without them.

* * *

After he made the last call, James placed the cell phone back into his pocket before getting in the rental car. He adjusted the rearview mirror and backed the silver convertible out of the parking space. "I'm hungry. Ready to grab a bite to eat?"

Neka nodded while gazing out the window at the passing view. "I'm starving."

"First stop—food. Since we have errands to run, I told mother not to expect us before three."

She frowned. "What errands?"

James glanced at her and smiled before driving off the parking lot. "Nothing serious. I'm giving us alone time before introducing you to my parents. I thought that would help you adjust."

Closing her eyes, she let out a long breath. He frowned when she didn't speak.

Breakfast wasn't the only affair his mother had scheduled for the day. She'd overruled his desire for a quiet evening with plans of her own. Despite wanting his mother to be happy, he had to keep Neka away from his brothers and their wives until she'd regained her footing.

"Brandie brought the kids over for breakfast this morning. They're excited to meet you." He laughed at the stern stare she sent his way. "Okay, they're excited to meet Teri."

James slowed down, allowing four cars to go in front of him. He entered the ramp leading to Highway 70. "Mother invited dinner guests tonight at eight."

Neka jumped around in her seat. "Oh no, I don't want to meet everyone today."

Time alone with his folks would have proven her sincere nature before the doubters cast aspersions. Reality had a way of trumping expectations. "The guest list is short—only the immediate family."

27

Her gaze contained equal portions of alarm and despair. "What will we do for five hours?"

"First, we talk." Grinning, he joined the fast-moving traffic heading east. He coaxed her along when her teeth nipped her lower lip. "It's impossible to proceed unless we're in complete agreement. Presenting a united front before my family is essential. Our strong relationship will illustrate why I brought you home instead of Teri."

Neka examined her clasped hands in her lap. "How? Our talks haven't produced the best results so far."

"We're closer than you imagine. Thanks for explaining the talk with your mother. I understand now why you wanted to help me. The inevitable can be postponed, not eliminated." James patted her knee when she winced. He winked at her, smiling. "Come on, smile for me. I'm lost unless you flash those lovely dimples my way."

* * *

They found a little eatery at the mall. The spicy aroma of grilled meat mingling with brewing coffee, teas, and mochas made her stomach gurgle. Anxiety always made her hungry, and the revelation on the plane had buried her beneath a ton of stress.

Only James's close proximity kept her from falling apart. His nearness steadied her nerves, but it also made her worry she might unwittingly reveal that she loved him before she even had time to process her feelings. Her mouth nearly dropped open as she centered on James.

The flirty cashier wasn't helping. Neka realized she'd been holding her breath when the woman stopped staring at James and accepted his money, touching his hand a little too long.

He snatched his hand away and grabbed their bags from the counter, avoiding further eye contact with the cashier.

While leaving the eatery, she tapped his shoulder. "We're eating somewhere else?"

"Apparently the privacy's limited here." Laughing, he shook his head. "I like intimacy with my confessions."

Confessions? "Okay ..."

"Unless we reach a consensus, the next two weeks will prove futile."

Neka resolved to have no more introspection. Smiling, she raised crossed fingers on either side of her face until he laughed.

She looked around the mall. "It's too bad we're leaving. We passed several stores that aren't in Tulsa."

"Be careful what you wish for." He grinned and nudged open the door for her. "Let's eat before my stomach growls."

At the car, James set his load on the hood and opened her door. The thoughtful gesture eased her anxiety. But the promised discussion weighed heavy in her thoughts. Perspiration dotted her chest when he pushed back his seat. When she found herself gripping the armrest, she willed herself to relax.

"This smells delicious," she said.

James sat their drinks in cup holders and laid a napkin across her lap. Putting his order aside, he opened the other bag and sprinkled condiments on the dashboard, stashing napkins and straws on the console between their seats. He folded each bag and laid them on the floor at their feet.

Neka marveled at the control in these small actions. They ate in silence, and she sipped her tea, interested to see his next move.

* * *

Fifteen minutes later, James began cleaning up. "Finished?"

She tore off small pieces of her sandwich until popping the final bite into her mouth.

He spread his hands and smiled. "Sorry. A sandwich can't last forever."

Glancing at him, Neka carefully placed her trash inside the crumpled bag, slowly folded the top, and then laid it beside the others. It seemed she'd exhausted every time-consuming task she could think of to avoid their conversation. Sighing, she linked her hands on her lap, facing him like a sacrificial lamb.

He leaned on his arm, closing the space between them. Freshness radiated from Neka. He delighted in the berry scent on her breath from her tea. There was a simple soul quality about her he'd never observed in anyone else.

"I love your dimples." He grinned at her double blink at his non sequitur, enjoying the way her eyes sparkled with excitement at a moment's notice. "Neka, let me fill in the gaps. Do you know how old I am?"

She smiled. "We'll celebrate your thirtieth birthday in seven days."

"I'm surprised. Few people in Tulsa know much about me. Teri asked my birthday twice and then stopped asking." James smiled when Neka frowned. "I haven't celebrated a birthday in six years. Do you want to know anything in particular?"

Instead of bombarding him with questions like he'd expected, Neka slanted away. Sighing, he closed the gap again, fighting the desire to touch her. "Be honest with me, even if you find the subject distasteful."

Neka frowned before replying. "So, you know that Kelly and Michael are living with us until their home's completed, right? Well, Teri visited Kelly last Saturday, and I overheard the explanation about breaking off the engagement. She admitted the two of you weren't in love ..."

"And ..." James prompted when she grew silent. The clock was ticking away. They had to get past the preliminaries and into the heart of their discussion.

She looked away, head leaning on her shoulder. "Teri didn't divulge specific information but said you two agreed to a loveless marriage."

"And ..."

"Why didn't you ask for details at the airport? Your lack of curiosity about all this surprises me." She shook her head.

He threw his head back in laughter. A vibrant picture of himself reciting Teri and Kelly's conversation verbatim crossed his mind, but Neka would be unsatisfied with the results and demand interpretation of each word. "Teri confessed at the airport. You supplied the missing piece—that she'd been planning it at least a week in advance."

"That's all?"

"Why clutter my mind with the useless details of her decision?"

Shifting in her seat, she used her hands to convey the words and peered at him through half-closed eyes. "You don't feel compelled to understand her reasoning?"

"Her actions show her low opinion of me. Her mindset doesn't really matter." James shook his head, leaning closer. "I'm more interested in how *we* progress together."

"In her favor, she didn't reveal any secrets."

Tired of the Teri connection, he grunted disapproval. "No kudos for her. She had limited details to distribute among her cohorts. Until the proposal, I prevented her intrusion into private affairs. I'll share a secret that no one else in Tulsa knows. Seven years ago I suggested my father diversify his company into rehabs ahead of the five-year expansion plan he'd enacted."

Her shoulders relaxed at the changed topic. She loved talking shop. Their breath mingled together as she leaned closer. "What type of business?"

"Building contractors. I recommended renovating homes for rental property. Several months earlier, Father had taken a stab on the development side. Matt and I finished out our contracts at the time, while Father and Ryan assembled a team."

She tapped a finger against her lips. "Your brothers could've managed the building side and you do rehabs."

"You know the risk factors and the horrendous politics involved. He decided not to advance the initiative, citing finances."

His throat tightened. James had supplied his father with detailed funding options, even enlisting his godfather to join the project. McKinley Construction's inclusion would have covered the expenses. His father's objections had simply defied explanation.

It had been an excellent proposal, but it died because the idea had come from James. No other reason made sense.

"He could have bought one or two properties just to get started."

"That was the exact argument I used at the time. Father refused to allocate resources until completing the development. Slotting the deadline six to seven years down the road."

Neka cocked her head to one side. "Who set you up in Tulsa?"

His gaze met hers. "I invested in myself from a substantial inheritance left by my great aunt." The funds had become available on his twenty-third birthday. Two months later he'd moved to Oklahoma.

"Why choose Tulsa?"

Because living in separate households had failed to alleviate the pressure of working with dictatorial brothers. It took relocating to a city four hundred miles away to even the odds stacked against him.

James stared out the window. He should've chosen a different topic. Reopening these old wounds was only poisoning his resolve to maintain the peace with his family. They got along fine these days because no one discussed anything controversial.

"The Copleys are far from the family next door. Too much competition exists between the men. Throw in two wives—one a conniver and the other one a schemer ... well, you get the picture."

31

Neka's eyebrows rose.

Could she understand his family's cutthroat tendencies when it came to their business? Sometimes she hung out with her sisters, and most of her relatives attended the same church. His semi-estranged family might prove difficult for her to fathom.

"You have to understand, Ryan had already set the precedent. Just a month after leaving university, he suggested we move into the Illinois marketplace. Although the company lacked sufficient capital, Father ran with the idea. Thank God his expertise kept us afloat until we completed the projects."

Neka nodded, seeming to understand somewhat. Grimacing, James stretched out his legs. "Two years later Matt proposed we bid on an industrial park contract. Resources were already leveraged, but our father heralded his idea as brilliant. Once again, only his business skills snatched us from bankruptcy."

Jaw muscles worked overtime as he bit down. "He undertook two risky ventures but denied my proposal to rehab homes, which was stronger than either of theirs had been. Once he rejected me, Ryan and Matt threw me under the bus, ridiculing the proposal in my presence."

James relived the endless insults, thwarted expectations, and lack of support for the first time since leaving St. Louis. Whoever claimed revealing past hurts assuaged wounds had lied. It unleashed the same resentment he'd experienced seven years ago. He narrowed his eyes, frowning.

One event in particular revived his anger. At a family dinner, his godfather and his son—who happened to become Brandie's future husband—had justified expanding into rehabs. Ryan and Matt had smeared the entire campaign. Instead of choosing sides, his mother and godmother had only smoothed everyone's ruffled feathers. Only Brandie, who was just seventeen at the time, had spoken up on his behalf.

That was when he'd known it was time to move. After the dust had cleared, the dice had been cast. Tulsa, Oklahoma, would become his new home. They actually expected to belittle him and walk away unscathed.

But his anger subsided now at the empathy on Neka's sympathetic face.

"Although I had disagreed with their concepts, I had supported my brothers' efforts, no questions asked. The company benefited if their projects succeeded. Their crusade against me didn't end with a rejected proposal."

James shook his head, engrossed in personal pain. The memory engulfed him in a sea of discarded dreams. His cheeks pulsated in rapid succession.

She lifted her hand, then let it drop to her lap. The action spurred him to finish.

"During the following months they challenged my integrity, character, and knowledge of the construction industry. Father defended their campaign to malign me." He braced his back against the window. "So I proved my ideas were superior to the ones they proposed. Now people know I conceive and complete major projects. My success validates the rehab proposition had been an excellent idea from the start."

Chapter Five

Neka reenacted in her mind the eager young man fine-tuning his business plan, misconception buoying the belief his brothers supported his endeavors, and Mr. Copley crushing his youngest son with a demoralizing defeat. The puzzle piece completed the picture of this mysterious man people in Tulsa clamored to know.

Wealth and position weren't an issue for James Copley. Only his family's negative opinion of him stained his existence. He simply desired his family's love and respect. This explained his proposal to the wrong woman.

His pain awoke in her a fervent desire to protect him.

"How did they take your enormous success? God enabled you to succeed without outside financial backing or a support system in place."

James shrugged. "I'm told they applaud the accomplishments. The five-year plan expired two years ago. Father's ready to implement corporate leasing. Each son will direct one-third of the operation while he steers the helm."

"What about Copley Homes?"

He chuckled. "I'll keep the baby safe and secure in Tulsa."

Neka nodded and took a deep breath. She didn't want to ask, but she had to know.

"So how does the wife come into play? Why did you propose to Teri?"

* * *

"A seat at the table comes with a marriage stipulation, per my father. Somehow getting married proves I'm a team player." He shook his head. "Utter nonsense. Brandie and I have always been the ones who promote family unity."

"What if you nix tying the knot for now?"

"It knocks me out of the equation." James assessed the compassion in Neka's gaze.

People assumed his detachment revealed contempt toward them, but the truth was that his lack of emotion protected him from their derision. While the physical labor of building his company had mitigated his fears in the past, now this compensation offered him solace for the future.

Once his folks admitted he'd exceeded their expectations, he would finally take his place at the Copley Enterprise table. He harbored no ill will toward Ryan and Matt. Both men had worked for the last six years to undo their attack. But their mistakes had proved they lacked the tenacity to lead the company into the future.

Neka placed her hand on his arm and ran her fingers across his skin, asking softly, "Does your father plan to reorganize the company while you're in town?"

James swallowed hard at the tingle where her hand lay, and he nodded. "Next week, I'll have to deal with business during the day and can act as a tour guide in the evenings. But, if I'm denied a seat at the table on Monday morning, we'll tour the sites during the day."

Frowning, she seemed to mull it all over. "So showing up without a fiancée is pointless. I can't believe Teri would do this to you—you had an agreement! From now on, I'll remember she tried to ruin you every time I look at her."

His spirit soared at her indignation.

"Don't be so hard on Teri. I accept the blame for our engagement. My lifelong dream to work in the family business clouded my judgment. Neka ..." he hedged. Though she'd dropped the opportunity into his lap, his plan might bomb. He frowned as he leaned against the door. "What I'm about to reveal might spoil the friendship we've built."

"Nothing you reveal could ever break this bond." Shaking her head, she scanned his features, took a deep breath, and laughed at herself. "Is this the confessing you were talking about?"

Instead of rushing into a speech, he silently added her to the select few whose opinion counted. Not too many people roamed those hallowed halls. While he prolonged the inescapable, her features softened. Perhaps she imagined he was summoning up courage to speak.

After Neka gave him a reassuring smile, he shook off his apprehension. For the first time in his life, James desired to see his integrity upheld in someone else's heart.

He leaned against the door while she nibbled her lower lip. "Here's the short version. Right after Ryan and Matt rejected my rightful place in the company, I plotted to take them down and hear my father beg forgiveness for his callous distrust."

James hesitated, attempting to truthfully bare his grievance. He sighed as Neka massaged her right earlobe. *Information overload.* "Our relationship wasn't in a constant state of dysfunction. The Copleys present a united front to everyone outside our inner circle. Only the McKinleys witnessed the actual status of our disarray."

He chuckled in a low tone. "It's hard to confess it was just to defend my bruised ego. I spent the last six years in a precarious state of denial, rejecting how much I missed my family. One day I realized disenchantment mattered less than working with the people I love. And I want an active voice within the business I'm destined to co-own."

James allowed truth to reach his soul. The good in their relationships outshone the infighting. Until that moment, he'd devalued moments of peace he had shared with his family.

Neka bit down on her bottom lip and waited for him to continue.

"Four years ago, I projected the good-natured side of my character, but payback still festered underneath the surface. But after meeting you," he said as he studied her face, "I want to work to undo the separation I've cultivated for way too long."

When James finished talking, she ran fingers through her hair. A couple of times she opened her mouth to speak but ended up looking downward.

"What are you thinking?"

"How a person overrun with bitterness could exude such charisma." She blushed and shook her head. "This is hard to deal with, James. Let's change the subject. Did your father decide to reorganize the company to bring you home?"

"Even if he did, his actions were heavy-handed."

"The two of you are more alike than you care to acknowledge."

It felt like an invisible hand tightened around his throat. "Touché."

Neka lowered her voice to a whisper. "Your father loves you."

"True, but don't get all warm and fuzzy. His autocratic nature landed me on Ryan and Matt's radar. My gut tells me a power play's underway at Copley Enterprise. My time away in Tulsa puts me at a disadvantage."

"Maybe they'll welcome you home." She smiled.

But his life was too complicated to entertain such impractical notions. James waved his hand aside. "I wish it was that simple. My brothers possess deep resentments from their own failed ambitions. Time doesn't heal every wound for all people. Outside sources indicate the West County venture flopped."

Neka's eyes grew wide. "Are they in a financial crisis? I'd hate to see them collapse."

He shrugged. "The true financial picture will unfold Monday."

She studied James. "All those years spent nursing wounds aggravated the pain that forgiveness would've healed eons ago." She stroked his arm, and he leaned nearer.

"I admit to setting up roadblocks instead of forgiving them, though I can't undo the breach." He hesitated. "Teri's actions today tie my hands."

Neka shook her head, not meeting his gaze. "It sounds like the next two weeks will be a possible war zone. Someone who loves you would stick it out, but Teri's resolve might've waned. She did you a favor by staying home."

"Even if her absence costs me my seat at the table?"

She nodded. "The absence of love failed to bind you together through difficulties."

James folded his arms. "In other words, you see her actions as justifiable."

"Level with me. Would you have proposed to her if the need hadn't arisen?" Neka's gaze didn't falter.

He frowned, not liking the direction this conversation was taking.

"You can't just use people for your own end."

"Then we must agree jilting me at the eleventh hour pays me back in spades. Applaud her. She accomplished her objective." The constriction around his throat lowered to his chest. The muscles in his stomach clenched as controlled anger seized him. Propped against the door, he watched her juggle sympathy between him and Teri, and all the anger went out of him.

Neka was the quintessential paragon of virtue in his eyes. He would have never believed he would be cementing a future with her in a rental car parked outside a mall.

He trailed his fingers across her cheek. His voice soft now, he said, "My past mistakes brought emptiness into each day. Going home to join the business allows these old wounds to mend. Father will send me packing unless ..."

She moved toward him and smiled encouragingly.

James swallowed hard. He leaned over and took her hand. It was now or never.

"Unless I convince you to become my wife."

38

* * *

Neka gasped.

Had James just proposed to her?

Her mom's encouraging words rushed through her mind. Could this be the change she'd seen coming?

In the midst of her thoughts, James rotated his thumb across her fingers. "For selfish reasons I rejected genuine relations with any woman. Out of the ones I dated, Teri possessed some sense of family. The folks would deem it possible, if not probable, that I intended to marry her."

"Did you date many women?" A lump in her throat made it hard to talk.

"Believe me. Regardless of my dating preferences, I respect traditional values." He clasped her hands. His hands were so warm, and the warmth spread through her. "I should've braved your rejection and courted you the moment I decided to marry."

She tried to smile, but she could barely breathe.

James hesitated. "You have all the qualities I've ever wanted in a wife. Godliness, lovability, and intelligence. Plus so many more I'd never thought of."

Though his praise lifted her spirit, Neka longed for something more.

Could she dare to believe he could love her?

She balanced his respect against the lack of deeper affection. When yearning for love, high regard fell flat.

He tilted his head to one side before continuing. "I trust you to raise our children. You have a strong hand and nurturing heart."

Their children? Nervous laughter bubbled up inside her and spilled out.

"Your peers agonized over my seeking you out."

"I've overheard many theories on the subject. I knew you played nice with me because I'm Kelly's little sister."

The hue of his eyes darkened. Did her evaluation surprise him?

"People make social faux pas every day. Do I *play nice* with anyone else?"

Blinking several times, she shook her head. "I'm the only one I know of."

He sighed. "You know I favor you above others. You've always received preferential treatment from me."

And then he smiled, brighter than she had ever seen. The smile reached his eyes, highlighting their golden glow. Her anxiety melted.

"Will you join your life with mine?" James caressed her cheek, smiling, and she leaned into his hand. "Forever."

Like a revved up engine, Neka's mind and body went into overdrive. She tried to sort out everything he had just said while buzzing sounds vibrated in her ears.

James Copley—*the* James Copley—had just proposed. Without pleading a brain freeze and taking it back.

Her mom's promises were proving spot on. Her shoulder's drooped. She couldn't lay her decision at her mom's feet—there's no way this is what she meant. People self-fulfilled their desires all the time. James simply stared ahead instead of gaping at her. Smiling, Neka allotted another thoughtful act to his favor.

Father, I love this man. Though I didn't expect a proposal today, I wanted to date him. Is helping James heal this old pain an assignment from You? Oh Lord, I'm so happy. The man I love asked me to marry him. I am blessed.

James turned to her with an expression she couldn't discern. It was a look she'd noticed before but never grasped its meaning. Nonetheless, she basked in the warmth of his proposal. She couldn't leave him to face his family alone. She loved him, and he needed her.

"Yes, James, I'll marry you."

He embraced her, and she was overcome by a strange mixture of sadness and pleasure. She tensed. This was nothing like the strong hugs given in the past. He cradled her in his arms, then he placed featherlight kisses on the tip of her nose and dimples. Pausing inches from her mouth, he brushed a kiss across her lips, hugging her until the tension melted away.

Neka's heart hammered against her ribs, and her bones felt like cooked pasta. She peered at James through eyes half-closed. He silently scanned her features as if engraving them into his memory.

Did her love show through her eyes and render him speechless?

"I feel awkward." Laughing, she glanced at her watch. "The phone might ring any second. How will you explain the broken engagement?"

"Ah, reality intrudes." Tapping his fingers on the steering wheel, James chuckled. "Let's chart a straight course. I'm interested in your response to Karen and Lawrence."

She raised her eyebrows. "But your parents are the ones expecting a different fiancée."

"Your parents will demand you return home on the next flight to Tulsa." James held up his hand when she frowned. "Don't suggest we play it by ear as you did on the plane."

Remaining calm, Neka almost giggled at his sincerity. "My mom and dad don't behave in ridiculous fashions."

"Don't ignore me." His eyes narrowed, but a smile played at his lips. "I know how they are."

She tensed at the reminder that James had spent vast amounts of time with her dad. "The simple decision to help you does present problems."

Although her parents were always available for counsel, they typically waited until their daughters requested advice now that they were adults. "If God ordained our marriage, He'll clear the pathway for us. That explains why we spent so much time together."

James frowned a little, but Neka's excitement was growing. She loved everything about this man, from the lock of hair hovering over his right eyebrow to the crescent-shaped scar above his lip that he'd received playing Little League baseball.

The man she loved had asked her to marry him. Nothing could ruin this day.

* * *

James was unconvinced that he had secured Neka's loyalty.

He weighed their options. Her commitment might disappear if her parents launched a counterattack. Even her sisters could jump into the fray. Neka had always followed their lead.

But he had traveled too far with her to backtrack now. He thought of their kiss, and heat trailed down his back. Her hesitancy made him want more, the kind of contact that would necessitate a honeymoon reveal.

But right now he had to plan for the inevitable Lacey retaliation. "Do you promise to remain in St. Louis until we fly out together in two weeks?"

Neka looked away from his searching eyes. Using one finger, he gently turned her face back to his. "I understand the strain of an adult child speaking with parents in the face of criticism. You're not alone anymore. Use me as a buffer. I can weather their reproach. Once they see how happy we are, their reservations will fade."

She sighed. "My parents already like you, but yours don't even know me. Will they accept our engagement?"

Why didn't she recognize the difference in their circumstances? "I'm not the twenty-one-year-old youngest daughter of a close-knit family. I'll tell the folks God saved their son from a dreadful mistake and present you to them. You'll receive a warm welcome and enchant them as you've captivated me."

He was satisfied that his low tone had soothed her apprehensions until she jumped when her own voice sounded throughout the car.

"Neka, pick up the phone."

She blushed. Was her heated face because of her cell phone's youthful ringtone? Apparently, his skepticism won out over her complacency as a wobbly finger slid across the phone's screen. After a woebegone glance at James, she took a deep breath.

"Hello, Mom ..."

Chapter Six

"Honey, I reread your letter several times. Why did you travel out of town without warning us? How does Teri and James's relationship involve you?"

"To support a friend, Mom." Neka's mouth hung open. The anxiety in her mom's voice shocked her. "Imagine the outcome for James if everyone abandoned him."

She flopped against the seat, picturing her mom counting to ten, the same practice she instilled into her girls.

"But why did you interject yourself into a couple's private affairs?"

She blinked in fast succession. "I couldn't allow him to board the flight alone. He carried the full weight of her deception on his shoulders."

"They're broad shoulders. James is an adult. Where is God in all of this?"

Under her mother's opposition, Neka's excitement waned a little. If her mom sounded upset, Dad would be livid. Until now, he and James had possessed a superb friendship. "Couldn't this trip begin the change you promised God would bring?"

"Don't lay your imprudence on me," her mother snapped. "The choices you make determine whether it's you or the Holy Spirit in control. If I asked you to return home today, would you agree?"

Frustrated, Neka buried her face into her hand. Tears filled her eyes. "How can I? I came to help him."

"Then your answer is no." Mom sighed. "Give me his parents' names and contact information."

Brushing teardrops from her cheeks, she accepted the handkerchief James offered. "May I call you later on?"

"Aren't you and James together?"

"We are but—"

"My disappointment in your behavior precedes concern over any embarrassment."

43

Neka laid her head against the window. There's no way she could announce her good news. A mother who disapproved of her traveling with James wouldn't welcome their engagement. Eyes closed, she tried but failed to think of a way to make amends. "How can you speak to me this way?"

"Instead of cross-examining me, explain traveling out of town without a word." Karen sighed so loudly that Neka winced. "Why would you hide your travel plans? Since we just celebrated your twenty-first birthday in April, your father and I couldn't forbid you from taking a trip in June."

Tears flowed down her cheeks in steady streams. Rushing from the car, she walked around in circles, explaining the beliefs that prompted her departure. After her mom had poked holes in every premise, Neka stared at the pavement.

Her mother ended by asking, "Is James aware of your feelings?"

"I didn't tell him."

"Just listen." Karen took a deep breath. "Protect yourself by guarding secret things until you return home. We'll have a quiet talk underneath our favorite tree."

She gazed at James with sad eyes as she got back into the car. "I promise. Something tells me sleep will escape me tonight. I love you so much ... so long."

Neka slid the cell phone into her purse, then she closed her eyes. "Thank you, Jesus."

He tucked a strand of hair behind her ears. "Pretty bad, huh?"

Nodding, she reflected on the conversation with her mom. Tears ran beneath her lids and down her cheeks. James removed the handkerchief from her hands, wiped her tears, and poked a dimple.

"Does Lawrence know we're together?"

Her hair dislodged when she shook her head. "Mom won't disrupt his day with bad news. Generally, she waits until he comes home from work. We'll talk after dinner tonight."

"Expect a call before tonight. Once Kelly finds out you're in St. Louis, she'll fill in the blanks from her conversation with Teri."

Without looking up, she shook her head. "Forget their friendship. Kelly won't disclose my whereabouts to anyone but Michael."

"I referred to her current information." He paused. "Lawrence doesn't possess your mother's natural grace. He'll demand to speak to me."

The thought of her father's reaction made her lightheaded. "I can picture Dad's slow-burning anger—annoyed that I'm here and incensed that I grieved his wife in the process. On the airplane I deluded myself that they would accept my account without backlash. I really believed your parents were the stumbling blocks."

Closing her eyes again, she ended their discussion.

* * *

For once, James wished he'd miscalculated someone else's reaction. Being right paled against what he'd just witnessed. Despite how taxing everything was for her, he was proud of Neka—and hopeful. Leaving home without notice showed a willingness to do things her own way and revealed a desire to reduce other people's resistance to her plans.

He watched her methodically massaging her earlobe, and tension seized his shoulders as he resisted the urge to pull Neka into his arms. He understood her pain. His mother had cried when he'd rented an apartment in Tulsa. Those tears had almost stopped his plans to start over.

But was Neka thinking of ways to patch things up with her parents or how to purge him from her life?

By assisting him, she caused enough chaos to disrupt the Laceys' weekend. Though he helped her whenever possible, she bore the burden of this situation alone.

Neka just sat there, staring out the window. James gripped the steering wheel tighter. Reshaping his plan, he drove to their destination in silence. When he turned into the parking lot, she examined the two-story building.

"Where are we?" She looked into the mirror and shuddered at her reflection. "I'll stay inside the car."

Neka took some lotion from her handbag and began to massage some into her arms. His eyes tracked every movement.

His abdomen tightened. No tear stains streaked her cheeks. Instead of detracting from her beauty, her sadness lent a delicate aura. She glowed as if inner turmoil added their own emollients to her skin.

She gazed at him. "I'll wait here for you."

Despite his gaze being glued to the fingers massaging lotion over her arms, James was determined to get their day back on track. Again. He chuckled. "So you trust me to pick out your engagement ring?"

45

She looked from the mirror to him and then at the building. "The jeweler's inside?"

Tearing his gaze from her ministrations, James surveyed her expression. "This is the official Copley family jewelry store. Wentzel's is one of the largest privately owned jewelers in the country and the most prominent one in the area."

Neka coughed as if the breath caught in her throat. "You're buying it now?"

"You already forgot accepting my proposal earlier?"

Her unease melted before his eyes, and she smiled. "So you're ready to buy a ring this time?"

Teri's ringless finger flashed in his mind. At this rate, a respectable estimation of his character might vanish altogether. All the negative revelations that morning had muddied the waters. Bolstering her favor was up to him.

"This is the perfect time to cement our relationship." James shot her his most charming smile, but his body jerked when she returned one even more enchanting. "Remember? Yes means forever."

"I remember." Tears filled her eyes again, but she was still smiling. She stretched out her palms toward him, then stopped the motion and clasped her hands together.

* * *

Inside the store, Neka took in the upscale setting. Bright lights illuminated the delicate stones displayed on black velvet. Filing the decor away for future reference, she turned to James. "The room is huge! What's on the second level?"

"On one side of the building there's a bistro and two boutiques with bridal and evening attire along with accessories. An auditorium and banquet room take up the other end."

She was becoming so excited that she didn't know where to begin. Her gaze swept the cases. "Are we purchasing a wedding band for you?"

"For all to witness." James visibly relaxed his shoulders, which she hadn't even realized were so tense. "Soon others will acknowledge we belong together too."

While he spoke, an elegant woman tapped him on the shoulder from behind. A simple black dress draped with a silver shawl highlighted her striking features. She was beautiful.

"James Copley, did you pop the question, and this stunning young lady said yes?"

"If not, you would've embarrassed us all for nothing. We flew in this morning, which makes you our first stop after breakfast." Gold flecks glowing in his eyes, he laughed and kissed the woman's cheek. Neka tensed at the affection between the two, but James pulled her closer. "Nikhol Lacey agreed to bind herself to me forever. Sweets, Mimi harassed me from kindergarten through senior year. Her grandparents built this establishment thirty-eight years ago."

Mimi grasped James around the waist. "He does mean forever. Only close friends can attest to his jealous nature. James dated girls he didn't mind losing."

His eyebrow rose. "Don't fill her head with drivel. Do you have a salesperson picked out?"

"Okay, Kent's lagging in sales this week. I'll send him over."

Mimi smiled and touched Neka's hand before moving away. "My husband, Clint, and James are old friends. Please come over at two next Saturday and spend the day with us."

Neka glanced at James before nodding. "Thanks for the invite. I'm looking forward to getting to know James's friends."

James was content to trail behind Neka. After a few minutes of peering into cases, she stood still in the middle of the aisle tapping a finger on her lip. "They're all so fussy."

James stopped in front of a display case she hadn't inspected. "You passed right by this entire section."

She came to stand beside him, placed her arm through his, and peeked through the glass top. "These rings do fit my taste better. Look at this gorgeous one on the second tier."

Stooping lower, she made a closer inspection.

"I found it." She squeezed his arm and leaned back on her heels. "I really like the third one from the left."

James beckoned Kent, who hurried over and unlocked the sliding door. "That bright smile conveys you found your heart's desire."

Neka clapped her hands, then clasped them beneath her chin. "It's a dream come true."

James leading me to the perfect ring has to bode well for our future.

Kent glanced at her, grinning. Using gentle motions, he extracted the ring from its cushion and held it toward the light. Laughing, he glanced at Neka when James stretched out his hand. "You're right. It's a flawless choice—a twenty-four-karat white-gold round-top pavé diamond semi-mount."

James tilted the ring to different angles before peering into the display cabinet. "Sure you want to wake up to this ring every morning for the rest of your life?"

"I love the setting. The side stones twinkle like stars." Neka was mesmerized by the emotional roller coaster of the day and by the ring's delicate beauty. She paused. "Wait, don't you approve of my choice?"

He chuckled. "If you like it, I love it."

She put a hand on her hip. "Then why are you frowning at it?"

James laughed again and reached for her finger. "I wanted you to make a fussier choice. But if you're certain I'm holding your dream ring in my hand ..."

He paused as if giving her a second chance to change her mind. When she remained silent, he placed the ring on her finger, surveying her reaction.

Neka waved her hand in front of her face. Laughing, she winked at James wriggling her fingers from side to side. She was too overcome to speak. This morning she'd left home thinking she was helping her friend, and now she was picking out an engagement ring with the man she loved.

James looked at Kent. "I guess we're finished here. We'll take this one today and a customized wedding band within two weeks."

It was real. She was getting married. She held back her tears, even though they were tears of joy. She didn't want to cry any more today. Instead, she smiled at Kent. "We need a matching band for James."

The salesman nodded approval. "Your purchase will be ready for pickup this afternoon. We'll have your second order completed next Wednesday."

As James removed the ring from her finger, Neka peeked up at him. "So you approve of my choice?"

He gazed down at her. "The ensemble heralds the virtues of its owner—simple yet beautiful and unique." He kissed the tip of her nose.

Once Kent measured their fingers he completed the transaction. He walked them to the front of the store while talking nonstop. Neka waved good-bye to Mimi. Holding the door open, Kent shook their hands with quick pumps. "Thank you, Neka and James for visiting us today. The ring will be ready after two."

Neka couldn't wait.

* * *

James parked the car in the same mall spot they had vacated an hour ago. "Care to tell me what you promised your mother?"

Refusing to look at him, she glanced out the window. After a few seconds, her gaze shifted to her toes.

Somehow he had to stop her from becoming wedged between him and her family. While considering a course of action, he realized that to Neka, honoring the vow to her mother was more important than satisfying his curiosity. The realization that he placed a dismal fifth behind her parents and sisters sucked air from his lungs.

She seemed to still be fishing around for an answer, but instead she asked, "Do your parents live far?"

"About twenty minutes from here. Let's shop until it's time to pick up your ring."

Blast this tightening around his throat. Though that sensation hadn't occurred in five years, he'd already experienced it a few times today. Forget about rating fifth place in Neka's heart. Not enough time had passed to expect anything different.

Helping her out of the car, James tilted her face toward his.

"You've experienced quite an unsettling day. Let's help those sad parts fade away and build enough happy memories to last a lifetime." He hesitated, scanning her features and brushing a thumb over her lips. "Next year we'll celebrate our anniversary with no regrets. God gives his children victory over every obstacle."

A tiny light sprung into her eyes.

"Proclaiming faith in His power always encourages me." Tears welled in her eyes, but she shook them off. "I long to please Him, but I keep messing up. Just like this morning; my best efforts sometimes miss the mark."

She took a deep breath. Hand in hand, they strolled into the mall.

Chapter Seven

As they sauntered through the lobby, the sweet aroma of the bakery permeated the air. Riding the escalator to the second level, they passed by countless shops she ignored until James stopped in front of a hair salon. When he stepped toward the doorway, Neka pulled back, refusing to move forward.

"Let's talk to a stylist. For years, you've wanted to try a different look." He smiled when she squinted her eyes, peering at him through half-closed lids. "Consider me the wish granter."

"You remembered." She studied him without speaking. The expression on her face warmed his body from head to toe. "Do they know how to style African-American hair?"

"Let's go inside. Someone's sure to meet with your approval. I'll read a magazine while I wait to see your new hairdo."

"I'll take your word for it."

Forty-five minutes later she tapped him on the shoulder, patting the top of her head.

"What do you think?"

Speechless, James rose to his feet, astounded by the transformation a simple haircut produced. He'd only expected the stylist to trim the edges, but her hair was at least two inches shorter. When she first went back, he'd watched her hair drop to the floor at her feet. But after the initial shock wore off, he chose a seat blocking his view.

He whistled low, and it brought a smile to her face. Ever since he'd met Neka, she had talked about cutting her hair, but keeping it longer enabled her to hide away from the world. The shorter hair highlighted her beautiful long neck. How had anyone ever overlooked her beauty?

"It really shows off those almond-shaped eyes."

Neka exhaled the breath she held, feathering fingers over her hair. "Do I look okay?"

"Better than okay. You're gorgeous." Involuntarily he leaned closer.

After paying the bill, he retraced their steps until they reached the nail shop next door to the bakery on the lower level.

"While you were with the hair stylist, I set up an appointment for a manicure and pedicure." James smiled when she stared at him without moving. "Sweets, you deserve to be pampered. Let me repair the damage caused this morning by your willingness to help me."

She bit her lower lip. "James—"

"Don't shy away from good treatment. Enjoy the attention." Tilting his head to the side, he observed her reaction. He was definitely winning her over. "We're engaged now. It's my job to help you tick off your dreams. I hear shopping is a panacea."

Neka glanced into the shop. James understood her resistance. Only fools indulged themselves when imagining the world collapsing around them.

Nevertheless, she crept through the door without a backward glance, still nibbling her bottom lip. He heaved a sigh straight from his gut, then spied comfortable chairs outside the store. Her trusting gaze haunted him. Running his fingers along the armrest, he crafted a speedy revision of his plans.

He pictured a vibrant Neka bouncing from the store, pleased with the personal touch, and he hoped the shopping would lighten her load. Going home to Tulsa was out of the question and would only increase her problems. Staying the course was still the best option.

Forty-five minutes later she sat next to him in the lobby area. "I'm finished."

James put aside the pamphlet he'd been reading. He was glad she was wearing sandals to show off her cute little feet and toes, even cuter now with painted nails. She still hung her head but held out her hands for his inspection.

The downcast face concerned him. He couldn't leave her alone for extended periods. James placed an arm around her shoulder, acutely aware of how small she felt in his arms. "Are you ready to continue our journey into unknown regions?"

His soothing tone seemed to calm her nerves. Neka flashed him a half-smile and dimpled cheeks. "I do like to shop."

"Yes, but we'll spree this afternoon." He chuckled, and tension he didn't know was there eased from his shoulders.

"Is there a difference?"

"I kept a pair of shoes notched with miles of trailing behind Mother and Brandie through these very halls. How are you holding up?"

"I'm fine unless I replay the disappointment in my mom's voice." Eyes full of remorse, she shook her head. "Thank God I didn't bail on them altogether. I was scheduled off today and completed my assignments Wednesday. Kelly can adjust my workload if any new projects come in."

Since Neka loved her job, he dwelled on the topic. "How many other interior designers does Lacey Corp employ?"

"Two others besides me and Kelly, plus four additional stylists spread between two subsidiaries."

* * *

Golden flecks intensified his gaze. Shopping with James was soothing her troubles. Neka's qualms decreased as she leisurely peered at store displays, imagining their new life together. Her nose twitched as she sniffed a third scented candle.

Her largest concern right now was keeping James unaware that she loved him, since her mother had made her promise. Thank God she hadn't blurted out the truth during their flight so her dignity remained intact. James would never discover the truth unless she tipped her hand in some way. Mom had guessed her secret but she would only tell Dad. Everyone else hearing the announcement would think them deeply in love.

Growing his business network had demanded so much of her dad's time when she was young that he'd handed his wife the reins to manage their household as she pleased. They learned at an early age not to complicate his life with foolishness, and he had preached against character weakness since she had first learned to crawl. Until today, Neka had always lived drama-free.

She glanced at James, surprised by the tingling surging through her toes. She really did feel better and prettier with some pampering.

He eyed her. "Where next?"

"This one that one and the one over there." Laughing, she pointed to every other shop they passed.

"Then I'd better find a comfortable seat in the lobby while you shop. Let's visit the stores they don't have in Tulsa. Since they're probably all over the mall, let's take a quick look at the directory."

"I wish Kelly and Tammy were here. They only let me buy the styles that flatter me." Neka jotted down several locations before recapping her pen. She liked shopping but was happy just being with him.

"Living with a sister means I can definitely tell what looks good on a woman." James tightened his arm around her waist. "Especially the one I'm going to marry."

"You know you never answered my earlier question. How many women did you date before proposing to Teri?" Squinting her eyes at him, she smiled.

"Less than you may think."

She stopped walking, waiting for an answer. "That's not a number."

"Fine." James let out a melodramatic sigh and laughed. "Three including Ms. Campbell."

Neka raised her eyebrows and glanced away before he could glimpse the love in her gaze. "What attracted you to them?"

As soon as she said it, she wished she hadn't.

He chuckled and pulled her into resuming their stroll. "How can I think of other women when my mind is filled with you?"

"Good answer." She happily joined his laughter.

Their light conversation kept her negative thoughts at bay. Being with James always gave her such joy. He was the only person outside of her family who understood her. But until that morning, their close contact had never caused a physical response in her body. James had hugged her in the past, but today he wrapped his arm around her shoulder, keeping her at his side. The connection almost made her forget that he hadn't said he loved her.

At the shoe store, Neka picked up several flats until James coaxed her to a high-heel display. She shook her head at each pair until three caught her attention. Pleased with her selections, a black handbag with hidden zippers jumped out at her on her way to check out. She plunked it on the counter next to the shoes and then smiled at James.

She swung their hands as they left the store. He glanced at her. She scowled, thinking about the shoes he insisted she buy. The sensible flats she'd set her heart on flashed in her mind. "Hopefully I won't trip over my feet when I wear those shoes."

"You won't trip wearing two-inch heels. You've got good motor skills." He chuckled, shaking his head and then capturing her gaze. "Besides, they make your legs look amazing. Thanks for accepting these small tokens of my affection."

Unable to contain her delight, she squeezed his hand. "Compliments pave the way to starved hearts." *Oops, too much information.*

James stopped in the middle of the crowd, forcing other shoppers to skirt around them. The light in his eyes drew her nearer. "Today was destined to be harrowing even with Teri's presence. But you've changed the focus of my day. I've even quit imagining my father's and brothers' rebuttal. Thank you."

The sincerity of his words struck home, more so because she sensed he instantly regretted speaking them. James began a rambling conversation of no consequence.

She knew it! He did enjoy spending alone time together.

* * *

Later, Neka eyed herself in every window, enthused at the fashionable woman who stared back at her. Buying clothes had never been this fun before. That James thought her beautiful made up for years of feeling alone.

"Wearing that outfit when you meet my mother will help you feel like the strong, confident woman you are. She wears pearls while vacuuming the carpet." He laughed.

His laughter made her heart flutter. "Really? No, you're joking. The laidback James Copley has June Cleaver for his mother?"

"Not really. Mother abhors carpet." He laughed again. "She's not as homey as Karen Lacey, but she made our house a home. Until today, she's always been my staunchest supporter."

Neka couldn't help her huge grin. "You mean me?"

"Mother and Brandie must take second and third place behind my fiancée."

Still laughing, they entered a natural-makeup shop. A middle-aged lady with a detached stare picked up a writing pad and met them at the door. Her lightly made up face convinced Neka she would use a soft touch.

"Hello, my name is Brooke. How can I help you?"

"I'm Neka. This is James. He's my fiancé, and he is fulfilling my every want today from the last four years. You're our last stop."

Shrewd eyes assessed him. "A man who remembers any conversation not relating to him is rare. Over a four-year-span is unheard of. Keep him."

Neka laid a finger against her lips. "Shhh. I don't want him to get a big head."

"I'm pretty sure it's too late for that. Expensive clothes, dark-blond hair, golden eyes, and a muscular physique ... he must fight off women."

Neka blinked at the woman's assessment of her fiancé. Clearly they needed to change the subject. "I want makeup for my eyes and lips, please. I prefer earth tones."

Brooke's tone changed immediately. "How about experimenting with brighter shades too? We can always remove any you don't like."

While complimenting her clear complexion, the makeup artist asked about her cleansing routine and skillfully outlined various products the store sold. Fifteen minutes later, Neka swiveled away from the counter and slid off the stool. "Do you think anyone from home will recognize me?"

James studied her face. "She simply enhanced the loveliness we already admired."

A surge of energy spread throughout her body. Glancing at Brooke, she pointed to James. "He's on a roll."

The makeup artist walked them to the door, laughing. "Remember he's a keeper."

When they got out to the car, James placed all the bags in the trunk, closed it with a snap, and examined her appearance. "Despite the chaotic beginning to our day, I like sharing my old stomping grounds with you."

* * *

"I scored big this morning. A new hairdo, pretty fingers and toes, and a different style of clothes, plus shoes and purses. Brooke was fantastic. I love my chic new look." She snapped her seat belt into place and twiddled her thumbs in her lap, then raised her head, smiling. "Until today, I doubted anyone could experience happiness and sadness in unison. You were right, though. Shopping calmed my nerves before meeting your mother and stopped me from reliving the harsh blow I dealt Mom. Thank you. For everything."

James backed the car out of the parking space. "Your parents dote on you. I'm sure your family bonds are intact."

What did the future hold with such a tremulous start? Answers would unfold daily.

Her stomach quivered. Family unity had always existed through the highs and lows of everyday life. The Laceys joined forces during hard times. Breaking rank had never been an option for any of them. Nothing stopped their ability to band together.

She glanced at James, who was concentrating on the traffic. The addition of Michael and Kenny to the family had only improved family interactions. What would James bring to the table?

Karen had requested that she return home. To accept James's proposal and then leave without solidifying the relationship made Neka nervous. What if she left the city and he rescinded the offer? But why marry a man who proposed out of need instead of love? Once the problem smoothed over, he might abandon her. She might be setting the stage for the biggest downfall of her life.

Perspiration dotted her chest. She couldn't leave. How did she make her family realize that she was the one who set the ball into motion? The bliss she experienced inside the mall sealed the deal. She and James had laughed throughout their afternoon, and she still felt the tingle of his arm around her shoulders.

James joined the fast-moving traffic on the highway. "So, are we having a large or small ceremony?"

Neka blinked. She'd always known exactly how she wanted her wedding—it was in her dreams both day and night. She turned to face him.

"Let's keep it intimate, only inviting close friends and family members. I'll ask my sisters to be matron of honor and bridesmaid. I wish there was a spot for my cousin Hazelle, but I only need two attendants. Since I don't have nieces and nephews, we'll skip the flower girl and ring bearer altogether." Neka frowned at him. "There's one other thing. I refuse to invite anyone to our wedding who doesn't like us."

He stared at her longer than he should while driving. "Now that particular requirement might prove tricky. Will we exclude family members who fall into that category?"

She squinted her eyes, thinking. "Not if it's your brothers and their wives." She pointed her finger at him. "But it means everyone else, including cousins, aunts, and uncles."

"What offense brought on this decree?"

"Don't think I came up with the idea overnight. It took me years to reach this conclusion." Neka hesitated when he laughed. "What's funny?"

As if to regain composure he gripped the steering wheel tighter. "It took years to arrive at that verdict?"

Their laughter filled the car. "Okay, so I'm only twenty-one. Since childhood, I've attended weddings where guests gossiped about the happy couple while sitting in church pews. Surface relationships don't matter to me. Only well-wishers will be asked to attend."

"Your firm position surprises me, but I like the idea."

"I'm glad you agree. Our ceremony will be sweet and simple, the church full of the Lord's presence."

James stole a quick glance. "I've never heard a woman mention God in connection with her wedding ceremony. I'll keep my guest list short."

Glad that he agreed with her ideas, Neka leaned closer.

* * *

James grinned. The light glowing in Neka's eyes and her eager smile rekindled a joy he had long forgotten; his top priority had to be setting the date today. Not even his mother would tolerate two failed engagements within six months. He must pick up the ring. He'd glue it to her finger if he had to. A swift ceremony would seal the deal. There were too many uncontrollable variables in Tulsa, and he refused to endure a year of knotted shoulder muscles.

No, at the end of the month, he had to be in St. Louis with his bride.

James glanced at her, willing her to agree. "Starting a new job in the midst of moving puts us in a time crunch. By forgoing the honeymoon until September, we'll experience a smoother transition."

Neka didn't attempt to hide her shock. "You want us to marry in three months?"

"Sooner, actually." He slowed the car, moving into the outer lane. "My job begins July fifth. Ideally, I'd like to be settled into our home before then."

She tapped a finger on her lips. "Relocating from another state does present problems."

"Glad you agree. I planned to buy a house this visit and move in at the end of the month." James lessened his grip on the steering wheel and reached for her hand. "If we fly home on the fifteenth and marry the twenty-third we can travel on schedule the following week."

Only fools neglected their blessings. A quick wedding would also squash anyone's—mainly the Laceys'—efforts to undermine their relationship.

There was no going back. He'd experienced his best day in eight years today, despite the urgent trials of the morning. Man, what a turnaround. It seemed God heard his prayers after all.

* * *

At a loss for words, Neka adjusted her seat-belt buckle. Did he really believe she would marry him in less than a month? It was impossible. Unless ...

Excitement surged through her body. Maybe James loved her too much to leave Tulsa without her.

But her fervor died in seconds. Looking downward, she clasped her hands on her lap. Only in perfect worlds do wishes come true.

Could her mom pull the wedding together in three weeks? No, she'd say they were rushing headlong over a cliff and request more time. "What about Copley Homes? Have you hired someone to manage your properties?"

"I've employed the same staff for six years. Occasional stopovers should suffice." He glanced at the clock on the dashboard. "An intimate ceremony is preferable to the showy weddings I've attended. Check whether our date's available at your church."

Her resolve waned. Why the big rush? Neka shook her head to clear her mind. "I'll ask. The fireside room *will* create a cozy atmosphere."

"We agree on the date?"

She considered the possibilities, chin resting on her fist. She was easy-going, but James was piling one challenge upon another. Even if she risked losing him she had to slow down his pace. "No. I'm sorry. But arriving home June fifteenth only gives me a week to buy a dress, set up the catering, and mail out invitations."

"You want a small ceremony and only plan to invite close family members and friends." James shot her a glance. "By tomorrow, they'll all know our marriage plans."

"How do I do everything in time if I'm in St. Louis for two weeks?"

"Three gowns are required. What could be simpler?"

"You don't understand the delicacies of group shopping. First we agree on which dresses to buy—"

"Since you're paying, you pick out the gowns."

59

Neka laughed. "Oh please, in an alternate universe maybe. What about food?"

He smiled wryly. "Ladies in your congregation can prepare a superb feast without a year's notice. Buffet tables complete our checklist ahead of schedule. Hazelle's parents' floral shop can supply enough flowers for twenty weddings."

"You make the impossible sound too simple." She smiled at the simplicity of his plan. Was she just setting up roadblocks and complicating the simple ceremony she'd always wanted? Frowning, Neka stared out the window until she realized the real problem. "But I want an autumn wedding. I love fall colors."

"Incorporate them into our summer ceremony."

Aghast, she shook her head in an emphatic "no."

"Sweets, I'm unable to change my start date. If I remain in Tulsa, my family will reorganize the company without my input."

"I knew you were leaving Tulsa on the twenty-ninth." Neka tapped fingers together as she stared off into space. "But Teri wasn't moving with you."

James turned to her for a moment and smiled. "You're not Teri."

"But you planned to leave alone." Laying hands on the dashboard, she studied him. "Maybe that's still the best plan."

Chapter Eight

Neka was so stubborn. Shades of Lawrence Lacey were seeping through her sweet façade. Did she share other personality traits with her father? He hoped Karen's influence dominated her thinking.

"Unlike with Teri, the two of us are partners. Forever, remember? We'll attend Little League games, piano recitals, Christmas plays, and all of our children's activities." He almost pulled into the parking lot they passed to plead his case without distractions. "I know this is a series of firsts for you, but it's a huge lifestyle change for me too. You're taking me on a path I've never been down."

"I'm honored God answered your prayers in me."

His heart almost stopped at the beauty of the way her eyes sparkled. She stretched her hand toward him; her hopeful expression begged understanding. "I botched this trip from the start with my parents. My mom doesn't know I'm engaged, and I can't proceed without her involvement." Neka looked away but then glanced at James. "What if my family and I decorate our house before you move in?"

James recognized the olive branch she offered. But the Laceys preparing a house for Neka and him to call home would signify their support for the marriage—and that would be a miracle.

"An excellent idea. In fact, make it a real family affair. Include Mother and Brandie in your decorating scheme too." He glanced at her until she nodded.

He turned into Wentzel's parking lot and stopped at the side entrance.

"I can't wait to see my ring on your finger."

* * *

Neka couldn't stop looking at the ring. She held it at different angles, in different lights in the car. It was the most beautiful thing she'd ever seen.

61

Driving down Highway 40, James pointed out the sights. "Turtle Park is on your right. Brandie takes her four-year-old daughter, Yancey, there all the time."

Neka turned in her seat, pulling her eyes away from the ring just in time to see the unusual playground. "Ooh, look at the turtle shapes. Some are huge. I like the muted colors."

He glanced at the park too, like he was seeing it through her eyes. "There are large and small turtle statues the children play on. Sometimes the place gets so crowded in the summer you can't find a parking space."

James exited the highway, then drove down Oakland, turning left at the corner. Once they crossed the overpass, he pointed out more sights. Stopped at a traffic light, he turned to her, smiling. "I grew up in this neighborhood. We're five minutes from my folks' house."

Was it his smile or her nerves making her stomach do flips? Neka wrung her hands in her lap. She was always a hit with older people and children, so those family members should accept her. But teenagers and other adults usually moved away after minutes of conversation. If everyone else would dislike her, making a splash with his parents was even more important.

Her lack of friendships during high school had been stressful. Even now, she only hung out with Hazelle, her sisters, or alone. Parties had become easier once James had befriended her. Not only had his presence provided male companionship, his helpful advice sustained her through college. He'd cautioned her to avoid people who mocked her beliefs, and that advice had solidified her choice to live at home.

Since Hazelle got married last year, she'd become a virtual hermit. Running around with Kelly and Tammy had its downside—they never allowed her to make decisions without their immediate feedback.

In fact, Neka was surprised she hadn't heard from them yet about her actions today. She checked the volume on her cell phone and frowned. Maybe Mom asked them not to call until she spoke to Dad. Would they have listened?

What about the Copleys? Her first meeting with her future in-laws would demand her active participation. She squirmed in her seat. How would she stack up against his past dates?

She glanced at James. Though her love for him had increased so much today, she couldn't really be happy knowing she'd treated her parents so badly.

Lord, let my family forgive the rash behavior and let his family like me.

While stopped at another traffic light, James stroked her knee. He held her gaze with that special smile he reserved only for her. The tender expression eased her nerves, but her heartbeat quickened anyway.

When the light changed, he eased into a commentary about the neighborhood before making a right turn on a cobbled road lined with outdoor cafes. In Tulsa, only Brookside or maybe Cherry Street came close to this artsy district. A woman in cutoff jeans and cowboy boots walked a dog too large for her to handle. A man wearing a pea-green smock painted a seascape in his makeshift studio. On the next corner, a whiskered gentleman leaned against a storefront playing the saxophone. Neka nodded in agreement as an older couple placed a bill into the cigar box at his side.

Finally, James drove through gates to an old neighborhood. "There are fourteen homes that were built in the early 1900s, either before or after the 1908 World's Fair. The streets are privately owned by residents. Twenty-two years ago, my parents purchased the Montgomery estate. The Copleys represent the second family line to live in the house."

He took his time and inched the car along. A wide variety of trees dotted the road, beginning with the sweetgums at the gated entrance, their spiky green fruit visible from the car. Farther down the street, she noted ash trees and Bradford pears interspersed with huge old maples. The homes offered various architectural designs from colonial to Victorian. Each situated on about an acre of land, the stately homes and their yards resembled a small park-like setting.

James's demeanor was always laidback, but perhaps his family was more well-off than she'd imagined.

Pulling down the sun visor, she examined her reflection in the mirror. She was glad she wore the clothes James purchased at the mall.

Her interior designer mind took over the moment she scanned the spacious foyer that doubled as a versatile living area. A trey ceiling and recessed lighting turned the open space into an attractive room. Kelly had completed decorations on a single-family dwelling with a foyer about the same size last week. Taking out her cell phone, she captured the image for her sister. Maybe Kelly would respond with a call.

On the right side, a light-gray love seat and two white chairs faced one another in a conversation pit, a dark-pink throw on the back of one. Olive-green shades topped the oval lamps set on accent tables. Stuffed between the chairs, a mauve upholstered ottoman completed the homey scene.

The other side of the room was an office nook with an oak desk and tan chairs. Furniture placement made the area appear larger than the actual square footage, while the olive green and rose-colored rug united both sections into a showplace. She knew they entertained all but intimate friends in this space.

As James led her down a long hallway, Neka gave each room a quick peek. The living and dining room connected on the left. An opened door revealed a library and office to the right. Before they reached the end, a tall woman, blond hair sprinkled with gray, welcomed them with outstretched arms. Dropping Neka's hand, James stepped into his mother's line of vision.

"You chose the perfect time to arrive. I just removed the last batch of cookies from the oven. Welcome home, son." Mrs. Copley flowed into his arms.

They embraced for several seconds until he gave her an extra squeeze and they broke apart.

"You're as beautiful as ever. I've missed you." James hugged her again, resting his chin on her head.

The woman's husky voice breezed into the air. "Frequent visits might've validated that statement. Stopovers only whet the appetite for more contact."

He chuckled. "Mother, meet your future daughter, Nikhol Lacey."

His mother's hands dropped from his shoulders. Sidestepping him, she stared at Neka, a question in her gaze.

James nudged Neka into a sheltering arm. "Sweets, Francine Copley is the backbone of our family."

Face-flushed Neka held out her hand. "Hello, Mrs. Copley. James has told me wonderful stories about you over the years."

Fran's gaze flickered over Neka, who wriggled on her feet before Fran shook her outstretched hand. "Excuse my manners."

Fran's stare pinned her son to his spot. "For a month we heard a different name. We expected Teri Campbell, the person you depicted to a T last night, or so I thought. Of course, there's a logical explanation for changing fiancée's overnight."

She cast Neka a sardonic look as she led them into the den.

* * *

"Put Mother's pithy comments down to exasperation. Her opinion of me isn't quite that small," James whispered as they settled on the mint-green sofa. He draped his arm around Neka's shoulder and hugged her against his side. "The worst of the storm passed during the introductions. I guarantee Father and the others will know our story before meeting you in person. Brandie's a ready ally. Her husband, David, is my best friend since preschool days." He paused, riveted by the love shining forth unhindered in her eyes.

From the corner of his eyes, he saw his mother monitoring their interaction. She cleared her throat as she carried a small teal tray loaded with goodies. "I brought snacks to sustain us until dinner. God knows we'll need the nourishment."

James took the tray, handed Neka a drink, and then set his glass on the accent table beside the sofa. Fran gathered her refreshments and sat down in a chair facing them, eyeing Neka.

Without looking at James's mother, Neka bit into a cookie and licked her lips, as if giving him time to sit beside her. "They're still warm. Thank you. I love chocolate chip cookies. And the fresh lemonade's delicious."

James returned to his seat and studied his mother. She glared back at him.

His mother was playing hardball. He reminded himself that her approval would minimize his father's opposition. "Mother, thank you for the warm welcome. But please, accept my apology. Last night when you asked for a description of my fiancée, I described Teri, even though she wasn't coming. Before you ask, I wanted to shield Neka from biased opinions regarding our relationship. So, I failed to mention her before today."

He swallowed his drink, surveying Fran as she sipped lemonade with a guarded expression. James sighed and rolled his shoulders. This day couldn't end soon enough for him. Though she loved James, his mother always sided with his father.

"Father's job offer sounded like a godsend until he issued the 'get married' command."

"Yes, those cumbersome details."

His eyes narrowed. "Since no special lady emerged among the women I dated, I proposed to Teri. But our engagement wasn't ... rewarding."

65

"I figured a problem existed when I wasn't allowed to congratulate your fiancée." Fran nodded. Both her hands squeezed the armrest. Her voice cracked. "Either you hid her or your mother."

James stared in disbelief and then smiled at his mother, not wanting to show how her comment had hurt him. "Hiding you from anyone is inconceivable."

She waved him off. "Brandie joked you'd finagled some poor woman into deceiving Gene and plotted to break it off in the end."

He grunted. Accommodating his father's irrational demand wasn't the same as deception. He leaned forward. "I missed you."

"Twenty minutes ago, my heart ached whenever I reflected on lost time." Fran turned to Neka. "Since James brought you into my home, I choose to speak without inhibitions. Our family suffered a needless separation because four men refused to stand down."

She sighed and looked away. "I called James every Sunday that no one in the family visited him in Tulsa."

"I welcomed each call. Our Sunday-morning ritual set the mood for the upcoming week." Unable to take back their shattered relationship, the low tone of his voice asked forgiveness for his part. "Only holidays were hard. I'd always spent Thanksgiving and Christmas within these walls. I enjoyed our family celebrations."

"We want you home." Fran gazed at Neka with half-closed eyes. "After the wedding, you'll have the gift of a wife beside you."

"I'm thankful." The idea of a future with Teri had killed his spirit.

Skepticism highlighted Neka's expression. What bothered her about their conversation?

James grasped her hand. "I finally found my soulmate. In fact, our paths would have eventually crossed without the move to Tulsa."

Fran set down her glass. "I almost clapped. You've spun the most believable, farfetched tales since you could talk. Like fine wine, they get better with age but become less tolerable."

James distanced himself from her disfavor. His mother could rip his determination to shreds. "Mother—"

Fran cut him off. "Though your words seem heartfelt, these questions still exist: When did the engagement end? How soon afterward did you propose to Neka? A lovely ring is on her finger, but when did you place it there?"

He squeezed Neka's hand. This had to be hard for her. "Mother, I met the Laceys when I first moved to Tulsa."

"Then why not propose to Neka instead of Teri?" She gazed at Neka. "How well do you know my son? Were you aware that he's never introduced the girls he dated to his family? Only David knew which ones he took out."

Smiling, Neka shook her head. James calculated the odds of his mother losing steam before recounting his entire life story.

Instead, the room grew silent. He remained quiet, refusing to add fuel to the fire of his mother's anger. To air troubles in front of strangers was unheard of in this household. She clearly wasn't buying any of it.

They both stared at Neka. During the entire discussion, she chewed cookies, watching them as if a theater performance unfolded.

"Young lady, why did you accept his proposal?" Fran stared at the ring. "Though I won't ask the date he proposed, I'm sure you agree the engagement defies credibility."

Finished, she placed her feet on a footstool and leaned against the cushion.

Chapter Nine

Biting into a cookie, Neka let the chocolate melt in her mouth. She refused to respond like a deer trapped in headlights. Sipping her drink, she considered her reply.

James had delivered an optimistic overview of their relationship filled with partial truths. Although Mrs. Copley was a little abrasive, her reticence seemed natural. How would her mom react under the same pressure? Didn't her future mother-in-law deserve the truth regarding their liaison? Could she accomplish this feat without betraying her fiancé's confidence?

She took a deep breath and received an encouraging squeeze from James. He'd shown genuine emotion after Mrs. Copley suggested he hid her from Teri. It was obvious that the comment wounded him, despite his smile. Their interaction showed that they shared a loving if tense relationship.

She twisted her ring around her finger. It sparkled even more in the indirect lighting.

"Even though we share a unique friendship, his proposal shocked me." Neka smiled at Fran's curious expression. "I met James a few months before my seventeenth birthday. Now I'm just a twenty-one-year-old homebody who attends church-related functions or those given by close family members."

Fran crossed her ankles and glanced at James. "I can't imagine a personable young lady like you as an introvert."

"This pariah can empty a room in seconds." She laughed, trying to sound natural, though her heart was pounding in her ears. "I discovered James had proposed to Teri because he needed a wife by overhearing a conversation between her and my sister Kelly. Since the need existed after she broke off the engagement, I intervened on his behalf."

Fran stared off to the side. "You didn't already have a boyfriend?"

"James is the only man that I've spent much time with." She blinked several times and didn't make eye contact. Being alone had hurt, even if she was the one who refused the requests. "He dances with me at parties and calls me sweets or sweetie. I like both names."

Disbelief appeared in his mother's eyes. Fran pursed her lips into an almost sneer. "Friendship doesn't explain marrying a man who doesn't love you. The arrangement didn't offend you?"

"Call me fanciful." Neka brought a cookie close to her mouth and glanced at James. He smiled reassuringly. "It's like those old romance novels, where couples enter into marriages of convenience, fall in love, and live happily ever after. It's intriguing when individuals scale mountains together."

"What about James and Teri—a happy union or a failure?"

Neka nodded. "Wrong for one another from the start. They're blessed the engagement ended."

Fran gazed at James, although she wasn't speaking to him. "There must be other motives for agreeing to this marriage."

Why would she think there were other reasons? Neka frowned, thinking about the previous exchange between mother and son. "Mrs. Copley, will you discuss our conversation with anyone else?"

Fran shook her head. "I share secrets with Gene only. Four children taught us the necessity of privacy. James can vouch for that."

He squeezed Neka's hand. "Only Father will hear about what was discussed here."

Leaning forward, she took a deep breath and rested her forearms on her lap. "My mom said that a new direction dawned for me and I should embrace God's destiny. I believe marrying James ushers in this change. We are a great team and can do wonderful things together."

Fran sat up at her words but then relaxed her shoulders, surveying her son. "That's not what I expected. Although I can't believe your mother agreed with this interpretation, basically putting you into a loveless marriage."

Neka looked down. Karen Lacey approving a hasty engagement? No way.

James's mother started to speak, then changed her mind. She seemed to misinterpret Neka's sudden sadness as embarrassment.

"Well, from your mouth to God's ear." Fran stood, extending her arms to stretch. Her elbow joints popped. She glanced at her son. "Did you bring the luggage inside?"

Shaking his head, James headed for the door, pulling Neka behind him. "Which room was prepared for my fiancée?" he asked his mother.

Fran glanced at Neka. "I didn't set up separate bedrooms, assuming Teri would share one with you."

Neka froze.

Overcome with laughter, James shook his head, regaining composure. "Now I'm surprised. Before moving to Tulsa, you would've barred me from visiting if I'd even hinted at a liaison under this roof."

His gaze flickered over Neka, and he winced.

"You've shocked Neka. Her grandfather's a retired minister. Uncle Joe pastors the church his father founded." He studied her downcast face.

She felt jittery, like her whole body was wiggling but no one could see.

"Brandie's room is available. You'll be comfortable there. I'll escort you upstairs while James retrieves the luggage." She beckoned Neka. Leading her from the den, Fran glanced over her shoulder. "The room is next to James's and overlooks the garden in the back. I think you'll like it."

While following Fran upstairs with stiff movements, Neka pondered the bedroom issue. She knew some professing Christians had sex outside of marriage. But why did Fran equate their actions with James? If she believed in God, why would she agree to that? Placing them in the same bedroom gave her seal of approval.

Her parents would never condone anyone fornicating inside their home. Of course, Fran couldn't control his actions, but her tolerating sin under her roof worried Neka. Did she regularly disregard biblical principles?

Neka stopped mid-step. Did James have sex with the women he dated?

In the numerous conversations where the topic was raised, he had never challenged her views. She thought he completely agreed with her own position that sex outside of marriage was a sin. Opinions contradicting God's word were insignificant.

Different scenarios flooded her mind as she mounted the steps. Had he actually slept with the women he'd taken out? This brought a whole new dimension to Teri's actions.

Neka frowned, not liking where her thoughts led.

In the car, James had revealed an element of his personality she'd never detected. Until four years ago, bitterness had consumed him. Resentment toward family members could develop while growing up. But indulging in sexual activity before marriage was a conscious act. Surely James didn't condone that.

Oh, Lord. Do I know this man?

No wonder Christians experienced a lack of power the early church possessed. Disobedience abounded, and not enough people called it out. At the door, Neka caught a curious expression on Fran's face. She must have zoned out. His mother stood in the doorway, staring at her as if she were a space cadet. She needed to leave thoughts of James's inclinations alone until a better time.

This day had twisted and turned all over the place. She smiled at Mrs. Copley, then entered the room and fell in love. "What an adorable space! I have a window seat like this one at home."

She bounced on the cushion, smiling. Some of her favorite colors were included in the design scheme.

A burnt-orange throw blanket popped life into the space. The curtains were a breezy fluff of material in deep beige that accentuated the smoky-beige area rug. Walls were painted dark beige with one dark-brown horizontal stripe on three walls. Four olive-green stripes adorned the end wall that housed a built-in bookcase and desk. Patting the seat cushion, she smiled happily at the peaceful surroundings.

Pleased at her reaction, Mrs. Copley opened the bay window. A fresh breeze circulated the area. "Only Gene will hear the details of your engagement. Thank God James proposed and you received him."

Happy to be accepted, Neka smiled.

"I see a definite change in my son's attitude. He weathered his mother's provocations in good humor." Fran turned to her. "May I have a hug?"

Surprised, Neka returned the embrace just as James entered the room. Setting down the luggage in front of the armoire, he seemed to enjoy the scene.

Fran wiped her eyes. "God answered my prayer in your fiancée."

"She does represent that godly influence you say I need."

"Since their birth I've asked God to surround them with principled people. Welcome to the family. The Copleys have followed our own path for far too long." Fran sat on the bed. "I want details. Have you set a wedding date?"

Neka tensed, refusing to look at James. "Not yet."

He stepped up his campaign for an early wedding. "I still think the fourth Saturday in June is the perfect date for an intimate ceremony."

Fran nodded her agreement. "Will it take place here or in Tulsa?"

"In Tulsa." Neka hoped the quick reply would stop him from egging on his mother.

"We can travel to Tulsa without a hassle." Fran rested her head on a finger. "An intimate affair might work. Pulling the ceremony together in four weeks is a big job."

Neka glanced at James. She thought they'd settled the issue in the car. Why must he take them down this road again? "My sister Kelly's in her sixth month. She may decline to participate. I want both my sisters to stand with me."

"Most women do slow down in the second trimester. Of course David will be the best man." Fingering the throw, she peered at her son. "Perhaps you'll choose one of your brothers for the groomsman?"

"Perhaps ... but doubtful."

Fran laughed at Neka's startled expression. "That's an improvement, at least. Normally he gives negative responses right away when it comes to his brothers."

Fran's enthusiasm offset her combatant manner downstairs. The attitude change invigorated Neka. Exhaling deeply, she gazed at the beautiful garden.

"The groom's parents pay for the rehearsal dinner the evening before the nuptials. Brandie and I can help you purchase your ensemble in St. Louis. We'll have the invitations engraved and mailed on Monday. That will give the invitees three week's notice."

Neka considered her alternatives. Should she pick the date James requested or wait for her mom's contribution? Hard-learned lessons from the morning stopped her from making any more rash decisions. "I promised to call my mom after dinner with your contact information. I hope that's okay?"

Fran nodded her approval. "I demanded the same info from Brandie before she was married."

Neka's tension melted. "Mom still requests my sister's hotel arrangements when they travel. Though Kelly married two years ago, she forks over her itinerary before leaving town."

Laugh lines formed around Fran's eyes. "We're alike in that regard. Cell phones notwithstanding, I obtain hotel information whenever the children leave the city." She studied her son, frowning. "Out of the eight visits James receives each year, we should've included a holiday trip."

Gazing at James, Neka vowed every holiday would become a major event in their marriage. He wouldn't have any more lonely holidays. "I'll run the wedding date by Mom tonight."

His mother glanced at her watch. "Four thirty. Gene gets home around five. Neka, you and James come downstairs at six. Gene must meet you before the children arrive for dinner."

Neka's stomach fluttered at the idea of meeting the rest of the family, and she sighed. "Thank you, Mrs. Copley."

Refusing to look James in the eye, she examined the garden after his mother left them alone. Eyes narrowing as if in contemplation, he headed toward the door.

"I'll get your bags from my bedroom so you can unpack."

Curled up on the window seat, she thought about James. His mother claimed he was a changed man and credited her for his transformation. Did their sporadic contact improve his character? Laughing, she laid her head against the glass.

Okay, Lord. I won't take credit for answered prayer.

Maybe it had produced positive change for both of them.

Why would he juggle three women instead of concentrating on one? Then again, why had she prayed for dates and then turned everyone down? She knew the answer to that one.

The men asking weren't James.

Would the answer to the first puzzle rest on meeting his family? He'd matured in six years—why not them?

Sometimes even family members failed to recognize character growth when it happened. Had he indeed changed? Appearing laidback today proved he didn't stray from his convictions. But he'd annoyed her with his expectation that she talk about the wedding with his mother while her own mom remained clueless. And his undermining her position annoyed her even more. What did he hope to gain by rushing into marriage?

James knocked on the door, then entered laden with packages. Deft movements deposited bags on the bed and hung dresses inside the closet. When he finished, he faced her on the window seat.

"Miss me?" He kissed her cheek.

Grinning, she pantomimed melting at his touch. Her legs really did feel all warm and liquidy, but he didn't need to know that.

James laughed. "This frustrating day hasn't broken your high spirits."

"Shout it out for the resiliency of youth. Twenty-one-year-olds withstand." Sobering, she leaned her head on the window frame. The tenderness in his gaze almost stole her breath.

Maybe her earlier musings were wrong. Maybe he didn't have ulterior motives.

Could he love her after all?

She had only realized she loved him after a cataclysmic revelation. What might foster the same reaction in him?

* * *

James leaned his back against the wall. "How're you holding up?"

"My gigantic mistake this morning is hard to get past."

"One day won't change love built up over a lifetime. I'm sure neither of your parents will hold a grudge."

Smiling, she grasped his hand. The gesture warmed him. It seemed that she was always submitting to his touch, but before today, she'd never reached out to him.

"Do you understand my discussing our engagement with Mom before making plans?"

"I appreciate the reasoning. But we have to go forward together."

She flopped back. "I know."

"But—"

"No buts. We're still single."

He scooted closer. His goal wasn't to separate her from loved ones but to cement their commitment. "I know our extended families share in important aspects of our lives. But being engaged means decisions should reflect us as a couple."

Clasping her fingers in her lap, she closed her eyes. "My mom reminded me that everyone is blessed when following proper procedures."

"I agree, but sometimes you have to ignore counsel, even from people with proven track records."

He wanted to protect Neka and bind her to himself. *God make it so.*

Guilt might cause her to cave in under pressure from Lawrence. Due to her earlier conversation with Karen, she'd resist any attempts to break their hold. He must allow them to push her to him. Life with Neka held so much promise, and her presence ensured him the top position in the family business with minimum resistance. Giving her up now was unthinkable.

Glancing at the clock on the nightstand, his mind moved a chessman on an imaginary board. It was time to rally the troops, bring Brandie and David to the forefront, and let them lead the charge.

Chapter Ten

Neka felt glued to the window seat. The whirlwind morning had left her frazzled. Her mind suffered from too much stimulation in a short time period. Where did James get his boundless energy? She felt washed out, but he'd sauntered from the bedroom as if he led a stress-free existence. She wilted under this pressure, but it seemed like he relaxed. She shook her head and smiled.

Before leaving her bedroom, James made it clear that compromising wasn't on the agenda. He'd kissed her hand and told her, "We'll win Karen and Lawrence over before long."

Neka sighed. His guarded expression proved to her that events had spiraled out of control. The conversation between him and his mother confirmed it. His father's position was carved in stone. An audience loomed in less than an hour with this man who was stuck in his perceptions.

She cringed at the thought. How could she weather another intense interview with a self-possessed parent? The session in the den showed that Fran sat in judgment on their relationship.

In fairness, if James had come clean with his mother at first, the explanation that he had proposed to Teri to secure a place in the business might've been enough. Maybe his father's marriage stipulation still clouded his judgment.

But now, any more details may destabilize the whole thing. Shaking her head in her hands, Neka sighed. At this point, further information would only emphasize his previous deceit with Teri.

It hurt her heart to think that way of James. Again, she wondered if she knew him as well as she thought.

After her big eye-opener on the plane, all she'd expected from this trip was for him to see her as someone worth dating. Eventually, she hoped he'd fall in love and they would live happily ever after.

So, if he told the truth and his father repented ... their engagement became obsolete.

And then Neka could test James's real feelings without his operating in survival mode.

Smothered underneath a mountain of emotions, Neka fought to regain her balance. Her gaze trailed over the meticulously landscaped garden. She just now realized that she'd fallen in love with him the moment he'd introduced himself. And all this time, the man who captured the imaginations of every woman had fancied her. Okay, maybe not to date but ...

She opened and refastened her watchband several times.

I love him, Lord, and he likes me and respects me. We have fun together. Can that be enough?

Neka methodically massaged her earlobe as she willed God to minister to her. She squeezed her eyelids together, wiping a few stray tears from her cheeks.

Marrying James felt right. But maybe she'd accepted his offer for the wrong reasons. If so, did that make saying yes the wrong choice? Teardrops pooled in her palms. Her head hurt.

Why am I here?

The discussion that started the journey rushed to mind. She'd wanted to defend James, but maybe she'd received the wrong message. Rocking her body against the wall of the window seat, Neka replayed a scene through her mind: two women talking outside as she listened from the upstairs sunroom of her home.

"Serves him right, don't you think?" Tossing copper curls, Teri had grinned at an unamused Kelly, who'd only stared at her in disbelief.

"No way. End the relationship if marriage is off the table. Why play games?"

Teri had glanced away and then studied her friend.

"Our situation is complicated." She'd paused. "James and I aren't in love—"

Neka had slapped a hand over her mouth and grasped the ledge for support, her legs like wet noodles.

Kelly had broken into her argument. "Now that's another thing—"

"Let me finish." Jangling keys, Teri had leaned away. "Because we share the same vision, joining forces makes sense."

"Who does that make sense to? You need to call him. Today."

"Three good reasons exist for doing it my way." Teri had ticked off the list on her fingers. "Number one: I accepted an awesome position at work. Number two: James might renege on our deal if his family dislikes me. Number three: A Cynthia Ward will always stand in the shadows. Ugh, I hate infidelity."

"At least we agree on something. So build on the goodness of honesty." Kelly sat down on a chair while rubbing her stomach. "End the relationship today. Don't abandon him at the airport."

Teri had pursed her lips, then she laughed. "Lighten up, Kel. I'm showing up at six o'clock on Friday morning."

Neka had shuddered at the lighthearted laughter and closed her eyes, noting the date and time.

They'd moved into the house, closing the door behind them.

Sighing at the memory, Neka closed her eyes. "I guess reason escaped me until now."

All she had really understood the first time was Teri's blatant hypocrisy. In her mind back then, Teri stood guilty as charged while Neka vindicated James. Now James's role leaped to the forefront. He'd schemed to enter into the family business using deceptive measures. Red flags littered the playing field, and she'd overlooked each one.

Red flags? She suppressed a giggle. James's jargon was rubbing off on her. Everything was a war to him.

Neka rose to her knees and laid her forehead against the glass. Fairness demanded consideration of all sides this time around.

Really, what had his dad expected when he gave him that kind of ultimatum? He'd known his son wasn't dating anyone special. A woman he loved would have been introduced to the family. He'd cornered his son into the very shenanigans he probably detested.

Earlier, Neka's mom had accused her of self-fulfilling the inspiring words she'd been given. Stunned, Neka laid her head against the window. Her mind returned to the afternoon in the garden. Instead of encouraging herself in the Lord as King David did in scripture, Neka had spent over an hour crying underneath the weeping willow tree.

Oh Lord, help me. Instead of seeking God's path as her mom had expected, she'd used the assurance as validation to pursue James. Her mom's constant warning reverberated throughout her soul. "Always guard the perimeters of your life."

Father, how do I come back from this mistake? Especially since I believe he's the one You ordained me to marry.

Exhausted, Neka fell onto the bed. She glanced at her watch.

Five thirty. Better get dressed.

* * *

His hand on the doorknob, James hesitated before exiting the room. This uncertainty surprised him. Satisfaction flowed through every fiber of his being right now. This victory was flourishing above his highest expectation. An iffy proposition now thrived due to one person's disloyalty. Now getting married proved imminent.

And to Neka instead. What a coup.

From the moment he'd spied her standing in line, he'd felt off balance. He'd never been one for anything superficial, and proposing to Teri had plagued him. But the threat of permanent annihilation from a leadership role in his father's company haunted him day and night.

He shifted his shoulders because his muscles tightened at the mere thought of defeat. Last night he'd lain awake, fine-tuning the design. And now his success was only minutes away. What could go wrong?

Neka was in the next bedroom, waiting for the man bent on calling the shots. Weariness had lined her features before they parted to dress for the evening. Confrontations lurked ahead with his father, siblings, and her parents.

Neka.

There wasn't enough time to devise a plan that released her from involvement. His stomach clenched at the thought. He couldn't chance sending her home alone. Doing so might interfere with the harmony building between them.

A few times at the mall he'd forgotten the intensity of the next two weeks. Even the showdown at dinner tonight. What if he ignored the clamors of the day and drifted into the yearnings of the moment?

Shaking his head, he frowned. Not in this life.

For six years, he'd worked hard with minimum play, tumbling into bed drained, only to start over the next morning. His mind steeled against the weakness surging through his body. It had afforded him a booming business with superb prospects, and his family would accept him now that he'd proven his business acumen. But the price his perseverance demanded could never be repaid.

And then his loneliness had fled at the airport that morning.

Since meeting Neka, James had frequented events he expected her to attend. Her mixture of serenity and exuberance fascinated him. He showed up at church socials and home parties he'd never think of joining otherwise. At least his presence saved her from gossip mongers and finger pointers.

The image of Neka hugging his mother tugged at his core.

Maybe it was good she would be involved in this mess. She was stronger and more confident than she believed. Together they would slay the Copley dragon.

His neck muscles stiffened as he pictured her troubled gaze. But observing her father taught him to pounce before the water rippled. The man never ceased the momentum of an offensive. Denying his opponent the ability to mount a defense increased his ability to dictate terms.

Eyes closed, he leaned against the doorframe. The ardent pupil won out. He and his sweetie must weather this storm. They'd already practiced four years in advance. He brushed aside his ambivalence, left the room, and knocked on her door.

James scanned Neka in admiration when she opened the door. Her smile was completely empty of any conceited notions. Instead, her obvious affection dazzled him. No one deserved such guileless devotion. The simplicity of the moment bound him to her.

Everything about her pleased him. The black and silver mini dress held her petite frame perfectly. She was confident in the two-inch heels she'd berated. Lovely light-brown eyes captivated him like a man in a trance. Smooth latte skin begged a caress.

He sighed despite himself, but it sounded more like a gasp. "You're gorgeous. I love your legs. You've ... uh ... worn your dresses too long."

"Not anymore." Frowning at the exposed skin, she removed the cell phone from the nightstand.

James almost advised her to leave it in the room. But why delay the inevitable? Perhaps her parents would call before the guests arrived for dinner.

Neka's thoughts raced ahead to meeting James's father. James kissed her hand, and it trembled. "Thinking about your father waiting downstairs makes me nervous."

He captured her fingers in his hand. "Your concerns are groundless. Mother adores you, and he respects her assessments of people."

His encouragement boosted her confidence.

"Your mother extended a warm welcome in spite of the shock. But I've yet to meet your famed siblings."

James squeezed her hand. "Brandie and David can't wait to meet you."

"Will they like me after the introductions? I'm terrible at making friends." Neka sighed.

"Lay that fairy tale to rest. People living outside God's word just resent you for referencing the commands they choose to disobey."

Pausing on the stairs, she gave him a somber look. So he had discerned the conflict with her detractors. Since she and James shared similar views, why did those same people like him?

What if she and James disagreed on more than she thought? Her pulse quickened. Neka thought about what his mother had said and searched for a way to broach the topic, but then she changed her mind. Tomorrow would be a better time to discuss faith issues.

James ran his hand down her arm, invoking a shiver. "I'm proud that you strive to obey God's word, though I can't uphold some of your convictions. Too many hypocrites preach against abortion, homosexuality, and other heavy hitters, conveniently forgetting that gossipers, liars, and slanderers also share in the lake of fire."

"That's a pat argument for people who don't want to obey God."

"Does that statement make my opinion any less factual? I admit people who practice sin often shun and ridicule anyone trying to follow scripture."

"Like repeating wedding vows before engaging in sexual activities?"

It seemed God wanted them to talk about it now.

She hesitated, gathering strength for the confrontation. Touching her lips, she paused. "James, did you have sex with the women you dated, like your mother's comment implied?"

Just like that, he was detached. His face went blank. "Does it matter?"

"It does to me."

Stuffing his hands into his pockets, he leaned against the wall, studying her with half-closed eyes. Neka failed to pinpoint his expression, but she'd never seen that one before. He searched her face as if to unearth hidden objections.

"From the moment you accepted my proposal, I consigned myself to a celibate lifestyle until we get married. I ... trust that answered your question. Now, let's go downstairs."

Neka complied, fighting against the desire to seek clarity. Like an automaton, she ambled down the stairs until reaching the bottom step. Why belabor the point? James had supplied the answer she'd sought.

He had engaged in sex outside of marriage.

She fought back tears. Obedience to godly principles mattered to Neka. She was far from perfect, but at least she tried. She'd never imagined he'd slept with Teri and the other women he'd dated. Not challenging her position left the impression that James agreed: No one should have sex outside of marriage. Why hadn't he voiced opposing views during their discussions?

She'd accepted his proposal in a hurry and was starting to think she should have put him off a while.

James returned to their previous topic, as if the conversation had never happened. "David said he and Brandie should arrive at seven. My sister wanted them to be the first ones to greet you."

"Really?" Her head lifted. The news pleased her, despite the heaviness.

His lips curved into her special smile, and he took her hand. Bypassing the den, he continued down the hallway. "Just to warn you, she lined up enough outings to occupy your time for two weeks."

Neka laughed and glanced at their clasped hands. "Good. I'm looking forward to having my days full while you work."

In the kitchen, several variations of gray, beige, brown, white, and green decorated the space. The aroma of baked cookies still permeated the air though the oven was cold. "I don't see dinner preparations underway. I expected a lot of bustle, even if caterers were hired."

"The building behind the garden serves as a gathering place for dinners and parties. They're in tiptop form down the lane." He grinned, and her tension eased again.

Fran spoke from the sunroom. "I placed sodas in the fridge. Help yourselves and bring us a can."

James peered inside the refrigerator. He removed four cans from the shelf, setting them on the same tray used earlier in the den. Glancing at her, he abandoned his handiwork and grabbed her hands, the warmth in his gaze conveying the caring words he didn't speak.

Courage fueled by his comfort erased her uncertainty from their talk on the stairs. No more jumping to conclusions.

A new day had dawned that morning. She loved him, and he would grow to cherish her. She could do this.

Smiling, Neka dropped his hands and headed toward the sunroom. Another opportunity existed to confront difficulties instead of cowering in fear. Pausing in the doorway, she stepped into the room once she sensed he stood behind her.

Chapter Eleven

The rugged man waiting inside the doorway shocked Neka. Gene Copley was like a storybook character of a rough-and-ready man. Fran rested on a love seat facing a sofa. Neka glanced at the man regarding her from behind black-rimmed glasses. Neka liked the glasses. They added a touch of civility to his face.

"Hello, Neka." He extended his hand. "Please, take a seat."

Though there were other chairs available, he pointed to the sofa. His gaze jumped to the son he hadn't seen in a year. Once she moved away, they spoke in low voices for a moment.

James placed the tray on the table and settled next to her. His features were set, as if chiseled in sandstone. He smiled at her without uttering a word to his parents. Overcome with shyness, she avoided their eyes and examined the area.

When the silence continued, she peeked at his parents. Fran's glances at her husband spoke volumes. Perhaps the scene wouldn't pan out as she'd hoped. Gene avoided his wife's gaze, emptying his can in a few gulps.

Neka shifted in her seat. *Now what?*

The seconds ticked by. Finally, she popped the top and sipped her drink, hoping one of them would start up a conversation. Tension throbbed around them like a living entity. She shot a quick glance at James. He gave her the airport smile, the one void of emotion.

Back to square one.

Unlike in the den, he refused to jumpstart the dialogue. She gritted her teeth and placed her can on the tray, giving his parents a wobbly smile. She cleared her throat.

"I love your kitchen." Neka cleared her throat again to steady her nerves. Her gaze scanned the room before returning to his mother. "Old charm plus modern conveniences."

Fran stretched her neck to the side, stealing a peep into the kitchen area. Her hands puffed the sides of her graying blond hair. "Maybe we should expand the color scheme. I worry that everything appears overstated."

Smiling, Neka scanned the area. James could jump in any time. "Oh no, it's perfect, just like this room. Natural light brightens the space from outside. Soft color combinations extend the sunroom into the garden flanked on the south lawn." She slid away from James. "You have a peaceful home. I like the design."

Grinning, Fran touched her husband's arm. "James chose an enchanting young lady to marry."

He laid his spectacles on the table and grinned at Neka, but his eyes were cold. "Your comments reveal you understand the business. I'm acquainted with Lawrence Lacey, a land developer in Oklahoma. Is he a relative of yours?"

James stiffened beside her. His head tilted to the side, studying his father.

Gene's sharp eyes didn't miss the response. Neither did his mother. Fran leaned into her husband as if to temper his behavior. When he gazed at Neka again, his demeanor had changed. Discomfiting his son pleased him.

Neka scooted forward. "Yes, he's my father. How did you meet? He works in Missouri but doesn't take on projects north of Springfield."

"We met at a trade convention twenty-five years ago. He's an honorable man. Lawrence headlines our trade and is respected industry wide."

Grinning, she turned to James. "Does Dad know you're Gene Copley's son?"

He shook his head, frowning and studying his father through half-closed eyes.

"I never realized they were acquainted. To my knowledge, Lawrence hasn't made the connection." Though he spoke to Neka, his gaze never left his father's face. "In the business world, Lawrence has an impeccable reputation."

Something was terribly wrong, but she didn't understand what. She tried not to tremble as she picked up her soda can. Fran stared off into space, and James withdrew while Gene crossed his arms. All pretense of a happy reunion had disappeared.

What had happened? She felt like she had missed something.

As awkward as this was for her, she knew Gene's behavior caused James pain, despite his blank expression.

"Thanks for the info." Neka willed her voice not to shake. "How terrible if he hounded his daughters about ethical practices then neglected them himself."

A question entered Gene's brown eyes, dividing his inspection between her and his son. "Rest assured, his honesty withstands the test of time." He centered his gaze upon James. "May we accomplish as much."

"Mr. Copley, I'm aware of the flipside to those accolades. Some brand him a hard bargainer. Others denounce him as a difficult man to negotiate with. As my mom often explains, God's still working on him."

Gene laughed. "The only people who'd say that must have tried to take him and failed." He eyed James. "Neka, give us an estimation of your fiancé's work ethics."

Neka glanced at his parents, smiling. "From all the comments I hear bandied about, my James is maturing daily."

James's eyes gleamed with suppressed laughter. He kissed her cheek and chuckled.

But Gene grunted disapproval. "In other words, no one has knighted him for ethical behavior."

James sighed, but it sounded like he'd taken a punch to the gut.

Though she remained silent, Fran cringed. Her fingers tapped out a pattern on Gene's thigh. Smile set in place, she concentrated on Neka. "And no one has branded him a scalawag."

Before the conflict could escalate further, Neka's ringtone filled the air.

Her stomach tensed. She retrieved her cell phone from the table. The speculative glance his parents gave one another disturbed her.

She breathed deeply, then slid her thumb across the screen.

"Hello, Dad."

"When are you coming home?" Her father's precise diction was discouraging.

Perspiration lined her back and chest. "In two weeks, on June fifteenth."

"The next flight to Tulsa departs at eight-ten tomorrow morning. Your mother and I want you home by noon."

"Dad, I'm not free to talk right now—"

"Then seek privacy. I'll wait."

Neka opened her eyes wide. Even when disappointed, he remained pleasant. He'd never spoken to her in harsh tones. She gazed at James and then closed her eyes before facing his parents.

Her tone was so low she feared they'd have to strain to make out the words. "Mr. and Mrs. Copley, please excuse me for a moment."

The next command caused her to squirm in her seat. She glanced at James, then closed her eyes, mentally counting to ten.

"I'm sorry, I meant we both need to speak to my dad."

She whispered into the phone. "I'll hang up and call back in a few minutes. So long."

James rose from his seat and pulled her up, whispering in her ear. "We'll return the call from the den."

He winked at his mother and clutched Neka's hand, leading her from the sunroom.

The heaviness filling the den threatened to suffocate her. She glanced at her watch as precious minutes ticked away. Outwardly, she was calm, except for her foot tapping a rhythm on the floor. Although her dad wanted to speak to both her and James, she wished for a private talk with her mom and dad. Gaze glued to her watch's dial, she reached for the doorknob, hoping James was winding down his final appeal.

Her father wouldn't wait much longer. That he hadn't called back was a miracle. This was one argument she wouldn't lose. A healthy relationship with her parents depended on her speaking to them alone.

Eyes narrowed, James pressed home his argument. "Lawrence requested a group discussion. Let's face your parents together."

Neka turned the doorknob. Ready to leave the den, she shook her head, hating to disappoint him. "Everything in me says to talk to them alone."

He wanted to understand—she could see it in his eyes.

"He'll demand a conference with me before ending the call."

Halfway through the doorway, she swung back to him and smiled, hoping to lessen the impact of saying no.

"I'll explain you'll contact him once we're done." She paused, smiling again. "I have to speak to them on my own."

"Neka, we pledged to become one. Don't detach from me."

The earnest request almost weakened her determination. Somehow the most confident man in the world needed reassurance. She wanted to rush to him, to soothe away his doubts. Instead, she replied from her heart.

"I won't. We're in this one together."

The house that had felt so homey twenty minutes ago now made her feel strange. Uncertainty seeped through the walls. Neka crept up the stairs, quite aware she should hasten her steps. The doorbell could ring any moment. Thank God the interviews with his parents were finished. Defending herself against imaginary opposition had sapped her energy.

But the real resistance still lay ahead. Her parents' vehement objection shocked her. Over the last three years, they'd discussed each issue in depth before locking in a viewpoint. Then again, this was a bigger issue than they'd faced before.

Once inside the room, Neka paced, counting to ten. As her confidence increased, she marveled at her calm. Comfortable now, she sat on the bed smiling.

"Hi, Dad. I'm alone in the bedroom so we can speak in private. I told Mom I'd call after dinner with the Copleys' contact information..."

A little later, she rested her forehead against the door. Regret had replaced her happiness as she told them about their engagement and plans to wed as soon as possible. Her dad actually questioned her relationship with James before today. He ripped off question after insulting question.

"It didn't occur to you that a desperate man could easily substitute one woman for another?"

Neka felt like her stomach wrenched in half.

He acknowledged knowing James was Gene Copley's son, saying, "How could I miss a Copley hailing from St. Louis with vast construction knowledge?" She frowned. Why withhold that information from James for six years?

Worse still, their conversation deteriorated when she tried to pacify their fears. She considered her placation reasonable. The discourse hammered in her mind. "Please, I'm not a stupid person. I don't just trust everyone I meet. I won't reject sound advice over some perceived grievance. James has earned my confidence. A strong connection to him won't cancel out twenty-one years with my family. Nor can I disregard our relationship because I love you."

His retort stung her ears. "Karen, I warned you this day would come. I blame myself for missing her crush on Copley." He steamrolled over her mom's objection, saying, "Neka spends too much time alone. She stays sequestered in the house on weekends and evenings, devouring romance novels. She doesn't have a life outside of the family. She's ripe for the picking and too easily sweet-talked."

That hurt. Neka flopped onto the mattress so hard she bounced. The proclamation devalued her worth. Surely he didn't mean it the way it sounded. He was just upset. But her response was out of her mouth before her mind caught up with her words.

"What? Dad, I hope your statement isn't an estimation of my worth. I'm not some dusty relic from the past. I live an active life. I visit the nursing home, hospital, and a rehabilitation facility. I'm an excellent employee for Lacey Corp five days a week. I attend prayer meeting and volunteer at the adult day care center. I live a quiet lifestyle by design, not out of necessity. I'm not trapped inside some fantasyland of my own imagination."

After spouting off, she rolled onto her stomach, burying her face in the cover.

Her mom minimized his comment. "Neka, calm down. Stop misinterpreting your father's words." Then she added, "Honey, you directed your footsteps from start to finish. Jesus anoints our steps when we follow the Holy Spirit. You should have known something was wrong with your actions the moment you felt the need to conceal your plans. Have you asked yourself how you could leave home without a word?"

The fight left her. Her desire to help James had overridden wisdom. Yet she opposed her mom's suggestion that James wasn't a Christian. His parents raised him in a godly household. Of course, no one followed Jesus by osmosis, but he attended church every Sunday. He talked about God and quoted appropriate scriptures on many occasions. Didn't most followers of Christ struggle to control their own fate?

Neka ran fingers through her hair when her mom pointed out that church attendance and quoting scripture verses didn't signify salvation. She froze and was unable to move.

Oh Lord, help me.

After the heavy exchanges, her dad said, "Sweetheart, he has redeeming qualities but lacks the proper response when cornered. This morning, he should have thanked you for your concern and flew out of Tulsa alone."

When her mom agreed he'd showed her kindness in the past, the dam broke. She reminded them of the pain of being rejected by her peers since middle school. Tears flowed down her cheeks at the memory.

"I've been so frustrated, Mom. Okay, I turn people off. Tammy says it's too much God talk for ordinary folks to stomach." Her hand massaged her earlobe. She'd never covered this ground with anyone before. She grabbed the box of tissues from the nightstand, then sat on the edge of the bed. "My own clay feet sparked the quest for obedience. But I hear what you're saying. A real life depends on following God's instructions. This is between me and God. It has nothing to do with any of them."

Her mom's soft sigh intervened. "Honey, please calm down. You're too far away from home for this discussion."

The conversation ended with a request for James to call back before the guests arrived. She promised to call them after everyone left with a play-by-play of the gathering.

The conversation she'd anticipated never happened. Both parents had decimated every claim she offered in her defense.

Neka wished God would grant her a redo. She would change every decision she'd made since yesterday evening. Even the promise to marry the man she loved. Happiness had kept her from delaying her answer until a later time. She'd been blinded by love.

Slumped against the door, she prayed, "Father, help me control this monster I created."

James knocked on the door ten minutes later. He'd gone into his room to call her parents and asked her to wait upstairs in case his brothers arrived early. She patted the window seat, hoping he would sit close to her.

"The conversation ended in a hurry," she said. "On a good note, I hope."

While sitting down, he appeared to weigh his words before speaking. "Well enough. Lawrence asked a few in-depth questions."

Staring at him, she massaged her earlobe. "Mom too?"

James nodded, and Neka bounced up on the cushion when he remained silent. "James, what did he ask? How did my mom respond?"

His blank expression gave nothing away. "Here are the highlights: Both parents remain displeased you're in St. Louis. They challenge our engagement and oppose a wedding taking place this month. I'm confident they'll fill you in tonight."

Mixed emotions already seized her about the phone call later that night. Far from comforting, his words fueled her apprehension. "I suppose you supplied the info Mom requested."

James nodded and kissed her cheek. "Relax, sweetie. This excruciating day is almost over."

Critiquing her feelings, she stared at the floor. "Do you remember the scripture *weeping may endure for a night but joy cometh in the morning*?"

He nodded, and she continued. "Do you foresee joyfulness at sunrise?" She lifted her head to discern his expression.

He stroked one dimpled cheek with his thumb. Despite herself, she shivered at his touch. "Your parents' love is still there, as God intended. This division has disrupted everyone's calm, but it won't stop their love. Beside, I'm the villain, remember?"

James squeezed her hand, giving her a slow wink.

"Learn from my mistakes. Instead of dealing with the miscommunications in my family, I just moved to Oklahoma. Those very same issues confront us today." He intertwined his fingers with hers. "If you run away from this problem, we'll just have to relive it in the future."

Neka pondered his statement. Her gaze searched his face for signs of approval. "I promise to move forward tomorrow. There will be joy in the morning."

She smiled, and he kissed her cheek, making her blush.

* * *

His lips lingered on the smooth skin of her cheek. Neka reclined against the wall. She might fall over if he loosened his grip on her hand.

Though James realized that Neka hoped he and her parents would come to trust one another, her comments implied she might depart for Tulsa in the morning. Still, she was standing her ground, even despite the pressure thus far. For now, it was better to let the Lacey drama rest and deal with the Copley saga unfolding downstairs.

With a quick squeeze, he released his hold.

"Follow your heart. I won't coerce you." He helped her stand up. "Brandie and David should arrive any minute. Let's extend our welcome."

Chapter Twelve

"I hear you were saved from a train wreck and rebounded on the fast track." Brandie breezed into the foyer, laughing. While his sister's twinkling blue eyes scanned the couple's faces, her husband eyed their clasped hands before closing the door. Brandie kissed James's cheek and then smiled at Neka while waiting for the introductions.

"Two of my three favorite women stand beside me. Neka, Brandie is the Copleys' personal ray of sunshine. David McKinley and I crawled around together as kids." He looked at his friend. "Man, I found the best part of me. This is Nikhol Lacey."

Neka extended her hand. "Friends and family call me Neka."

"That ring is gorgeous!" Ignoring the outstretched hand, Brandie embraced her.

Returning the hug, Neka felt an immediate bond to this gracious woman, and it only increased when David kissed her cheek. The tender look between James and his sister thrilled her.

Brandie and David were a dazzling couple. A blue-eyed, dark-haired beauty, Brandie exuded joy and self-confidence. The same height as James, blond David was the strong, silent type. Intense blue eyes added to the serious demeanor, complementing his wife's bubbly personality.

David went straight to his agenda. "Since the others are on their way, let's hold our discussion outside until they arrive."

A lighthearted talk about the house's color schemes ensued on the way outdoors. Fresh flowers perfumed the air with delicate fragrances as they huddled on the winding path leading to a building at the end of the walkway.

"I checked the records Brandie provided this evening. The company is bleeding cash. The Illinois warehouse wraps up early August. Nothing else is slated."

James stared into space. "West County?"

"West C's on hold until further notice." David glanced at Neka.

"That explains the hemorrhage." James gazed at his sister, then studied his friend. "The current foundation allows a strong push into rehabs. That will stem the flow."

David nodded. "A win is salvageable. West C's disarray should facilitate modifications."

James studied his sister. "We must incorporate rehabs pronto to rise above our competitors."

Stepping back, Brandie distanced herself from the circle. "Forget about money. Profit margins don't matter. As David indicated, West C has immense potential."

Business was always about profit. Of course, the desire to provide a needed service started the process, and then hopefully ended with a good company. But they had to have a positive cash flow to thrive, and diversification was a great way to do that. The way Neka saw it, two issues existed. The company was losing money, and the family disagreed on the fix.

"I have an idea," Neka said. She'd barely stopped herself from raising her hand. When everyone turned their gaze to her, she wanted to shrink, but her tension eased as James squeezed her shoulder encouragingly.

Brandie closed the gap in the circle, still agitated. "I'd love to hear your opinion."

"I recommend finishing the West C venture as soon as possible." She glanced at James, who nodded. A thrill went through her at his support for her idea. "Rental income ensures a steady cash flow while completing major projects."

James pounced on the opening she provided. "Add your influence to the daily operations, Brandie. Doing it now ensures you'll have a company left to inherit."

David's head tilted a fraction of an inch. The action reminded Neka of a Doberman, alert eyes watching the slightest move. Thank God that David wasn't lethal.

After several seconds, he nodded. "Go on."

Though no one else was around, James lowered his voice. The sparkle in his eye showed his excitement. "We don't have time to mull over your decision. Implementing the model I've seen at Lacey Corp is imperative, and it has to be this weekend. Their network covers the full spectrum of real estate development."

He glanced at Neka, then smiled at his sister. "Convince the folks to give you an equal say in shaping our future. Insist we separate the company into four integral parts before restructuring begins—"

"What?" Brandie said quickly, hands collapsed at her side.

Neka's knees felt weak. Did brotherly love drive his desire to include Brandie on Monday? Or was self-interest shifting the field in his favor? In the parking lot, James had claimed his vengeful thoughts had been discarded, but now she wasn't so sure.

David squeezed Brandie's arm. "Let him finish."

"Of course, this statement is off the cuff," James downplayed his suggestion. "But I propose Copley Enterprise purchase McKinley Construction. The buyout allows David to direct one fourth of the operation on Brandie's behalf, beginning Monday."

The breath caught in Neka's throat. This move balanced his family's lopsided arrangement that existed six years ago. It would no longer be two against one, and he would make sure his voice was heard.

David's low-pitched whistle vibrated through the air. Gesturing toward his friend, he turned to Neka. "You just witnessed James at his best. Your fiancé stage manages everything he touches. He lets them think they're the ones in control, while the puppet master pulls the strings, manipulating the scenario from start to finish."

Neka refrained from massaging the ache over her right eye.

Lord, please help me to understand James's quirky behavior.

* * *

James studied David. He was the consummate opponent. Thank God they played on the same team.

"Actually, Neka came up with the idea years ago." He let his words sink in before continuing. "A gentlemen's agreement between our folks this weekend seals the deal."

David glanced at his wife when she pulled his sleeve. "What's the idea? Your brothers won't allow you an ally with equal authority."

Brandie snapped her fingers. "Mother promised we can count on her backing if no one jeopardizes Ryan and Matt's positions."

David grimaced. "What's her definition of jeopardize?"

Light laughter eased the tension.

"I'm confident she'll back any idea that gives us an equal voice at the table."

Entwining his fingers with Neka's, James assessed the question in her gaze. David's charge deflated her optimism because she didn't know its dual purpose. He tore his gaze away and studied the couple whispering to one another until Neka tapped his arm, wide-eyed.

"You need to mention the merger tonight so Brandie and David can voice their approval. Both of you have keen business sense. So present a united front after dinner." She smiled at David. "You'll make a formidable team standing together Monday morning."

For the second time, Neka had predicted his game plan. Except for a few minor tweaks, she played his hand without any prompting. Pleased with her foresight, he whispered into her ear.

"I only need one person beside me. I'm so glad you came with me on this trip." He wrapped an arm around her waist, the warmth of her seeping into him. "I agree except for one minor detail. Brandie should broach the topic during dinner."

"Me?"

"They'll listen to you. Stay focused on our folks. Only their opinion matters. They're shrewd enough to snap up the offer before the evening ends."

"James always makes things seem simpler than they are." Brandie rolled her gaze upward.

He wagged his finger at her. "Father understands his livelihood could trickle down the drain unless he diversifies."

Expectation flooded her face. "Will he listen to me?"

James grinned. "When hasn't he hearkened to your every word? Count on my backup, if needed."

"Okay, I'll ad-lib during dinner."

"Then I guess it's a done deal. We're in." David brushed his lips across Brandie's.

The two men shook hands. David rubbing his hands together in expectancy caused Brandie to burst into uncontrollable laughter. "My father-in-law rubs his hands like that whenever he's excited. David won't appreciate me saying this, but he adopts a new trait of his father's every year."

Stifling giggles, she touched Neka's arm. James's heart skipped a beat at the loving gesture between the women.

"I don't want to distort your view of Matt and Ryan. We love each other, and I like Sandi and Celia. They're devoted to my brothers and raise six of the eight most adorable children in the world."

Neka grasped Brandie's hand, smiling. "Disagreements happen in every family, including mine."

* * *

Walking back to the house, Neka reflected on the obvious. James had another motive for agreeing to his father's conditions. Though fighting for acceptance, he wanted their approval ... on his terms. His running the company might be the only way they could prove their respect. Unsure where his maneuverings led, one point couldn't be denied. Another ugly struggle would poison the family for years to come.

She glanced at James, wondering about his motivation. Maybe he welcomed an altercation because he'd abandoned the fight six years ago. In truth, she didn't know where any of them stood. Her parents could help her muddle through the maze on their call tonight. The thought of talking to her parents again made her head hurt.

As she considered several scenarios, four people standing at the door jolted her mind to the present. Ryan, Matt, and their wives.

James placed his arm around Neka's waist as they entered the sunroom. Neka studied the brothers and their wives. Based on James's character descriptions, what they might look like had been distorted in her mind. But they seemed perfectly normal.

One of the couples sat on the sofa, eyeing her, while the other pair backed up a little so everyone could file into the room. The man smiled. His black hair was an inch longer than James's. He was handsome, just like his younger brother, and so was the one sitting on the sofa holding his wife's hand. Both women wore designer clothes. She wondered which one of them was the ... what had James said? Right, which was the schemer, and which was the conniver.

She peeked at her toes. A quick glance at Brandie revealed she also wore the latest styles. Before that moment, Neka hadn't noticed her clothes and was even more thankful for her new wardrobe.

The taller man's smile deepened. She could tell this man smiled a lot. Laugh lines crinkled on the edge of dark-brown eyes. "We were about to join the discussion."

A woman with cropped blond hair addressed James. "Ryan and I are eager to meet your fiancée. Introduce us."

Smiling down, James drew Neka closer. The protective gesture lessened her apprehension. "Neka, meet the lovely Sandi and Ryan." He indicated the seated couple staring them down. "On the sofa are Matt and the indomitable Celia."

Celia's light-brown hair shook as she laughed. She glanced at her husband and then back at James. "I don't know if I like my introduction. So am I spirited or stubborn?"

"Ask me that question at the end of the evening." James emitted a low chuckle, but his arm tightened almost imperceptibly at Neka's waist. He swiveled a little to meet the eyes of each person. "Sandi, Celia, Ryan, and Matt, I'm honored to introduce the bright spot in my life for four years, Nikhol Lacey. We call her Neka."

Stepping forward, Ryan held out a hand that Neka quickly grasped. "Welcome to the family, Neka."

"Thank you." Though the smile never wavered, Neka knew he took her measure in an instant.

He shook his brother's hand and stared at him without blinking. "The expertise you bring to the table gives us a definite edge over competitors."

James nodded, then smiled at Neka, obviously pleased at Ryan's compliment. Ryan regarded her too. "Sandi and I expect to spend time getting to know you. We're only a phone call away. The next two weeks will end in a blur. Good times are over too fast."

"I'm happy to be here."

Her trembling stomach eased a little as Sandi stepped forward, inspecting Neka before giving her a hug. "I'm free during the day if you find yourself with time to kill."

"Thank you, Sandi. James always talks about his family. I'm honored to meet you and Ryan."

Matt rose from the sofa, approaching the couple with measured steps. The muscles in his arms bulged through his sleeves. A crew cut emphasized his rugged physique. Just like his smiling elder brother, his gaze delved into the depths of her soul.

"On the drive over I envisioned a high-society type. Instead, this bashful young woman is greeting me." Glancing at James, he extended his hand. "Add Celia's and my good wishes. Join us for dinner next week. Any day you choose. Decide over the weekend, and James can let me know Monday."

"Thank you. We'll choose a date this weekend."

As he turned away, Celia's voice called from across the room. "Our children are excited about meeting Uncle James's fiancée. Give me a list of your favorite foods before we leave tonight."

Celia's smile didn't falter even though she looked right through Neka.

Neka smiled. "I will."

She was finally done with the hard parts. *Thank you, Jesus.*

God had carried her past the introductions gracefully and would continue through dinner and in her call to her parents. The Copleys' tension was like the division she'd seeded within her own family. She had to mend the relationship with her parents straight away.

Her shoulders slumped. She inhaled a deep breath. God had never forsaken her throughout the process.

Chapter Thirteen

James's parents came in and took their seats at the table. Everyone else followed.

Gene bowed his head in prayer. "Father, with thanksgiving we celebrate James and Neka's engagement. Bless their union, our time together, and the food we'll enjoy. Reward the hands that prepared and serve our meal in Jesus's name. Amen."

When he finished speaking, Gene glanced around the table at his guests. He sighed, grinning at his wife. "I'm a happy man. Only the grandchildren are missing from our meal."

Fran captured his gaze and spoke through steepled hands against her lips. "Indeed we are blessed."

Brandie peered at her mother. "Everything smells delicious. I'm starved."

"Thank you, dear. I'll pass your remarks to Corinne. She'll take pleasure in the compliment."

The family discussed a safe topic—the children.

Celia cast her napkin beside Matt's plate. "Mark your calendars. Lindsey's first dance recital is coming up on June fifteenth, and Brandie's hoping Yancey will request dance lessons once she sees her older cousin live on stage."

David speared a grilled tomato from Brandie's plate. "I'm repelling your push. Kids need to show interest before they are made to practice for hours."

"Like forcing her to practice the piano she hates to play?" Removing the tomato from his fork, she stuffed it into her mouth.

The light in his eyes danced when he chuckled. "That's different. Every parent should demand their children take up an instrument. My mother pressed me into playing clarinet, and I turned out marvelous."

Fran clapped her hands, then glanced at Neka. "We're taking six tickets. Our granddaughter is a magnificent ballerina—a child prodigy possessing natural grace few children attain."

Neka smiled. "I wish we could attend, but we're flying out that afternoon."

A lively debate ensued about the pros and cons of their children's activities. Happy the subject took the focus off her, Neka's shallow breaths subsided. As the animated chatter continued, she turned to the culinary feast. She appreciated an excellent meal. But she didn't drink, so she left the vintage Pinot Noir untouched and listened to Sandi's mashed potato soup recipe.

Capturing Neka's eye, Celia turned the attention to James. "Don't you think calling Neka sweets and sweetie is a bit extreme?"

Silence met her words, and all eyes turned to Neka. Her heart pounded in her ears, and she lowered her eyes. James placed his hand on hers.

Matt quickly veered the discussion into another arena. "Remind me to approve Jake's leave on Monday."

When Ryan fell right in as if the topic hadn't altered, Neka sighed in relief. James smiled at her and squeezed her hand.

"Is he asking for two weeks off this time?" Though speaking to Matt, Ryan's gaze never left Sandi's face. "They said his daughter's surgery was a success."

Celia's knife clanged on the plate. "You usually don't refer to your women by pet names."

An amused grin played on James's lips as he focused on Celia. "You know, there's a big problem with people today who think uninformed opinions are better than having none."

Startled, she glared at him. "You've never called your dates by nicknames before."

"Remind me again how many times we've double dated." James cut his potatoes.

Batting her eyelashes, Celia cocked her head to one side. Matt covered her hand with his. "Celia ..."

She pulled her hand away and stared at James. "Is this part of the change we're told you've made over the years?"

"Please excuse us." Matt slid back his chair. When Celia refused to move, he avoided eye contact with everyone else and remained seated.

Emboldened, Celia lowered her voice to a taunt. "Like switching fiancées after a four-week engagement."

Glaring at his wife, Matt slammed his napkin onto the table just as a lazy grin spread across James's face. Neka tensed for the backlash, but instead of issuing one of his classic diatribes, he simply turned aside.

Hands on the table, Fran leaned forward. "Why insult Neka by bringing up another woman in her presence?"

"Mother, she intended no harm." Matt's half-closed eyes turned to Neka. "Please accept my apology."

Neka couldn't decide whether Matt was angry, embarrassed, or both. She just wanted to hide under the table.

Celia glared down the table at Sandi, who quietly sipped her wine.

"Of course Matt's correct. I meant no criticism of Neka." Her words were contrite, but unrepentant eyes stared across the table. "I apologize for my clumsy attempt to understand."

Brandie frowned. "Understand what?"

"The questions good manners insist we leave unasked." Celia sighed and turned to James again. "Why are we eating dinner with Neka instead of Teri?"

Face flushed, Brandie pushed her plate away. "You had to say it again, didn't you?" She rolled her gaze to Sandi. "Who else wants to explore their private affairs?"

Sandi met the dare with silence. Hooking her arm through Ryan's, she laid her head on his shoulder.

"David and I spent an hour talking to this lovely lady before dinner," Brandie said. "Only the thought of securing a friendship crossed our minds." She glanced at her husband. Her tinkling laugh matched the sound of the spoon tapping her glass. "Mom, Dad ... I have aspirations for Copley Enterprise."

Ryan and Matt glanced at James before looking at their sister. Gene's scowl practically dared his sons to speak. "Speak your mind, kitten."

"You taught us all to love our company. James moving away stole the essence of what you engineered, but his return shows everyone needs input in the reorganization." Brandie swirled ice cubes in her water glass. Frowning, she closed her eyes as if hearing an inner voice inside her head. "I want a seat at the table beside my brothers. Let's fashion four distinct units: land development, structural building, corporate leasing, and renovations."

Neka watched everyone's reactions. Ryan's gaze never left James's face. Dismayed, Sandi stared at her husband. Matt almost choked on his wine.

Celia looked like a fish that had jumped out of the bowl before being rescued from suffocation.

Gene glared at James before turning to Brandie. "Well, you stated your case with confidence."

Fran tore her gaze away from James, who stayed focused on Brandie but squeezed Neka's hand lightly. "I'm eager to know the particulars. You've talked nonstop about the meeting on Monday plus the joys of watching your children grow up."

Brandie set down her water glass. "I apologize for the mixed messages. I still don't want to work outside the home until Cody starts kindergarten. But the company's success demands we make changes while James is present."

"Go on."

She opened her mouth, but no words came out. Resting her forehead in her hand, she stared at her mother.

"I'm a little overwhelmed by this significant moment. Mom, I lived your struggle to preserve our family while Dad walked a tightrope to support his children." Leaning back and taking a deep breath, she focused on her father. "Except for completing the warehouse, the job log is clear. A clean slate indicates preparation for corporate leasing. Build the momentum with a readymade workforce. Buyout McKinley Construction and utilize David's employees to hit the ground running. Let him operate on my behalf beginning Monday."

It seemed Brandie's proposition muted their voices. The stillness in the room was unnerving. Waiting for someone to speak, Neka smiled at James when he ran his thumb over her fingers. Without mounting an objection, Ryan and Matt exchanged exasperated looks.

However, Neka identified with Brandie's appeal for representation. With all this antagonism, they really needed someone with a rational viewpoint.

Sandi rubbed her hands up and down her sleeveless arms. "Last week Ryan said we may lay off workers. You want us to purchase another construction company in the midst of downsizing?"

Brandie's eyebrows rose. "Implementing rehabs will increase the workload."

"Different skills are required between the two jobs. We can't justify hiring additional workers while sending loyal staff to the unemployment line." Ryan glowered at David. "That's the reality we face if we purchase his parents' business."

"I gather you two weighed the pros and cons beforehand." Gene stared at David and grinned broadly. "You'll go from managing the entire operation to accepting direction."

"And profit in the process." David beamed, but Matt grunted.

"If we purchase McKinley Construction, the staff belongs to us."

"Managing a fourth of the operation in Brandie's interest makes them my workers."

Gene glanced at Fran. "Charles and Maureen sanctioned the sale?"

"Prudence required we determine your willingness first." David grinned.

"We once contemplated merging companies." Gene gripped his glass in his hand. "Many businesses succeed following that model."

Matt's strained voice interrupted. "But the quick growth has ruined a substantial number of companies when they can't sustain the push."

Gene's gaze scanned the table before settling on Fran. "We must proceed without destabilizing either business."

Neka's pulse raced. Had they just jumped the second hurdle? She glanced at Gene just as he winked at his wife.

Fran peered at Brandie. "Time is a valuable commodity we have precious little of." Studying Matt and Ryan, she paused, then spoke to David. "Speak with your parents tonight. Tell them brunch is on us tomorrow. If they're free for the day, we'll extend our visit."

"What an exciting evening!" Brandie jumped up to hug her father as David scooted back his chair. She scurried around the table to kiss her mother's cheek and sped across the room, pivoting at the door. "Neka, I organized activities every day for two weeks except weekends." She waved, then followed her husband out the door.

Fran laughed. "Gene, I'm excited like Brandie. I just know that Charles McKinley will call you tonight."

Ryan raised a hand halfway in the air. "May I voice an opinion?"

Gene glared at his son. "No, wise guy, we'll hash out specifics over brunch tomorrow."

When a noise in the entryway drew Gene's attention, he beckoned the man waiting to be acknowledged. The server rolled the dessert tray into the room, stopping next to Gene's chair. "We lost two guests," Gene told him.

They ate dessert in silence. Whatever excitement Fran had felt seemed to seep away after the server left the room. Neka continually examined everyone's faces. No one appeared happy, not even James. He was probably absorbed in planning the next step. It seemed that his parents weren't the only ones caught in the crossfire. Brandie probably worked overtime to keep relationships alive with Matt and Ryan. They definitely were not the family next-door.

Frowning, Neka squirmed in her seat. Whoever knew silence could resound in a room? It was time to move the conversation to a positive topic.

She cleared her throat. "Mr. Copley, sometimes Lacey Corp gets feelers outside of our service area. We rejected bidding on developments in Eureka and Rolla."

Shrewd eyes narrowed. "What are the particulars?"

"Eureka will build an industrial park and credit union, while Rolla will undertake a major residential expansion."

Matt's eyes lit up. "What's the target date?"

"They break ground in mid-August in Rolla and early September in Eureka."

Laughing, Gene rubbed his chin. "Oh boy, I'm tempted. But these breaks must pass us by."

"Do you work in planning?" Ryan asked as he captured her gaze.

She shook her head. "Acquisitions sends weekly emails listing potential projects."

James squeezed her fingers when Ryan and Matt's cagey expressions indicated they counted the advantages of his return home.

Chapter Fourteen

After dinner, she and James went to the guest room. Neka almost purred as he methodically massaged her ankle. This special moment surpassed her wildest imaginations. It was so innocent but so intimate that it almost robbed the oxygen from the room.

Countless times she'd sat in corners as women vied for his attention. How would they react to hearing she was the one who finally captured it? Helping James had plunged her into a crazy storm of opposing personalities. There was no way she could have foreseen the turmoil that traveling to St. Louis would bring about. Too many opposing viewpoints resided within one family.

Her defenses were slowly melting. The foot massage released tension throughout her body. Eyes closed, she succumbed to the enticing sensations. "Ah ... thank you. Your fingers feel so good."

Her eyes sprung open.

"I—I mean—" Blushing, she threw up her hand. "I ... never realized how much ..."

She cleared her throat.

James laughed and tilted his head to the side as if he enjoyed her stammering words.

"This is just the first time I've tackled a week's worth of activity in one day." Closing her eyes, she allowed inertia to lull her again.

Oh Lord, what an unbelievable, mystifying condition.

* * *

James flexed his shoulder muscles, breaking his trance. He had to admit that touching her this way felt pretty good to him, too. He blamed his sharpened awareness on exhaustion. Her expression was so soft and open. It replaced his harsh realities with hope.

Life with Neka guaranteed stability; without her, emptiness loomed. Dating three women had provided less pleasure than one day filled with her wholesome company. Tonight he went down an unfamiliar path. In the drive to advance his cause, James revived long-lost dreams and disregarded visions.

He glanced at his watch. Calling her parents gripped his mind. Dinner had ended earlier than predicted. Everyone dashed to their cars, probably impatient to discuss the proposal in private. Now he wanted nothing more than to hold her until they drifted into sleep. Contentment tugged at his heart.

James grinned. He'd almost forgotten his lifetime goal.

As if detecting his feelings, Neka smiled. "A penny for them. In a matter of seconds, your facial expression changed numerous times." Bridging her fingers together, she supported her chin. "Private times are for sharing confidences."

James chuckled. "I just experienced an extraordinary desire to kiss your ankle."

Confusion crossed her face, like he'd spoken in a foreign language. She shifted toward him as if closer contact removed the mystique. "Why?"

He tried to look as serious as he could. "It's a good place to start."

Using the headboard as leverage, Neka tried to snatch her foot away, but he refused to relinquish his hold. He just laughed again and shook his head.

"All evening I wanted for us to spend time alone, but not for ... sexual gratification." When he resumed his massage, she settled back down.

Neka had handled herself well at dinner. She was an even better match than he'd imagined. Poor Teri had been outclassed by her friend's youngest sister.

Unaware of his thoughts, Neka smiled at him. "I'm thanking God ahead of time and praying the McKinleys agree to merge."

He nodded. "As expected, the proposal's introduction to the folks survived without a hiccup. Still, framing the reconstruction of both companies will require diligence and tender care."

"You always talk shop using construction jargon, game-playing metaphors, or medieval terminology," Neka said as she shook her head.

Suppressed laughter escaped when he shook his head in denial. Lights sparkled in her eyes. "Brandie was awesome."

James had cherished Brandie's performance but had grown concerned with the near emotional breakdown. His sister's compassionate nature embraced them all. "I'm proud of her. She possesses a definite stage presence."

Neka laughed and tucked her legs underneath her. "Matt requested us to dine at his house next week. People shouldn't snub family members without justifiable cause. Though Celia is annoying, avoiding her will disrupt your family's peace, but including Celia as if nothing happened will foster unity. God can build harmony between us."

"I like it." He'd uncovered a kindred spirit who stayed the course through adversity. "Pray for a smooth transition. We blindsided them at dinner. Tonight they'll stockpile ample ammunition for a full assault."

Neka sighed and closed her eyes, like she wanted to shut out the world and everything bad it possessed.

James couldn't stop the phone call with her parents tonight, but he could still convince her to stay. They were perfect together. Tomorrow he'd get her out of the house.

He stroked her cheek when she gazed at him. "Sweetie, Saturday and Sunday belong to us. Tomorrow, let's hunt for a house and have some fun. After all, this is a two-week vacation."

"Yeah, but you have to work." She frowned. "Where did you disappear to during dessert?"

"I didn't want anyone's focus trained on me." James eased away, studying her expression. "Why do you ask?"

"I'm interested in your intentions regarding Copley Enterprise and Monday's meeting. Ryan and Matt are capable business men. Who do you perceive at the helm in ten years? Either one of them or yourself?"

Rising from the bed in one fluid movement, he strolled to the window before replying. "Do I win a prize if I answer correctly?"

Tilting her head, she examined her hands. "No, but you could lose one if you don't."

Outside, the darkness matched the bleakness inside the bedroom, a stark departure from their harmony a few minutes ago. Over the years, he'd booted women attempting to mold him into their idea of the perfect mate. But Neka had always followed his lead. Whenever he wound down their discussions, she ended them with a smile.

109

Was her resolve waning now? He studied her reflection through the glass. "You forgot to add Brandie into the equation."

"David's taking her place. How about him?"

Tightness gripped his abdomen. "Let's stick with Matt and Ryan."

Looking downward, she clasped her hands together. "Do you plan to run Copley Enterprise once your father retires?"

Sitting beside her on the bed, he laid his forehead against hers. Their breath mingled as he answered her question. "Not in a hostile takeover attempt."

"Why should you lead and not one of them?" she asked. The light of compassion in her gaze contradicted the disapproval behind her words.

A furious tightness constricted his shoulders. His fingers applied pressure to the knotted muscles. "Is it prideful to admit I'm better qualified for the position?"

"Not if it's true."

"In my mind or Ryan and Matt's?"

She ran her fingers halfway down his arms. "How about letting God direct your father's decision?"

James captured her hands, locking them into place. She met his eyes.

"And if Father doesn't listen?"

"We'll pray that he does."

Breaking contact, James leaned against the headboard. "No problem, then. God put this dream in my heart twenty years ago." He paused when she looked at him, then averted her gaze. "I'll fill you in on the plans for Saturday and Sunday."

* * *

Did James ever slow down?

Her brother in-law had once said that James lived for the fight but resided in the future, concentrating on whatever promise lay ahead. As soon as he realized a dream, it was replaced by another prize beyond his reach. She'd dismissed it all as absurd, but now she had to wonder if Michael had it right all along.

Eyes sparkling, he weaved his vision for their weekend.

"Our tour around the city will whet your appetite for the St. Louis experience. Plus, we'll locate the perfect home before returning to Tulsa." Sighing,

110

he grabbed her hand. "You look confused. God brought us through a dreadful day. There's no better way to prepare for bed than having you by my side."

After he left her room, Neka crawled beneath the cover, stifling a yawn. She was almost too tired to pray. Her first day in St. Louis had confused and exhausted her, physically and emotionally.

"Father, thank you for keeping me safe. May Your kingdom come, Your will be done in all Your creation as it is in heaven. Always bring glory and honor to Your name. Please bless my conversation with Mom and Dad. When I open my mouth, speak through me. You are my Rock and Fortress. For the glory of Your name, lead and guide me. Don't allow me to lean to my own understanding. I want to acknowledge You in all my ways. Please direct my steps today and forever. In Jesus's name. Amen."

Picking up her cell phone, she pushed the call button and closed her eyes. As the phone rang, Neka dozed off and frowned at her mom's voice.

"Hello, baby, it's only ten fifteen. We expected a much later call."

Hand rubbing her eyes, she smiled at the familiar tone. "Dinner's mayhem sapped everyone's strength so they left early to regroup before the next battle."

"Not the peaceful meal we prayed for?"

Neka yawned. "Excuse me. The evening proved surreal in significant ways." Her body contorted under the cover as she stretched tired muscles. She shook herself awake. "During dinner I could hardly wait to talk to you and Dad, but tonight, I almost fell asleep while reading my Bible."

"Of course you're drained. Look at all you did today."

There was no disapproval in her mother's voice, but as Neka went back over it all in her mind, the checklist distressed her. "Situations can appear in a different light from the outside. Life took me on a roller-coaster ride today. It was like I lived outside my body while events whirled around me."

"Your mind employed safety mechanisms to blunt the trauma." Her father's deep voice cut in.

"Hi, Dad. I didn't know you were listening."

"Really? We've waited all evening for this call. Since you're comfortable, give us the highs and lows of the day. We want to view occurrences from your perspective."

Tiredness fled. Her eyes popped open as she squirmed to sit upright. A private in-depth review boggled the mind. So how could she discuss events she struggled to explain to herself? Neka didn't think anyone could assimilate so many changes in a short time period.

"How much time am I allotted?"

"We've got all night. I laid my book aside when the phone rang. Now I'm propping my feet on a stool beside your father's. Tell us about your day."

This sounded more like the mother and father she poured her heart out to at home.

"Well, in that case ..."

Finding her second wind, Neka's hand arced into the air, conveying her day full of difficulties and abundant joy.

* * *

A peculiar lethargic state greeted Neka as her eyes slowly opened. Frowning at the clock, she tugged a pillow over her face. Eight twenty. For the last two years, she'd awoken at six o'clock regardless of the day and beat a path to the chaise in the sunroom, her unofficial spot to pray and read her Bible.

This morning she lingered in bed, rethinking the conversation with her parents. Their discussions were always challenging. She attempted to predict her father's response and weighed her words in advance. His precise questions always stimulated her thought process, replacing half-formed judgments with larger concepts. She knew she was blessed, even when he upset her.

But last night they communicated on a higher level than usual. Her father let her talk without grilling her on any topic. Their conversation flowed until her mom started talking more.

Maybe he was starting to see her more like Tammy or Kelly and not his little Neka.

After Dad had left the room, Neka had explained her "I think James might love me" theory. Her mom shot that idea down in a heartbeat. In spite of this setback, by the time her dad returned, they had mercifully laid her folly to rest and moved past her mistakes.

She blew out her breath in relief. It was true that James had multiple facets to his character that she hadn't suspected. Until yesterday, she'd always glimpsed Jesus in his actions.

"Father God, though this trip was flawed from the start, You sailed him through the upheaval unscathed. I pray I am correct in believing I followed

Your will by coming." She turned her head sideways. "Thank You, Lord. Please help me make better choices."

About an hour later, Neka closed her Bible just as a knock sounded on the door. James breezed into the room carrying a tray.

"Hello, sweetie."

She smiled as he kissed her dimple and then set the load on the cushion. Sitting across from her, he uncovered the platter.

Pleasing aromas made her stomach gurgle. James had prepared a feast. Dreams of eating breakfast in bed each morning swirled through her mind, and she had to suppress a giggle.

"Thanks for breakfast," she said. "I didn't know you could cook."

James blew a breath on his fingernails and rubbed them against his shirt. Neka laughed, and he grinned.

"I'm a splendid chef, but this was a cheat meal. I laid bacon and eggs on the griddle, placed biscuits and hash browns into the oven, and then poured ready-made orange juice into glasses. It took longer to decorate the tray than it did to cook the food."

He winked before bowing his head for grace. "Father, bless our first breakfast together and all the ones to follow. Lead us to the right home to purchase. Make this a peaceful day void of surprises."

Over playful small talk, they piled their plates with food. Neka loved looking at homes, but those evaluations usually benefitted the company. Since she and her sisters had selected acreage on her parents' estate, it seemed odd to search for a house in another city. Kelly and Michael's home would be completed next month, while Tammy and Kenny had a target date set in late August.

Averting her gaze from James, she chewed her hash browns in silence. In theory, relocating to another city thrilled her, but she was afraid the reality would pale in comparison to her expectations.

She'd woken up with a different mindset this morning, after her parents had forgiven her mistakes.

"Do your parents sleep late on Saturdays?" she asked James. "It doesn't sound like anyone else is up."

"They locked themselves inside the office before dawn. Data preparation for the meeting is a top priority." James broke a biscuit in half. "Plans have changed. Lunch is at the McKinleys' house. Maureen invited us to join them for dinner at six. I accepted the invitation on our behalf."

Scooping eggs onto a fork, she nodded approval. "I look forward to meeting David's parents. Are they like him?"

"He's a mixture of the two." James studied her as he sipped his drink. "You seem puzzled. If you're wrestling with specific issues, lay them on me."

Keeping the man she'd promised to marry in the dark wouldn't do. Lowering her fork, she sought the right words. "Kelly and Tammy haven't tried to contact me. For both of them not to call or at least return my messages is strange."

"What do you think is going on?"

She shrugged. "Even when they're mad, they still talk to me. This lack of communication is just weird. I guess I'll ask Mom tonight if I don't hear from them today."

"Don't read too much into it. You three have a great relationship. I bet they'll get in touch before tonight." James squeezed her fingers, and she smiled at his comforting her. "How did the discussion go with your parents?"

"They're awesome. I'm glad we made plans to talk after everything settled down. They asked me to critique the day from start to finish. But even having the best parents in the world didn't make it any easier to make sense of all that." She bubbled up with laughter but sobered quickly. "We put all mistakes to the forgiven pile. Now I need for them to forget them altogether."

He paused. "What did you tell them?"

* * *

James noted Neka's downward glance. An edited version of her story should roll from her lips any moment. A June wedding never stood any chance with her parents. But she was still wearing his ring, which meant there were no interruptions in their engagement. Yet.

He gently rolled his neck to keep his shoulders loose. They were sore from being so tight yesterday.

"I skimmed over the entire day, but I detailed your proposal and my acceptance. They disagreed with a quick ceremony—no surprise there—but they never tried to dissuade me from getting married." Soft laughter teased his ears. "I guess that describes our conversation in a nutshell."

A miniscule nutshell. It was hopeless to expect to reverse a lifetime of loyalty overnight. However, maybe her deep love for her parents was beneficial to him. Maybe her devotion to them predicted a long future with her. But he had to break her habit of clamming up when he pressed her for details.

"Ready to go?"

"I am." Smiling, she stuffed a forkful of hash browns into her mouth.

Chapter Fifteen

James was a first-rate tour guide and dished out lots of interesting facts on the drive downtown. Peppered with insider information, now she really wanted to learn more about the city. St. Louis was only four hundred miles from Tulsa, but she'd never considered living in another town.

Neka examined a horse-drawn carriage as they walked past where drivers waited for tourists. She imagined exploring the area in a buggy seated next to James. A giggle rose up as her excitement soared, and she clamped her lips to keep from looking like an excited child.

The prospect of life married to her dream man thrilled her. But leaving the family she loved exposed the flip side of saying yes. She still wasn't sure how to balance her old life with the new.

In the design world, it was easy. She'd fall in love with a space and fashion it in seconds. But important decisions should never be made with heightened emotions, especially lifelong choices. They were better with some distance from the headiness of first love.

Well, it was a little late for that assessment now. Casting her gaze at the buggies, she wished for simpler times. The Gateway Arch came into view. Somehow pictures had failed to do justice to it. Sunlight cast a brilliant luster against the gleaming steel gray. No other building competed to dominate the view, so it stood magnificently on its own, like the main attraction in an amusement park.

James pointed to the Mississippi River. "Since there's a smattering of people, let's take a stroll on the riverfront before riding to the top."

They headed down the sloped sidewalk. Satisfied, Neka thought their budding romance resembled her parents' wonderful marriage. Even in business, they operated as a team.

Taking her hand in his, James said, "Travelers called St. Louis the gateway to the West because it was a stopping point for settlers migrating west during

117

the 1800s." He looked around. "I enjoy submerging myself in historical tales. Reading about their lives causes me to wonder what the books will record about us."

This was the James she'd come to love. Their conversations held no boundaries. Squinting her eyes, she wondered if he viewed those intimate discussions as a weakness. Always open, the cagey side of his personality had surfaced on this trip. She wondered what other issues he had that she was unaware of.

But she knew his deepest yearnings, those secrets he hid away from everyone else. That was what really mattered. They had the rest of their lives to get to know each other better.

James studied her expression when she stopped swinging their hands. "What's occupying your thoughts, sweets? You're clearly not listening to me."

Laughing, she glanced up at him. "I'm sorry. Besides taking in the sights, I'm thinking about us."

"Since your thoughts fully engaged you, I hope they were pleasant." He narrowed his eyes in mock suspicion as he contemplated her reply. They laughed.

Neka delighted in the laughter she heard more in two days than in the entire time she'd known him. Shouldn't he be stressed instead of lighthearted? "All thoughts of you are pleasant, even when they give me ... moments," she said.

"I promise to stop any action that upsets you. Your approval means more to me than anything else—even presiding over the family business." Grasping her chin lightly, his hazel eyes were full of sincerity for a moment before coolness entered his somber gaze and he masked his emotions again.

But the small glimpse into his soul replenished Neka's desire to spend her life with him. Caring about her opinion would lead to love. She just knew it.

James scanned the hill. "I see tourists. Time to go up." He pointed to the Arch.

Encouraged, she followed his lead.

* * *

James scanned the city from one of the sixteen windows in the observation deck at the top. The sun was strong, and it was hot, even for June. The swel-

118

tering heat had impeded their progress in the uphill climb from the riverfront. Sweat was glistening on his skin before they even reached the Jefferson National Expansion Memorial.

But somehow Neka looked fresher than ever. He wrapped her hair around his finger while she examined a barge floating on the river. "Are you enjoying yourself?"

"I'm thrilled to be out of that tram. It was the longest four minutes of my life!" Her eyes glittered as her gaze swept the area. Her dimples deepened, and she batted her eyelids at him. "How about using the stairs on the way down?"

He laughed at her ploy. "I hate to disappoint you, but I don't share your penchant for walking down one thousand seventy-six steps. Visitors must use the tram elevator. Only maintenance personnel use the stairways."

Neka frowned and watched as a group of teenagers moved down the slope to the elevator. "The park ranger said you get to the bottom in three minutes. Losing a minute off of the descent works for me."

James chuckled at her flexibility. She was never out of sorts for long and always returned in full force, bubbly as ever. Even her shyness fled in his presence. Around him, she expressed her ideas and observations without hesitation. She was so inquisitive that he'd had to take the role of tour guide as they explored the city.

He examined the horizon, trying to see the sights as she must see them. "I'm glad we have a clear day with high visibility. We can see thirty miles into another state. Do you like the Illinois side?"

"I enjoy looking across the river." She turned back to him, eyes wide, and pointed to boats anchored at the dock. "Do they provide excursions on those riverboats?"

Something in him loosened at her excitement. "We keep the *Becky Thatcher* and *Tom Sawyer* busy. They run sightseeing, dinner, and Sunday brunch tours. They also provide several theme cruises."

"I wanted to stop off as we passed by but thought it better to beat out the crowd headed toward the Arch. I've never sailed on a riverboat before. Is it sailing on riverboats?" Frowning, she faced him and then turned back before he could answer, scanning the Mississippi. "It's dirty. The Arkansas River has cleaner water."

James feigned indignation. "Do you realize you're insulting a national treasure? The Mississippi River is famous for its mud. How many stories have you heard spun around the Arkansas River?"

Her body shook with laughter in quite a pleasing way. "If the citizens of St. Louis search for acclaim, mud is as good a commodity as anything else."

"Do not cast aspersions upon other people's jewels." He laughed and glanced at the riverboats as the next comment almost choked him. "Clearly an excursion on the muddy Mississippi beckons. Let's skip the helicopter tour on this trip."

Her eyes opened wide. "Hey, let's ride a carriage instead. Several horse and buggies lined the street on our way to the Arch."

James hadn't ventured near the downtown area for years before moving away, and now he was going to have a carriage ride and a riverboat ride in one day. "A buggy? Sure, why not? Chalk up another first for your fiancé. I must run a tally; the list is beginning to grow."

"I'm good for you." Neka caught a fingernail between her teeth. "And ... you're even better for me."

She studied his features through half-closed eyes.

The intensity of her gaze mesmerized him. If time could be suspended, this was the moment. But it couldn't, so he glanced away. He composed himself by probing the change in her expression. "A penny for them."

Neka grinned as if at a private joke. "This is a forever moment. I'm etching this scene within my heart. These are the memories we'll regale our children with as they grow up."

It was almost as though she'd read his mind. James could ooze charm on command, but he was folding at her confession. For a moment, as the sunlight reflected in her eyes, his pleasure with her derailed his reserve. Her smile acted like a vise securing his heart.

"Do you remember my question to you yesterday?" Neka asked.

"Which one?"

"I asked if you thought that joy would come in the morning. Thank God it did." The low timbre in her voice enticed him further.

Hands locked together, they turned around to the other side of the observation deck. James glanced at Neka, the only woman who might supply the happily ever after he craved. Accelerating the courtship set the pace for this now-romantic vacation. A shudder broke the spell and brought his perilous position to mind. Tonight, Neka would talk to her parents again, who were more likely than not committed to ending their relationship. How much division could they achieve long distance?

Neka squeezed his hand when they reached the windows that provided a panorama view of the Missouri landscape.

Neka sighed and glanced at James out of the corner of her eye. "Since football season is over, we can't attend a Rams game." Her body shook from withheld laughter. "What about those people strolling toward Busch Stadium?"

Grinning, he looked away. "The Lacey women do love their sports. Your father definitely didn't allow the lack of sons to deny him sports enthusiasts in his home."

She nodded, pointing toward the park. "So was that a yes to a quick walk to the ballpark this afternoon?"

"Sorry, our schedule's already full. The Cardinals are in a homestretch, so there's plenty of time to catch a game. We'll check their schedule online."

Contented with his answer, she peered out the window to study the city. "What's next after our cruise?"

"Fulfilling your wishes." He smiled and stroked her cheek. "We go straight to the buggies for our carriage ride. Afterward, we'll eat lunch at a restaurant in Laclede's Landing."

"I can't wait to sample the food." She leaned into his touch, and his heart raced for a moment. "What about houses?"

"Six today. The first appointment begins at three. They're located in the same area as the McKinleys' home."

Waiting for the elevator, James frowned at her suddenly worried expression. He wrapped an arm around her waist, determined to keep her happy all day today. But she trembled in his embrace. James grasped her hand when the door opened. Neka refused to budge. Instead, she peered inside the egg-shaped cubicle, counting to ten. Eyes closed, she whispered, "Thank you, Jesus," then stepped inside.

* * *

A tour coach pulled into the parking lot while they crossed the street. Neka tiptoed over cobblestones leading to the anchored *Tom Sawyer*. Fear of rolling down the sloped walkway in her new shoes impeded her progress. First an airless tram ride and now uneven ground. Why hadn't she noticed the flawed pavement when they passed by earlier? Watching elderly couples disembark from the bus, she stumbled and clutched his arm.

He glanced at the wedged-heel shoes. "You're wearing sensible shoes. You won't fall."

Neka gripped his arm tighter. "I don't want to roll headlong into the river."

"You swim."

She sighed when his eyebrow rose. The summer after they'd met, he'd played volleyball in their swimming pool. Seventeen-year-old Neka had joined the fun, wearing cutoff blue jeans and a sleeveless Oklahoma Thunder T-shirt.

"In shallow water."

"People can drown in a tablespoon of water."

Her free hand swiped his arm. "Stop repeating that old wives' tale."

"Ah, a non-believer. Ever hear of laryngospasm?"

"No." Neka jumped up on the ramp leading to the riverboat. She laughed and wiped moisture from her forehead, turning away from his inquiring gaze.

Of course, James had attended several parties where she'd flitted in and out of the water. So, she understood the unasked question. Though her sisters were avid swimmers, Neka gave the illusion of being one. In truth, she never graduated from the shallow end of the L-shaped pool.

However, fear had never been a part of her life, just as water had never frightened her before now. Their family took vacations every other year. Picture albums bulged with photos of her riding down trails, rafting, hiking, and similar pursuits. Yesterday's hectic events unsettled her emotional system but not anymore. Before leaving St. Louis, she would fearlessly repeat the tram ride and cobblestone track.

"We'll swim together on the deep side this summer." He turned to the lady behind the ticket window. "Two."

* * *

Neka pored over photos the photographer had taken as they boarded the boat. "Ooh, these are lovely. I can't wait to download the ones I took. We'll fill a photo album showcasing our vacation."

"Beautiful lady." James peered over her shoulder. "You're very photogenic."

Each picture highlighted how natural they looked together. Tearing her eyes away, she waved the pictures in her hand. Thank God for camera phones. Today's precious moments would be tomorrow's keepsake memories. "I'd hoped to send Mom a few shots tonight. I might mail her a photo album featuring downtown St. Louis."

"Good idea. We'll fill up one for Mother too." When she hesitated, James moved them off the platform onto the cobblestones. Frowning, he touched her cheek when she stared at him, her lower lip nipped between her teeth. "What's wrong, sweets? Neka, don't ever hold back your feelings. Level with me at all times."

His gentleness released a floodgate of emotions. Though baring weaknesses proved the kiss of death for many couples, she refused to marry a man who lacked compassion.

"You noticed me trying to manage fear today." Before staring into his eyes, she studied her shoes. "Actually, it cropped up yesterday before I dashed into the restroom at the airport."

The color of his eyes darkened to a hue she hadn't seen. Grabbing her hand, he led her up the sloped walkway to the narrow road. After crossing the street, they climbed the hill until he gently pulled her down on the grass beside him.

"Talk to me."

Without a doubt, James cared about her. That knowledge alone strengthened the impulse to stand beside him against adversity. Her heart melted when he played with her fingers.

"To conquer this fear, I need to repeat the tram ride and walk down the cobblestones alone."

As they sat in silence, Neka stared across the river, sorting through her feelings. Her lips trembled as she smiled at James. "May we come back to the riverfront before leaving St. Louis?"

The positive smile nearly outshone the kindness exuding from his gaze. It seemed he understood the challenge of facing imaginary terrors.

Strong fingers stroked her cheek. "How about today? Though I vow not to touch you, I'll walk beside you the entire way."

Standing together, they headed down the hillside.

"First we retrace our steps to the *Tom Sawyer*. Then we'll take a ride up and down the tram. Agreed?"

Nodding, she willed tears not to fall. She had the reassurance that she sought. James might truly love her.

123

Chapter Sixteen

The horse-drawn buggy slowed as it passed in front of Busch Stadium. Neka craned her neck from side to side like a searchlight. "Look at all the people. They must have a sellout crowd."

James checked out the fans surrounding the ballpark. "The Cardinals had a good season last year."

Once the light changed, the carriage moved down the street, turning right at the traffic signal. The area teemed with groups standing together and individuals walking alone.

"Is it always this busy?"

"It is during the spring and summer, especially around restaurants and hotels."

Three couples snapped pictures in a huge parking lot. His hometown had changed since he moved away. Playing tourist helped James readapt to the area as well. It also gave him time to reflect on his dismal performance with Neka since leaving Tulsa.

His missing her overwhelming anxiety for two days in a row stung. Being an astute observer had rescued him from untold complications. This time his vaunted clear-sightedness proved a miserable failure. Instead of basking in triumph, God taught him a lesson in humanity. Self-interest had left his fiancée unprotected.

He rested his chin on her head after she leaned her back against him. Their friendship created a sense of belonging for both of them. It had also smoothed the way for the shift in their relationship yesterday.

Years of dating multiple women who also dated other men had made him cynical. Neka brought an innocence into his life that broke through that barrier in a way that unsettled him. They had a sense of companionship he'd longed to experience but actively avoided with other women. He knew it was hypocritical—he'd engaged in sex since his teens, but he liked that he was

125

marrying a woman who would only lower her inhibitions for him. Glancing at the scenery, James added lost dreams revived to the mental scorecard he compiled.

"The St. Louis Rams dome is just ahead."

Neka grasped his fingers, smiling. They were living life at its highest peak right now. He shoved Monday morning further away.

* * *

Entranced by his nearness in the dimly lit cellar, Neka gazed at James, who poured on the charm. Had he romanced her in the past without her knowing? She looked around the restaurant to hide her adoration.

"This was a marvelous choice. I love pasta."

"What else do you love?" His voice was soft.

Heat crept up her face, and she was glad for the dim lighting. "Everything about this morning because my fiancé made it special. Fiancé—I like saying that word."

His tone lowered to a whisper. "You are welcome to say it whenever the urge hits."

It felt like a conspiracy, and she laughed breathlessly. Somehow this man possessed a power over her that no one else had. They'd strolled side by side across the cobblestones lining the riverfront for half a mile. After that, they rode up and down the tram twice before departing for the carriage ride.

James never complained about the lost time. He'd simply rescheduled the three earliest appointments for next Tuesday. There just wasn't enough time to add in more activities for that evening. If love hadn't already seized her heart, his tender attentions today would have cinched her loyalty forever.

Satisfied, she surrendered to the happiness encompassing her life.

"I will never forget today. And now I'm having lunch by candlelight at an intimate table for two seated across from *my fiancé*." When he gave her special smile at her words, peace overwhelmed her.

"See? I aim to please."

* * *

Driving to the McKinley home, James assessed the day. The calm, amenable Neka from this morning had disappeared after lunch. Already behind schedule, her disengagement while viewing houses had forced them to view even more properties next week. Perhaps he could spark her interest.

"How about the colonial you cooed over on Pershing Place?"

Turning her face toward the side window, she shrugged. "I liked them all but they were a bit grand for our first home."

"People buy starters when they can't afford to purchase their dream house the first time out."

"What about our place in Tulsa?" she asked out of nowhere.

"We're keeping the condo."

Face resting against the cushion, she shook her head.

"What about the house I planned to build on my parents' estate? Kelly and Michael built their home across the lane, while Tammy and Kenny broke ground on the hillside." Neka nodded at his glance. "Let's choose a different parcel if you don't like the site I picked."

"Your parents purchased enough land for future generations? I didn't know that."

"Lacey Corp also opens up additional avenues."

Almost involuntarily, he switched into his detachment mode with a new variation. "Did I overlook a vital detail about the company?"

One look at her set features tightened his sore shoulder muscles into hard knots. The last forty-eight hours had tossed her moods in several directions.

"An issue needs settling before Monday. Since Kelly, Tammy, and I don't have the business backgrounds—or the desire—to take the position, we need someone ready to step in after Dad retires."

"Is everyone still set on starting a foundation in five years?"

"We need to run with it now. Dad wants to administer the organization, and sometimes he can be stingy."

James chuckled. "It's envisioning his hard-earned dollars getting wasted. You Lacey girls outlined a money-guzzling operation. Perhaps he hopes to save his grandchildren from poverty."

Neka frowned. "Kelly married an architect, and Tammy's marrying an attorney in September. Those facts make you the only son-in-law equipped to take over."

His feigned indifference didn't reach his neck muscles, which at this point were beginning to demand relief. All morning he'd yearned to truly blend their lives together, but now this revelation chipped away at that unity.

Had it even been real?

The thought irritated him, bursting bubbles he didn't know he'd made. Did she agree to marry him to secure a CEO for Lacey Corp?

Of course, their network had crossed his mind, but he never entertained thoughts of taking over. It would simply undercut his current obligations. Despite the respect he'd get from directing their prestigious organization, he wouldn't detour his master plan. Neka's double alliance was becoming a distraction.

Squinting, she touched his arm. "Penny for them?"

He squeezed her fingers. "Why would your parents bestow that honor on a man they disapprove of?"

"They'll want leadership to stay within our family. Our marriage achieves that goal." She hesitated, watching his face. "Now how do you feel?"

"Unconvinced."

"My dad mentored you in the business for six years. He treated you like a son. Several times a year he claims you're perfect for the job."

Chuckling, he glanced at her. "Did he express those sentiments last night?"

"No, but he didn't retract them either. Lacey Corp didn't figure into our conversation at all."

"Lawrence keeps his network uppermost in his mind at all times."

She smiled and shook her head. "Just ... please remember us while negotiating Copley Enterprise's future."

James stopped in the circular driveway of a massive ranch-style home. There were too many vehicles parked in the side lot. "I see my folks' sedan. The black SUV is Brandie's. I don't recognize the other two cars."

"Did they invite Matt and Ryan?"

"Those cars don't belong to either of them." James assisted her from the car. "Come on, my lovely."

Brandie appeared at the door before they reached the porch. "You two are the last ones to arrive."

Once inside, they followed her down steps to a sunken level. James tapped Brandie's shoulder. "How many guests did they invite?"

"Take a look." Moving aside, she allowed Neka to precede her into the family room.

* * *

Glancing at James, Neka burst into laughter, then hurried across the room. "Mom, Dad! What are you doing here?"

Tension melted as she embraced her mother, who was rising to greet her.

Eyes closed, Karen held her in her arms. "Thank you, Lord."

When she moved, Lawrence's strong arms hugged Neka longer than usual. "We missed you."

Neka buried her face in his chest. The unemotional man kissed her head before letting her go.

Thank You, Lord. Thank You. I can weather this storm.

"Hi, Neka."

Swinging around, her mouth dropped open as her sisters approached. Willing tears not to fall, her gaze swept the room. Kenny and Michael had traveled with them. However, Tammy's beautiful green eyes lacked their customary vibrancy.

"I'm sorry I ignored your phone calls. I wanted to surprise you." She hugged her younger sister, backed away to smile, and then pulled her closer. "I could hardly wait to see you."

Waiting her turn, Kelly's gorgeous features filled with worry. "We'll talk later." Her lips brushed against Neka's cheek. "I love you. And I like your new look."

Shaking her head, Neka stumbled into James standing behind her. Her happiness spiraled out of control. She held her breath as he approached her mom. Karen accepted the hug but didn't return the embrace. Lawrence shook hands, but the words "your move" seemed to fill his eyes. Though everyone appeared friendly, they were keeping their distance.

James acknowledged her sisters with a nod. But neither sister greeted him in return. Kelly turned away, then sat beside Michael, who was bobbing his sandy head. Tammy settled on the love seat next to Kenny, regarding James with a speculative expression on his dark-brown face.

Oh no! Does anyone else sense the friction?

Neka studied James's mother and Maureen McKinley on the sofa. Fran's pursed lips indicated she'd noticed their disdain. Maureen looked bewildered. She'd obviously seen the snub too.

Though concerned about James's relationship with the family, Neka stayed calm.

Maureen gestured toward her. "Welcome to the family, dear. Fran said our godson was engaged to a charming young lady."

Neka glanced around when Brandie touched her on the shoulder. Her broad grin brightened the gloom. "James spent so much time here that my mother and father-in-law practically raised him."

She smiled. "I'm glad to meet you, Mrs. McKinley, though your dinner guests amaze me."

Maureen's high-pitched titter vibrated in her ears. "Karen and Lawrence flew in this morning, and have been at our house since lunch. After the meal, Lawrence revealed that the rest of the family flew in this afternoon and were attending a doubleheader tomorrow." She grinned at the small group sitting close together. "So I invited them to join the festivities."

Charles McKinley hugged Neka, scanning her features as if committing them to memory. "This dinner party is an engagement celebration."

Neka grinned. "Thank you both. We appreciate your well-wishes."

"You made a wise choice." He shook James's hand, patting him on the back. Observing James's reserved smile, he regarded Neka. "Our godson will make you an exceptional husband. You said yes to a good man."

"Thank you."

Charles glanced at Neka's parents. "No doubt you're wondering why we're gathered here today." Laughing as if he'd made a joke, he pointed to a wide ottoman and sat in his recliner. "Take a seat. I'll stick to the high points. Last night, Gene called after Lawrence offered to buy both companies—with stipulations."

James's hand tightened on her shoulder. Neka also felt the disbelief that flashed in his eyes. Nothing Charles said made sense. They put together a buyout overnight? Her mom wouldn't hop a plane without prior notice unless ...

Did God tell her to come?

"Rumors attesting his swift execution are understated. Over lunch, he unveiled a cohesive strategy to absorb both companies." Charles studied James. "Now for those conditions. Gene and I agreed to join the advisory board. Your father said he wanted our years of experience in the boardroom."

Neka shifted in her seat. She failed to comprehend some silent communication that passed between the two men.

"The final provision includes buying Copley Homes."

* * *

Buying Copley Homes had been a prerequisite all along. Even before Lawrence had demanded to talk to James before dinner yesterday, his mentor had plotted to enlarge Lacey Corp's network at his family's expense. Remembering the conversation in the car a few minutes ago, James inspected Neka's face. But her dubious expression quelled any suspicion of prior knowledge. This entire situation had caught her off guard.

Neka studied her father. James realized that except for her, everyone watched him.

Brandie practically pulsated with excitement. David's easy grin acknowledged that he stood to receive quite a financial gain. Maureen and James's mother beseeched him with their eyes to sell. Charles had always believed dawdling over the inevitable helped no one. And his father silently challenged him to quit stalling and sign on the dotted line.

The expectations differed on the Lacey front. Tammy dared him to disagree with their plans. Kenny's shrewd gaze weighed odds. Kelly and Michael wanted him to say no. For the first time since James met Karen Lacey, she wore a deadpan expression like a pro.

Lawrence simply studied him, unreadable. Buying three companies in one day was his trademark. It was the signature move that every major player in the land-development industry anticipated. Adjusting troublesome situations into a win was his specialty. Playing ball would double Lacey Corp's profits within twelve months because they had enough revenue to fully utilize their newest acquisitions.

Though longing to massage his aching muscles, he refused to tip his hand. It was time to regroup. His languid rise from the ottoman caught Neka's gaze.

"My fiancée and I will confer in private. Excuse us."

She gripped his outstretched hand. Withdrawing from the room, James kept walking until they exited the house. Outside, he leaned against a trellis, running his fingers over its thorny vines.

* * *

Unable to read his thoughts, Neka watched James in silence. His pent-up energy belied the calm demeanor.

131

"I didn't know they were coming." Blinking, she tried to recapture their perfect afternoon. She stepped closer to reach out a hand but dropped it to her side.

"I trust you."

"Thank God." She let out a breath she didn't know she'd been holding.

"Lawrence gave us a bird's eye view of the world according to him, his classic response to those pesky little trials one encounters in life. The man turns conditions to his advantage at every turn."

Neka failed to understand his attitude. Though shocking, the benefits far outweighed any disadvantages. Surely he'd evaluated the pluses in the family room.

"He brokered a substantial deal that profits everyone," she said.

James's narrowed eyes resembled slits. "How so?"

"The proposal has merit and answers prayers. God is so good. Now you'll manage four organizations."

* * *

It was true that selling their companies to Lacey Corp would surpass his expectations. The McKinley and Copley families would reap substantial monetary gain, even if the West C losses meant his father would have to settle for less than the company's actual value. McKinley Construction would demand top dollar, but Copley Homes beat its value.

"Last night you talked to your parents."

She nodded. "For about ninety minutes. Dad left the room for a while, but he couldn't conceive, formulate, and propose a plan in that timespan."

"He's a skilled negotiator. I'm sure Lawrence developed his agenda after my conversation with him and Karen. Adding the other businesses while you talked, he fine-tuned his strategy. The die was cast when he exited the room."

"My dad normally has a team that charts the course of mergers. Handling this one solo must mean God is directing his steps."

Neka believed everyone until their wickedness smacked her in the face. Normally James liked that about her, but right now ... "This action sets a precedent for the future."

"This can't be an ordinary business deal. My mom came with him without prior notice. Or do you accuse her of deception as well?"

132

Gaze softening, he stroked her cheek. "Your mother is in St. Louis because you are here. But now that she's seen you, she'll pay attention to your father's manipulations."

She crossed her arms. "Like you told Brandie and David, this merger is a winner for every party involved."

Her candor staggered him. Agreeing put him under her father's thumb, stripping their ownership to furnish jobs within companies they built.

James evaluated the timeline again. Lawrence had received news of their trip around five thirty. Before eleven, he'd devised a plan to buy out three businesses he'd never considered until yesterday.

The man had devised a scheme to defeat him in less than six hours. Instinct drove his actions, not the Holy Spirit.

But was the instinct about business or keeping him from Neka?

Frowning, James shook his head. Retaliation didn't fit this scenario. This was a game Lawrence played daily and usually won. "Do you expect me to make a hasty decision on something that affects the rest of our lives?"

Closing her eyes, she turned away. "You expected me to."

Lawrence was turning everyone against him. He'd offered everyone their lifelong dreams and planned to dash their ambitions if James refused to sell. Fighting against a motivated foe was a move he couldn't have foreseen.

And his life with Neka dangled like a pendulum.

It was time for a new playing deck. First Neka had to see Lawrence not as a saint but as the man he really was—a tall but necessary order.

He tipped her face up to him. Hope overflowed from her eyes. An answering need rose within him. This lady was worth the effort it would take to speak those vows. "Your father is displeased with me. If I sell Copley Homes, you and I may have to start over."

Her look tugged at his heart. "My father is tough but not ruthless," she said.

"You speak as the daughter who loves him."

Neka turned her head away. "He trusts you to manage Lacey Corp's future. If he has a hidden agenda ... Jesus is faithful to fight every battle when we trust Him."

James stroked her cheek. "Your father operates by instinct."

"And love." She wasn't budging.

"The jury's out on that one concerning me."

Neka met his eyes. "But not me."

"He loves you, but these hostile actions don't speak to his thinking of me like a son." He ran his finger down her nose and then pulled her close. "I won't stand in the way of anyone's dreams. Let's go inside and wow them with our unity."

Chapter Seventeen

Smudging circles across the glass of the window seat, Neka mulled over the McKinleys' dinner party. The pleasure filling her spirit couldn't be denied. Just knowing her family was a few blocks away bolstered her courage.

Ryan had called ten minutes ago, and James took the call in the den. Every dread caused by the conflict with his brothers had evaporated that evening. Lacey Corp purchased Copley Enterprise. James fortified his future, despite his suspicion that her father had nefarious reasons that sparked the bid. This purchase was a gift from God.

"Thank you, Jesus."

Better still, instead of cherry-picking specified assets to purchase, he assumed full liability for each company—something he'd never attempted before.

On Monday, Dad would release a twenty-four-month business plan. Neka prayed it would alleviate James's needless concerns. His upcoming role within the network secured their future. She'd never heard of her dad treating employees unfairly. He understood the personal risk for her if he ignored James when they restructured.

After a quick knock on the open door, James stepped into the room. "Do you always sit in your window seat at home?"

He seemed more relaxed than when they'd parted downstairs in the foyer. She nodded. "How did the talk go with Ryan?"

"Not too bad. When Matt called, I set us up on three-way. At first he claimed the buyout sidelined him and Ryan." He smiled when she raised her eyebrows. He sat and massaged his shoulder. "But they understand my precarious position. Monday morning holds uncertainties for everyone on our side."

What would convince him he didn't need to worry? Like Excalibur, God embedded his position into stone. Words of encouragement came easy.

135

She walked around him and massaged his shoulders for him. "Though Monday may be worrying, dare to believe God directs Dad's steps. The day can't close without God's blessing you. Call me with the praise report right after the meeting."

But her excitement from earlier faded. Listless, Neka stared into the starless night full of wishes. Did she possess the courage to stand on the same convictions she asked of him?

Their engagement ensured James a role in the family business. Since yesterday, she'd wavered on the wisdom of saying yes without serious consideration. But she wasn't ready to call it quits. Her whole being screamed out that James loved her, and that deserved a chance.

She kept kneading James's shoulders, and a little sigh escaped his lips.

"Our engagement locked you into a position with Copley Enterprise," she began. "Selling the companies removes that ... burden." She blew out a long breath. "Look, I refuse to hold you hostage." Her lips trembled. "Consider yourself released from the obligation to marry me."

What had she just said? The notion had only entered her mind a second ago. But it was too late to take it back.

* * *

James brought her around in front of him and lifted her right hand as he had in the car when he proposed.

"I meant it when I told David you're the soul mate I'd longed for. I won't insult you with meaningless love declarations." He looked into her eyes. "I know that we'll be happy together. I want to marry you."

And when he said it, he knew it was true. He wanted this woman at his side forever.

"Marry me. Mother our children. Let me wake up in the mornings snuggled against you. Allow me to spend the day picturing you lying next to me through the night." Cupping her face in his hands, he kissed the tip of her nose and both dimples.

"You're always mindful and attentive to me." Neka swallowed hard as tear-filled eyes held his gaze. She hesitated and licked her lips. "Ask yourself why you care so much."

He studied her. Surely the desire for unity was more powerful than declarations of undying love. Emotions were fickle, but commitment endured.

Asking her to marry him calmed a slew of fears, the most important being that he might never have a family of his own. Now that the perfect lady was available, there was no going back.

"How about setting a wedding date?"

Her eyelids fluttered a couple of times as she changed position. "May I borrow the car? I remember the directions to my parents' hotel."

James hadn't considered she'd want to talk to her parents in person. The Laceys flying in presented even more obstacles.

"I was thinking more like promising not to hang up without making firm plans."

She laughed, but it died out when he failed to join in.

"I give you my word to press the point. I'll sleep better if we speak in person." Neka paused, seeming to come to a decision. "I don't hear any movement downstairs. Do you think your parents went to bed?"

His whole body tensed. He didn't even want her speaking to her parents over the phone without him. He just couldn't sanction a private discussion face-to-face. But if he refused, it would be a win in their column.

"I don't expect anyone to drop off to sleep right away."

Neka sat with her legs tucked beneath her. She looked so young. He didn't like the idea of her driving around a strange city alone at night. He knew her father wouldn't either.

But she would insist on going alone, just like she had insisted on talking with them yesterday without him. A phone call to her sisters would bring one of them to the house in fifteen minutes. The firsts were racking up. James wanted to accompany and protect her.

Her dimples flashed as she reached out her hand for the keys.

* * *

Neka walked into the hotel room and hugged her mom. Wriggling fingers at her dad, she sat in a chair facing them. Although she should be upset, she felt ridiculously happy.

"Thanks for letting me stop by on short notice."

"You're welcome to visit no matter where we stay." Her mother curled her legs on the cushion and leaned into her husband's embrace. "Why so formal?"

137

She squinted and looked between her parents. She couldn't pretend to be upset when she was ecstatic with the turn of events. Still, her parents were wrong not to alert her to their plans. She deserved a heads up before the fact.

Tilting her head to the side, she studied the couple who complemented one another in disposition and appearance. She was as beautiful as he was handsome. Her mom's dark-brown hair and mocha complexion enhanced her glowing light-brown eyes. His blue eyes combined with silver-blond hair exuded a coldness that was far from his true personality.

"Today was crammed with activity and too many surprises."

Karen smiled. "I trust you found our coming to St. Louis a pleasant one."

"I have mixed emotions about being followed here." She frowned, thinking of a respectful way to voice displeasure. "That's what you all did, Mom."

Her body tensed for the denial, but the love emanating from Karen's gaze calmed her frustration.

"I confess. Before your departure we hadn't planned on a visit to this city."

"Taking over three companies wasn't on Dad's program either," Neka provided.

"Takeover is such an unforgiving word. How about buying?" Karen's eyes twinkled as she smiled. "This isn't a hostile bid. Your father purchased businesses with each owner's express approval."

The indulgent look on her mom's face made her squirm in the seat. "Yes, but one of them agreed under duress."

She shrugged. "If he hadn't responded, it would have halted negotiations for everyone."

Neka hung her head, fighting to remember what annoyed her about the transaction. Except for James's objection, the solution proved spot on. But he might have been more receptive to the idea if they had been upfront about it.

"It wasn't much of a choice. Saying no would have shattered his family's dreams."

Closing her eyes, Karen exhaled a long breath before gazing at her daughter. "James isn't a dream filler. We make choices in life. God gave us the ability to choose."

Neka frowned. "He gave us the right to do so."

"We only have the right to choose Him." Karen slowly shook her head. She glanced at the silent man sitting beside her. "Do you imagine James said yes to safeguard their ambitions?"

Gazing at her dad, Neka nodded. "Yes, I do."

The carefree mood shifted to an underlying heaviness. Did her response disappoint them? *Thank you, Jesus, for allowing me to come in person. We needed this time together.*

"Your fiancé gambled Copley Homes for future gain."

Neka looked away. Maybe he'd bet the odds for a greater prize, though many factors caused him to give in. "Will he succeed?"

"Only God knows."

She slumped and stared into space. But after a moment, she sat upright, staring at her dad. Why didn't he speak? Did he remain quiet because she wouldn't like what he had to say?

"I need clarity. James fears Dad might cut him off once they sign contracts."

"I rather hope you trust your father's humanity."

She ran her hand through her hair, then across her shoulders. "This merger answers my prayers. Everybody wins, us especially. Our marriage makes James an immediate family member. Dad can leave the company under his control after his retirement."

Karen's feet hit the floor. "You agreed to marry James so Lawrence could install him over Lacey Corp?"

"Of course not!"

Jumping from her seat, Neka paced around the room. Halfway through the ten count, she threw up her hands. Nothing was working today. Facing in the opposite direction, she braced against the wall.

Lawrence spoke when she resumed her seat. "Pouting should be beneath a woman considering a wedding in a few weeks. You've told us what James thinks. Now give us your perspective on all this."

Neka clasped her hands on her lap and smiled. "Dad, most of his family members wanted to combine resources eons ago. You accomplished that goal and ended the standoff between James and his brothers."

"All good, correct?" Karen's compassionate gaze undid her.

She fell backward on the cushion. "Yes, Mom, but why include his company in the deal?"

"It benefits the network," her dad said. "Does the sale of Copley Homes present a sticking point?"

She closed her eyes. Why must her dad ask questions he knew the answers to? "No one explained how the sale affects him."

"I'll produce a cohesive business plan Monday." He stared at her. She felt like he was looking into her soul. "Why did you accept his proposal?"

Eyes cast downward, she smiled. "I love him. God put us together. One day Michael will head the planning division and Kenny the legal department, while James learns the ropes to navigate our future."

He chuckled. "Do you always tie up other people's lives into tidy parcels?"

The affection in his gaze brought tears to her eyes. "Until yesterday I never thought my dreams would come true."

Karen glanced at Lawrence but turned to Neka. "Honey, how can you pray over the hopes of other people and not believe God will answer those same desires for you?" she asked.

Instead of answering, Neka bowed her head. How did she admit that until yesterday her dreams were mundane? She'd never envisioned James in her life. Just a "husband" who never had a face. No, her dreams were quite general at best. Friends, dates, and living what she'd always termed "a normal life." Fear had kept her from delving deeper into emotions definitely too painful to comprehend.

Sighing, Neka studied her mother, surprised by the hopeful expression. Mother and daughter gazed at one another until Karen shook her head and leaned into the cushion.

"Did you stop by to discuss the wedding?" Karen asked with a smile.

"Thanks, Mom. I got off track and need an answer before morning."

"Tammy announced her wedding plans eight months ago. It wouldn't be fair to upstage her. And please, allow us transition time while we plan yours. It makes losing you easier to bear." Karen clenched her husband's hand. Smiling, she glanced at him. "Blending three companies into our culture will require optimal productivity companywide."

"Even without a buyout I should have thought about your first two reasons." Her contrite gaze begged forgiveness. "Fear of losing James makes the earlier date attractive."

Her mother closed her eyes, causing Neka to shudder. Did Neka's insecurities hurt her mom? Lately her decisions complicated way too many lives. Even she couldn't explain her behavior since last Thursday. Her life was unfolding as if from an unrehearsed script. Maybe opening up to the people who knew her best would settle her thoughts.

Taking a deep breath, Neka gave Karen a half smile. "Mom, I decided to travel with James Thursday night. Yet I scheduled myself off work on Friday and cleared my workload Wednesday." Closing her eyes, she slumped in the chair again. "Believe me, I had no prior thoughts of leaving."

Karen leaned forward. "A handsome man made socializing easier and showed you kindness. Attempting to warn James of trouble didn't work. When private thoughts interrupt normal behavior, it's time to seek wise counsel."

Lawrence shifted positions. "You might have still left after talking to us, but you would have received a rebuttal to your plans. Sometimes dissenting voices protect us from impulsive actions."

Leaving her chair, Neka squeezed between them. Lawrence stretched an arm across the back of the couch. Sighing, Neka closed her eyes. Sitting near her parents brought a comfort nothing else could.

"There's something else I need to talk to you about." Somehow she must relay the anxiety attacks without casting blame on James. "My body has deserted me this weekend. Yesterday at the airport my heartbeat accelerated, and my stomach went haywire. One moment I was talking to James, the next I fled to the restroom in a wave of panic."

Tears trickled down her cheeks when Karen took her hand.

"On the tram ride in the Arch I almost suffocated from lack of oxygen. Try acting normal while convinced you're dying. Worse still, I almost fainted walking over cobblestones leading to the *Tom Sawyer*. I feared drowning in the Mississippi River. Just like yesterday, all was well, and then fear seized me."

Squinting, she glanced at her dad. "James rode up and down the tram with me two times and walked over cobblestones on the riverfront until I was unafraid."

"This may sound harsh, but he either cared or protected his interest."

Grasping Neka's fingers, Karen frowned at Lawrence.

Neka's head lolled on her chest as tears fell onto her mom's hands.

She had a lot to pray about.

Frowning, Karen squeezed Neka's fingers as if coming to a decision. "Do you still want to discuss a wedding date? If so, don't mention June."

Neka leaned against the cushion. "I always wanted a fall wedding."

Her mother nodded. "You've always said the Saturday after Thanksgiving." Karen's lowered voice made Neka lean closer. "Honey, you say God wants you to marry James. Well, standing on faith requires walking in obedience to His word."

141

"I understand."

"Let's hope so. Your travels this weekend might have ended in tragedy. Instead of taking you home, we're about to discuss a wedding date for the ceremony we disagree should take place." She tried to smile. "How about Saturday after Thanksgiving next year?"

Laughing, Neka's eyes brightened. "No, Mom, after Thanksgiving *this* year."

"Now it's my turn to agree." Karen's smile filled the empty places.

Neka liked being squashed in the middle of her parents. It brought back childhood memories. This was the type of marriage she wanted with James. Before long he would acknowledge how much he loved her. Her eyes squeezed tight. *Lord, make it soon.*

"You're tired. I'll leave." She captured her parents' hands, bringing them to her lips.

Driving from the hotel, Neka contemplated the future from her parents' perspective. She sympathized with her father, who would be presenting a business synopsis in thirty hours. Even with a pending deadline, he used valuable time to hold her hand. Though exhausted, her mom had accompanied her to the car.

If she truly believed God had arranged this marriage, she must accept He had everything under control. Surely tonight ended the winding road she'd stepped on Friday morning.

As she pulled into the Copleys' driveway, the lone figure leaning against a column made Neka grin. He'd never declared his love in words, but James waited outside at one o'clock in the morning.

This was the person she wanted her future linked to—a man who cared about her welfare.

Opening the door, he helped her from the car. "Did you turn off your cell phone? I was about to call your folks."

Neka climbed the stairs, rifling through her purse. "I may have run out of charge."

Outside her room, James released her hand when she yawned. "Get a good night's sleep. We'll talk in the morning."

Chapter Eighteen

Staring out the window, Neka fought back tears. All morning she'd anticipated a heart-to-heart talk with her sisters that hadn't materialized. Maybe she'd been wrong to accompany them today.

"From the time I stepped into this car, you've slammed James."

Tammy glared at her through the rearview mirror. "Kenny and I had plans this weekend, which didn't include sleepless nights and a visit to St. Louis."

Gazing out the window, Neka muttered under her breath. "Then you should've stayed home."

"No, you should have. Look Miss Fleet Foot, your escapade disrupted many lives this weekend." She blew the horn at a car crossing into their lane. "Dad flew in an entire team to facilitate the meeting Monday."

Neka digested the scope of the operation tomorrow. She'd been naïve to think her father could handle all this alone. Sighing, she remembered her words to James the night before—that her dad's solo act meant God directed his steps. Only to find out he flew in members of his transition team. Would James remember her previous words?

Closing her eyes, she laid her head against the cushion. "How did they assemble a team so fast?"

Tammy pulled into a parking space and got out. "The second game will start in a few hours, so it's too late to shop, but we'll fill you in on all the details over lunch."

Kelly joined Tammy outside the car. "No junk food. I want a healthy meal. I'll order carry-out for Michael."

Walking away, they turned around when Neka stayed by the car. Huddled together, they stared at one another until Tammy embraced Neka and brushed aside fallen tears. "Squabbling was not in the script."

"Chalk up our horrible manners to fatigue." Kelly kissed Neka's cheek, then hugged her from the side. Tammy took Neka's arm, and the sisters strolled toward the mall. "James called you sweets the first day you met. At my birthday party, he added sweetie. I always thought his interest was in more than just friendship."

"Why didn't you tell me? I would have told you."

Tammy's green eyes danced for the first time that weekend. "Not if you were twenty-one and I was seventeen."

Neka stared at Kelly. She shook her head, smiling.

"Sorry, I assumed he placed you on the same level with his younger sister." She shrugged. "Let's hope I was wrong."

Neka studied Tammy again. This next question proved crucial but could very well backfire. "Do you still hold that same view?"

Her body tensed for the reply.

Tammy glanced at the smiling Kelly, then she nodded. "I do—but with reservations. Let's go inside before Kelly topples over." She locked arms with her older sister when Kelly rubbed her lower back. "Kel, you're starting to waddle when you walk. Forget about what Annie says—you know most obstetricians claim newborns weigh around seven pounds. But your baby will be at least ten."

* * *

"Gimme!" Two-year-old Cody's screams sliced the air as he fell on the grass, kicking his feet. Yancey leaned over him holding out a bright red ball.

James's eyes narrowed at the ruckus. His thoughts floated back to the airport scene two days ago. Until now, his niece and nephew had always seemed like perfect children.

Brandie picked up her son and kissed tearstained cheeks, frowning at grass stains on his T-shirt. She settled him on her hip and pointed to a cushioned seat. "You know the drill."

Yancey looked at the bench and scowled. She began to speak, then stopped when Brandie's eyes narrowed. Instead of mounting a defense, she pouted over to the cushioned seat, squeezing her eyelids together in an attempt to generate tears.

Still holding Cody, Brandie sat on the glider and allowed the gentle motion to lull him to sleep. She laughed at the horror on James's face.

"That expression is hilarious." Brandie laughed at James, and then pointed her finger at David, who stole a quick glance at Yancey. "Take a look at my husband. We are you and Neka in five years flat. Get used to having children underfoot."

Aghast, James shook his head. "Too soon. We'll need the time to adjust to one another."

"Believe me, you'll adapt faster than you imagine." Brandie placed her hand across her mouth, suppressing laughter. She grinned at her husband. "Ask your friend."

David chuckled when James glowered at him and pointed to his children. "These two skipped their afternoon nap, and it's well past their bedtime."

James's double take caused the couple to erupt into laughter. He stared at his sister in disbelief. "He sounds like you. Married five years, and you've already stolen his voice."

"Wait until you lose your own."

Brandie burst into laughter again when he made a cross with his fingers and held it in front of his face.

"I'm surprised they stayed awake this long. Once Yancey falls asleep I'll move them inside." She smiled at her daughter, eyes aglow with affection. "Another ten minutes and she's a goner."

James was tired too. It had been a long afternoon. The picture of the buyout had blurred after talking with his attorney several times that day.

He grunted in discontent. They wouldn't really know anything until Monday.

* * *

James got out of the car when he saw the vehicle coming to a stop in front of his parents' house. Perfect timing. He missed Neka. What had started as their trip together had turned into a family affair. He wasn't happy to share his fiancée with a family hoping to break them apart.

Though losing her wasn't an option, he refused to analyze the craving for her presence. Instead, he hugged her the moment she stepped out of the car.

"I had a wonderful time." Neka waved when Michael started the engine, then she smiled up at James and wrapped her arms around his waist. She peered inside the car again. "We're taking in an evening game next week."

Although her sisters didn't greet him, they didn't disrespect him with open disdain. That was progress. But once again, displeasure highlighted

Kelly and Michael's faces. How did they achieve perfect harmony in their facial expressions? Tammy still challenged him to some unknown duel.

However, curiosity intensified in Kenny's features. "Did you know the Cardinals won both games?"

James acknowledged the peace overture. Tammy and Kelly had a right to feel affronted. "I heard the score. We listened to the last stretch at Brandie's house."

Repairing the breach in the relationship with her family required patience. In time, he would prove himself to be the straightforward man they'd known.

He focused his attention on Neka's smiling face as they strolled straight through the house to the kitchen.

James studied the room as if seeing it for the first time. "Did you enjoy the Cardinals game?"

"Yeah, at capacity crowd." She leaned on the granite island and joined his perusal of the space. "We ate lunch at the mall before the second game."

One eyebrow rose. "Why did you decide against attending the first one?"

"Blame Kelly. She didn't want to sit through a doubleheader. Like being pregnant is an excuse." She rolled her eyes and laughed.

Before he could respond, Fran stepped into the kitchen, scowling. She stalked to the island and glared at Neka. Perplexed by the aggressive posture, Neka watched her until Gene stepped into the kitchen and halted beside his wife.

Then Fran's gaze never left James's face. "Lawrence called your father and Charles this evening. He changed the venue to the hotel on Market Street at nine o'clock. He requested us to arrive with our attorney at seven to close the deal." She paused, contorting her lips. "Lawrence indicated you were contacted today."

James winked at Neka, then he glanced at his mother. "I spoke with my lawyer several times. He relayed the location change. He will conference in from Tulsa."

She pursed her lips and grunted. "Did he inform you Lawrence flew employees in yesterday to attend the second meeting?"

Now what?

How would she extinguish the doubt factor? Neka's hands arced in the air, framing her words. "Merging three organizations this far from our home base is a major transaction for Lacey Corp." Her gaze moved from Gene to Fran. "Dad hoped to reassure you the transition team can handle the task."

146

When they remained silent, she focused her attention on James.

"You know his meticulous nature. Swift caution is his motto." She touched his arm, trying to gauge his thoughts. "Our engagement is a factor too."

James stroked her shoulder, although she knew his thoughts lay elsewhere. "When did you discover a change in plans?"

Neka smiled, relieved that he seemed to believe her. "This afternoon on the ride to the mall, my sisters filled me in on the change of plans."

He glanced at his father. "I noticed the men were absent but supposed your sisters wanted to chat in private."

"They did." She sighed and nodded her head.

She discerned the skepticism on his parents' faces. She wished they'd recall her status as a guest. She stood in their kitchen, not an interrogation room. If Gene had spoken to the man with the answers, why not question him? Most of her information was secondhand.

James smiled at her through his distraction. "No one discounts anything you say. You're reporting the information at your disposal."

"Wait a minute." Fran folded arms across her chest. Her pursed lips and narrowed eyes deepened the wrinkles on her face. "What positions do you and the rest of the family hold?"

"My mom and Tammy are real estate brokers. Kelly and I do interior design."

Fran turned away. "Lawrence flew in staff ahead of our commitment to sell."

The censorious tone disturbed Neka. She just wanted to find common ground.

"Tonight Dad said that everyone grasped Lacey Corp's setup without a tutorial," Neka said with a smile, hoping for a similar response. "The quick agreement sealed his good opinion."

Fran didn't return the smile. "All to his benefit, of course. Sure, we stand to profit, but business deals inevitably favor one party over the other."

"I can't deny that my dad stands to reap enormous gains from the purchases." Shrugging, Neka gazed at James. "You talked to Blake several times today. He didn't mention his parents were in St. Louis when you spoke?"

"And Blake is ...?" Fran interrupted.

"Blake Latham is my attorney and Kenny's brother. Their father is Lawrence's attorney, and Michael's father is Lacey Corp's accountant. It's quite a family affair. Kenny's and Michael's mothers hold managerial positions inside the network. I knew Mr. Latham flew into town. Blake stood me proud today, addressing issues outside of the original offer." The innocuous glance he bestowed on both parents silenced his mother's grilling. When he turned his attention to Neka, it was clear he was done with this conversation.

"Ready for bed, or do you want to watch a movie?"

Neka avoided meeting his parents' eyes and dashed for the doorway.

"Wait." Fran hurried across the room, blocking her exit. "Forgive my rudeness. You are a guest in our home, and it wasn't aimed at your parents."

James's mother gave a breathy sigh and leaned against the door. The energy seemed to seep from her on the spot. She turned pale as if her life blood trickled away.

"I enjoyed meeting your family and agree our business venture will prove beneficial." The words sprang from Fran's mouth without much conviction. "The last three days have taken their toll on everyone. An even longer week looms ahead."

* * *

"Care to predict the outcome of the meeting in the morning?"

Neka smiled. Monday was the beginning of a brand-new day, a bright tomorrow, and endless promises in Christ. She gazed into James's doubt-filled eyes.

"Only that the day will bless us."

In the kitchen, he'd defended her to his parents, even though he questioned her dad's motives. Trust was a mighty foundation to build a relationship on.

Neka gazed around the room without focusing on anything in particular. Last night she missed an opportunity to discuss the wedding date with him. And that morning there wasn't sufficient time to hold a lengthy discussion before going to church.

That he hid his curiosity well couldn't be denied. She had valid reasons for waiting until tonight. But the fiasco downstairs made each one appear suspect.

"I chose a wedding date last night and ... I hope you agree." When he frowned, Neka hesitated, giving him a chance to speak. He didn't. "It wouldn't be fair to select a day prior to Tammy's wedding in September. Since my mom made valid objections, I agreed to wait for our ceremony."

One eyebrow shot up. "Until when?"

"Well, it's impossible to *really* choose one without your agreement." She wasn't good at hiding things when face-to-face. She smiled.

Chuckling, James pointed a finger at her. "So, my lady, what day did you select once I agree?"

Eyes twinkling with delight, Neka burst into laughter. He found her out quick enough. "How about the Saturday after Thanksgiving?"

* * *

"Why on that particular day?"

A lazy smile belied James's complex thoughts. He knew Lawrence had never anticipated his daughter leaving him. For some unknown reason, her father expected James to ditch Neka. James couldn't imagine what circumstance might provoke him to do that.

"Well, I already told you I love fall colors. And Thanksgiving Day is the start of my favorite holiday season. We'll listen to Christmas music, decorate our home, and spend our evenings buying gifts for our families." She rested her chin on his hand. "This is the first year I'll buy toys for nieces and nephews. And you can come with me to the adult day care center I visit twice a week and help distribute their presents."

Inclusion in her everyday activities stimulated his imagination. His sleeping niece and nephew came to mind. Every time she projected their future, it was like magic. The warm images stirred a yearning to really let go and lay his heart on the line. What if …

Shaking his head, he dispelled the thought. "I'll take advantage of every opportunity to spend time with you."

"We'll celebrate the birth of Christ reading scriptures before the fireplace on Christmas Eve." Her gaze took on that faraway look people assumed when visions unfolded in their mind's eyes. Her smile dazzled. She touched his arm lightly. "The last reason is … your missed holiday celebrations. I want to start our life right by honoring family traditions during that season."

He was speechless in the face of her compassion. Even after a tremendous upheaval, she'd remembered his lonesome holidays. Only Neka could make him change his mind with her kindness and sincerity.

The Laceys had won the second round. So be it.

But the split up they advocated wouldn't happen.

"You paint a picture of what I want too." Lifting their hands, he tweaked her nose. "I'll sweep you away to a private retreat during the reception."

She flashed those dimples, and it intoxicated him like a fine wine. Her sparkling eyes filled him with a warmth he'd never known.

"Thanks for making juggling you and my family simple. I'll support you whenever possible."

The shy smile tugged at his heart, and he knew nothing could ever convince him to leave her.

* * *

Laying her Bible on the nightstand, Neka closed her eyes and prayed, giving thanks and asking for God's guidance. She slid underneath the cover thinking about James. Since the day they met, no other man stood a chance of winning her affection.

Tammy had said he'd liked her all along. If so, why didn't he ever ask her out? He juggled three women instead of settling for one. If he was interested, why did he begin dating Teri a month after Neka's nineteenth birthday?

Thinking of birthdays, she texted Brandie. She'd need her help planning James's party on Friday.

She flopped onto her back. Was he asleep, or was he wide awake too, only contemplating the meeting in the morning? Signing over Copley Homes contradicted the position he'd staked out in the mall parking lot on Friday.

So many changes had occurred since then. James had accepted the November wedding without a hassle. She'd almost leaped from the bed shouting with joy. Before he left her bedroom, they had overcome the huge obstacle of when to get married. In one day, James and Neka had crossed many milestones together.

Their connection was growing. By November, it would never be broken. Serious prayers were needed.

"Father, please help us. We need You. Complete Your course for our lives in us and through us. Make our lives count for Your kingdom and our service effective for Your body. Create within us a clean heart and renew the right spirit within us. Teach us how to choose correctly in every issue of life.

In looking, cause us to see. In listening, cause us to hear. Father, conform us into the image of Your dear Son. Make us women and men of integrity and good character. In Jesus's name. Amen."

Chapter Nineteen

Sliding into the chair next to Kelly inside the meeting room, Neka observed the bustle. While all the principal players were sequestered in the smaller meeting area across the hallway, everyone else roamed about this larger conference room. Some pointed to their name tags while others selected food from three refreshment stations. Everywhere, excited participants waited to hear the news that the deal was done. Tulsa's crew mingled with Copleys and McKinleys as if they'd known one another for years. Pocket groups discussed the merger, and laughter rang amidst animated debates.

Surprisingly, there were no frowns or smirks from anyone, even the Copley wives. Stylishly dressed as always, Celia and Sandi carried on lively discussions with various people. Ryan joked with the marketing head, while Matt engaged in dialogue with Lacey Corp's building inspector. Brandie and David talked to Tammy and Kenny at the juice bar. The intense expressions on their faces underscored their conversation's delicate nature.

About to make a fruit bar run, Neka glanced at Kelly when a voice called out that the meeting was over. Sighing, she scooted her seat back for a better view as everyone filtered into the room.

Hands clasped, the McKinleys strolled in in high spirits. Gene curved an arm around Fran's waist, laughing at whatever remark she'd made. Grinning together, Neka's mom and dad stood inside the doorway.

Her gaze lighted on James, unsmiling and walking alone. Her heart pounded in her ears. What could've gone wrong? Did some unexpected snag emerge?

Examining the languid movements, Neka reconsidered her first impression. It would be easier to decipher his facial expressions if he retained one longer than a second. His friendly greeting to Kelly and Michael conveyed geniality.

Kissing her cheek, he pointed to the next table. "That one has the Copley name on it."

Neka rose, sensing all eyes were watching them. Unaccustomed to intense scrutiny, she sped to the other table and sat down fast. One day she'd get use to the stares James commanded.

* * *

Surveying the room, James was happy that Neka seemed to be unaware some transition team members knew Teri had announced their engagement four weeks ago. Neka didn't need to be any more nervous than she already was.

His gaze centered on his family. Each member integrated with Lacey Corp staff like they held prominent positions within the network. Last night he hadn't imagined the proceedings would be a harmonious affair. The lack of contention illustrated the merger's real status. Invested wisely, his earnings from the sale promised to sustain Neka and him throughout their lifetimes.

Several individuals stared at them, probably wishing they knew when his engagement to Teri had ended. He knew no one in either family would talk. Tilting Neka's face toward his, he brushed his lips across hers. Eyes sparkling, her gaze darted around the room.

"Well? How did it go?" Her valiant smile reminded him of her comeback spirit. She always showed up at social events, even when she was ignored by everyone but family members. She knew one day her peers would accept her.

Leaning forward, he whispered into her ear, even though they sat alone at the table: "Does God always respond to your pleas so quickly?"

She composed her face, but it still radiated glee. He couldn't help but flash that special smile she loved.

"Miracles still happen. Sometimes we forget who's really in charge. Being consumed with ourselves makes it easy to omit Him from our days."

James had to admit to not spending adequate time with God. He frowned. Until that moment, the thought had never crossed his mind. As with most people, he humbled himself amidst difficulties when his need was greatest. Had he ever prayed without some problem at hand?

Movement at the head table caught his eye.

Lawrence opened the proceedings after conferring with Charles and Gene. "Good morning. We welcome you to our first insiders' meeting in

152

St. Louis. Thirty-two people, including family members, advisors, and vital employees are in attendance. Many others are conferencing in from the Tulsa office. Today Lacey Corp passed a tremendous milestone in its twenty-three-year history. Over the weekend, we purchased two major companies miles away from our home base. Introductions are in order."

Sitting down, he gave attention to Charles, who was standing up. Each advisory board member introduced themselves and their guests. When Gene introduced Fran, she announced, "Last Friday, our youngest son, James, brought home our future daughter-in-law, Nikhol."

James stared at the monitor as applause thundered from the screen. The Tulsa faction was fired up.

A woman called out, "Way to go, Neka."

When Neka glanced at James, a man chimed in, "She's blushing."

"Jeff won't know how to take the engagement news." Another woman laughed.

Eyebrow raised, James studied a puzzled Neka. Jeff. He'd have to find out who Jeff was. His mother passed the floor back to Lawrence, and the introductions continued to the other advisors.

Family politics engrossed James's imagination. How would the McKinleys and Copleys fit into the scheme? Neka chose that exact moment to peer down the table, fingers massaging her earlobe in a steady rhythm. Evidently her thoughts ran along the same line. Guessing games played out in real time.

"Now I'll introduce our power center, the core of our organization, along with their Tulsa counterparts. These employees will fill the gap until the St. Louis office is fully staffed."

Smiling, Neka glanced at James. "Here we go."

Lawrence continued to introduce administrative assistants, his advisors, and department managers.

Squeezing Neka's fingers, James withdrew within his designated private zone and wondered if the mechanics that drove the Lacey empire would be revealed. For six years, Lawrence had spoon-fed him tidbits of information. Today he planned to gorge on uncovered facts.

Lawrence concluded the introductions, saying, "Key members of our transition team flew to St. Louis while their counterparts worked from Tulsa. Due to the efforts of tireless individuals, the contract proved satisfactory to all parties. An invitation to our celebration breakfast means you have a stake in the outcome. Two of our six coordinators, Mindy and Bernadette, prepared a brief overview of our organization."

James looked at the coordinators, who were eyeing David. Though he thought that both women were happily married, the overt looks signaled their apparent interest in his brother-in-law. Even Neka glanced from one to the other, then stole a peek at James's friend. She studied him for a few seconds, then gazed at her father, frowning.

Lawrence glanced at the computer screen. Then, scanning the occupants at the McKinley and Copley tables, he smiled. "Are there any questions?" He took his seat and fielded questions for thirty minutes, highlighting their separate marketing, engineering, architectural, inspection, and surveyor firms and plans for the two coordinators to relocate to St. Louis to ease the transition.

Ryan caught James's eye. The question in his brother's gaze summed up James's own feelings. How often did people decide to move their families overnight?

Celia whispered to Matt before asking another question. "Have you decided which employees to retain?" she said to Lawrence.

"All our workers stay put."

Lawrence began to detail his twenty-four-month business plan. One of the coordinators, a plump brunette with a bob haircut—James thought her name was Mindy—consulted notes from a stack of color-coordinated folders. His eyes narrowed when she thumbed through index cards, though he felt sure she didn't really need to. She removed papers from a green folder, passing them down the table on both sides of her.

Mindy said, "This morning our project manager submitted bids for assignments in Eureka and Rolla, Missouri. If successful, she'll circulate particulars next week."

Lawrence had definitely come out swinging. While eating dessert after dinner Friday evening, Neka had told everyone that Lawrence refused to bid on those jobs in Eureka and Rolla. Scribbling on a notepad, he studied the man who took Lacey Corp from showing no interest to submitting bids within three days. Naturally, he underbid all three projects to score a win.

Although the information flowed, they were still holding back. If they planned to retain all staff members, why not speak freely? Who was the question mark in the room?

154

Leaning closer, Neka tapped his arm. "I can't wait to hear the positions for the people present."

The light in her eyes restored the hope that had faded during the earlier meeting. Lawrence's earlier presentation had failed to imbue any trust.

Everyone appeared to be on the same page. Brandie peered down the tables at Mindy. "What's the layout for St. Louis?"

Mindy looked at the slim, curly-haired woman sitting beside her. "Bernadette prepared a brief synopsis of our network."

Pulling her laptop in front of her, Bernadette read from a file. "McKinley Construction will expand to accommodate both companies' equipment and increased workforce. All permanent field employees, rehabbers, maintenance workers, and cleaners will report to this location. Their workplace will include seventeen additional staff members."

"Copley Enterprise will move their warehouse to the other facility. The building will house a total of forty-five employees. Expansion of the existing structure and parking lot is necessary. Our attorney Diana will maintain an on-site office."

Celia interrupted. "Why would a construction company increase their clerical personnel?"

"Additional workers will occupy several positions. Our St. Louis division will operate in Missouri's six bordering states. Construction begins next Monday at both locations." She paused as murmurs broke out among the families. "Copley Homes's staffers move into our Tulsa office Friday. James's prime real estate will be leased."

The meeting went on, outlining the plans to acquire enough buildings to get rehabs going strong and tour the West County project.

Neka tapped his arm. "See? I told you the transition team was well organized."

The happiness in her gaze almost engulfed him. Trust in her father never wavered. When circumstances offered opportunities to doubt, she discovered new reasons to continue believing.

His stomach clenched. Would she extend that same confidence toward him? Needing to secure the connection, he clasped her hand, willing himself not to give it another thought.

Lawrence rose to his feet. His natural grin eased the tension that had crept into the room during the presentation. "I trust the overview provided insight into our culture and the scope of our vision for the future. I appreciate everyone attending the meeting."

Cheers reigned out from the monitor.

"Much has been accomplished in a limited time frame. Imagine what the future holds as we focus on the prize." He lowered his voice. "Success is the goal I reach for. Thanks again for coming on board."

James tapped his pen against the notepad. Bravo. Snake oil salesmen beware. The hype filling the room spilled enough grease to slide them out the door. None of the speakers spoke substantively.

Who would lead St. Louis?

Lawrence gazed at James as if he'd heard the thought. "It's time to move forward. The third meeting begins in fifteen minutes."

Surprise registered on several faces, including the staff from Tulsa. "We'll stay connected online to help answer queries. You have department heads, in-house staffers, attorneys, and accountants at your disposal both here and there. Utilize their availability, then allow the team to assimilate our newest acquisitions."

James glanced at his watch, hoping his family recognized what the challenge represented. He tuned in as Lawrence addressed his wife: "You and the girls can run this outfit without me."

James turned to Neka. "Let's talk in private."

Heading for the exit, they accepted congratulations from everyone they passed. Outside the room, he moved down the hallway until they reached an alcove shielded on three sides. He gazed at her with a blank stare.

"Who is Jeff, and why should our engagement concern him?"

Neka blinked twice. Evidently she'd expected a different topic. She shrugged.

"I only know two Jeff's at Lacey Corp. One is a married design analyst who works in planning. The other one transferred to renovations three weeks ago. I hardly know either one." Touching his arm, she smiled, and slivers of light danced in her eyes. "Now give me your thoughts on the meeting."

He grunted. He'd allow the conversation switch, but he wasn't done with the Jeff issue. "The staff did their homework, came prepared to impress, and succeeded."

Neka leaned against the wall. "Your parents seemed pleased."

His noncommittal gaze didn't falter. "Their gratification was one of the only high spots in the procedures. What's the plan for the day?"

Her downcast face hid her disappointment poorly, but she responded with her customary buoyancy. "My mom lined up properties to visit for renovation. Her term for dilapidated rejects is rough diamonds. She scratched lunch and plans to invite your mom and godmother. I should make it home before five."

Home. Heat spread through him. Grabbing her hands, he kissed her knuckles. "Include Brandie in the outings set for this week. Keep the evening free. We'll discuss the finer points over dinner."

His gaze followed the men walking into the smaller conference room.

Neka nodded, and her gaze followed his. "You're up."

She touched his arm. "You are incredibly relaxed."

He pulled her close and kissed her cheek. His body always calmed before a battle. It reminded him that an eminent clash waited down the hall. Suddenly he only wanted to be here with her.

"Call me when you can. I can't wait to hear the good news." Her eyes were bright and held a hint of laughter. "I think a pleasant surprise awaits you."

Despite himself, he almost believed her. He stared into her light-filled eyes. Knowing Neka loved him blunted years of feeling unlovable after his family's betrayal. This was the reason he'd singled her out all these years. Her quiet faith dispelled the disbelief and made him a prisoner of hope.

Minutes later, James slipped into the seat next to David, determined to remain aloof even when provoked. His senses seemed amplified and made peace with the storm raging inside him. Unlike his brothers, he welcomed the chance to witness his mentor in action, even if he planned to test the younger men's resolve.

Lawrence removed folders from his briefcase and leaned back in his chair. His expression made it seem like he searched for the perfect word, but those actions meant nothing to James. He knew this man never fished around for the correct phrase to use.

Briefly scanning their faces, Lawrence sat upright. "Men, there's a rough road ahead of us. A point man must direct operations from St. Louis. Every department head at this location will report to that person. Gene and Charles are on hand, but they have a different set of priorities. My decision is final, and I made it based on information supplied from various sources."

Instantly, James realized this third meeting centered on him. It was a personal message. But his tenacity had always provided the strength to weather storms.

Lawrence opened a folder, then directed his gaze upon Ryan. "Lacey Corp has two objectives. Making a splash in unknown territory and strengthening relationships already established." He offered Ryan the title of out-of-state project director, St. Louis, a taxing but doable position. Gifted with the ability to knock down walls and open doors facilitating the grand design, his strengths lay in the proposed commission.

James studied Matt when Lawrence glanced his way. Skepticism embedded itself in Matt's features when he was offered the job site director, St. Louis, position. His brother viewed the job as a glorified foreman. But, really, the job held tremendous power and would allow him to secure the respect of workers far and wide.

"On board?" Lawrence shook each man's hand as they agreed.

David glanced at James when Lawrence tucked two folders into his briefcase and reached for the third. Until that moment, James had failed to notice three folders had lain on the table instead of four.

His jaw muscles tightened, and it felt like all the air had left the room.

The job in the remaining folder belonged to David.

Chapter Twenty

Neka rode in the backseat, going over different scenarios of the third meeting. James came out on top every time. Surely he would lead the St. Louis division and report directly to her dad.

Her lips curved in delight as she pictured them flitting back and forth between the two cities. The best of both worlds. She'd retain a lasting bond with her family while building a new one with the Copleys and McKinleys.

Checking her cell phone again, she sighed, thinking the discussion should have ended two hours ago. "How do you think the conference is going?"

Karen occupied the passenger seat while Tammy drove. In the back, Kelly sprawled across the other end. Up ahead, Brandie led their caravan with Fran and Maureen.

Her mother glanced back. "Since the first meeting set the standard, I expect positive results."

Neka squinted against the sunlight. "How much of Dad's plans are you privy to?"

The laughter in her mom's voice made her smile. "All of them."

"Spit it out, Neka." Kelly elbowed her in the side. "What are you hinting at?"

She scooted closer to the door. "Okay, I admit to a touch of anxiety. Did Dad hand James control of the St. Louis office?"

Laughing, Tammy peeped at their mom. "You know the unwritten rule to never ask questions about pending resolutions."

Neka thumped her finger and thumb at her sister's back. "Please tell me."

Karen sighed. "Unless you curb the curiosity, the day is going to drag on."

She needed to stop wavering back and forth and have the faith she always told others to have. Dad was an honest man who heard from God.

But, Lord, will he listen?

Kelly nodded to the car ahead of them. "I'd love to ride invisible in that car. After the meeting this morning, I can't imagine their estimation of us."

Tammy adjusted her speed and glanced at her sister in the rearview mirror. "They have to admit we're capable. I mean, what else could they possibly say?"

"That we're arrogant, high-handed, and over-confident." Kelly shook her head. "I spotted that expression on at least two faces from time to time."

Tammy turned right at the corner. "Sandi and Celia, right? One day they'll realize we're not the villains they think."

Karen glanced over her shoulder. "Or else they'll conclude we're passionate in our vision, resolute in our pursuit, and proficient in our execution," she said.

Neka smiled to herself, thankful for the support her family always gave one another. Before long, the Copleys and McKinleys would join their ranks. Just as Kenny's and Michael's parents were advisors and longtime friends.

Please, Lord, bless us.

* * *

That afternoon, Neka tried to make sense of the scene unfolding in a haze. Everything began after Brandie's cell phone rang. Smiling, she listened a few seconds, then she said, "What?" and rushed away. As Brandie walked away, Neka heard her say, "Elaborate, David! You can't drop outrageous news and then say you'll fill me in later."

Next, Fran's cell phone vibrated. She greeted Ryan, then stalked off without a word to anyone. Once Brandie turned around and spotted her mother heading to the SUV, she ran across the grass, cutting her off.

The two women hurried toward their vehicle, leaving the rest of the group to follow behind. Brandie kept looking at them over her shoulder, gauging their progress. Maureen sped ahead of them, reaching the car just as Fran closed the door.

Neka's heart sank.

What unwelcome news did they receive? She glanced at her cell phone. No messages. What happened to James's report?

At last, Karen stopped short of the vehicle. "Is everything okay?"

Brandie breathed deeply, as if trying to appear normal. "Oh yes, everything's fine. Karen, thanks for allowing us to view properties with you. We'll head home if you all can make it to the hotel without any problems."

160

"If we get lost, GPS will guide the way," Tammy answered.

Karen touched her arm. "We're glad you stuck with us this long. Gem hunting depletes the energy in a hurry. Tell Fran I'll touch base with her this evening." She smiled at Maureen. "Thanks for joining our scavenger hunt."

Relief flooded Maureen's face. "We appreciate the invitation. I hope to visit with you ladies again before Friday."

They entered the car but didn't drive off.

Neka thought she should probably speak to Fran. Recalling the cold scene in the kitchen the night before, she glanced at her mom and then started for the car. Kelly caught her arm, shaking her head.

"Let them go."

Finally, the occupants waved good-bye as the car pulled away from the curb.

Tammy glanced at Kelly. "They ended our outing in a rush. It appears those phone calls didn't bring joyful tidings."

What did all this mystery mean for James? And what would that mean for their future? Neka wished he would call.

When they were done looking at properties, the exhausted group exited the car and trooped along to the hotel entrance. Since no one answered their calls, only Neka's mom knew why half their group quit early.

Tammy bent her head and whispered, "Maybe James already left."

Neka sighed. For the last two hours, Tammy and Kelly had badgered her not to return to the Copleys' home, encouraging her to get a hotel room and then fly back with them Friday afternoon.

Why should she run away from James? If his position raised concern within his family, he would need her to remain in St. Louis for another week.

"Then drop me off at the Copleys' house."

"Ugh." Rolling her eyes, Tammy departed to the other side of Kelly.

Biting her lip, Neka opened the glass door. The ladies marched through the lobby until reaching the conference room around the corner. Activity swarmed the massive space. Workstations had been set in place, transforming the area into makeshift offices.

Kelly's quick scan around the room failed to locate Michael. "Bummer. The trip to West County took up more time than expected. The entire planning department is missing."

Her arms hugging her slim body, Neka hovered inside the doorway. She spotted James and David talking on the far side of the room. The two friends spoke together in an amiable discussion.

All must have been well, after all. Maybe the problem was with Matt or Ryan. Pacing her steps, she gave them plenty of time to see her approach.

Spying Neka, James ended his conversation and closed the gap between them. Draping an arm around her shoulder, he kissed her cheek. "How did the shopping expedition go? Find any prospects to purchase?"

"We viewed several possibilities." She smiled as David joined them. She playfully slapped James's arm. "You didn't call me. Were you saving the good news for later?"

* * *

The tension he'd been holding in his shoulders released.

James stared at David. He couldn't be angry. McKinley Construction flourished under his steady hand. Too bad his qualifications equaled James's achievements. Only one man could lead St. Louis, and in Lawrence's estimation, David proved to be that man.

If he had to suffer the loss, thank God the victor deserved the crown.

"Congratulate David. Lawrence chose him to head the Missouri division."

Shifting her focus to the other man, she held out her hand. Her genuine smile brought out her dimples. "You'll enjoy working with my dad."

"Thanks, Neka. I'm impressed with your reply. Most people fail to handle unwelcome news with grit and a smile." David retained her hand within his grasp for a moment. Staring at his friend, he backed away. "I'll leave you two alone."

Her shoulders drooped after David's departure, and James took Neka in both arms. Though she hid behind her bubbly exterior, she always unwound for him. Hurt radiated from her eyes as she fought to regain control.

She'd clearly been convinced Lawrence would give him the job, but he never expected that. Unsure of what he had actually expected to happen, clearly, bestowing him with honors wasn't it.

Most people in her father's predicament would drive a wedge between the happy couple. Isolate him in St. Louis and keep her in Tulsa. But Lawrence demanded a ringside seat at their courtship.

James scanned the large room and, as expected, most eyes were focused their way. "Come on. A little alone time is in order."

He explained the assigned positions as they strolled to the door.

Neka nodded as he spoke. "From what I know of your brothers, they are the best men for those tasks. Those key positions wield a lot of power."

James planted them in the same alcove they had used earlier that morning and leaned his back against the wall. "God answered your prayers, my lady. Your father created a new position most suitable for a son-in-law." He kept his face neutral. "Take a look at the operations director, Tulsa."

Hands clasped together, Neka jumped up and down like an excited child, and he couldn't help but chuckle at her enthusiasm.

"Thank you, Jesus. With you and David at the helm, Dad is free to fine-tune both outfits while you learn the ropes." She closed her eyes, reveling in the news. "I'm proud you're the next ranking officer in the network. Even Mom will report to you."

James damped his irritation down for Neka's sake. Would she understand that her father had hampered his ingenuity by burying him underneath a ton of bureaucracy? His senses were exhilarated when he pummeled to the top through unprecedented hardship. Half the allure of returning to St. Louis was combining two average companies into an unbeatable powerhouse and even a potential competitor to Lacey Corp.

All that had vanished that morning.

Neka squinted at him. "You're not impressed. I don't understand. Most men work a lifetime for the same opportunity, but you're not even thirty."

His hand clenched into a fist in his pocket, but he kept his tone level. "Your father accomplished many goals with this last maneuver. The obvious one being he intentionally clipped my wings. How do I top his success?"

Mouth parted, Neka stared at him, shaking her head. "Your complaint is that my dad thought you worthy to direct a company he poured his life into? If so, I hope the other objections fare better."

He bit down hard. Of course she didn't understand.

Laying a hand on his upper arm, she smiled. "Instead of surpassing his deeds, why not improve on them? You and David are innovative thinkers. The challenge is clear—take Lacey Corp to the next level."

Imagine his friend's retort when he explained Neka decreed they elevate the construction industry above its current peak. Somehow this whole situation had gotten away from him. Lawrence had played him, dangling the carrot to bait him into inaction. For once, another person's craftiness obscured the path he'd planned to take.

James sighed. Still, he'd proposed to a keeper. Regardless of Lawrence's heavy hand, would she guard her heart for him?

"I'll relay your sentiments before the next meeting. I made dinner reservations for seven thirty." Glancing at his watch, he retraced his steps down the hallway.

* * *

Neka sashayed in front of the cheval mirror, wearing a close-fitting teal dress. It was stylish but not something she would normally wear. Frowning, she slipped on the dreaded heels, hoping to cheer up James.

Satisfied with her appearance, she sat on a wingback chair. Once she and James returned home, the department heads would report straight to him. What a conquest.

But could there be fallout connected with his promotion?

The fall from the heights of excitement had come quickly, threatening to steal her joy. As in the previous three days, happiness had proved elusive. She couldn't understand why.

Miracles had piled up four days in a row. On Friday, the man she loved had asked her to marry him. On Saturday, she agreed on the wedding date with her parents. On Sunday, her sisters promised to work on their relationship with him. Today, the president of Lacey Corp installed him into the director's seat.

God had answered her prayers in spectacular ways. But none of this promised that James's love would manifest given time. Crossing her ankles, she considered the women flocking after James Copley, business owner. Would their pursuit intensify for the operations director of a multifaceted corporation?

Neka felt like the timid eighth-grade version of herself, who discovered friends only tolerated her because of Hazelle. Life in St. Louis had represented a new beginning. Brandie and David actually liked her. James's friend Mimi accepted her because of him. At church yesterday, several people issued dinner invitations during their brief visit.

In this city, she'd found acceptance. People judged her for themselves, not with misinformation from questionable sources. James's hometown nourished her in substantial ways.

And her expectations increased every time they were together. She just knew that soon he would entrust her with his heart. She'd already handed hers to him years ago.

Tulsa might drain the reservoir she'd begun to build. At least three women he'd dated still lived there. She couldn't even think about his confession and the extent of his relationships with those women.

That admission had knocked her off the soapbox against his former fiancée. Her prosaic interpretation of his seeing Cynthia Ward after proposing to Teri didn't seem so simple now. Though Teri's conduct appalled Neka, she sympathized with the frustration.

She rested the back of her hand on her eyelids. Would Teri balk at his marrying her? Would she assume that they were ... intimate too? His idea of a June twenty-third ceremony would have alleviated facing the women he'd recently dated.

Neka ignored his knock but stood up, fluffing out her hair. Previous thoughts robbed her of energy and the will to revive herself.

"Ready to leave, sweets?" James peeked into the bedroom, then gave an exaggerated whistle. He stepped inside the room when she failed to answer. "What's wrong?"

She shrugged, then spread out her hands. "Everything. I've been thinking about us."

"Then you should be pleased. I am." He kissed her hand.

Neka couldn't talk about it right now. She just wanted to enjoy their dinner. "It's six forty-five. We'd better go."

Grabbing a beige crocheted wrap off the bed, she drew up beside him. "Give me a play-by-play of the meetings today. Ryan told your mother all the assignments were handed out except for your position. You and Dad left for lunch before he called her. Did the two of you enjoy a nice one-on-one over the meal?"

He laughed. "You really know how to close down discussions you don't want to engage in. You've turned dodging questions into an art form." He kissed her forehead, then sighed, grasping her elbow. "I won't derail your mad dash not to be alone with me. Let's go."

Oh Lord, I blew it.

"James—"

"We can continue this conversation in the car." Hand on her elbow, they walked down the stairs in silence.

* * *

Driving off the circular drive, James wanted to wait for her to begin the conversation wherever she wished. But he ended the standoff before leaving the neighborhood.

"We've covered too much ground for you to shut me out now. All this transformation of multiple lives ... it proves we belong together."

"I agree. But I also understand God rewards obedience ..."

"Go on."

"Friday you explained your dissatisfaction with the church. I have a problem with some Christians too. The early church operated in power when they obeyed God. Sometimes people call me Saint Nikhol behind my back." She looked out the window. "Some even mock me to my face. It doesn't faze me, though. It isn't them I hope to keep on the narrow path—it's me."

James bit down hard at the mention of anyone mocking her. Where was she going with this? "Is this the reason you never defend yourself when anyone insults you?"

She turned sideways in her seat to face him. "Like you told Brandie, I play to an audience of one. But it is ongoing work. Every morning I spend time with God, but by lunch, I've often forgotten the scriptures I read to begin my day. Those experiences sharpen my understanding of how Christians can gossip and criticize as much as people who deny Christ."

He'd never thought of it that way. It explained so much about why his belief system fell short of the messages he heard every Sunday. "Then you admit obeying scripture doesn't come easy."

"We walk in victory when we spend time with Him and in His word. Instead, a lot of us want the world to accept a Savior we refuse to obey." Glancing off, she nibbled her lip and then faced him. "Call me foolish, but I don't care to chitchat with women you slept with. And there's no avoiding Teri."

Frowning, James slowly nodded his head. Neka shied away from all confrontations, attempting to make herself invisible when trouble surfaced on any front. Teri's flair for dramatics could present complications at first. "Un-

166

fortunately, Teri will make her presence known. In time, you may also run into other women I dated."

Instead of his agreement pleasing her, it appeared to distress her further.

She hung her head before replying. "It would be easier if it weren't complicated by ..."

James tapped fingers on the steering wheel. The accusation levied against his character took him by surprise. How could any man who worked around the clock play endless bedroom games? "Don't imagine I had sex with every woman I dated."

Letting out a relieved sigh, she pressed her back to the cushion. "I'm glad to know you didn't."

"Look, this is a terrible admission, but it won't bother them or me. I understand my old lifestyle poses problems for you, but I can't undo what's done. Doors to other women closed the moment you agreed to marry me."

Chewing on her thumb, she glanced at him. "Do you get the point?"

"I do possess a modicum of understanding."

"I didn't intend to insult you, but God-given rules set us above the drippings offered by this world. Though I try hard not to harm anyone with my choices, the recent ones complicated the lives of various families. I ... I just don't want someone else's decisions to hurt me."

Neka's active explanation of her beliefs was so different than listening to a sermon in a crowded room. Around her, he felt a connection to the beliefs he professed to hold. Despite his problems with her family, this woman always got straight to his soul in a way no one else ever had. It unsettled him, but he always felt stronger afterward.

"So our activities can either strengthen or weaken our conviction levels."

Neka laid her head against the window. "I read the Bible day and night to sift my day through the light of His word. Though I make big mistakes, I'll keep trying to get it right. Living in His presence outstrips the discipline it takes to stay there."

"We're not at a stalemate. Marrying me won't mean a drastic change from the lifestyle you want. I respect your beliefs more than you know. They were the first qualities I admired about you." Picking up her hand, he smiled but kept his gaze on the road. "Stop inventing problems for us—we already have too many real ones."

Chapter Twenty-One

Neka closed her Bible and stared out the window at the manicured lawn. Yesterday marked the end of her first week in St. Louis. Her parents would fly home this afternoon.

Thank God she'd convinced her sisters to attend James's surprise birthday party tomorrow. What a fantastic turn of events. Though they could be friendlier, neither sister rejected his efforts to make amends.

Stepping up to the plate, he'd wooed her family like a pro. He laid his reservations aside, and Operation Heal the Breach consumed his time. His regret over wounding his friendships led each step. Though her family proved a hard sell, she was sure his sincere peace offerings would restore their bruised relationships. It might just take some time.

Last Friday she'd crept away from home like a runaway. But this morning an engaged woman welcomed the start of a new life.

So far, no legalities had surfaced to hinder the merger process. A steady influx of employees from Tulsa was smoothing the transition. Except for a lovelier-than-expected dinner at Matt's house on Wednesday, she and James kept the evenings free for themselves. Exhausted, everyone appreciated a stress-free environment after their hectic workday.

However, today was going to be different. Brandie, Kelly, and Tammy pledged to help her shop and decorate the recreation building for the festivities. She laughed. She would do everything she could to make him forget his previous pitiful celebrations.

* * *

A few hours later, the shopping was done. Tammy hung the last row of tiny lanterns strung together by a delicate cord.

"Finished." She tilted her head to the side, examining their handiwork. "Your concept came alive. This place is a dream."

Hands clasped beneath her chin, Brandie perused the room and smiled.

"Give me a hug." She threw arms around the beaming Neka. "You're such a good designer. This room will blow James away."

Kelly opened the door, taking another glance around the room. "Are you sure he won't come near this place before tomorrow morning?"

Neka turned the key in the lock, then tucked it into her pocket. She put a finger to her lips. "I'm hiding both keys under my mattress when we go back into the house."

They all laughed.

* * *

"What the—?"

James jerked upright in bed, throwing back the cover. Numerous spherical shapes suspended from the ceiling came into focus. He fell on his back, laughing in delight.

Sometime during the night Neka must have released helium-filled balloons into his bedroom. Somehow they managed to congregate just above his bed. He was a light sleeper. He couldn't believe he didn't wake up the moment she'd opened the door.

Was he too tired to wake up or too satisfied to care? Her thoughtfulness ushered in an excitement he hadn't experienced since his childhood. Shaking his head, he studied the balloons. Without counting them, he knew there were thirty.

Despite the ups and downs of the harrowing week, his birthday began with a bang. He looked forward to the day for no other reason than he got to share it with an incredible person. Just for today, business would take a back seat.

David had made inroads into his job. Everyone strove to smooth his pathway to success, and he accepted it with grace. Would he get the same reception on his return to Tulsa? Three division heads set the pace for the company and would soon report to him. Would they accept directions from a younger, less-experienced man? Karen supported her husband's choice, but the co-owner had nothing to prove.

Accepting Neka's challenge, James sought to raise the level of play at Lacey Corp. It would establish his leadership throughout the network. Several project ideas had emerged over the last few days that might set the tone for his leadership for years to come.

A soft knock on the door shifted his thoughts back.

He shook his head. Right. Business was taking a back seat today.

Without waiting for permission, Neka cracked opened the door and peered inside, grinning. "I heard the yell, but you didn't run across the floor screaming, so I figured you stayed in bed."

Still laughing, she scooped up a circular tray from the floor. Flower petals and glitter covered the bottom. On top was a covered bowl—breakfast in bed? An envelope and small wrapped gift roused his imagination. Placing it on the nightstand, her gaze flickered across his face.

James was paralyzed by the love in her eyes. He'd always detested emotional weakness, but her vulnerability filled the empty space inside him. His senses filled with her as she rubbed her cheek against his. The moment was so tender, and it underscored the pointless life he'd lived before this whirlwind courtship.

"I've never embraced an unshaven man while he lay in bed." Neka leaned back, smiling, then she studied him when he didn't speak.

Their shared affection had unbalanced him some since they'd met. When she was seventeen, she was like his little sister. But since then, the attraction had somehow shifted when he wasn't looking.

Time with Neka appeased the restlessness he couldn't control any other way. It pacified something in him. Today their relationship promised the family he'd wanted but never expected to have.

But it also led him to avenues he had no wish to explore. Love turned strong men into peons. Each time he reached an unexpected summit with this lady, another curveball headed his way. He'd have to shore up his battered resistance if this was any indication as to how the day would go.

"I wrote you a song." Eyes twinkling, Neka sat upright. She cleared her throat and began to sing.

> *This is your season.*
> *This is your year our Lord Jesus is standing near.*
> *His Holy Spirit brings elation,*
> *His assurance you'll attain salvation.*

He fulfills each purpose prepared just for you,
So put Him first in all that you do.
What's your birthday message for the year?
You'll reap God's rewards as you keep Him near.

She sang like … he didn't even know what. It was the most delightful thing he'd ever heard.

Closing the gap between them, she cupped his face between her hands. "Enjoy your day. Celebrating thirty is an important milestone."

Springing from the bed, she removed the envelope from the tray. "Open this one first." He broke the seal, and she hurried out of the room before he could read it.

James stared at the closed door before turning the homemade card side to side. A dimpled stick figure Neka—he could tell by the hair—offered thirty balloons as a stick James kneeled on one knee with a ring in hand.

In calligraphy, she'd written: "Dress in casual clothes and meet me at the recreation building in thirty minutes."

Smiling, he uncovered the bowl. Sweet aromas from his favorite fruits wafted out. James selected a watermelon wedge from among the grapes and diced pineapples, savoring how her affection made it taste that much sweeter.

Thirty balloons, a homemade card, and an original birthday song in less than fifteen minutes. He couldn't imagine what she had planned at the recreation building.

He pushed the tray aside, frowning. Unwittingly he'd stumbled into a well-laid trap. Stalking into the bathroom, he left the gift untouched amidst flower petals and glitter.

But a few minutes later, towel wrapped around his waist, James opened the package, revealing a smaller ring box inside. He extracted a gold pinkie ring mounted with their birthstones.

He sighed. Neka acted out of love, not a hidden agenda. Once again, he reinforced his weakening self-discipline.

Rose petals of every color led him down the pathway to the building. Before he reached the steps, Neka appeared at the door, dressed in an alluring outfit that they had not purchased together. Silver and gold earrings dangled from her ears, and multicolored bracelets clanged together on both arms. She even wore a new pair of heels he'd never seen.

She was stunning.

Inside the room, burgundy and white curtains formed a canopy against the far wall. Gray pillows covered the floor on one side, and a blazing fire in the fireplace completed the cozy scene.

Neka pointed to cushions underneath the canopy. "Please take a seat while I serve your meal."

He dutifully sat where she pointed, but his gaze followed her movements as she set food on a low table and then wedged in beside him.

These decorations must have taken a considerable amount of time. Who helped her transform this plain room into an oasis?

James groaned inwardly as another chunk of his armor suffered a quick demise. He'd always scorned unnecessary birthday preparations, but he couldn't help but welcome her special attention.

Neka captivated his thoughts yet robbed him of speech. That someone cared enough to burden themselves for his enjoyment humbled him. Words of surrender stuck in his throat.

Plenty of women had attempted to ingratiate themselves into his life, but Neka only acted out of affection. There wasn't anything to gain from this act.

He swallowed hard, glad they were already engaged, because his need for her far outweighed her love for him.

His stomach turned somersaults when she lifted the server top. Fried potatoes and onions, breakfast steak, and toasted bread strips begged him to take a bite. The last time he ate this meal was during his parents' visit last year. Mint sprigs hung on the rims of frosted glasses.

"What are we drinking?"

Neka lowered her voice as if exposing national secrets. "Juice splash."

He raised an eyebrow, and she laughed.

Chuckling, James sampled the multilayered drink. "Delicious. What's in it?"

She whispered again. "White grape and raspberry juice with a dash of lemon."

Peering melodramatically underneath a pillow, he lowered his voice to match her tone and leaned close. "How did you stumble upon such a tasty beverage?"

"I mixed several juices until finding the right combination." Neka's eyes darted side to side, and then she burst into laughter.

The next item on the agenda was paddling across Post-Dispatch Lake in Forest Park. It was a beautiful day to mix with nature. Ducks, geese, and swans floated on the water while schools of fish swam beneath the surface. The leisurely pace brought some relaxation into what had been a hectic work week.

Too bad the boathouse didn't rent canoes. The whole idea came from a desire to watch James's muscles propelling them across the water. Neka stifled a giggle, knowing she'd have to explain herself.

If not for the party tonight, they could come back for a moonlight ride. Lights from the restaurant and lakeside patio would lend a dreamy ambiance perfect for a romantic excursion.

This place was a must-stop the next time she visited St. Louis. Invitations received after church last Sunday already claimed two days of the upcoming week. Mimi demanded a visit too because Neka had cancelled their trip today to spend James's whole birthday alone. Thankfully, the amiable woman had called him to cancel their plans and would attend the party tonight.

Every detail was planned. Tammy and Brandie had promised to host until she arrived. Neka had contracted with a church to allow guests to park in their lot and rented a bus to transport them to and from the Copley home. She wouldn't let cars parked in the driveway ruin the surprise.

Her body tingled at the thought. One day, she had noticed Charles McKinley rubbing his hands together; was it because they had itched with excitement like hers did right now?

James's eyelids drooped. Apparently the paddling was bringing a lot of relaxation.

She noticed subtle changes in his features since last Friday. He looked younger and yet somehow more mature.

Their companionable silence squelched any desire to pepper the moment with speech. She smiled. Her parents could sit together for hours without speaking. When she was planning the day, she'd imagined they would discuss their future. But unlike the tense quiet on the plane, James seemed content as they paddled and held hands.

She was too—more than she could ever remember.

After they'd paddled back to the dock, he swung their hands like Neka often did as they stepped off the boat. It was marvelous to see him loose and having fun, and her spirit soared.

After leaving the lake, James parked in the underground garage for the St. Louis Art Museum. In the main lobby, he placed his arm around Neka's shoulder, pointing to the directory. "Sweets, there aren't enough hours in a day to view everything. It would probably take weeks."

The brochure said they had over thirty-thousand works and several exhibitions, so she supposed he was right. "We can try."

He chuckled. "How about we each choose a collection to walk through? The Native American collection features prehistoric, historic, and contemporary art of indigenous peoples of North America." He paused, glancing at her.

She read from the pamphlet. "The Decorative Arts and Design Collection house examples of European and American furniture. You can view architectural elements and period rooms from the Renaissance to the present day." She looked up at him, batting her lashes playfully. "Think we can see everything in an hour?"

Laugh lines formed around his mouth. In that moment, he looked a lot like Ryan. "Wishful thinking, my dear. How about two?"

Neka marveled at the slow pace James set in place. Though he always sauntered, today he stopped every few feet, pointing out items he would usually ignore, some interest and excitement actually peeking through his mask.

* * *

James opened the door for Neka to enter. She'd picked a four-star seafood restaurant for their lunch. The boat excursion and tour of the art museum had boggled his mind. He didn't know how she'd managed to cram planning today into her congested work schedule this week.

She must have scouted their outings, decorated the rec building, and purchased his ring, balloons, flowers, and a new outfit—right along with drawing up designs for the rehab properties. This morning she'd sprinkled petals on the walkway and prepared his breakfast before nine o'clock. She was a little dynamo.

He shook his head, wondering what would be next.

After handing the menu to the waiter, he noticed Neka stared at him while her body shook with suppressed laughter. In spite of himself, he chuckled, hoping the joke wasn't on him. "What's funny?"

Pointing at him, giggles erupted with such force that she placed a hand over her mouth to stifle the noise.

Never one to laugh at himself, her spontaneous mirth unleashed a joy he couldn't deny. "Why are we laughing?"

The question set off another round of giggles. James barely suppressed his lips from curving into a smile.

Still waiting for their meal, James considered their easy companionship. Nothing about this day fit into his well-scripted life. Even though he drove them around, she simply refused to disclose the next destination until they settled inside the car. Not one to follow anyone's lead, today he followed Neka around as if they were tied together.

But the joy in her face indicated her plans proceeded on schedule, and that made it all worthwhile.

Stop worrying, man. Let another experienced driver control the wheel.

Though young, she was whipping him into shape.

His grin faded. Wayward thoughts had a habit of bursting pipe dreams.

Their server brought their meals before Neka explained what she had been laughing about, but her mouth dropped open when the food reach the table. Biting her lip to keep from laughing, her body wriggled. Once the server moved away, Neka dabbed her eyes with a napkin.

"That's so much food! I thought you ordered enough food for two people, and you did." Her eyes scanned the plates lined up on his side of the table. "I've never seen you eat like that. I guess joyful people possess hearty appetites."

He laughed with her, and the warmth in her eyes made him feel stronger than any meal ever could.

Their relationship had intensified since their trip downtown last Saturday. Neither of them had to work now to drum up the magic. He hoped to get Neka to himself for the rest of the day. If she declared that was it time to go home after he acknowledged his need ...

James felt a tightening in his shoulders that he hadn't experienced in three days.

After their late lunch they went to the movies, and then it was time to go back.

He shut the door after Neka stepped inside the house and then pulled her back against him. Closing his eyes, he kissed the top of her head, enfolding the remarkable creature in his arms. At every stop during the day, he had waited for the ax that never fell. Their entire day smacked with promise for their future.

James normally directed the conversation, but he'd been quiet most of the day. Words simply failed to deliver the reactions overflowing his being.

Shifting in his arms, she pulled away, grasping his hand. Her teary eyes released a floodgate of emotion inside him.

He brushed his lips across her fingers. "Today I celebrated the best day of my life. The one I prayed to see but never believed would materialize."

If eyes could declare love, hers did.

Neka tugged his hand.

"I have one last surprise." Leading them through the hallway, she smiled up at him. "We'll end our evening celebrating in our secret haven. I brought soft music to play in the background."

The rose petals on the footpath hadn't wilted. It was another miracle that his mother hadn't swept them away. Perhaps his wasn't the only heart affected by a flawless day.

Unlocking the door, Neka backed into the room, gazing into his eyes. As he flipped a light switch, a chorus shouted, "Happy Birthday, James!"

Except for his future in-laws and the children, everyone important in his life was present. Glancing at Neka clinging to his arm, he began devising her birthday celebration in April. Maybe in the Bahamas.

Brandie scurried across the room, tugging her husband behind her. At a loss for words, the two siblings simply stared at each other. The support in David's gaze released James's reserve. Looking around at the well-wishers, the hush in the room amazed James. It seemed that everyone understood the significant moment.

"Each person within this room represents a major part of my life." He glanced at Neka. "This morning I opened my eyes to a panoramic view of what real living offers. We indulged in pursuits I hadn't chased in too many years and had an incredible day. My adorable fiancée singlehandedly restored dreams I didn't recall losing."

Amazement lined the faces of everyone present.

Shaking his head, Ryan stared at Sandi and said in a stage whisper, "Someone kidnapped my brother. I swear he would've never spoken those words a week ago."

Everyone laughed.

A little self-conscious at his revelation, James chuckled and maneuvered farther into the room. "So what do we do at parties?"

Several voices shouted out, "Have fun!"

"All right, but remember that the relationships we nurture today strengthen our tomorrows."

Celebrating with his friends and family was the perfect end to a perfect day. They mingled, and Neka was more comfortable than he'd ever seen her at a social function.

Chapter Twenty-Two

When the bus driver knocked on the door at ten o'clock, their guests grabbed their belongings and prepared to leave. Standing outside, Neka and James said good-bye to everyone amid handshakes, hugs, well wishes, and plans for the coming days.

Mimi and Clint departed with their sisters, Marcia and Laurie, also long-time friends of James. Mimi embraced Neka before hugging James. "Don't forget we're grilling at my house Wednesday at seven o'clock."

Neka nodded. "We're coming. Thanks for changing your plans on short notice."

Clint winked at Neka before shaking James's hand. "We enjoyed mixing old with new. I look forward to seeing your family again in November." They waved as they strolled down the pathway.

"If ever a deer was caught in headlights, brother."

James laughed at Matt's joke. "Let's see your reaction when twenty-four voices yell out of nowhere."

Celia glanced at her husband, smiling. "I don't think he will hide behind me."

"I wrapped my arms around Neka to keep her safe."

Winking at Neka, Sandi leaned into Ryan. "I think she might've felt better protected standing behind you."

Grinning, Ryan gazed at Neka too. "The choice is yours. Do you feel more protected standing behind James or being wrapped in his arms?"

Neka's grin widened. "I'm secure knowing he's in the room."

Laughing, the couples moved away as the Copley and McKinley families' attorney, Russell Hodges, and his wife, Anita, walked out with their parents, who were also old family friends. The small party stopped in front of James.

"This celebration culminates an extraordinary week." Russell smiled at Neka. "Though we're hammering out a few legalities, the transition was smooth."

179

James nodded. "I'm glad you all came."

"Give your parents our regards," Anita said, and she embraced Neka. "The entire family expects an invitation to the wedding."

Neka beamed. "Wonderful. Thanks for joining our celebration tonight."

Maureen and Fran walked up ahead of Gene and Charles.

"We'll see you two at the house, dear," Fran said as she touched Neka's arm.

Maureen kissed her cheek, smiling. "Brunch will be at a different restaurant after church tomorrow."

Brandie laughed. "I cast my vote for a Chinese buffet. Ignore David—he wants Italian."

Neka laughed. "Chinese buffet. I'm always hungry after services."

David ended his side conversation with James. He nudged Brandie. "You win this time. See you both tomorrow."

Charles and Gene added their good-byes without a prolonged discussion.

Neka grinned when Kelly hugged her from the side. "Thanks for inviting us. We enjoyed the party."

She patted her sister's protruding tummy. "What an excellent ending to a marvelous day. The only negative was Mom and Dad going home yesterday."

Tammy hugged her. "They were already committed for this evening."

"I'll borrow the car and see you off in the morning."

Michael grinned at James's guarded expression. "Sleep in, Neka. We'll see you in Tulsa next weekend."

Shaking her head no, Neka smiled when James touched her shoulder. "Okay, Michael. See you all Friday. So long."

Kenny chuckled. "I'm shocked you folded so easily."

After Tammy and Kelly chorused, "So long," they hurried away.

Smiling to himself, James reached inside the door and turned off the lights.

"I love the way your family says 'so long' instead of 'good-bye.'" He tilted Neka's face toward his. "From this day forward, I promise never to leave your side without declaring I'm coming back to you."

She stretched her arms and yawned. "Hugging Anita's and Russell's parents reminded me that my grandparents haven't met you yet. I'll have to plan a small announcement party shortly after we return home."

Kissing her smiling lips, he turned the key in the lock. He put his arm around her waist, and they walked back to the house together.

On the plane the next Friday, Neka fastened her seat belt and reviewed the last five days of her trip. She could hardly wait to return home with the man she loved by her side. Thank God the whirlwind vacation—which ended up being more work than play—was behind them.

A call from her cousin after the party had brought events into perspective. Hazelle's mother had dropped the engagement bombshell over Sunday dinner.

Relieved to talk to her cousin, Neka opened up without justifying her actions. Rehashing events with a person who understood how her mind worked was easy.

Of course, Hazelle just had to point out Neka had acted out of character. But she'd also suspected James harbored special feelings for her all along. She'd apparently only kept the knowledge to herself because she was afraid she could be mistaken.

Summarizing the last two weeks, Neka realized why she'd been so afraid those first two days. Her whole system had just been overloaded with stress. She wasn't used to that.

Lord, thank you for taking care of me.

James had been different since his "birthday extravaganza," as he called it. He'd taken extra care with her and welcomed her input into his business. Neka liked being his sounding board. His creative mind revved up her own imagination.

To call this indescribable week eventful was an understatement. Occupied with hard work days, they dined with a different family every night. Yesterday was their only chance to relax at home, watching comedy videos with his parents and the McKinley families. It was a comforting end to two consecutive weeks of frenzied activities.

His family had changed toward her too. With the main stress of the merger past them, they welcomed her with open arms. Even Celia and Sandi were ... well, they were *less* awful.

James took Neka's hand once the flight attendant rolled her cart down the aisle. "Next month I'll present an initiative to Lawrence outlining expansion opportunities. I decided to combine several ventures. David has an alternate plan, so we'll draft separate proposals on the same proposition."

She frowned. She didn't want competition to damage James's and David's friendship the way it had hurt his relationship with family. "Why is he sharing in your project?"

James raised an eyebrow. "Both locations will be affected by the outcome."

"But the idea belongs to you and should be presented as such."

He grasped her hand, smiling. "I prefer to present a group effort going forward."

Neka was pleasantly surprised by the sincerity of his statement. He didn't seem to have any hidden motivation. She steepled their hands under her chin. "Give me a few particulars."

He went into detail about his plan to build communities for senior citizens and middle-class families in unincorporated areas miles outside of densely populated cities. He went on to explain more of his vision—recreational centers, medical facilities, schools, libraries, and museums.

Practically dancing in her seat, she clapped her hands. "Medical care could be free to seniors. Most residents with children can pay for the services. No need to make money—just charge enough to cover our overhead."

Neka laid her head against the cushion. The opportunities to elevate people's living conditions were endless. Thinking about the endless possibilities, she touched his arm. "The foundation can underwrite grocery stores and gas stations to help defray company costs. Grocery stores will only sell organic products." Smiling, she took a breath. "Now Dad has to set up the foundation."

Laughter filled his gaze. "Not if you tell him your plans to bankrupt his company."

"God blesses people so they can be a blessing."

James chuckled. "So don't squander His goodwill. You expect the foundation to cover company costs while the company funds the foundation?"

"My practical James, we just need to establish the organization."

He kissed the tip of her nose. "My generous Neka, we can't fund the organization if we bankrupt the business."

* * *

Waving good-bye to James when he dropped her off at home, Neka followed happy sounds coming from the kitchen.

"I'm home," she called.

Nostalgia took over while she walked through these rooms she loved. Before her trip to St. Louis, she took this place for granted. In just five months, she would have to infuse into a new house the family atmosphere her parents had given this one, giving her children the same loving protection this place had always afforded her.

"Surprise!"

Hands pressed against her chest, Neka jumped. Smiling faces welcomed her home. Granny Singleton and Grandmother Lacey sat at the table in the alcove. Hazelle and Neka's other cousin Bridget occupied stools at the center island. Kelly leaned against the refrigerator, salad bowl in hand. Tammy stood in the doorway leading to the sunroom, clutching cutlery.

Her mother set a casserole dish on the stovetop and then hugged her daughter. "Welcome home, honey. I invited your grandmothers over for lunch and your cousins graciously brought them by."

Neka embraced her mother. She loved that Karen never missed an occasion to bring both sides of the family together. In a short time, watching her mom perform routine chores every day would become a fond memory.

Sighing, she set her purse on the counter, reflecting on James's surprise birthday party. Just like then, there were no cars to give away the celebration brewing inside the house.

"Where did you park?"

"Behind the garage." Bridget laughed. "Mother planned an engagement get-together for next Saturday. So make sure you and James keep the evening free."

Neka nodded. Aunt Trudy never missed an opportunity to throw a fabulous party. Now Neka could forget about planning an announcement party.

"Hi, Granny Singleton. Thanks for welcoming me home." Neka stooped to kiss the gray-haired woman on the cheek. The Singleton family had always provided their children a simple lifestyle.

She turned to her dad's mother. The austere white-haired woman had blossomed into a loving grandmother sometime after Neka's seventh birthday. "Thanks for coming, Grandmother."

"Show us the ring." Grandmother Lacey's tone demanded instant obedience. She examined the twinkling gems. "This is the perfect one for you. Its glitter matches the sparkle in those beautiful light-brown eyes." She swiped her face with a napkin and cleared her throat. "Did your young man escort you inside?"

Neka was robbed of speech by the compliment and tears and stared into her grandmother's eyes until the older lady embraced her. Laying a cheek against her grandmother's bosom, Neka spoke softly. "He went to his house but will come back later. Please stay to meet him."

Standing, she smiled at Granny. "Do you and grandmother remember his visits to our church?"

Bridget spoke before either woman could answer. Her blond curls went in all directions when she nodded. "How do you forget a man who ignores you, then spends every second with your younger cousin? I had to accept a few dates to get over the rejection."

Neka laughed. The lovely Bridget was never at a loss for admirers. Men swarmed around her like a platoon besieging a fort. "You're the third person to tell me you knew he was smitten before I did."

She hoped they were right.

Hazelle laughed. "Next time I'll speak up instead of playing it safe."

Kelly rubbed her huge belly. "Spending time together at social functions doesn't make the perfect match. Everyone used discretion, as they should have."

Bridget almost fell from her chair. "Come on, Kelly. True love won't be denied. I expected this announcement two years ago."

Removing a large pitcher from the refrigerator, Kelly gazed at her cousin. "I dated Michael for six years before getting married. There weren't many surprises in store for me, especially since we grew up together."

Tammy spoke from the doorway. "It doesn't hurt to move slowly when setting the course for the rest of your life."

Hazelle winked at Neka. "Maybe, but not every love story moves at the same pace."

Eating the food for thought, Neka flashed her ring to the gray-haired lady observing their interaction. Granny grabbed her hand, refusing to turn it loose. "That's a beautiful love token he gave to my beautiful granddaughter."

"Thank you, Granny. I'll drive you and grandmother home before five if you stick around to meet James."

"Carl can heat up leftovers for a snack." Granny folded her hands onto her lap.

Grandmother Lacey stared at Neka through half-closed eyes. "Introduce me to the man who stole your heart. I told Karen you'd fall hard once you met the right fellow." She smiled at Karen. "Your father pooh-poohed the idea, but I'm seldom wrong."

"And never modest." Tammy helped her up from the cushion then escorted her into the sunroom, calling over her shoulder, "Come on in, folks. I set up two tables for lunch."

Granny stood up after the others left the room, squeezing Neka's hand. "Normally, couples date before agreeing to marry. He is the young man you visited with at church socials?"

Though the penetrating eyes made her nervous, Neka smiled and nodded. "You spotted us talking together?"

"Women's gazes followed him straight to you. It's okay to slow down. Not now doesn't mean not ever." Granny laid an arm on Neka's shoulder until she noticed Karen standing in the doorway. "Remember these words when needed."

Patting Karen's arm, Granny left them alone.

Neka waited until her mom moved closer. "Do you agree?"

Her mom's gaze roamed over her face for a long moment.

"The fairy tale is over. Tulsa will test his commitment and yours." She paused, looking at the doorway to the sunroom. "Everyone's stuck outside their comfort zone on this one. Kelly almost buried Teri alive when she questioned your relationship with James." Her voice lowered. "Cynthia Ward introduced herself to Tammy at a restaurant Tuesday."

Neka massaged her earlobe at a loss for words. News about their engagement was already common knowledge. "How did Tammy react?"

Karen leaned against the table. "From all accounts, not well. Tammy froze her out. Has Cynthia contacted James?" She frowned when Neka looked down without answering. Gesturing toward the door, her mom headed that way. "Talk to your sisters later. They may be able to shed more light."

When Neka failed to move, Karen beckoned her from the threshold. "Come on, guest of honor. We're holding up the celebration meal."

185

Chapter Twenty-Three

Neka cornered her sisters in the kitchen when everyone left the room. "What happened at the restaurant on Tuesday?"

Sitting at the table, Tammy unloaded. "I was having dinner with the Lathams when Cynthia searched for you but found me. She actually strutted over and asked me when you were coming home. She sure doesn't shy away from confrontations."

"Has James mentioned their relationship?" Kelly touched Neka's shoulder.

Neka felt foolish. Only his lack of celibacy had been discussed.

Kelly glanced at Tammy. "I suppose he cut off contact so she resorted to investigative work."

"Did she ever approach Teri?" Neka tried to make sense of Cynthia accosting Tammy.

Tammy shook her head as she drummed her fingers. "Teri's ego precedes her. You're an unknown to Cynthia."

Kelly nodded. "Maybe she didn't expect the engagement to Teri to stick. Now she's scavenging for information, and you're the prey."

"She's not the stalker type but definitely a persistent woman who wants James back." Tammy clasped Neka's fingers and glanced at the clock on the wall. "What time is he coming by?"

"He'll be here any minute."

"Demand the information you deserve. Be firm. Pin him down and do not let him off the hook. Ask him about Peggy Kennedy too." Tammy frowned and took a deep breath as if to control her temper when Neka slumped against the cushion. "You're unaware of that one, huh?"

Neka pulled out the chair next to her when Kelly's shoulders drooped. "Sit down, Kel. What do you know about her?"

Her sister eased into the seat. "She's a fifth-grade English teacher at a middle school in a small town. Kenny and Michael met her in college and say she's a nice lady."

"Peggy interrogated Kenny while we shopped at the health food store two days ago," Tammy said as she leaned back on the cushion.

Kelly gave a wry grin. "Michael and I need to get out more. Stuck inside this house, no one can waylay us."

Tammy winked at Kelly. "God's teaching me the 'let your words be few' lesson."

Neka frowned. "Mom said you froze Cynthia out."

"I did, right after I told her what I really thought."

Neka's face rested in her hands while her mind searched for answers. She knew there had been other women, but now they all had names. Teri, Cynthia, and Peggy. How did he keep three women at bay?

James hated sharing anything about himself. She knew she'd have to face all this eventually, but she'd hoped to have more time.

Like her mom had said, the fairy tale was over.

"Stay at home for a while." Kelly touched Neka's arm. She hesitated, glancing at Tammy. "Someone told Cynthia your favorite restaurants and design stores. Peggy's been questioning everyone that she even thinks may know you."

Neka's mouth dropped opened. "I don't plan to spend the next fifty years incognito."

They all left, and Neka went out the front door to wait for James. He needed to call them off. Today. He'd drafted a plan to enter his family's business against enormous opposition. For him, getting rid of ambitious women seeking marriage should be child's play.

Sitting on the steps, she considered the situation. Since James dated Teri for two years, he could have dated Cynthia or Peggy even longer. He was thirty, after all, and had probably been dating for years. Surely he knew that emotions became entangled over time. It didn't matter whether or not they were aware of one another. Most people believed they would win out in the end.

Why was she standing outside? James pulled up to the curb as Neka dashed across the lawn to meet him.

Though tears glistened in her eyes, James knew she was angry and wondered what could have transpired in two hours to upset her. Neka was not a dramatic person—something must have set her off.

"Cynthia Ward and Peggy Kennedy have been interrogating my sister."

He frowned and narrowed his eyes. "They came here today?"

She shook her head. "Tuesday, Cynthia accosted Tammy about our return date. The next day Peggy approached her and Kenny at the health food store, wanting to know all about me. Why are they stalking me?"

"I'll talk to them." James gritted his teeth and took her hand. "I informed both ladies that we were engaged the Friday you agreed to marry me."

She glanced away. "Did they contact you since then?"

"I ignored the calls and text messages. This won't last."

"In St. Louis you told me Teri would be an obstacle and that I may run into other women from your past." She pulled her hand from his grasp, retracing her steps across the lawn. "But I don't like being stalked."

"I promise to take care of this today." He jogged to catch up to her and caught her arm. Without looking at him, she tried to move forward. "Neka, don't pull away from me."

She swung around to face him. "Then let go." His hand dropped immediately. "That's not good enough. What's going on with them?"

James raised an eyebrow. "You're asking me to explain another person's actions?"

"Please give it a shot."

Taking a deep breath, he knew he had no right to be indignant. Neka had given him the best two weeks of his life. For once, business and family gelled into a cohesive whole. The courtesy call he'd placed two weeks ago should have ended his obligation to either woman.

"Proposing to Teri gave them false hopes. I don't know why. You'll have answers in abundance tonight." His eyes narrowed when she remained silent. "Do you want me to leave?"

Her face told him everything. "My grandmothers are inside. The welcome-home party expects to meet you."

James put on a blank expression, unable to process the hurt she'd dealt him. He'd rushed through his mail and eaten a hasty meal to return to her in record time. And now she all but dismissed him.

"So you would ask me to leave if not for your grandmothers?"

Neka studied her shoes before meeting his gaze. "This problem is about you and them—not me. Should I expect to be a sideshow for someone's entertainment?"

It felt like she'd punched him in the gut. He schooled his face. "You providing entertainment for Peggy and Cynthia will never happen."

She sighed heavily and threw up her hands. "Then explain why this happened."

"I dated them longer than Teri."

"So they claim ownership?"

He touched her arm to keep from exploding in irritation. "I'll leave after I meet your family and stop by later with more information than you'll care to hear."

Neka glanced away. "I doubt that's true."

"Please trust me. I promise we'll talk tonight." His palm stroked her arm.

Nodding, she strolled into her house, and he trailed behind her.

* * *

A melodious tone rang throughout the house, prompting Karen to glance at her watch. "Nine thirty. I wonder who's visiting this late in the evening."

Neka folded the last pillowcase, then stored the liquid detergent inside the cabinet. "James promised to get rid of my stalkers and report his success tonight. Where's Dad?"

"In bed," her mom replied. "I'm heading up to join him."

Neka spotted her dad descending the stairs. "I'm sure its James." She pointed to the silhouette in the tinted glass. "See? It's him." Staring until her dad went back upstairs, she sprinted forward. "Come in."

James didn't budge. "No kiss for keeping my promise?"

Neka brushed her lips against his cheek, then left him to secure the lock. He followed her into the family room as she settled on the love seat and pointed to the chair. Ignoring the offer, he sat down beside her. She leaned away from his resolute expression.

"Don't build up a defense against me. Old habits are hard to break. Talking about personal things is hard for me. I'm used to keeping my own counsel."

She sighed, tucking her legs beneath her. "Marriage means more than sleeping in the same bed and raising children together."

"Have you forgotten our two weeks of bliss despite the business challenges?" His finger stroked her cheek.

Neka closed her eyes to shut out the pain that peeked out of his gaze. Seeing it left her heart bare. "This hit me fifteen minutes after you dropped me off."

James squeezed her fingers. "My parents enjoy a solid marriage, as do my godparents. And although she disagreed with many decisions, Mother permitted my father's pandering to Ryan and Matt. My godfather repressed lifelong dreams because his wife feared he might suffer another stroke."

"James—"

His raised hand silenced her. "Letting misconceptions fester disrupts many households, as it did mine. I didn't want to marry until I found the lady with all the qualities I was looking for—my perfect partner. I was determined not to settle for second best, and I dated flawed women until my dream mate appeared. Only I failed to recognize her until a predicament dropped you into my lap."

Her heart pounded. He did love her. He'd practically said so. Hadn't he?

Did his parents know that he felt rejected? His only real flaw was a penchant to influence situations in his favor. She believed he'd developed this trait when he had to learn to fend for himself. It's what made him so good at business, but it wasn't an endearing trait in a husband.

But at what age did parents' responsibility for their children's behavior end?

"Cynthia and Peggy know now that you were the one I searched for over the years. Also, they understand the police will appear on their doorstep if they stalk you anymore." He paused, smirking. "How's that for clearing everything up?"

Neka gasped. James had threatened to call the police. "You'd really make a formal complaint? Isn't that a little heavy-handed for women who don't constitute a physical threat?"

But she thanked God he'd taken her seriously. Due to the mess with his female friends, she'd doubted the wisdom of agreeing to marry him so quickly for the first time in days.

His soft laughter lightened the mood. " 'Police' is a useful word when used on law-abiding citizens. I'd told them on the first date marriage wasn't an option. I won't buy into their fantasies. Like Teri, they dated other men too."

Neka unwound her legs and relaxed against the love seat. She narrowed her eyes. "Do you promise they'll stop looking for me now?"

He nodded. "A chance meeting may exist in our future, but they won't instigate one. Cynthia and Peggy understand I don't make threats." He tilted his head to the side. "Any more reservations?"

She shook her head. "You answered my major question—why you dated them."

"Desperation fled the moment you accepted me into your life." He brought her hand to his lips. Then he jerked away, unable to hide his emotions before she caught them.

Neka whispered into his ear. "It's okay, James. We can trust each other."

Chapter Twenty-Four

Other than Neka's parents, everyone was in the family room, though they were enjoying different activities. For the last month, it had become their unofficial recreational area. They all needed a respite from work overload. Activity within Lacey Corp had only grown in momentum instead of diminishing. Competition between two cities had spurred everyone to excellence.

Spending time with the Lacey family also gave James another avenue to healing the breach. His friendship with Kelly and Michael had improved greatly since their return to Tulsa, and Neka was sure the others weren't far behind.

Neka relaxed against the love seat after five days of nonstop assignments. James sat beside her on the floor, flipping through home magazines. Tammy and Kenny pored over a five-hundred-piece puzzle they'd vowed to complete that weekend. Kelly and Michael reclined on the sofa, absorbed in the little one exercising its limbs in Kelly's belly.

No one stirred when the doorbell sounded. Not until Karen said, "They're in the family room, Teri. Go on in."

Neka and James raised their heads at the same time.

Tammy jumped to her feet, but Kenny grabbed her hand. "We won't finish if you refuse to sit down."

His entreaty accomplished its goal. Tammy wrapped her arms around him and watched the door. She glanced at Kelly, who stared at the entryway, engrossed in her friend's arrival. Pulling his wife closer, Michael brushed her hair away from her face.

Neka tensed despite being unafraid about the encounter. At least Teri made contact at her home. But she couldn't help but wonder how many times she'd driven by before catching them all together. She shivered.

Teri floated into the room, gazing at Neka and James, then glancing at Kelly. Hand held up even with her face, she laughed.

193

"I come in peace." Flashing a bright smile, she sat on a lounger facing the pair, twirling keys on her fingers. "Hello, friends. Someone told me the happy couple came home a few weeks ago. I gave them ample time to unwind before offering my congratulations."

Neka turned to James, who nodded for her to speak first. "Thank you. We appreciate all well-wishers."

Teri's eyebrows lifted as her mouth gaped open.

"We?" She frowned at Kelly. "Well, James's significant other speaks on his behalf these days."

She leaned against the cushion, grinning, as James's eyes narrowed.

Tammy glared. "I thought you came to offer congratulations. If not, get to the point and leave."

Fingers spread over Teri's lips, and she laughed.

"Ouch. As usual, your manners need improvement." Tammy scooted back the chair, but Teri hesitated before she rose. "I know about Cynthia and the restaurant. You showed Neka doesn't stand alone."

"And ..." Tammy was still seething.

Looking downward, Teri sighed and then peered at Neka.

"Well done, young friend. I saw you going into Lacey Corp Thursday." Teri inspected her from head to toe. Neka lifted her chin slightly. She would not let this woman tear her down. "Styling your hair off your face gives you a pixie quality. The tailored clothes accentuate your slim figure. Show me the engagement ring people rave about. Of course, they inquire why I never sported one."

Frowning, Neka glanced at James. Did he mistake Teri's real feelings when they'd dated?

Teri's emotions etched lines on her pretty face. "Kel, I'm disappointed you didn't invite me to the July fourth hoopla. I hear the reclusive Laceys cordoned off an entire block to shoot off fireworks at your cousin's house. Normally, no one in this family brings attention to themselves." Teri glanced at James and then back at Kelly. "Who decided on a neighborhood celebration?"

When Kelly remained silent, Teri focused on Neka. "Did you set a wedding date?"

Neka glanced at Kelly before answering happily. "The last Saturday in November."

"Can I anticipate an invitation?"

"No." Kelly rose from the seat as quickly as she could, still needing Michael's help. "May I speak to you alone?"

The sadness in Teri's eyes changed the atmosphere in the room to one of empathy. She stared at her friend for a moment then turned away. "James, might I talk to you in private?"

"You said it all at the airport six weeks ago."

"Not quite. We have an unexpected development we need to discuss."

For a moment, Neka couldn't move—couldn't even breathe—at the heavy implication in Teri's voice. When James stirred, Neka stood and walked across the room, knowing all eyes followed her progress. She only felt numb.

At the French doors, she peered outside as the weeping willow tree beckoned. She studied Teri, who was clanging keys, through the reflection in the glass.

"If you want to speak with James in private, please visit him at his house," Neka said to Teri. "Since you came to my home, state your business."

Everyone was still and silent. James rose to his feet and waited for the reply.

"So the kitten scratches when riled." Teri sprang from her seat and darted across the room. She smirked at James. "I won't engage Neka, since my argument is with you. Your fiancée welcomed me into your home. Expect a visit."

Teri winced at his derisive chuckle and turned around, facing him.

"Let's end that idea before you show up on my doorstep unannounced." He nodded at Kelly. "Your friend offered you a way out. You should take it and leave gracefully."

"Okay, let's go there." Anger flashed in her icy blue eyes. Huffing, Teri stared at Neka. "James proposed to me in a scheme to take over his family business."

Holding up her hand, Neka intercepted Kelly before she could interrupt. "Let her speak."

"Your fiancé proposed because he needed a wife to facilitate his plan to run the family business. Clarity hit four days ago—I was duped." Fingers disheveled her copper hair. "You were his goal all along. These are his comments regarding you and your family."

Shaking her head, she ticked the list off on her fingers.

"He said most fellows discounted your appeal but you constituted safe ground. Any corporate raider welcomed your dishing out company secrets."

195

She glanced at Kelly and Tammy. "He admitted the men who netted the daughter's hearts won the business in the end."

Neka kept her eyes on Teri, refusing to question James in front of her. Teri continued, her voice rising in pitch.

"He plotted to maneuver the friendship he'd cultivated into a love relationship all along. My dumping him just sped up the process he'd already set in order. James deserves his safety net removed, not you. Stop fooling yourself that he loves you." Tears filled her eyes as she shook her keys. "One day you'll thank me. I've been kinder to you than I was to myself."

Apparently done, Teri stood there a moment, and then hurried out the door. Kelly gazed at Neka before she and Michael followed behind her.

Neka still couldn't look at James. Teri's accusations robbed her of hope that he might love her without his recognizing the truth. But that was Neka's story and not his. Self-deception mattered, even if she might win his heart in the end.

* * *

James grieved over his loss as if a loved one had passed away. The light in Neka's eyes had died when Teri unleashed her venom. Spouting his comments out of context, she'd delivered an award-winning performance. It seemed spontaneous, but he knew she'd practiced days—maybe weeks—in advance. Though they sympathized with her desperation, he sensed none of them bought her speech.

No one but Neka.

Even after their perfect time in St. Louis, Neka believed the worse. It had taken him weeks to get her back to normal after Cynthia and Peggy soured their first day home. It was essential that he mount a defense before Neka wallowed in the false accusations.

"Listen, if I don't dispute her allegations, they'll linger with your family." He touched her fingers. "Come with me while I contest her claims before she escapes."

Karen and Lawrence stood in the foyer now, listening to the discourse taking place. While Michael's disapproving expression showed, he wasn't buying into the discussion. Kelly spoke as Teri silently shook her head, her defiant glare daring James to refute her claims.

He nodded to Neka's parents and cleared his throat. "My preference is to handle my affairs in private. Though I won't disrespect your home, these accusations need quick rebuttals."

Animosity flared in Teri's gaze as she gestured to the small assembly. "I've known these people since kindergarten. You can't damage my friendship with Kelly or anyone else in this room."

James clasped Neka's hand, ignoring everyone but his fiancée. Staring into her eyes, he wished he could usher Teri out of the house. Did he observe vulnerability within the defiant woman? Had it been there all along, escaping his notice until now?

"I did say these things, but not in the context she would have you believe. Teri enjoyed talking about your family. Whenever she mentioned you were dateless, I explained men rebelled against your views on righteous living."

Teri threw up her hands, edging closer, but Kelly tugged her arm. She brushed the hand away, scowling at James. "Oh please, everyone comments on Neka's lack of dates so don't pretend I'm an anomaly."

Disregarding her defense, he stayed focused on Neka. "One day some of her friends complained that college students brought nothing to the table in marriage. I told them wholesome individuals such as you constitute safe ground for any spouse."

Teri was practically shouting now. "Is that all you have? We referred to groundless people spreading their love around. No one included your saintly fiancée in the dialogue."

If the woman hoped to gain support, belittling Neka wasn't going to help. Yet James didn't let himself look smug.

"Teri grumbled that you occupied my time at parties because I was a corporate raider ferreting company secrets. I explained that I 'wasted' time with a woman who never divulged information that wasn't readily available to anyone."

Teri clapped slowly, and it echoed through the foyer.

Before she could speak again, he continued, holding Neka's gaze. "Teri frequently criticized you and your sister's reluctance to run the business." He hesitated when she groaned and inched toward the front door. "I explained Kelly married a planning genius and Tammy was engaged to a brilliant lawyer. I assured her that you would choose the perfect spouse. God blessed your choices because the men who won your hearts would navigate Lacey Corp."

Now Teri looked like she wished for an escape route. James glanced at Neka's parents' reactions to the devastating scene. Karen crept nearer to the woman fighting an inner war to overcome condemnation. Kelly's eyes filled with tears watching her friend's features.

Various expressions flickered across Teri's face until pride won out over despair. Regaining self-control, she tossed her hair over her shoulders.

"I refuse to suffocate on pity." Her sad eyes studied Neka. "I warned you. Marry him at your peril."

Karen and Kelly reached the door as Teri fumbled for the doorknob. Tears streaming down her cheeks, she peered at Tammy. She jerked her head and stormed outside while the three women followed after her.

James turned back to Neka. Silence in the foyer rivaled the weariness which seemed to overtake her now. Her gaze singled out the insightful man jingling coins in his pocket. What was Lawrence thinking?

Neka looked at her dad. "May I speak to you a moment?"

Not waiting for an answer, she pulled her hand from James's and rushed up the stairs ahead of her father.

* * *

Neka was sitting on her favorite resting spot when her father entered the sunroom.

"Move a chair closer to the chaise. I don't want our voices to carry downstairs." A movement in the doorway caught her eye. "Mom, we came upstairs to talk alone. I'm glad you came back inside. How's Teri?"

"I left her talking with Kelly and Tammy." Karen pulled up a seat next to Lawrence. "How are you?"

Instead of answering, Neka covered her face with her hands.

"Confused. Teri initiated the traumatic episode downstairs." Shaking her head, she tried to sort out the ill-fated scene. What had happened in the family room? Why would Teri do this?

She shook her head slowly. "Nothing has added up since Teri's arrival. She waltzed into the family room stating she wanted to congratulate us, then she sowed dissent the entire time. James confronted her in self-defense, but Teri was unprepared for the confrontation she'd instigated."

Her back braced against the cushion, Neka explained what they'd missed downstairs. When she finished speaking, she studied their reactions.

Karen tilted her head, staring at her daughter. "Teri was a guest in our home."

Neka glanced from one to the other. "But why cause a scene? She broke off their engagement in the worse way possible."

"She craves devotion, so his neglect drew her in." Leaning forward, Karen patted Neka's knee. She glanced at her husband. "Teri will rebound because family and friends will surround her. None of us will gossip about it, and that will give her time to regroup."

Neka's parents' expressions made it clear that they wanted to help her, but she tied their hands in some way. What was the obstacle?

Her father raised his eyebrows. "Problem-handling gives insight into a person's character."

"You don't think he handled it well?"

Lawrence shook his head. "Overkill. He destroyed her credibility. In the future, none of us will take her seriously."

"I believed his version."

"I question his intent, not his account."

Neka frowned.

"Mom, what do you think?"

Karen shrugged. "The downstairs episode was regrettable."

"I should probably see Teri off." Neka ran from the room before giving them a chance to respond. Zipping down the steps, she passed the talking men and sped out the front door. Her steam disappeared on reaching her sisters as they watched Teri drive away.

"Oh no, I'm too late."

Tammy glanced at her. "Too late for what?"

Why did I rush outside? She shrugged her shoulders. "I'm not sure. Upstairs I felt an overwhelming desire to say good-bye."

Kelly hugged her. "You handled your business in the family room. Still, Teri underwent a terrible loss. Unfortunately, her foolishness undermines whatever she was trying to do with James. What a mess. I'll text her later."

Her gaze followed the men's progress when they ventured outside the house. Both sisters took their significant others back inside. Left alone, Neka moved away from James, who was staring at her with unreadable eyes.

Though despair threatened to swallow her, this time he wasn't the problem.

199

He'd surpassed all expectations in his new job. Her mom and the other two division heads commended his quick adjustment within the company. He even contributed to the new location's speedy development. His business aptitude allowed her dad to spend two days a week in St. Louis since the merger took place, and that really helped David adjust to Lacey Corp culture in a short timespan.

The Eureka, Rolla, and West C plans were all ahead of schedule.

James had worked hard to prove himself to her and her family. The two of them spent Wednesdays and every weekend together. He had joined her church. It was his suggestion they eat breakfast together at his condo before attending services. They ate brunch at a different eatery each week and dinner at her home. Some Saturdays they drove around town seeking out new activities, even attending a medieval reenactment one weekend. Others they just engaged in some down time with her family.

Neka loved him so much that her heart felt like it would explode.

So what was wrong?

* * *

Moving nearer, James acknowledged more than physical distance separated him and Neka since Teri's charade began. Her deception would succeed if the ruse divided them. "Do your parents understand she led me into a trap I couldn't escape?"

Still studying him, she nodded. "They didn't intervene because you deserved a chance to disprove those charges."

Skepticism entered his gaze. "But?"

"No buts. It was just painful to watch."

Not for him. Teri brought this on herself.

But her timing was awful. Last night he and Neka had played an insane version of Monopoly at Hazelle's house. At work, coworkers accepted their engagement with sincerity. Church members welcomed him into the congregation, saying they'd seen an engagement coming whenever he visited.

Teri's deplorable conduct threatened to unravel all their work blending their lives into one. Problems she manufactured had brought them together, but mayhem she invented wouldn't undermine their relationship.

"You're disconnecting. Talk to me." He longed to ask her to believe in him. He believed in her. How many times did he have to prove himself?

200

Sighing, Neka kicked loose twigs across the lawn. "Let's walk around the house to the weeping willow tree."

Without waiting for a reply, she cut across the driveway and around the house until they reached her favorite outdoor spot. She sat and squinted up at him.

"If Teri hadn't broken off the engagement, the two of you might be married by now."

Could he expose the defects in his armor and retain her trust? He had thought about it more times that he could count. Would she extend the same abiding empathy that she did for her father? Or would he lose the one person who mattered in the life he wanted to create?

"That engagement would've ended in St. Louis."

Her eyebrows knit together. "How? Marriage fulfilled your father's mandate."

"I never planned to marry her." His shoulders were so tense that it hurt to talk.

She frowned. "That's a bold statement coming from the man who asked her to marry him."

Hesitating, he took her hand and swallowed hard, willing his muscles to relax.

"From the beginning, my mother and Teri were destined to clash. Since Mother is never willing to suffer nonsense from non-family members or acquaintances, she would've stopped the craziness and reeled her husband in line after the introductions." He cupped her cheeks in his palms. "Father never stood a chance once her last son threatened to bring another manipulative woman into the family."

The alarm in Neka's eyes astounded him as she knocked his hands from her face. "You're talking in riddles, but I'm not sure I want you to get to the point."

He leaned closer. "I had no interest in marrying Teri. We never set a date, and she never received a ring. I dated her to escape my loneliness and asked her to marry me, knowing my mother would never allow it."

When Neka closed her eyes, James gazed at the rose bushes and took a deep breath. "I was trying to outsmart my father's demand that I marry. At the end of the day, futile actions are unsustainable."

His confession settled so many unasked questions. She had never imagined Teri failed to pin down a date because he never intended to marry her.

He and Teri were two peas from the same pod, manipulating circumstances as if people existed as a means to their personal ends. Yet James didn't need to continue the engagement with Neka, unless ...

Closing her eyes, Neka sat up straighter. Maybe Hazelle had been right after all.

She shook her head before the thought could gain traction. There was no denying James behaved miserably before St. Louis, but since then, he seemed to have changed. Could they move past this latest roadblock?

"What if Teri is in love? The earlier drama proves her attachment."

His eyes searched her face. "I didn't take advantage of an innocent. Visions of financial gains drove her actions."

"Don't underplay the cruelty." Neka looked away. "Whatever her mentality was, it doesn't absolve your actions. Teri announced her engagement to everyone. How did you expect her to explain a breakup to all those people?"

Remorse filling his gaze, he lowered his tone to just above a whisper. "I wouldn't have contradicted her version of events."

"I don't question your willingness to accept that burden. But it's too little too late."

The pain in his eyes extinguished her fury. What he did was deplorable, and Neka couldn't condone it. But he'd set the scheme into action before God had softened his heart.

Father, help me.

James cupped her chin in his hand, and he couldn't hide the weariness in his eyes.

"Sweets, if I could replay my life with today's wisdom, I'd make better choices." He moved close enough for his breath to warm her face. "She knew it was all a business arrangement, so I planned to compensate her lost time."

Exhaling a long sigh, she lowered her gaze. James laid his forehead against hers.

"I'm a changed man."

Tears rolled down her cheeks as she laid her head on his shoulder. "I know."

Neka thought her heart might rip from her body. Her marvelous idea in St. Louis wasn't working now that they were home. In theory, marriages of convenience were romantic. Maybe it was just because it seemed to come from a simpler time.

But in reality, marriage arrangements presented a living hell when the person in love sought love in return.

She wanted nothing less than his love. Today. Not years later after she grew on him. St. Louis cast a spell over both of them as harmony melded them together. The magical moments depicted their future and not the reality of today. While in St. Louis, she expected to hear love declarations. But back in their real world in Tulsa, James protected himself with endless work.

So many lives had changed because she'd refused godly advice. Now she was trapped into honoring her word to marry a man who might not love her.

Granny had said not now didn't mean not ever. They needed a transition period to get to know one another before standing at the altar. She needed an escape clause without losing James forever.

* * *

James was so relieved to be honest with Neka. Her scorn paled in comparison to coming clean.

But really, he wanted her to cast her convictions aside and take his side. Each time they'd reached a stalemate, he'd given in. The time had come to negotiate the difference.

Tilting her face toward his, their eyes met as he worked to identify her end game. "How about we go get double scoops of French vanilla ice cream in a cake cone?"

A smile curved her lips as she turned away. "Good. We can discuss delaying the wedding until next November."

James just discovered that Neka issued ultimatums with a smile. It seemed the goodwill built over six weeks had vanished with one wave of Teri's hand, right along with bridging the gap with her family. If he lost ground with his fiancée, improving the relationship with her sisters was over. And where they led, Neka seemed to follow.

While growing up, the close-knit sisters had born multilayered difficulties that resulted in what James termed to be a form of codependency. Being children of an interracial marriage gave them stumbling blocks sometimes difficult to overcome.

Supporting one another developed into living interchangeable lives. Though he weaned her away from them daily, the progress faltered at times. From all accounts, maturing brought about the needed changes. First Kelly's marriage, and then Tammy's engagement shrunk the ties somewhat. Even his engagement to Neka had caused the three of them to stop living in one another's shadow. Although they seemed less tight, any upsets brought out the cheerleaders in a hurry.

Frowning, he acknowledged it was time to even the odds. Too many naysayers in close proximity undid his efforts at every turn.

Chapter Twenty-Five

Covering the cake plate, Neka glanced at Fran. For three weeks, Neka had picked up James's parents from the airport after work on Friday, driving them to his condo. Dinner was always on the table when they arrived. During their visits, they took the opportunity to get to know her other family members and friends too. But after dinner on Fridays, Neka and James watched movies with his parents until he followed her home around eleven o'clock. The special treatment reinforced Neka's "he really loves me" moments.

On Saturdays, she and Fran typically prepared dessert and side dishes together in the kitchen. Today Fran studied Gene's and James's interaction from the window. Smiling as the two men enjoyed companionship on the deck, she turned to Neka. "Solidarity is finally building between those two. God blessed us. He allowed the sale of the business, which caused the problem, without taking it completely away."

Neka slowly walked to the window to stand next to Fran. It seemed James wasn't the only family member craving unity. He'd told her so many times how he wanted a closer relationship with his family. Now he constantly hung out outside on the deck, soaking up the companionship that had eluded him in the past.

Thank you, Father. Jesus is the gift that keeps on giving.

She smiled at Fran. "Let's join them."

Fran shook her head. "You go on. I prefer observing them from here."

Neka hastened outside and wrapped her arms around James from behind. She rested her cheek on his back. They'd had their share of misunderstandings, but her love for him had only grown. Her smile deepened when he clasped her hands, securing them against him. After a while, she lounged in a chair, listening to their lively debate until Gene winked at her and grinned.

"We're done here. Bring everything inside."

He trailed away, leaving them alone. He and Fran did that a lot.

As much as she loved his parents, being alone with James was her favorite thing in the world. His gaze followed his father to the house, then he turned to Neka. "It's nice talking to my father without locking horns every fifteen minutes."

His eyes shone with happiness. Neka had to stop herself from leaping off the cushion and hugging him again. There was nothing like answered prayer.

She gathered the meat and grilled vegetables to carry inside. While James tidied up the workstation, her thoughts sifted through the accounts of his childhood she'd heard over the last few weeks.

Viewing him more objectively these days, she accepted his ability to compartmentalize his life. It was how he survived a dysfunctional childhood. They explained how he promised never to bring home a girl that he couldn't marry. And he never did until she visited their home some fifteen years later.

Further exchange revealed Ryan and Matt also had issues with relationships, presumably explaining their choices in wives. It seems Gene and Fran discovered that their children forming sound judgment required help on their part, and they had intervened with Brandie. Maybe it took them that many years to develop good parenting skills.

She glanced at James, relaxed and loading cooking utensils into the dishwasher. Thank God he'd mellowed out since those young-adult years.

During dinner, the conversation became a little heated as she and his mother critiqued recent movies. Fran's surprise that Neka had seen new releases without James had Neka explaining the long hours he spent at work. From that point, Neka discussed the new friends she hung out with in the evenings.

Settling in the living room, Fran fixed an apologetic gaze on Neka. "Sorry, dear, for upsetting your fiancé. My innocent question about your becoming a social butterfly unleashed a storm."

Neka laughed. "It's okay. I think James secretly wants me to sit at home every evening with nothing to do while he works crazy hours."

James glared at Neka playfully. "Isn't that what you did BSTL?"

She tilted her head to the side, laughing, and glanced at his parents, explaining. "Before St. Louis. Humongous changes have taken place since then."

"So how do you spend your evenings?" Fran gazed from Neka to James. "After St. Louis, that is."

"I still read, but since I've made a few friends ..." She smiled at James. "Sometimes we go to the movies or shopping to fill in time until he's free."

Gene frowned at his son. "I'm sure he'd prefer you to read romance novels until he's available."

A hush spread over the room when James frowned at his father. Gene's narrowed eyes studied Neka. Something in the direct gaze begged her to pay attention.

Eyes half-closed, Neka leaned forward, blocking everything else from her mind. Her pulse accelerated in a different way than it had during the anxiety-filled first two days in St. Louis.

"James clutches to everything he can't bear to lose."

Fran kissed her husband's cheek. "I agree."

Neka glanced at James, who was looking out the window. His blank expression was back, as it sometimes was around his parents.

For now, the simple statements appeased the ache of wanting James to declare his love. But his parents' assurance wouldn't satisfy his lack of affirmation for long.

At least it partly explained his flat-out refusal to postpone the wedding until next year. She'd brought it up a few times now, and he always shut the conversation down completely.

Standing, Fran pulled her husband up. "I think Gene and I have intruded into your private affairs enough for one night. We'll leave you two alone."

James draped his arm around Neka's shoulder. Though her heartbeat pounded in her ears, an incredible calm controlled her body. He kissed the tip of her nose, then her dimples. Her body pulsated with his attentions. Gazing into her eyes, he kissed her knuckles and then clasped her hands to his chest.

"I love you, sweets. Thank you for taking me into your life. My only hope is to secure your love forever."

The longing in his eyes fulfilled three months of hoping and praying that the man she'd pledged to marry loved her in return. Tears flowed over Neka's cheeks. She would never forget this moment.

James loved her. He loved her. Thank God he loved her.

She threw her arms around his neck. "I've always loved you."

Relief flooded his eyes in a second. What had he imagined?

Enfolded in each other's arms, their shared peace molded them together. She finally felt that she'd been justified in her actions after weeks of wavering back and forth.

Going to St. Louis without notification had been wrong, no doubt. But thank God He worked it out for His glory and their good. Now their relationship was on solid ground—no more rocky moments.

* * *

A few days later, Neka parked her car down the street from James's condo. Yesterday she'd made plans to attend a jewelry party that evening. But after receiving a text that he was closing shop at five thirty, she'd altered her plans in a hurry. Gathering supplies from the back seat, she hastened to the porch in search of the perfect spot to spring her surprise.

She hid her basket in the alcove beneath his window, plastered her body against the building, and rang the doorbell, suppressing giggles. Holding herself flat against the concrete, she had a similar vantage point as James. A black marble tray contained silver and gold glitter fashioned into two interlocking hearts. A lavender regal orchid dazzled in the middle of the design. Muffled laughter shook her body until James stepped outside the door. Instead of picking up his gift, he swiveled, facing her.

"Hello, sweets."

Laughing, she threw up one hand and poked him with her basket. "James, you were supposed to look up and down the street and wonder who left the present."

"No one else is this thoughtful." He kissed her cheek, chuckling.

Her body warmed at the light touch, but she pretended to pout. "Someone else could've been thinking about you."

James stroked the side of her face, and the warmth flowed through her body. "Only my fiancée would provide a picture-perfect ending to an otherwise tedious day. Still going to the jewelry party?"

"I'd much rather spend my time with you." The pleasure on his face told her she'd made the right decision.

"Come in. I was about to make a sandwich."

"Then I arrived just in time to rescue you from the mundane." Inside, she noted shadows across his features that she'd failed to notice outside. Since coming home, he'd turned his living room into a makeshift office. Sitting beside the laptop were three large file folders crammed with drawings and outlines.

She sighed. "You worked ten hours today and still brought work home from the office."

"Lacey Corp is like an octopus spreading its tentacles in every direction." James glanced at the overstuffed briefcase hidden under the table and frowned when Neka swiftly restored the room back to its primary function. "Factor in the latest proposition, and I'm shelved for the foreseeable future."

He looked around until he spotted the purple basket she'd carried inside. They reached for it at the same time. She swatted his hand when he lifted up the top, then she pointed to the sofa.

"Grab a seat I'll bring your food out in a jiffy," she said.

She was on cloud nine as his throaty chuckle followed her into the kitchen.

Having prepared the food at her house meant a quick heat up would suffice. Still, she took her time making it special. While their dinner warmed, she hung a mint sprig on the rims of two glasses but skipped the frosting this time. The timer sounded just as she poured their drinks.

Neka paused inside the room, shaking her head at the fatigued man sprawled on the sofa. James had fallen asleep in less than fifteen minutes. The peaceful expression belied that he once manipulated the lives of so many people. Thank God he'd left that person in St. Louis.

Tiptoeing across the room, she placed the tray on the coffee table. Leaving the dishes covered, she curled up at the end of the sofa and watched him sleep.

* * *

Neka kicked off shoes when she got home. It felt good to sit. She'd had a long day too. She had to learn to curb her bleeding-heart tendencies for sure, or other people would take advantage of her. It seemed you were never too old to learn a lesson.

A cell phone rang, and it took her a moment to realize it was hers. The new melodious ringtone took some getting used to.

An excited voice broke through the line when she answered. "Hello, did I catch you at a bad time? Excuse me for a moment. David just walked in the door. Hi, honey, I'm warning Neka we're Tulsa-bound and I expect a personal tour of the city."

Neka scooted off the chaise, smiling. "James said David might spend a few days in Tulsa for meetings."

Brandie laughed. "No way. We're in for two weeks."

Frowning, she sat back down. James was late with the news. "Though I'm not complaining, why so long?"

The pause implied Neka should have already heard the news.

"The advisory board meets the week before we arrive. Then Lawrence will implement David's and James's initiatives." Brandie paused again. There was a smile in her voice when she resumed speaking. "You're a godsend. Thanks for daring them to take Lacey Corp to the next level. The challenge sparked their imaginations more than ever."

Being asked to the party last annoyed her. "When did you find out?"

"David called me once the conference session with Lawrence and James ended."

Only then did Neka remember the unanswered messages on her cell phone. No wonder James had called several times. Apparently she wasn't too old to have to learn to check her voicemail either. "Well, they stepped up to the plate big time. When are you all coming?"

"In two weeks. They hope to have these conferences wrapped up before Tammy's wedding."

"James didn't mention the consultations would start in September."

"Your dad made the announcement at the end of the day. David phoned on his way home from work. I rushed to call you while the children napped."

Either her fiancé had planned a huge celebration tonight, or he didn't think she rated enough to get a heads up. What was he thinking? Didn't he know his sister would call? Neka glanced at her watch. "They're asleep at dinner time. You must have worn them out earlier."

Laughter bubbled through the phone. "We ran around today with mother. As they say, wonders never cease, including my parents' visits to see James the last few weekends. By the way, they love your church."

Neka strolled to the window, biting her lip to keep from asking more questions.

"We love them back. I'm happy they devoted so much time to James this summer." She laid her forehead against the glass. "Fran talks nonstop about the wedding."

"I can imagine her excitement when she's with you. Thanks for including her. She didn't play any role in Ryan or Matt's weddings."

This was news to Neka. She thought Fran enjoyed a healthy relationship with her daughters-in-law. "How come?"

"Both families planned the rehearsal dinner without her input and then forked over the bill. How's the ceremony coming along?"

Shifting emotions kept her off balance, so she hesitated. She'd asked Hazelle to be her matron of honor. Now two bridesmaids needed escorts. The improved relationship with Ryan and Matt prompted the suggestion that James ask them to be groomsmen. Brandie's inclusion would provide a role for his favorite sibling. Blake, James's attorney and Kenny's brother, promised to escort Brandie down the aisle if she agreed.

"I was going to call you this weekend. We want you and your brothers included in the ceremony. How about being a bridesmaid in November?"

Shuffling around the room, Neka anticipated Brandie's response.

"Oh my goodness, I didn't expect it, but of course I will! I'm glad you wanted me."

She frowned. "We'll get you measured for your dress when you come to town."

"Yesterday we received an invitation to Tammy's wedding. I feel connected with the Lacey family. We don't share that kind of relationship with Celia's or Sandi's relatives."

Resolve to include them in family events surfaced. "Care to stay with us during your visit?"

"Thanks, though I must decline. Let's see how my brother holds up with little feet underway for two weeks straight. Will you see him this evening?"

"Yep."

"I'll let you go then. See you in two weeks."

Neka sauntered back to the chaise, swamped by the fallout of speedy judgments. Her determination to postpone the ceremony had collided with Fran's enthusiasm for the wedding. Although his parents' frequent visits benefited James, they didn't help with her plans to delay the marriage another year. It only added more fuel to his arguments for getting married this year.

At this point, she'd all but given up. And professing his love had greatly reduced her misgivings. Most of her nagging doubts vanished as August settled their relationship into a harmonized pattern.

But being in love didn't negate the truth. Spending more time together would strengthen their relationship before getting married. Because he worked late every evening, dinner on Wednesdays and weekends with his parents were all they had. Interesting how Fran and Gene began visiting after the showdown with Teri took place.

She cringed whenever thoughts of Teri's meltdown entered her mind. Neka had heard she'd rebounded from her dangerous place. Kelly said Teri attended church with her family and stayed out of the spotlight for now. Maybe some benefit would come from the nasty exchange.

Neka sighed. She'd turned her doubts over to God. It was in His hands now.

On a good note, Hazelle really helped her fashion her dream wedding. Married last year, the dew of love still clung to her spirit. The family floral shop turned sanctuaries and reception halls into nuptial paradises on a weekly basis. Her cousin's ideas would transform the fireside room into the intimate family gathering Neka had dreamed of.

"Thank You, Jesus, for blessing us beyond measure." She stood up and spun around, combining several dance steps as she twirled into the bathroom. A well-placed kick shut the door.

* * *

"Hey, put it back. I wasn't finished."

Folding her arms, Neka frowned when Karen removed the cookie jar from the counter and placed it on a shelf. Her mom stirred meat sauce she'd left to simmer.

"If I do, you won't have room for dinner."

"Mom, give me credit to know how many cookies I can eat without ruining my meal."

"I didn't touch the six cookies you already have on the napkin."

Neka laughed. She broke off another piece of cookie. "Hurry up, James. Watching Mom cook this food is making me hungrier."

Entering the kitchen, Lawrence nuzzled Karen's neck before taking the stool beside Neka. "You're making me hungry talking about eating. Perhaps your mother and I should join you."

Karen turned away from the stove, pointing her spatula at him.

"We're home for the night, dear. All day yesterday you begged to have this for dinner this evening." She removed a pan of biscuits from the double oven and set it on a rack. "You shall enjoy the meal I rushed home from work

212

to prepare. Thanks to the increased workload, I have to forego working half days for a while."

Lawrence threw back his head in laughter. "When faced with an ultimatum from a spatula-wielding woman, I always comply."

Neka nodded at the cookie jar. "Mom baked chocolate chip cookies earlier. They're still warm."

Karen glanced over her shoulder. Her eyes twinkled at her husband. "They're for dessert."

He glanced at Neka. "Now I get where you picked up that inflexible attitude. I'll work on reforming Karen later."

"Sorry, sweetheart. You're twenty-nine years too late." On her way to set the table, she feathered his lips with kisses.

Hope rose as Neka eyed the blissful couple. That would be her and James in twenty-nine years—comfortable with the knowledge they had a lifetime ahead of them. "What's the agenda for the upcoming meetings? Brandie said her family would spend two weeks in Tulsa."

Lawrence picked up a cookie. "I foresee a lengthy preparation session ahead. There are tough choices on every front."

"Though James and David share the same vision they have different concepts for execution." Neka slid the cookies closer to him. She hesitated. "Do you foresee any obstacles?"

"The correct question is whether we pursue either version. It's a massive undertaking, even for a thriving corporation."

Karen patted Neka's arm on the way to the table. "Creating mini cities works in theory, but there are a lot of possible pitfalls."

"I'm sure the outcome will overshadow the risky journey." Neka swung around in her chair. She glanced at her father. "Lacey Corp was founded on dicey ventures."

"Your dad has more obligations than when we started out."

Lawrence ate the last cookie, then he grinned, eyeing the cookie jar on the shelf. "Tomorrow the board will evaluate the project. If it passes scrutiny, the advisory committee will hammer out policy in a weeklong planning session. After the guidelines are set in place, our operation directors will join me in crafting the blueprint."

"What's the next step?"

"We'll present the results to division heads and then lay it out to managers and supervisors. After the outline is flawless, we unveil the project in the auditorium for a companywide rollout. The entire process should take four weeks."

"That's why the McKinleys are flying in this Friday." The doorbell rang before either parent could answer. "That's me."

She hugged them both before heading for the door. As she made her way, she realized she'd forgotten her handbag so she turned around and came back into the hallway. Voices came from the kitchen.

Her mom said, "Now fill in the blanks."

Lawrence paused before answering. "I need all hands on deck to ensure the presentation is successful. There's a lot to learn from that young man."

"Such as?"

"James rallies others around his agenda by giving them a stake in the outcome. I want each employee eager to come on board."

Karen sighed. "Surrounding Neka with spokespersons on his behalf has improved his disposition."

Lawrence led her to the table. "Withhold judgment a little longer. Oftentimes, breaking old habits hits an impasse. They've been engaged twelve weeks. A lot can happen before November."

James was waiting, so she left before she heard any more.

* * *

Once she opened the door, Neka glided into his arms. Filled with an indescribable ache, he buried his face into her hair. Swamping Neka with well-wishers who advocated for them to get married in November had forced them upon himself as well. Now he'd fallen prey to the dream weaving prearranged for her. He needed to connect with her more than ever. He hated the feeling of weakness, but it was getting easier to bear.

In the car, Neka faced him, touching his arm. "I talked to Dad. I think he'll accept the proposal."

James wished Lawrence was the easy sell she thought he was. "We stoked his competitive juices. New territory appeals to his pioneer spirit."

"I know we didn't get to talk about this last night." Neka nipped her lip between her teeth. "But I would've rather heard the news from you."

James was about to broach the topic himself. "I came to your office to take you to lunch but was told you left the building with Jeff Frazier at eleven fifteen."

The thought made him tighten his grip on the steering wheel.

"I forgot to turn on my cell phone after the meeting this morning. We ate lunch together."

"Long lunch?"

Frowning she shook her head. "No. Why?"

"I stopped by your office after one." He raised an eyebrow and gave her space to fill in the blanks.

"I had an assignment in Bixby. Hey, I didn't get to tell you my good news either. Brandie agreed to serve as a bridesmaid. When will you ask your brothers to be groomsmen?"

Neka changed the subject better than anyone he knew. He stopped short of praising her expertise. "I didn't realize you worked with field personnel."

"Sometimes they're around when I design interiors. Jeff hopes to transition into another field." She paused. "Should he opt for planning or residential? His current knowledge might advance him above other applicants in either division."

Unwilling to change subjects, he persisted. "Did you go back to the office?"

"I went home after Bixby."

Never a fount of information, her elusiveness demanded he dig further. He'd repeatedly heard Frazier's name coupled with hers before today. "What time did you arrive home?"

"Not too late. I think around four thirty." She turned to him, dimples flashing. "Brandie's excited about the visit. You'll love spending time with Cody and Yancey."

Neka's refusal to settle on his topic told him something had unsettled her. Frazier had showed interest in her before St. Louis. These days Neka was enchanting everyone. James had waited for her for so long. No upstart would snatch her heart away from him. Not after he had fallen in love with her.

He drummed out a beat on the steering wheel.

Slow down. You're entering dangerous terrain.

* * *

"This fish is delicious. James, we should eat here once a week."

"Familiarity might breed contempt. Can't chance that happening."

Neka pointed her finger at him, laughing. "That phenomenon pertains to relationships, not food. Fried fish and I shall never part ways."

James chuckled, narrowing his eyes. Then he was quiet for a long moment. "Did Frazier request your assistance changing careers?"

Her head jerked up. She thought they'd exhausted the Jeff discussion in the car. "On one occasion he mentioned rotting in the field, though I explained his current position might springboard him into related areas. The next day he emailed his job experience, so I wrote up a résumé for him." She nodded her head as she spoke. "A good one-page résumé can open doors."

"Have you arranged other dates with him?"

"I ate lunch with him today. I reserve dates for you." What was up with the interrogation? Neka had never given him any reason to doubt her. She laid down her fork.

James rested both hands on the table. "Answer the question."

Leaning against the cushion, she glanced away then stared at him. "He accompanied me to the house I decorated Tuesday. Why the sudden interest in my whereabouts?"

He abandoned the pretense of eating. "Stay away from Frazier. Let human resources personnel practice their trade without interference from you."

Neka's mouth hung open. "What?"

"Do you believe he just wants a hand up?"

She frowned at the panic in his eyes. "I did until today."

"What happened, Neka?"

"Jeff called me his 'special cutie' and asked for my cell phone number." Looking down, she drew her lips together. "Maybe I read too much into an innocent remark. But I didn't like his comment."

"Leave Frazier to me." Eyes narrowed into slits as he covered her hand. "I'll deal with him in the morning."

"That doesn't sound good."

James grinned. "His skills fit the contractor position Ryan promised to post next week. Since he desires to ensnare people with his words, he might as well learn from a master."

Happy he solved her problem, she resumed eating. "Shouldn't other opportunities arise once we implement the newest initiative?"

"Those positions won't materialize until next year." His narrowed eyes glowed when he grinned. "Frazier either accepts Ryan's offer or seeks employment outside the company."

216

"What if he chooses to keep his current position until the new jobs post?"

His gaze didn't falter. "The warning shot. Men will litter your life with unwelcome advances without the proper response from me."

She considered his statement. "You mean Jeff's out of a job if he doesn't relocate to St. Louis? What if I mistook his interest?"

Underneath the table, James touched her knee. "Today isn't the first time I've heard his name with yours."

Still, this seemed a bit harsh. Resting her forehead in her hand she shook her head. "Jeff is the only child of a single mom battling cancer. How can he leave his mother behind?"

"They have excellent hospitals in St. Louis." He paused, smiling encouragingly. "Keeping his present position isn't an option. He's gone by Friday. His mother can follow later if she wishes."

With the snap of her finger, she said, "How can you plan to change their lives like that?"

Chewing the last morsel of food, he tossed back his wine and dabbed the napkin across his mouth. "You told me once that actions can have unintended consequences. Pray that Frazier gives the next couple better treatment than he afforded us. Their relationship might not withstand the assault."

Breathing deeply, Neka covered her face with her hands. After a moment, she stared at him, shaking her head. "James—"

"Sweets, men have always found you attractive. Learn from this incident. As our wedding day approaches, some will try to steal you away from me." Leaning closer, he covered her hand with his. He kissed her hand, retaining it in his. "I love you. Let me shield you from them."

Unconvinced that his actions offered the best solution for the Frazier household—or that they even had the right to decide that—she weighed their options.

"The new position does represent a triple promotion if Jeff accepts the job. However, moving disrupts his mother's medical treatment." Staring into space, she massaged her earlobe, wondering what the right course was for the family. "Will Ryan make the offer?"

"He lacks on-the-job experience, but Ryan may give him a shot. I'll find out tonight."

Neka nodded noncommittally and prayed this wasn't the beginning of the return of the old James.

Chapter Twenty-Six

Dusk encircled them as they left the restaurant holding hands. Though neither one spoke on the drive to her house, tranquility permeated the atmosphere. Never in his life had James labored so hard not to offend someone else's belief system. Their viewpoints differed on a host of subjects, but James navigated them through prickly issues with the relationship intact.

Stopping in front of the mirror hanging above the plant stand, he stood behind Neka, then pulled the warmth of her body against him. Though she peacefully closed her eyes, the smile on her face didn't fool him for a moment. Her mind hunted for ways to save the hide of that undeserving man.

How could she fail to recognize his obvious attraction to her?

She was beautiful. There was no doubt about that. But her physical attributes were only a fraction of her appeal. She'd pushed herself outside her comfort zone, and it had enhanced her confidence daily. Neka no longer voiced her opinions to everyone she talked to. These days she defended her position without the judgmental tone she'd used in past discussions.

Grinning, James trailed fingers down the left side of her face. His stomach clenched as she caressed her cheek in his hand. Mesmerized by the innocence she projected, he cleared his throat and sighed.

"What do you see when you look in this mirror?"

Gazing at their reflection, she turned in his arms, resting her head on his chest.

"Us."

His body reacted strongly to the low tone of her voice. No, this woman had no idea about the power she held over anyone. Especially him.

* * *

Neka locked the door behind James, then dashed up the stairs. At the top of the landing, she bypassed her favorite hideout and raced down the hallway.

Seconds later, she entered her parents' bedroom without waiting for a reply to her knock.

"Good. You're still awake." Tossing off her sandals, she settled in the middle of their bed. Her gaze roved between the pair before cupping her cheeks in her hands. "Does James have the ability to fire employees he didn't hire?"

From their seat on the sofa, they glanced at one another and then Lawrence propped his legs on a footrest. "Why?"

Neka frowned. Maybe rushing upstairs wasn't such a good idea after all. Sometimes Dad disapproved when you interrupted a peaceful evening with his wife. Besides, her parents still hadn't really warmed up to James. She didn't want to undo any goodwill he managed to achieve, but she didn't have anyone else to turn to. "Can he fire employees who don't work for him?"

Tilting her head to the side, Karen laughed. "Every employer in Tulsa works for the operations director, me included."

"Mom ..." Neka scooted to the edge of the bed. Fully committed, there was no backing down. No one had the right to plan the life of another person. "Jeff Frazier from renovations ate lunch with me today. We had left the building before James came to take me to lunch. I hadn't made it back when he returned after one."

Lawrence chuckled. "If you ever left your cell phone on ..."

"Dad, please. I forgot to switch it on after the meeting this morning."

"Next time, place it on vibrate. So James tried in vain to reach you?"

She nodded. "Once I realized, I saw the missed calls but figured we would talk over dinner."

Neka sat on the floor at their feet. Moaning, she tapped a finger on her lips. "Don't laugh. I'm distraught my good deed backfired."

Karen patted her shoulder while grinning at Lawrence. "Perhaps we can help. What happened?"

"Jeff's looking for a career change and accompanied me to the two-story on Cincinnati Tuesday. After lunch today, I took him to the house in Bixby." She thought of James's overreaction. Neka hesitated at the sudden chill in the room. She leaned on her heels, looking between her parents. "He ruined our afternoon by calling me his 'special cutie' and requesting my cell phone number. Probably a harmless comment, but it made me uneasy."

"One, two, three, four, five—"

"Lawrence—" Karen stopped speaking when he held up his hand.

"Six, seven, eight, nine, ten … it didn't work. I'm still annoyed. Were you alone with him at either location?"

"Doug and his team worked at the Cincinnati house, but we were on our own today. He made the comment after I dropped him off at his car." Her gaze darted from one parent to the other. "I hadn't planned to take him with me. He asked to come along."

"And you agreed because …"

"He's just a coworker. I didn't think anything about it." The rebuke in her father's gaze bothered her. "It's going to cost him big time. If Ryan doesn't offer him the contractor position in St. Louis, Friday's his last day at Lacey Corp. Can James fire him?"

"The job offer is a concession to you."

If nothing else, her dad's steady stare and inflexible tone reflected total agreement with James. Sometimes it amazed her how much the two of them were alike. Jeff's days were definitely numbered. "He's the only child of a single mother undergoing chemotherapy."

Still no light of reason dawned in her dad's eyes. "Her doctor can make referrals if she decides to follow him to St. Louis," he replied.

Neka sat beside Karen. "Mom—"

Smiling, Karen touched her arm.

"It's a lost cause, honey. Twenty years ago Lawrence canceled a lucrative contract we desperately needed after the owner invited me to dinner." She glanced at her husband. "I still believe Connor had honorable intentions."

Lawrence just frowned at her.

"Lacey Corp must have an opening around Tulsa." Neka bit her bottom lip.

Karen wrapped an arm around her daughter's shoulder. "Honey, you can't fight over every difference of opinion. Spouses must learn to pick their battles."

Winking at his wife, Lawrence nodded.

Karen's expression softened at Neka's distress.

Still holding Lawrence's hand, she reached for Neka's, giving it a squeeze. Bending, she kissed Neka's cheek. "We'll pray for Jeff's mother's healing, plus a positive outcome for all participants."

The following morning Neka waited by the desk for the administrative assistant, Monica, to hang up the phone. She'd been thinking about James's comments from the night before. Someone linked her name to Jeff's before yesterday. That someone was probably a former Copley Homes employee, and before the merger, Monica Allen had been James's secretary. It had to be Monica. Only a former Copley Homes employee might speak against her.

Smiling, the woman with blue locks draping her left ear replaced the receiver. "Hi, I just took a call for your sister. Appliances ordered for the Madison Avenue triplex no longer work. At the request of the buyer, we're planning to change laundry nooks into small office areas."

Neka set her purse on the desk, frowning.

"I hate last-minute changes." She glanced at Monica, who picked up a pen prepared to jot down instructions. "A center island makes removing fourteen inches of counter space doable. Have Maria confirm measurements, then order a twenty-two-cubic-foot French door model with bottom freezer. It's a tight squeeze, but a slim-line stackable washer and dryer should fit the space."

Before she finished speaking, Kelly stumbled into the room. Neka supported her as she lurched forward. "What's wrong?"

Ashen and panting, Kelly gripped the desk.

"My water broke. Michael's on his way down to take me to the emergency room. Tammy's bringing the car to the front door. I heard your solution—go for it." Bewildered, she turned to Monica. Kelly gripped the desk edge tighter. "Only Neka will handle my designs. We already planned a remote tour of my workload."

She moaned as a contraction took her. Footsteps raced down the hallway as Michael ran into the reception area, rushing to her side.

"Your contractions are too close together. Come on. Everyone's meeting us at the hospital." He handed Neka his keys. "I'll drive Kel's car. Drop off mine at the house before heading over."

Out of breath, Tammy sidled up to the desk. "Okay, I parked right outside the front entrance. I called your doctor's office and caught Annie before she took her first patient. She's on her way to the hospital."

Kelly groaned in pain and doubled over before she reached the doorway. After she straightened, her husband swept her into his arms and hurried to the elevator. As they rounded the corner, she said, "Michael, I can walk now."

Tammy glanced at Neka. "Are you ready to leave?"

She shook her head, gesturing toward the door. "Let me talk to Monica first. I'll meet you in the lobby."

The assistant's gaze didn't falter as she studied Neka. She giggled nervously. "I know what you want to discuss. Tammy can listen. I may need a witness."

Neka shrugged her shoulders. "Your call. Were you here when James came by yesterday?"

Nodding, she glanced at the woman whose curious gazed darted between them. "I explained you went to lunch with Jeff Frazier and hadn't returned when he came back later."

"Before yesterday, someone implied we hung out together."

The wide-eyed woman raised both hands on the side of her face.

"Whoa. James and I discussed a career change for me into garden designs. I asked his advice about an internship with someone in landscaping." She glanced at Tammy, who observed Neka with narrowed eyes. "Your helping Jeff gave me the idea."

"You requested we initiate the program within Lacey Corp?" Neka squinted, looking away.

Sighing, Monica shook her head. "I had feelers out for myself, although the setup would benefit all interested personnel."

Was this the source of his misinformation? Neka picked up the work roster but then set it aside. Thoughts of establishing internships within the company crossed her mind. She smiled apologetically at Monica.

"Future possibilities may exist along those lines. Forget I asked. James didn't accuse you in any way."

"After six years of working as his secretary, I know him well. Peeved doesn't scratch the surface of his dissatisfaction with my performance." Panic fled Monica's face as she stood. She shrugged at Neka's surprised expression. "Not only did I fail to contact you, I didn't get Jeff's cell phone number from HR."

That startled Neka even more. "Would they release that information to another employee?"

"They would if the operations director made the inquiry," Tammy called over her shoulder as she stuffed Kelly's mail into a tote bag. Then, gazing at Monica, she snapped it shut. "Place a detailed outline describing an internship program in all three divisions on my desk. I'll discuss your proposal with James tomorrow. With a cohesive plan in place, he may go for the idea." She glanced at her sister. "Ready to go?"

As Neka nodded, Monica crossed fingers in the air. "Thanks, Tammy. I'll lay the report in your tray by five and offer myself as a study case to boot."

When both sisters walked away laughing, Neka waved good-bye at the pleased woman before disappearing around the corner.

* * *

Three hours later, James kissed Neka's cheek as he peered over her shoulder. "I understand how you feel. She's beautiful. I had arrived at the hospital right before Brandie delivered both Yancey and Cody."

Gaze glued to the sleeping baby, she wrapped an arm around his waist. "Uncle James flew in from Tulsa. How lovely. I just adore the butterfly designs on little Michey's blanket."

Kelly's labor had lasted two hours flat. Healthy six-pound, four-ounce Michelle Lisette Smith had kicked and screamed into the world an hour ago.

James kissed Neka's cheek without taking his gaze away from the baby. "Have you seen Kelly since the delivery?"

"Not yet. Did I mention the proud papa handed out baby work schedules last week? I'm on evening duty beginning Friday."

Chuckling, he shook his head. "That sounds like Michael."

Neka nodded.

She explained how Michael's detailed plan meant he and Kelly would have round-the-clock help for the first week. Smiling, she tapped a finger against the glass.

He laughed, and she elbowed his side. "After a week, they're on their own. Stop laughing."

Unable to stem the chuckles, he kissed her cheek.

Neka laid her head against his chest. "Do you want to congratulate Kelly and Michael?"

"I do. How about lunch? I passed Kenny and Tammy on my way in. They're heading to the office after they eat."

224

Neka smiled when Michey's body contorted into a yawn.

"I rode here with Tammy, but she left with Kenny, so Michael's sister Carla promised to drop me off at the office. Now Carla can visit longer if she wants." Her gaze grew dreamy every time she peered through the nursery window. "James, how many children do you think we should have? I want four: boy, girl, boy, girl." She smiled up at him. "I even have names picked out."

Grinning, James shook his head.

"My adorable niece made her debut the same week your first proposal unveils," she said. "Friday, the board will implement a new project." Smiling, she grabbed his arm.

He held her against his side, chuckling. "Hold on. They still have to decide which discussions should advance within their parameters." He laughed when she wagged her finger at him.

She glanced at Michey. "So the options are to axe the entire proposition, accept the Copley design, the McKinley plan, or a combination of both versions."

Apprehension flickered across his face. He'd lost the iron control over his expressions after they returned to Tulsa—at least with her. Emotions still died off in a flash, but Neka identified a few before they disappeared.

"Hey, I almost forgot to ask. Did Ryan agree to hire Jeff?"

He narrowed his eyes. "The door closed on that suggestion, but Matt offered the rehab foreman position. Frazier interviewed in June but withdrew his application due to his mother's diagnosis."

"Who filled the position then?"

"Pete Thurman. He worked for McKinley for a long time. However, he's moving to Colorado in December and wants a slower pace until retirement."

Eyes squeezed tight, Neka almost crossed her fingers. "So, he accepted?"

"Yes. Friday's his last day at the Tulsa office. There is a strong possibility his mother and grandparents may relocate to Missouri." He brushed his finger across her cheek. "If so, David promised to pick her up on the cleaning side. Jeff moves this weekend, and they'll settle in before fall."

"Mrs. Frazier works?"

"And standing on her feet eight hours a day for minimum wage, at that. Lacey Corp pays higher salaries plus provides benefits packages. Frazier understands the advantages to his family." James smiled at her. "Admit I'm an angel in disguise."

Thankful God had landed James on his feet again, she turned back to Michey. Her tiny hands curled into small fists while she yawned. Marrying next year meant James might occupy this exact spot in two years, watching their first child. Neka hoped she would do the Kelly thing and deliver in two hours.

Succumbing to daydreams, she jumped when a finger tapped her shoulder from behind. James had moved away, and in his place, Teri's amazed gaze stared at her friend's daughter.

"What a gorgeous baby, just like her mother. Look, she scrunched up her little face." Still looking at Michey, she nudged Neka. "I'm trading places with your sister next year."

Her gaze trailed to Teri's flat abdomen. "Anyone I know?"

"This summer I received two marriage proposals."

That was a speedy turnaround from a woman who was just engaged. James had said she dated other men. "Then I'll pray you choose the right man or none of the above."

Frowning, Teri switched her gaze to Neka.

Voice lowered, Neka leaned closer. "Heads turn whenever you enter a room. The perfect man for Teri Campbell might wait in the wings hoping to be noticed."

Teri stared at her in disbelief. "How did such an astute lady end up with a reprobate like James?"

"Teri..."

Avoiding eye contact, Teri studied the sleeping baby. "How's Kelly doing?"

Neka stepped away from the window. "We're on our way to congratulate the proud parents."

"Michey will keep me busy until you leave."

"We won't stay long." Neka moved away as Teri pressed her face against the window.

* * *

James closed his eyes, shutting out the world's constant demand to perform, threatening the mental safety net that had taken years to set in place. The calmness he'd perfected took a beating after proposing to Neka.

226

Since then, she'd upset his life by infusing joy and grief into each day. She made waking up each morning worthwhile but she broke through all of his defenses. Her wishes to delay the wedding disrupted the last part of the plan he'd envisioned for years.

Neka and the children who now held names completed the picture. He massaged his knotted shoulders while he tackled the other antagonist threatening his stability.

On Wednesday, board members voted to implement the project he toiled day and night to develop. The session today would decide which initiative to enact. All morning he'd crunched numbers to validate his ideas. It was a pointless exercise since arguments from both sides ended the day before, but it gave him a sense of control.

Early feedback indicated David's approach had more support. It seemed the board preferred a calm veer into small-city development instead of penetrating both marketplaces in simultaneous blitzes.

A glance at the clock revealed only five minutes had passed since the last time he'd looked. This was a pitiful end to an otherwise marvelous week.

Some failed to grasp the high stakes of the conference going on down the hall. But his godparents flying in with his parents this evening signaled a tremendous undertaking began that day. Monday the advisory board converged for a weeklong session.

Neka believed allowing David input on his vision was a mistake. Had he miscalculated by giving his best friend a spot in the limelight?

* * *

Gliding into the elevator, Neka kept her finger glued to the button. She had prayed throughout the short drive to the office that the meeting would adjourn before lunch. In her haste to see James, she practically careened into a tall woman waiting outside the elevator doors and then took a more dignified pace. But she bolted around the corner after passing two men debating some issue beside the water cooler. Her heels clicked on tiled floor as she scurried down the hallway to his office.

Her spirits sunk at the sight of James staring into space. He did that a lot lately. In unguarded moments, he looked like a person overloaded with hardship. She knocked on the door and smiled.

"Cheryl's away from her desk."

Meeting in the middle of the room, she lifted her face for his kiss. Every fiber in her body tingled at his touch. Time suspended every time he kissed her. However, this time something heightened the experience.

An urgency within him invited her to satisfy his hunger.

James maintained the embrace long after their kiss ended. Arms wrapped around her body, he leaned against her as if he needed her strength to stand upright. The significant moment quelled the questions she'd planned to ask. The tension assailing him weighed heavy in the room.

Neka stroked his arm. "The board will strike the best course for the network. No matter which version they adopt, you deserve honors for conceiving the idea."

He raised an eyebrow. "So I win whether or not they accept my proposal?"

She laid a finger on his lips. "Over three months ago I challenged you to take us to the next level. You accomplished the goal within weeks."

Tension visibly drained from his body.

"I'm proud of your efforts." She paused, smiling. "God chose you to hold the reigns for Lacey Corp. Love always finds a way."

"Your serenity penetrates the core of who I am." Closing his eyes, James leaned his forehead against hers and whispered, "That place where I shield myself from unimaginable hurt."

Neka struggled to breathe. She always prayed for openness, but his secrets overwhelmed her. James trusted her enough to expose his most-hidden fears.

"I thank God you have faith in me, sweets." He trailed a finger along her cheek, and his whole demeanor changed. "Here's my take on the outcome. Style shapes the essence of any company. A lost round sets a precedent for future negotiations concerning David and me."

Chapter Twenty-Seven

"What's the verdict?" James's mother asked before closing the car door.

Neka identified with the wistful look in Fran's eyes. She hadn't spoken to James since leaving his office over three hours ago. She shrugged, fastening her seat belt. "He hasn't contacted me, and I refuse to keep calling. My phoning every fifteen minutes might unnerve him."

Gene entered the back seat as she spoke. "A prudent decision we're all trying to follow. Charles and Maureen decided to check into their hotel before coming over." Clasping hands behind his head, he stretched out his legs. "James said your parents are dining with us this evening. We will know soon enough."

Neka glanced at him in the rearview mirror. "I picked up dessert on the way to the airport."

They drove along, making small talk. When Fran mentioned Brandie, Neka remembered her future sister-in-law waited for news as well. "How is she holding up under the pressure?"

"So-so. All of us realize that profound ramifications exist regardless of the outcome. Implementing David's plan undermines James's authority."

Neka glanced at Fran when she slowed downed for a stop sign. Though no one else's opinion mattered anymore, the censorious expression kept her from responding. Interim mishaps didn't shake the confidence that James would one day run Lacey Corp.

She trusted God on this one.

"Neka seems unconcerned about the outcome of the meeting. Do you agree with her nonchalance?" Fran stared into the back seat at her husband.

His hands spread out in appeasement.

"Lawrence moves fast on familiar terrain. We'll find out how he operates on uncharted ground." Leaning forward, he captured his wife's hand. "From where I sit, it could go either way. Both plans have aspects of his technique."

Pulling into the driveway, Neka shot out of the car. His parents' vacillating had spoiled any enthusiasm for company, and she longed for a quiet evening for two. Dessert in one hand, she grabbed a suitcase and headed up the walk ahead of his parents. James stepped outside as she reached the door. His blank expression gave nothing away.

"Any news?"

He removed the case from her hand, then reopened the door.

"Forty minutes ago, I left the office before the meeting ended." Studying his father lifting luggage from the trunk, he sat the suitcase inside the door. "We'll talk after I bring their bags inside."

Neka placed packages on the counter, frowning. James hadn't entered the pristine kitchen since coming home. Nibbling her bottom lip, she placed her hands on her hips, looking around the room. Six guests expected to eat a wholesome meal in about ninety minutes. The future unfurled before her eyes. Long days and evenings filled with unending tasks. Hordes of activity buried beneath countless commitments.

Neka had too much to do and too little time in which to do it.

She rearranged furniture and placed flowers around the space with practiced hands. Thank God she'd arranged the floral designs after work yesterday. Her well-trained gaze flitted around the area.

Back inside the kitchen, she tied on an apron she'd brought over after the first visit to his condo. It was a good thing the real food preparation had happened the previous evening. Autopilot served her well as she sprinkled paprika over a potato casserole before sliding it into the oven. Next she grated serrano peppers into a skillet before pouring in stir-fry vegetables. Engrossed in slicing bread, Neka jumped when James spoke to her from the doorway.

"My folks decided to rest until our guests arrive."

Nodding, she reached for the olive oil and dripped it over the vegetable mixture. "I suppose clearing off his desk for a week took its toll. Especially since Gene had one day to read through a seventy-five-page business plan. Plus, your father's and Charles's absence triples David's workload."

"He'll rise to the occasion."

His sharp tone penetrated through her multiple tasks. Sighing, Neka set the flame low and cupped his face in her hands. The anguish he failed to hide shocked her. "Only you demand excellence from yourself, and no one else. Most people never reach the perfection they want from others."

He kissed the tip of her nose, brushing his lips across her mouth. "Your continued support means everything to me."

Neka gazed into his eyes, which were filled with uncertainty. "I celebrate you, not your achievements. One project doesn't define a man. If the board chooses an alternate path, your leadership will still lead us to victory."

James drew Neka into the deepest kiss they'd shared. His firm hands caressed her back, and she shivered. When she pulled away, he groaned but released her. He seemed to be bereft without her nearness.

She moved robotically, but her body pulsated from his touch. She'd wanted to comfort him, not stimulate his libido. Stunned at her own reaction to a simple kiss, she chastised her lapse of judgment. She was not some schoolgirl; she understood sexual surrender.

Her voice quivered as she tried to banish the desire to fall into his arms again. "Time's running out. Better make the juice splash."

Full of regrets, she floated about the kitchen in a daze, refusing to undergo a tutorial in losing her self-respect. Awareness of his love almost vanquished her resolve. But the knowledge that he'd slept with other women made chastity more desirable than ever. There would be no sexual escapades outside the marriage bed. Period. Thank God she discovered her weakness in a setting adverse to seduction.

* * *

His body had adjusted to the lack of sexual gratification. Only teenagers seduced girls in the kitchen while their parents slept upstairs, but old habits die hard. He'd used physical pleasure as a panacea since he was seventeen.

James watched Neka. Her skill in the kitchen ensured a piping-hot meal would grace his buffet table on schedule.

Suddenly and surprisingly, his anger emerged—this woman irritated him beyond compare. Until five minutes ago, she'd fit his life as if made for him alone.

But she imposed herself into private sanctuaries no other person had ever dared to invade. Neka lived by all or nothing methods and required total surrender. She chipped away his core, draining his lifeblood in steady drips.

Lawrence.

The ache that wracked his soul seized his chest. She hoped to replicate her father in him.

231

Maureen peeked through the blinds at the sound of closing car doors and glanced at Neka when she remained seated. "Your parents are here."

The high voice filtered through Neka's gloom. While both sets of parents tried not to show partiality for their own son, the negativity in the room sapped her strength. Boosting everyone else's confidence had depleted hers.

On top of everything, James refused to look at her. Opening the door before the doorbell rang, she smiled into her mom's frowning face.

How did Karen always see whatever her daughters tried to hide?

With a smile she hoped looked genuine, Neka embraced her mom. "Come in. You're right on time."

Her father handed over two bottles of Riesling, chilled and ready to serve. Though she and her mom didn't drink, she beamed up at him when he hugged her. Wine served with dinner meant they had cause to celebrate.

Before her parents could settle on the love seat, Charles popped the number one question. He rubbed his hand together, grinning broadly. "What's the ruling on village building? Do we sprint or stroll?"

Glancing around the room, Lawrence stretched an arm around his wife. "The direct approach brings us home. I'll brief you if the dinner can hold five minutes. David was informed on the drive over."

Neka appraised James before nodding. "Sure."

"Sprinting requires running short distances at maximum speed. Strolling implies walking without plan or purpose." He stared at Charles with serious eyes. "Lacey Corps sets precedents others imitate. Spring is the target date."

Apparently pleased with the disclosure, Lawrence sat down.

Did that mean they were combining the plans?

She was about to ask, but a mutinous expression contorted James's features before they relaxed into a calm façade. Still smiling, Neka centered her attention on him. "I'll have dinner out in ten minutes. James, will you please assist me?"

In the kitchen, James considered her with a blank expression as the door swung shut. He froze people out to keep them off balance. His eyes were deep and unreadable, and she felt like she was falling into them. Averting her gaze, she cleared her throat. "What did my dad say that upset you?"

Her shoulders drooped as rationality hit against the wall he instantly put up. Instead of instilling confidence, the question seemed to provoke him. He clenched his jaw, and that seemed to be the only thing that kept his bitterness in check.

"Don't downplay the shrewdness on display in the living room. He didn't reveal anything." He paused when she inched away, looking downward. "Forget about the board—whose design did he choose? Which plan will we follow?"

Neka shook her head, trying to understand his anger. "Yes, the brief was minuscule, but I took it to mean that he'll blend both plans into a cohesive one. Doesn't that mean you both win?"

His pained expression brought tears to her eyes. Gene allowing Ryan and Matt's constant ridicule weighed heavier than she'd imagined. James measured his self-worth by the acclaim of other people. For him, success meant everyone applauded his accomplishments.

Lacey Corp adopting a project he proposed wasn't enough to sustain him. Her dad failed to acknowledge his brilliance openly.

Stiffening at her touch, he brushed her hand from his arm. "I poured my life into that proposal, leaving you on your own to dart about town without me."

His sneer dared her to disagree.

Neka sank beneath his contempt. It produced vivid reminders of repeatedly backing down every time someone hurt her feelings. Of putting on a smile instead of fighting back.

Tears formed as she sought ways to relieve his agony. "Though the information was scarce, he'll speak in-depth to both of you over the weekend."

James ran a hand through his hair. "I expected an outline tonight."

She wished she could make him realize there was nothing to prove. "Does it have to be an either-or proposition? Unfamiliar territory lies ahead. Why can't we take our time where it's new and rapidly set up familiar parts?"

"So he's feeling his way along?" He barked out a harsh laugh.

Sadness wrapped itself around Neka like a cloak as she searched for an escape from his sarcasm. "I won't play guessing games. A conference call with you and David will resolve the matter."

A tinge of hope sprang alive in his eyes, then died. "And if these phantom calls fail to materialize?"

She threw up both hands. "Just once, can't you be reasonable?"

Finally, Neka witnessed the turmoil he hid so well. His face mirrored his fierce battle to reclaim control. The emotions assaulting him tore her apart.

He'd spent a lifetime covering up the devastation threatening to destroy him. In the past, he'd faced adversity alone. Why couldn't he comprehend he had a partner in her?

Lord, show him love means more than sharing good times.

Emotions reigned in, he touched her cheek and frowned.

Neka leaned in, against her better judgment.

He ran a finger across her lips, eyes smoldering when she trembled. She stopped his hand, and his eyes flashed.

"Don't be angry. You know how I feel about this ..." She frowned. "You're trying to push me away—"

James held up his hand. "Reason will come to me if you find a place in your heart to stand beside me. Or am I relegated to the backroom when it comes to your family?"

He abruptly charged through the door, making it forcefully swing open and rush back into place.

Trembling, Neka slumped against the wall. He had worked himself into a fit of rage over something so easily explained. She wiped tears from her cheeks when her mom rushed into the kitchen. Karen's anger sobered her quickly.

"Are you okay? Honey, what happened?"

Wiping tears, she attempted a smile. "Please don't say anything. Just give me a few minutes, and I'll have the food out. Okay?"

Her mother just stared at her.

Neka rested her head on the refrigerator. "I'm okay, Mom. This is something I have to work out alone."

Inhaling deeply, Karen gathered her into her arms. Neka embraced her mom tightly and laid her face on her hair, swaying back and forth. The gentle motion brought back happy memories. Those loving arms could slay life's dragons. Kissing the top of her head, her mom left the kitchen.

* * *

Neka didn't know how she made it through the rest of the evening, but she did. Bewildered, she sped home after leaving the condo. Halfway to her house she realized James was behind her. Confusion changed to anger before reaching her neighborhood. No matter how many scriptures she quoted, her irritation remained.

Dinner had been ruined, despite efforts to salvage the damage he'd done. Their guests raced through the meal until his father begged an early night. Thank God someone put an end to it.

After disrupting everyone's evening, he had the audacity to ensure her safety getting home. She should've left with the guests and let him clean up his own kitchen. Neka fought the impulse to make him travel over half the city while placating his conscience.

Lord, did we travel this far to hit an impasse twelve weeks later? Did we blend lives together for nothing? Declaring his love failed to erase our problems. We're further apart than ever.

Parking crooked in front of the garage, she dashed across the lawn.

"Neka, wait."

His voice cut through her anguish. Key ready for a speedy entrance, she forged ahead until he grabbed her arm. Failing to break his hold, she spun around to face him.

"Let go."

His grip on her arm loosened, and she tapped her foot on the ground counting to ten in her head, immune to his tormented expression. For once he had failed to come up with a backup strategy.

"Please stand still so we can talk. Let's not end the evening in disagreement."

She crunched twigs beneath her shoes. "You disrespected me while we had guests—our families! What is there to talk about?"

His apologetic gaze begged forgiveness. "We got off on the wrong foot tonight ..."

"I didn't berate you." Neka kicked a loose branch across the lawn. She just wanted to go inside before she crumbled at his feet. Eyes half-closed, she covered her mouth to keep from crying out.

James held out his hand in conciliation but then backed up, shaking his head. His scathing expression glued her arms to her side. He turned aside, peering across the lawn, lips pressed tight.

"I don't need this. You refuse to talk to me? Fine. I won't beg for forgiveness from anyone. Good-bye," he called over his shoulder as he walked away. Right before sliding into the car seat, he paused, staring at her.

Exhaling, she rushed into speech. "Didn't you mean to say 'so long'?"

Sorrow clung to his face until he shut the door. As he sped away, Neka stretched out fingers as if they were magnets that could pull him back to her side.

Tears soaked her neck and collar. Her gaze followed his progress until the car disappeared around the bend. Alone, she cried until her mom appeared at her side. Even then, she refused to tear her focus away from the empty road.

Karen brushed tears away from her cheeks. "How long are you going stare at a vacant street? He's halfway home by now."

Neka hung her head, sobbing into her hands. "I think it's over."

Her mother's strong arm wrapped around her shoulder and guided her to the house. "Should the relationship have begun?"

"How can you ask that question? I experienced the best time of my life with him."

Still walking, Karen tilted her head to one side. "Really? Three months kowtowing to a sullen man overshadows twenty-one years of living with a family who cares about you?"

Fresh tears dripped from her cheeks. "Oh Mom, you know what I mean. Until a few hours ago, James exuded optimism."

"At the moment, he feels ill-used."

"Why? He has so much to be thankful for. Those ideas originated from him, not David."

"James is a conflicted man." Karen opened the door, then stepped aside. "Come inside."

Peeking into connecting rooms, Neka crept into the foyer. "I don't want Tammy and Dad to see me this way."

Karen placed a finger to her lips, then glanced up and down the hallway. "Shush! Head upstairs while I cut them off at the pass."

Giggles escaped Neka, in spite of the tears. "I love you, Mom. You always know the right words to say."

At the top of the stairs, she gazed at the closed doors and then slipped into her bedroom, unnoticed. Ambling around the space, she glided her hand across treasured objects from her childhood, seeking comfort but not finding it. She sat on the bed. A safe haven in the past, thoughts of James followed her into the room.

There was a knock at the door, and it opened before she could answer.

Carrying a tissue box, her mother kicked off her sandals and sat on the bed, facing her. Peace clashed with grief as Neka steadied her breathing. Karen patted her knee when fresh tears flowed.

"I hate seeing you cry over a man."

Neka grabbed a tissue from the box and blew her nose. "I'm sorry," she said softly between sobs. "But we ... we lost everything we built over one ... one disagreement. How does a relationship collapse on one misunderstanding?"

Head tilted to the side, Karen surveyed her. "You and James differ on a host of issues. Until recently, his lifestyle conflicted with your beliefs. Yet, some quality you possess attracted him."

Three months analyzing that same thing hadn't produced any results. "We've lived such different lives."

"What draws you to him?"

"He always treats me like I'm special."

Smiling, Karen leaned closer. "I think he admires your attributes that frustrate him the most." She paused as if carefully choosing her words. "Adversity allows the real James to remain hidden while his alter ego fortifies for battles he only imagines he has to wage."

Nothing added up anymore. His behavior defied reason. "He claims to seek godly wisdom."

"Like most people, he accepts the advice that agrees with his personal convictions."

"That was before St. Louis." Neka shook her head, frowning. "He travels a different road these days."

Karen's eyes narrowed. "When your destination is Kay Avenue, who cares whether you approach from Juniper Boulevard or Casey Road as long as you reach the target?"

"So ... when I think he's compromising, he isn't?"

"A man like James doesn't give in unless he's forced to stand down." She laughed when Neka shook her head. "Trust me. I married his mirror image four months after my eighteenth birthday."

Neka gasped. "Dad treats you like his queen."

Karen sighed, shaking her head. "Our peaceful existence came at a heavy price. Challenges existed from the beginning. Until we met, Lawrence only gave lip service to racial equality."

Perplexed, Neka feathered fingers through her hair. "What changed his mind?"

Her mother's brown eyes twinkled with suppressed laughter. "Meeting me opened up possibilities he never realized existed."

Pushing the tissue box aside, Neka scooted nearer to her mom. Finally, a topic pulled her mind away from James. "Tell me the first obstacle you faced together."

"Neither family sanctioned our marriage." She shook her head as if reliving the hostilities. "Your grandfather officiated, and my family attended the wedding, but only your Uncle Ed stood with your father."

Really? She'd never noticed her father's family treated them any differently than their cousins. As children, Bridgett and Katie practically lived at their house. It was hard to imagine they'd had a problem with an interracial marriage.

"When did the others have a change of heart?"

Karen's cheeks flashed the dimples Neka had inherited. "On both sides, I think their lovely nieces eased their fears somewhat."

"How does James now resemble Dad then?"

"Lawrence was a rough diamond too. It took years to polish him up. Don't laugh. Life was difficult early on." Karen set the tissue box on the nightstand and brushed Neka's hair away from her face. "At first your father avoided my family. Said he hated hypocrites—his code word for Christians. Now he realizes not everyone invoking Jesus's name knows Him."

Her parents' bumpy road had smoothed out in the end. Could she count on James's and hers to do that? If God destined them for one another ...

"James said good-bye."

"Your granny says every closed eye isn't sleep and every good-bye isn't gone."

"Meaning?"

"Experience and personal knowledge cause us to rely on what we know. We go astray when we believe in our own infallibility."

A gateway to hope imbued her spirit, but tears flowed down her cheeks. "His good-bye sounded final."

"At that moment it probably was. But a man with plans doesn't discard them on a whim." Karen stood beside the bed and raised her hand to quell the question forming in Neka's mind. "Just know that James expects life on his terms."

Frowning, she contemplated her mom's remark. "Tonight he placed that same label on Dad."

"I hear we often see in others what we fail to realize in ourselves."

Neka bit her lower lip. "You think he'll come back to me?"

Karen held out the tissue box. "Take a few and dry those tears. I don't believe he left you. Now let me ask you the question you should be asking: Will you accept him back once he returns?"

Considering the answer, Neka glanced away. Could she just sweep her heartbreak under the rug?

"My love remains the same."

"In those early years, I regretted getting married. Is he worth the years it'll take God to smooth out those rough edges?"

Neka rose to her knees, frowning. How could her mom ever have qualms about marrying the best husband in the world? She weighed her options. "If given the chance, would you do it differently?"

"You're not me. Listen, most people wouldn't understand the internal struggle gripping James." Firm fingers cupped Neka's chin. "There's a mysterious quality about him that draws people closer. A lot of women imagine they're the one to tame him. Quite a few men attempt to imitate him."

Neka frowned. "I don't understand."

"People rave about the positive changes in his personality. James often projected a friendliness that never existed." Karen tilted her head to the side as if examining Neka's reaction. "While we witness the progression in his character, you walk by his side through the process. Remember, not now doesn't mean not ever. Talk to God. Strength comes from Jesus."

Chapter Twenty-Eight

Neka sprang from the chaise when the doorbell sounded and dashed downstairs. Thank God no one else was home to view their reunion. Before opening the door, she examined her appearance in the mirror, making sure every strand of hair was in place.

Last night she'd sunk deeper into the jaws of despair. But this morning her enthusiasm intensified while reading her Bible.

Though James might be angry, love wouldn't disappear on command. Growing pains occurred in every relationship worth maintaining. For four years, they'd weathered life's storms together. Mending the breach today would only improve their relationship.

But one look at James undid her optimism. Overnight he'd built up a wall of aloofness impossible to scale. She'd never seen him like this. She couldn't even speak. While she searched for ways to interact, he stacked the deck against any worthwhile discussion with his hard expression.

If he wasn't there to make up, why had he come?

Neka moved away from the door, hoping he'd come inside. Grin set in place, he shut the door and leaned against the frame. Instead of speaking, his gaze flickered across her body as if engraving her in his memory. He slowly approached her.

If he was waiting for her to beg forgiveness, they would stand here all day. From now on, they would work at this relationship together or not at all.

"Yesterday wasn't one of my best moments. I dumped my disappointment on the only bright spot of my day." He trailed a finger over her left cheek. "Weeks of sleep deprivation undermined my common sense."

"Sleep deprivation." The words nearly stuck in her throat.

James dropped his hand. "Because my father rejected ... my last proposition, I poured myself into this new one. Our ideas contrasted, but they both

241

had strengths and weaknesses. This will be good for Lacey Corp but bad for my ego."

The mirthless chuckle reminded Neka of her mother's question from last night. How long would it take before years of self-doubt faded away? She was torn between easing his hurt and wanting him to break the chains that held him to his past.

She sighed. "The compromise allows us to implement the best concepts of both sides. Everyone profits from superb ideas from two intelligent men."

A tiny light glowing in hazel eyes was the only sign her comment struck home. Maybe their meeting wasn't a bust after all. Her spirit lifted when he smiled. "Are you hungry? I can have lunch ready in twenty minutes."

Her shoulders slumped when he shook his head.

"I'm on my way to the airport. David called in an S.O.S. this morning. Monday is the last day to purchase a small hotel and surrounding buildings close to downtown. If he fails to act, the owner will list the properties Tuesday. My flight departs in two hours." He hesitated, then drew her into his arms. "David never asks for help he doesn't need."

Neka laid her cheek against his chest without voicing dissent. Since James hunted for avenues to distance himself, she would send him off in peace.

Some time without him sounded good to her at this point. Their frequent squabbles over the last few days had stocked her delay-the-wedding storehouse. Time spent away from Neka might cause him to appreciate her viewpoint.

Or it might cause him to end the relationship altogether.

She smiled at him through tear-filled eyes. "I'll miss you."

Sorrow entered the steady gaze. Kissing her forehead, he pulled her closer. "I'll miss you more."

In ten minutes flat, she locked the door behind him, refusing to wave him off. The words "so long" rang in her ears.

* * *

By the following Friday, Lacey Corp buzzed with gossip. Everyone knew the advisory board met in the conference room next to her dad's office. Not part of that scene, Neka spent hours touring a property ready for renovation. After a mind-numbing day, she eased her feet from a new pair of heels.

Once again, she swiveled around to face the wall. Staring at the blank space brought a strange contentment.

Whenever she wasn't working, thoughts of James filled her mind. Each night before going to bed she received duty calls with mini progress reports. But it was always just business.

Of course, David purchased the property. Knowing him, the decision was made before speaking to James last Saturday. Whether James dispatched the S.O.S. or responded to it didn't matter. He was flying home tonight, and Brandie's family would drive down tomorrow.

Expelling a long breath, she stuffed her laptop into her satchel, too tired to move. It weighed heavily on her shoulder as she crossed the hall to her sister's office. Fatigue from handling Kelly's workload had depleted her passion for the job. Two weeks down—only ten more to go.

* * *

James replayed his parting scene with Neka as the plane back to Tulsa took off. Reaffirming their relationship was uppermost in his mind. He should've assisted David long distance. While he labored in another city, Neka slipped further away. It seemed her interest waned with each day.

Unable to find a comfortable position, he readjusted the seat for the tenth time.

Their separation held significant consequences for him. Neka yearned for the James she fell in love with—the image created during four years of wishful thinking. Unsatisfied with the real-life man, she raced to revamp him into her version of a godly husband.

Last Friday's overreactions erected obstacles that would be difficult to overcome. Friction had jeopardized their fragile romance from the start.

He sighed. Those baseless accusations demeaning Lawrence's wisdom embarrassed him now. Especially since her father had managed the company successfully for years before bringing him onboard.

Expecting Lacey Corp to incorporate his entire plan was unrealistic. Whichever path they chose, the idea had originated with him. Neka had figured out that he drafted the proposal alone. But Lawrence believed both men applied the same commitment to their plans.

He imagined the headwind if others recognized his abilities. Then naysayers couldn't undercut his contribution. But it was Lawrence's way to reward excellence without flattery. Continuous praise wasn't in his repertoire.

Hands curled into fists, he grappled with the core of the problem. He was a self-made man yet thrived on praise from peers. Only one person stood beside him in the storm he'd created before leaving Tulsa.

And the memory of her tear-filled eyes had assaulted his mind for a week.

James hated the shabby treatment he'd given Neka. Now she drifted away from him. Those unreturned calls forced him to stay in touch with her. This unusual conduct contradicted her usual desire to smooth everyone's ruffled feathers.

Was someone else advising her actions? If not, she avoided him on her own accord.

Rotating his head from side to side, he counted the cost of losing her.

God, remind her of how much I love her. I can't live without her.

He sipped his coffee, but it was too hot, and it spilled out of his mouth and over the empty seat in front of him. Mopping a handkerchief across his chin, James peered at stains dotting his shirt and slacks.

What had changed? Before they left St. Louis, he'd realized Neka fitted him to perfection. But his current thoughts made it seem like he'd always welcomed her into his life. He grimaced at the thought.

Had marrying her been an unknown hope, even before St. Louis?

James shook his head. Even four years ago, seventeen-year-old girls were not on his radar. But there was no denying the pretty teenager had grown into the beautiful woman he knew today.

Neka surpassed every youthful dream he'd ever had about who he'd marry. She would make a wonderful wife and an impeccable mother. Far from being a pushover, her genuine love for other people reduced his self-indulgence.

She'd never given in to the numerous men who'd sought her affection, ignoring invitations to dance at parties and refusing dates to various events. She failed to see that the boys who ridiculed her in high school hounded her for dates in college.

Men like Jeff Frazier. What other man hoped to steal her away? Like antennae, hair on the back of his neck rose.

James departed the plane, took a taxi home, and sprawled across the sofa. He prayed Neka would answer the phone. Nothing mattered more than securing the affection of the woman he loved.

On his trip to St. Louis, he'd alternated between missing her and blaming her for his woes. But the flight home had made everything clear. There would be no more understating the depths of his affection.

Finally, her voice sounded over the line. For the first time since he'd left Tulsa, she answered during the day. "Hello, sweets, I got home an hour ago. Still working?"

"You changed your flight. I'm printing designs for an office complex in Kelly's office."

"Holding up okay?"

"I'm fine."

James frowned. Where was the excitement at hearing his voice? Instead, she just sounded tired. Neka excelled at her job, but dealing with his stubbornness had exacerbated her massive workload.

"Preparations for a quiet dinner for two are underway in the kitchen." He paused, closing his eyes in a silent prayer. "I hope you left the evening open for us."

"What time do you want me to come over?"

Her tone still didn't change, but at least she didn't say no. His tension fled. God gave him a chance to make amends.

"The folks fly out this evening. I'll pick you up at six."

"See you then."

James stared at the silent cell phone. Neka couldn't wait to end the call. For the first time in years, he got on his knees to pray.

God, I need a miracle to turn this ship around ...

* * *

He finished his dinner preparations and showed up early to pick her up.

When he finally saw Neka, he swept her into his arms and held her against his chest. He had missed seeing her every day but hadn't realized until this moment just how much. It took a few seconds, but Neka laid her cheek on his shirt, relaxing in his arms.

He opened his eyes to see Tammy.

"Hello, James," Tammy said. "I'm about to visit the most adorable baby ever born."

The two sisters smiled at one another, and he managed a weak grin of his own.

"I guarantee that belief will change over the next two years." He felt the smile reach his eyes. "Is getting married in two weeks causing jitters?"

She laughed. "No way. I've been after Kenny since my fifteenth birthday."

Making small talk, the trio strolled down the pathway to his car. His gaze followed Tammy's scurry across the lane. Of course she'd hung around in case Neka needed her. He had to respect her love for her sister, but she could forget any hopes that he might ruin the best relationship of his life.

They settled into the car but rode without speaking. Her greeting showed that she wanted their relationship to recover. He glanced at her several times before breaking the silence. "Brandie's anxious to get fitted for her brides-maid dress. Did you set up an appointment?"

She nodded, staring out the window. "Thursday at six o'clock was the only evening everyone was free to grab a meal afterward. Your mother and Maureen bought their outfits yesterday."

He glanced at her. "Your mind is elsewhere. What are you thinking?"

Keeping her face averted, she smiled a little sadly. "How tired I am."

James searched for ways to spark her attention. "Our favorite home-cooked meal is warming in the oven."

Closing her eyes, Neka clasped her fingers against her lips. "Thank you."

Gripping the steering wheel, he slowed the car almost to a crawl. He pictured her standing in a field pulling petals off a daisy, saying, "He loves me; he loves me not," indifferent to the outcome. Perhaps he'd read too much into that hug.

"Look, I botched my apology before leaving Tulsa. This is my attempt to make amends."

Neka shook her head. "Can you? Can you patch up the breach? Won't it just split apart again?"

She practically turned her back to stare out her window.

He studied the road ahead through narrowed eyes. Good thing they were close to home. The home they would share together in less than three months.

Lord, make it so.

James glanced at Neka, thinking of ways to stimulate her interest. "Not if we come to a consensus."

She laughed tersely. "Is compromise the new word for getting your own way these days?"

Neka refused to cooperate. His shoulders tightened into knots, stiffening his neck.

James rotated his head slightly to relieve the pressure. "You're not going to make this easy for me, are you?"

Shifting in her seat, she faced him. "Not anymore. From the day I surprised you at the airport, I labored at this relationship. I elevated accommodating you into a work of art."

The hurt in her eyes made his stomach clench.

What type of reception had he expected? He'd spat out enough venom in the kitchen that would have crush the average person, ignored her in front of their families, virtually broken off the engagement, and then flown out of town, leaving her alone.

Until that moment, he'd only considered his neglect on the periphery of how events had affected him.

"I always cultivated our friendship." It was weak, and he knew it.

"What friendship? You've steered the helm since we met. For four years I lived my life according to James." Neka laid her hand on her forehead, shaking her head. Finally, she squinted at him. "You suggested I live at home instead of the dorm. You suggested I forget about dating until the right man asked me out. You suggested I stop trying to secure friendships. To allow people to gravitate toward me."

James pulled the car into his driveway, letting the engine idle. "You've lost me."

"Why did you befriend me?" She folded her arms.

He studied her. "So my previous answer isn't good enough anymore?"

"Nothing about our relationship is."

James flinched. "Not even your belief that God intends our marriage? Or have you discarded those beliefs right along with trusting me?"

She glanced away, looking downward. "I still believe God chose us for one another."

Leaning closer, he turned her face toward him. "So you threw out obedience to Him to enact your own schedule?"

"I thought we were having a conversation about you." Neka opened the car door.

James stepped out of the car. Tension throbbed between them as they left the driveway. He took her hand and led her into the kitchen.

* * *

Neka halted in the doorway, mesmerized by the romantic scene he'd created. James had removed the table extension, bringing two chairs closer together. Tiger lilies adorned the centerpiece. Either someone revealed her favorite flower, or he simply liked the bloom himself.

Whatever he'd prepared smelled terrific. The variety of aromas wafting through the air made identifying the main course impossible. She seated herself at the table while he poured their drinks. Their gaze met.

She laughed. "Juice splash. How did you know the recipe?"

"I've watched you make it plenty of times." He hung a mint sprig on her frosted glass.

He'd even remembered the garnish. It shouldn't have mattered that he'd planned this special evening for them, but somehow it did.

James placed the food on the table then joined her. He'd made the perfect meal for an imperfect couple.

He clasped her hand and bowed his head. "Father, bless our food and our lives together ... don't let me self-destruct."

Her eyes popped open, surveying him again. Did he refer to an emotional collapse?

Oh please, make it clear, Lord.

Light conversation carried them through dinner. She laughed at his stories about Yancey and Cody. When they were done eating, he scooted back his chair, and Neka yawned.

In the living room, they sat close together on the sofa. Eyes closed, she laid her head against the cushion. The weeklong friction between them seeped away. Harmony replaced her insecurities, and hope banished uncertainties. A magical mist of peace united them as one.

Neka lost the fight to hash out their differences as he hugged her to his chest. Images of his birthday celebration sprung to life as she drifted to sleep.

* * *

"Wake up, sleeping beauty."

She stirred, stretching her arms and opening her eyes as James stroked her face, smiling down at her. Sometime during the evening they'd shifted positions. He had one leg on the cushion and the other foot on the floor. She lay against him with both feet curled on the sofa.

"What time is it?"

He glanced at the silver clock hanging on the wall. "Ten thirty. I'll drive you home."

Amazement highlighted her features. "Did we resolve anything tonight?"

"What we already knew—we belong together." James chuckled.

She felt more relaxed, but nothing had changed. Instead of coming to terms, she'd just fallen asleep. "For how long?"

James ran his fingers through her hair as if searching for the perfect response. The intensity in his gaze surrounded her heart. "Forever, Neka. Trust me, it's forever."

She removed his hand from her hair, squeezing his fingers. "Not now doesn't mean not ever."

James jumped up and grabbed keys off the table. "It does to me."

Slipping on her shoes, Neka darted to the door. An ugly thought had bothered her since the Teri incident at her home. In weak moments, she couldn't help but wonder if James truly intended to marry her. Sometimes she was haunted by how he'd preplanned their own engagement to end. Now she had an answer—by dumping their inability to compromise at her feet.

She paused, laying her forehead against the door. "Are you saying the engagement is off if I want to change the date to next year?"

James sighed and looked away. "I don't deal well with ultimatums."

She blinked away tears. This was definitely not the evening she'd hoped for. Since there was nothing left to hold on to, why not end it now?

A scripture entered her mind. *Against all hope, Abraham in hope believed ...*

"Neither do I, James. Take me home."

Chapter Twenty-Nine

Neka enjoyed watching Brandie inspect her bridesmaid's dress for the third time since hanging it in the closet. Her future sister-in-law seemed pleased with the roaring twenties vintage-style design. Because Brandie lived in a different state and couldn't drop by for alterations, her dress was completely finished. Mrs. Goolsby was a dressmaker who attended her church and specialized in creating vintage-style clothing. She'd worked from measurements Neka supplied two weeks ago. Brandie's garment required a rush job for the collective fitting.

"Storing my dress at your house is an excellent idea." She turned around smiling but hesitated when she took in Neka's bowed head. "Something's wrong. You've moped about since we arrived last week."

Neka left the window seat and settled on the bed, leaning her back against the headboard. "I'm indecisive about a few things."

Brandie sat down beside her. "Is James the problem?"

Nodding, Neka evaded her gaze.

"Trust is earned by the nature of relationships as well as time." She leaned closer, laying a palm on Neka's knee. "Soon-to-be sister-in-law, I believe we're friends for life. Please confide in me."

Neka stared at her, considering. Should she entrust her private thoughts about James to his sister? Except for David, no one else in Tulsa knew him better than Brandie. She took a deep breath.

"We're inundated with problems at the moment." She paused, attempting to smile. "You understand James better than I do."

Brandie rubbed Neka's arm but remained silent.

She closed her eyes. It was easier to speak without witnessing the silent appeal for understanding. "It's impossible dealing with a man who refuses to compromise. He claims I'll neuter him for life if he doesn't resist my pull."

251

Neka opened her eyes, and Brandie's double take caused her to grin. "No kidding," Neka continued. "He used those exact words one day."

"What were you discussing?" Brandie leaned back on her elbows, frowning.

"Pushing back the wedding date a year." Neka twiddled her fingers, looking downward, and then studied Brandie.

Brandie grimaced. "Do you still want to marry my brother?"

Neka nodded and rubbed an area of pain developing above her right eyebrow. "But we need time to explore one another's weaknesses and strengths. At this rate, more than likely I'll only earn his contempt. I think he needs additional time before saying I do."

"He does and not you?"

Neka smiled. "I've always been sure about him."

Brandie ambled to the closet for the fourth time. Silence charged the room while she quietly fingered the fragile material. The action instilled doubts in Neka. Maybe prudence should've overcome frankness.

Only God knew where their relationship led. Keeping up appearances drained both of them. In reality, they hadn't spent any time alone since their disastrous dinner at his house. His family arrived the next day, surrounding them with more well-wishers. Neka hid inside the bubble of onlookers, afraid to speak to the man she loved without a crowd.

Incorporating a large city into the network required the Tulsa office to pull double duty. Now the operation directors essentially worked around the clock negotiating a project even bigger than the earlier deal in St. Louis. A couple of times James had visited her house with Brandie and crew in tow. During the day, she operated off-site more than at the office. While he was sequestered in conferences during the periods, she worked in-house.

Neka glanced up as Brandie sat down and reached for her hand. "James likes having his own way because he's ended up on the backburner too many times in the past."

"Eons ago." Neka shrugged. "It's time to grow up."

Tears turned Brandie's eyes glassy. She exhaled long and hard before continuing.

"In these areas, the little boy in his head hasn't caught up with the grown man within his heart." She hesitated. "Do you still want to marry my brother?"

Neka frowned. Why did Brandie repeat a question Neka had already answered? Neither she nor James sought an escape from the engagement. Tears filled her eyes.

"Next year."

Relaxing, Brandie smiled and then flicked her fingers. "If that's how you feel, pick the day of your choosing. If you remain with James, he won't risk losing you."

Neka squinted, contemplating the changed attitude. "I have no desire to leave him."

"Convince him of that."

She threw up her hands. "He won't let me."

"James responds strongly to rejection." Narrowing her eyes, Brandie hesitated. "Our house was like a war zone when we were younger. Matt and Ryan rebelled against his dominance while he warded off their sneak attacks. They never gave him a peaceful moment."

Neka gasped. "It was that bad?"

"His only break was when they protected him against someone else's grievances." She grasped Neka's hands. "James fell in love with you the first day you met."

"I used to hope so."

"Let the same faith that brought you to St. Louis lead you to the altar in November."

Neka looked away. "Please, Brandie ..."

"My brother prefers you to believe he fell in love since the engagement." She shrugged. "Maybe he's convinced himself too."

"In most areas James is a truthful man."

"Not in relationships. He hauls around a truckload of abandoned dreams." She leaned closer as if to convey a secret. "You know, most people bolt right before their greatest victory."

Neka closed her eyes as Brandie extended her version of the brother she loved. Falling captive to the hopeful words, she wanted to believe it was true but didn't know if she should.

* * *

The next day Neka headed to James's office to extend the olive branch. She prayed for an opening to change her role in the conflict. Nowadays, she admitted that four years of discussions at parties wasn't enough to build the proper framework for an enduring marriage. And both of their endless business demands prevented forging a united front before November.

The idea of getting married in eight weeks frightened her. Doing nothing was no longer an option.

James pushed his work to the side when Neka opened the door to his office. Encouraged, she stepped farther into the room. "Cheryl's away from her desk again. May I come in?"

Leaning in his chair, he studied her from head to toe. Curiosity dominated his expression. "I was fifteen minutes from looking for you."

"Good. I sensed we were of like minds today." Smiling, she sat on his desk. "Were you hoping to buy me lunch?"

"Actually, I wanted answers concerning Tammy's heart-to-heart an hour ago."

She wasn't expecting that. Her smile vanished. "What did you talk about?"

Standing, he closed the gap between them. "Why I spent the summer tormenting her sister." He paused. "Why did you tell her I didn't love you when I proposed?"

Neka gasped. In a weak moment, she'd confided in Tammy. Who revealed secrets to the person being discussed? "I won't apologize for telling the truth."

"That's news to spread around?"

"She already knew."

"She may have suspected; now she knows."

James examined her like she was a stranger, not with the blank expression he donned when threatened. At least some good came out of fifteen weeks of togetherness. She read him much better these days. Given another year, the mystique would disappear altogether. This time he was ready for a fight.

Deflated, she slid off the desk, avoiding the cross-examination. "Since you already staked out your position, I won't hang around for another rejection."

"Running off again?" He cut her off from the other side of the desk. "Tell me what changed since my proposal?"

When Neka pulled the door open, James pushed it closed. She let him, and he leaned his weight against the frame.

"Preparations for the rollout this week have been hectic. On Friday, we unveil the new project at a companywide meeting." He ran a finger down her cheek. "Once the sweep is over, you and I get back on course."

She took a couple of steps backward. "I never got off course."

"Then every problem is my fault?"

Neka welcomed the confrontation. By now, they should've operated in unity instead of the division they flirted with all summer. "I can honestly place the majority of our disagreements into your lap."

Head back, she parted her feet, waiting for the backlash.

James settled his gaze on a spot above her head. "What do you want?"

"We need more time getting to know one another." Neka faced him. "Change the wedding date until next year."

James leaned against the door. "Back there again, huh? And if I say no for the thirtieth time?"

Neka's hands spread in exasperation. "Why disagree? The reason for a hasty marriage no longer exists. You're free to chart your own course."

His jaw muscles moved in and out as he eyed her, frowning. "My own course. Which is ... what? According to you?"

"Doing whatever pleases James."

Anger cast a shadow over his features. "What if marrying you this November pleases me?"

Neka spread out her palms in silent appeal. "Then explain why it does. Can't you see I need clarity?"

James glanced at his watch. "I'm already late for a working lunch with your father and David. I'll stop by your house tonight before heading home."

The advisory board had formulated a draft, setting the groundwork in place. Once the actual process started, visits from James had decreased even more. Their conflict had only festered from the neglect. "Brandie said you and David haven't come home before midnight in over a week."

"Your father is a tough task master. Look, in two days the heavy workload will curtail." He hesitated when she glanced at the floor. "All I need is two more days—tops."

Memories flitted across her mind—her mom alone with her girls at music recitals, school plays, science fairs, and soccer games. Like her dad, James thrived on enlarging his territory. After this rollout, he would immerse himself in the project. Her gaze focused on him when he stroked her cheek.

"How about spending the day together Saturday?" His winsome smile begged her to agree. "What do you say, sweets?"

"Be here now." Neka shrugged. "That's all I want."

Golden lights glittered in his eyes. He cupped her cheeks between his palms. "I'd give up everything for you."

A gentle calm from his sincerity replaced her irritation. For a second, Neka closed her eyes. She loved this man struggling to escape years of emotional bondage. "Don't relinquish your dreams. Just allow me to share them."

His fingers fell from her face. The inner battle consuming him raged across his features. He stretched out his hands to her, then dropped them at his side. It seemed trusting her wasn't in the cards today. Ten minutes of his time might lay the foundation of peace for deeper discussions later.

Sadness filled her heart when he opened the door and stepped aside. Neka left the room without a backward glance.

* * *

Resting his forehead on the door, James listened to the click of her heels as she moved farther away. He'd spoiled the unity he wanted in just one conversation. Talking to her sister had made him want to see her more than ever. Their conversation had drudged up images of a woeful Neka experiencing pains from his withdrawal. He'd berated himself for the callous treatment until she floated into his office on top of the world.

He winced at the delusion. Her lightheartedness had incensed him, but it was just Neka rising above the mire he'd generated. She visited him in hopes of rallying together. Instead of meeting her halfway, he'd broadened the gap even more.

The only way to stop the separation was to do it now.

Cheryl turned around when James stepped outside the room. Her presence checked his intended action. It would be better to let her cool down first; they both needed time alone.

"Give Neka my itinerary if she calls."

Cheryl nodded. "I'll email your schedule before going to lunch."

"Don't set up any appointments for the next two weeks. I plan to clear off my desk before the weekend."

Putting on his suit jacket, James stared at the ton of work needing completion before tomorrow.

* * *

Neka closed her book when the doorbell rang, and she rushed to the top of the stairs. Her shoulders drooped when Hazelle's happy voice greeted Karen. "Hello, favorite aunt, can Neka come out to play on this lovely Friday?"

Laughter drifted up the stairs. "Go on up. She's in her hideout."

"The sunroom." Giggles erupted when they spoke at the same time.

Neka returned to her haven as Hazelle ran up the steps. Instead of coming to find her, she tapped on Tammy's bedroom door. "Ready for the big day Sunday?"

They discussed their plans for decorating the sanctuary and reception hall.

Neka poked her head into the room. She frowned when Tammy clasped her fingers beneath her chin trembling.

"Perfect! I'm soooo nervous."

Hazelle laughed. "Why? You decided to marry Kenny years ago."

Smiling, Tammy nodded. "I played scavenger hunt, leaving clues strewn across the years."

"He found them all." Hazelle winked at Neka.

Tammy sank to the trunk, wrapping her arms around her shoulders. "He finally wound his way back to me."

Neka couldn't believe her sister had ever doubted Kenny's love. The college sophomore showed up at a teenager's birthday party. True, he hung out in the kitchen with Michael, but he came.

Tearing her gaze from Tammy's dreamy features, Neka spoke to her cousin. "I'd planned to call you later tonight."

"Then we're in sync. I came to steal you away. Grab your purse; dessert's on me."

"What's the special occasion?" Tammy's gaze darted between the women.

"Rescue mission." Trying to appear mysterious, Hazelle's eyebrows rose up and down. "I'm saving Neka from herself."

"Sounds interesting." Tammy glanced at them. "If Neka weren't upset with me, I'd tag along."

Neka headed for the door. "I forgave you two days ago, though I would like to speak to Hazelle in private."

Tammy nodded, and after embracing their cousin, she closed the door behind them.

257

* * *

After they ate their ice cream, Hazelle rubbed an ice cube against the choco-late smudge on her white jersey. "I need a bib."

Thinking about her sisters, Neka viewed the ministrations in silence. Un-solicited advice from both of them had worn her out. Who could make sen-sible decisions with that kind of information overload? Fed up, she'd issued a silent decree. No more criticisms or accolades.

Her cousin was a neutral person who cared more about her than him.

Pleased with the results, Hazelle cast the ice cube aside. "Why do you want to cancel the wedding?"

Neka fought back tears. "It's James who wants to end the engagement, not me."

"He called it off?" Hazelle's eyes widened.

"Who knows? We haven't spoken since Wednesday."

Deep in thought, Neka glanced away. James and David had achieved great success that afternoon. Everyone in the auditorium applauded their Launch to Excellence meeting. As planned, having all hands on deck gave the em-ployees a sense of ownership in the new venture. Promotions were slated to begin early next year.

At the end of the program, her dad had dropped a bombshell on his op-erations directors. He announced back-to-back meetings with the advisory board today and tomorrow. Charles and Gene would conference in both days. Thus, James couldn't spend the day with her Saturday even if he wanted to. She hoped he would contact her that evening if he got a break between meetings.

Hazelle touched her hand. "Did you two argue?"

Laying her head against the cushion, she sorted out their latest quarrel. "More like disagreed. I want to marry next year. He wants the ceremony to continue as planned."

Her cousin sighed. "Why do you want to wait a year?"

Tears filled Neka's eyes. How did she explain her objections without dam-aging his character? James deserved loyalty from at least one person pro-fessing love. "Our relationship lacks compromise, as demonstrated by this present deadlock."

"What's his reason for not moving the date?"

She could only guess. Getting married was a lifetime decision no one should make lightly. She'd learned that the hard way. "I have no idea. I explain my reservations, but he refuses to reveal his motives."

Hazelle pushed her bowl aside. "To you, he's inflexible, and to him, you changed the rules."

"Stalemate."

"But self-imposed." She hesitated when Neka frowned. "Weeks ago we agreed about his personality transformation. He's always been the suave gentlemen, but now he's more accessible than ever."

"It's a tremendous amount of work in a short time."

Hazelle leaned closer. "What happens if you're displeased with his progress by next November? Do you delay another year?"

Neka slumped in her seat. Would she continue moving the date until James fulfilled her dreams? She wasn't asking for perfection—just communication without the pressure. "Granny said—"

Her cousin's raised hand cut off her response.

"Granny's a fount of wisdom you've ignored before." Hazelle laughed when Neka shook her head in denial. "You refused to live on campus and attend a Christian college."

Dimples flashed with Neka's broad grin. "James influenced my decision."

"You're withstanding him now. What does Aunt Karen say?"

Her parents advocated waiting until James learned to yield and she learned to stand her ground. "She agrees with Granny, only she compared us to her and Dad."

Hazelle laughed. "Now that's a story I'd love to hear from her perspective. My dad's version is biased. In their case, love conquered all."

Neka smiled in spite of herself. Since her mom's revelations, she often thought about her parents' romance. Until that day, she'd never considered that either family was against their marrying.

Did every couple have hurdles to overcome before reaching the altar? The high divorce rate indicated that many couples failed to count the costs before saying, "I do."

"Mom said—"

Hazelle threw up her hands. "In other words, James hasn't improved enough in a few weeks to win you over?"

Neka laid her forehead on a napkin. She peeped at her cousin. "If the game plan is to wear me down, you're succeeding."

Light glowed in Hazelle's eyes. She twined a lock of hair around a finger. "Will he develop enough to please you in a year?"

Being flawed herself, did she expect excellence from James? Or were her expectations reasonable? "Why suppose I can predict the future? I'm not God."

Her cousin could hardly contain her laughter. "Because you do it all the time. According to you, He ordained this union."

Maybe Neka was a little heavy-handed attributing events to God. Smiling, Neka traced circles on the table. "I stand by those beliefs."

"Did our loving Father consign you to a disastrous marriage?"

Neka massaged her earlobe in furious motions. "Hazelle ..."

"For nearly four months, you've stated God destined you to become one with James."

Neka wilted under the weight of her own argument. From the start, she'd believed the Lord had destined their marriage. Though her cousin's rebuttal made sense, what if God brought them together for the future and she dashed ahead of His plan?

Chapter Thirty

Tammy stepped from the dressing room decked in her wedding gown. Neka's hands flew to her cheeks.

"You're so beautiful!"

"Thanks." Her sister floated to Neka's side, grabbing her hands. "Your stubbornness annoys me. How can you refuse to be in Kelly's and my weddings, but expect us to stand up with you in November?"

Neka smiled. "I like viewing the front of the church from the back row."

"That'll change in two months." Eyes filled with concern, she squeezed Neka's fingers. "Sure you forgive me?"

"The same day it happened. Lately, I've become saturated with advice about James. I just want to be left alone for a while."

Tammy nodded. "I understand. Though I shouldn't have interfered, he responded well. Unlike Kelly, I've always believed he cared deeply for you. But sometimes love isn't enough." She covered her mouth. "Oops, I did it again. Sorry."

Neka tilted her head to the side, smiling. "Old habits are hard to break. You've bashed James since you met him."

"Old habits are hard to break. I'll repeat that comment to Kenny when we argue." Glancing at the wedding party in various stages of dress, she pulled Neka into the dressing room. "I'm about to leave Tulsa for a week. Talk to me."

Tempted to dump her unhappiness on a listening ear, she declined with a smile. "And ruin your day? Never."

"Contact me if you want to talk. I mean every word."

Once again, God reminded her she had the best family in the world. She could never take advantage of their kindness.

Neka rolled her eyes. "Oh yeah, your hubby will welcome S.O.S. calls throughout his honeymoon."

The sisters hugged, and Tammy reopened the door. "Stop talking nonsense. Kenny thinks of you as a sister."

Neka's eyes sparkled at the mental image of the newlywed tossing his bride's cell phone off the balcony.

"He'll stop if I ruin his wedding night." Laughing, she kissed the air next to her sister's cheek. "I don't want to smear your makeup."

With a final survey of the room, Neka waved good-bye.

She settled into a seat toward the back of the sanctuary. Her aunt's expert hands had turned the space into a nuptial wonderland. Beautiful bouquets bordered the room like a picture frame. As usual, the Singleton family performed a top-notch job.

Her planned November wedding plagued her mind. Lost in her thoughts, movement at the altar captured her attention. At last, Kenny and Blake exited the pastor's study. She closed her eyes, waiting for the organist to play the wedding march.

James should have occupied the chair beside her. Today marked an ideal time to experience a live event together. The right moment to—

Her eyes flew open as fingers tapped her shoulder. Without waiting for a response, James claimed the seat beside her. When his gaze slid past her, she turned around. Brandie and David entered the row from the opposite side of the room. Their actions boxed her in between them.

She'd forgotten they were staying in town to attend the wedding. She hadn't heard from Brandie since Tuesday. Teens in her church had babysat Yancey and Cody since their arrival. It must have been because of her argument with James. She was surprised he had even bothered to show up.

A hush enveloped the sanctuary as Mrs. Sanders played the tune Neka'd longed to hear. Heads turned in anticipation when Kenny's nieces started off the procession by strewing flowers along the white runner.

Snickers erupted when his nephew followed, holding the pillow sideways. Thank God Blake held the ring and not his son.

Leading off the adults, slim-again Kelly made an attractive picture draped on Michael's arm. Each couple kept in time with the music until the maid of honor strolled into place.

Tammy's friend Jenny glided down the aisle, smiling at onlookers until reaching the altar. When the music stopped, the moment had arrived. Everyone stared at the door as the bride came into view.

"Oh, she is so lovely," Brandie whispered.

No one could match the stunning woman commanding their admiration. Their dad's satisfied grin held reassurance when he caught Tammy's gaze.

Hands clasped beneath her chin, Neka observed their progress down the aisle. Before they reached Kenny, the setting took on a surreal quality, like she was viewing the ceremony from a tunnel instead of being in the midst of the scene itself.

She studied the group gathered at the altar, waiting for Uncle Joe's instructions. While he spoke, James brought her hand to his lips. He drew her against him when the couple repeated vows, cementing them as one.

Around the room, tears flowed freely when the pastor pronounced them husband and wife.

Squeezing her eyes together, Neka thanked God for answered prayer. Kenny and Tammy were married, just as her sister had always prayed. When she opened her eyes, James studied her with an awed expression.

Close to her ear, he whispered, "Please forgive me. I'll comply with whatever pleases you."

Her expectations swelled until she squashed them. Far from being pacifying, his words left an opening for later discussion.

* * *

After the ceremony, James and his family waited in the hotel lobby for Neka to arrive. In the reception hall, she skirted around throngs of well-wishers until reaching the front of the room. Securing the chair next to Hazelle and Lincoln, she spoke to several relatives seated around the table. Then her friendly cousin introduced everyone to Brandie and David. As the others made small talk, Neka replayed James's comment ad nauseam.

Why did he seek common ground today of all days? Until now, the word compromise wasn't in his vocabulary. Was his surrender prearranged? Had he discovered that marrying her next year worked to his advantage after all?

When they finished eating, James leaned close. "Let's talk away from the festivities. This reception will go on for another hour. May I pick you up at four?"

Her heart beat faster. "What about Brandie and David? Do you prefer talking in private at my house?"

"They're heading out after picking up the kids." He studied her for a few moments. His expression implied he half expected an adverse response.

She slowly nodded.

David rose and winked at Neka. Lines around his eyes crinkled as he smiled. "See you in two months."

Neka grinned even though James had just agreed to delay the wedding another year.

Brandie moved closer, and Neka leaped from her chair.

"We'll attempt a farewell to the newlyweds. Failure means you tell them thanks for including us in their special celebration." She hesitated, scanning the other occupants around the table. "May I call you tonight?"

"Call me whenever the urge hits." Neka noticed that the shakiness in her voice brought a frown to Brandie's face. "Regardless of the outcome, we're friends forever, right?" she added.

"More like sisters into eternity," Brandie corrected. Her gaze held unasked questions. She leaned closer. "I'm praying for you and James. God not only hears our prayers, He answers them."

With a parting glance, she wrapped her arms around David's waist as they followed James to the head table.

Hazelle crossed her fingers in her lap where Neka could see them. "Is it on again?"

The prospect looked favorable. Did she dare to believe? "He's picking me up at four to talk. I hope food's included."

"Why? You just ate a five-course meal."

"Stress makes me hungry." She shrugged. "Besides, he's an excellent cook."

* * *

Neka pushed her plate aside to follow James into the living room.

Now what? From the time he'd picked her up, his innocuous conversation transported her to that blissful last week in St. Louis. Back home, their promising beginning had collapsed so quickly. They frequently soared the heights and then descended into the pit all on the same day. Lying in bed at night, she always analyzed their many missed chances.

In theory, James complemented her personality in positive ways. Once he'd entered into her private world, the door had opened for others to follow. Casual friendships bloomed practically overnight. Life offered numerous prospects since leaving home the first Friday in June. Perhaps this last

Saturday in September flipped the page to an era of happiness. Even now, the softness of his gaze filled her with hope.

But his willingness to interact was just a start.

In response to her scrutiny, James grasped Neka's hand before speaking.

"If you still want to get married next year after our discussion, I'll sign on without further complaints." He rubbed the back of his hand against her cheek. "I only rejected the idea because ... I fear losing you."

The admission stung. He doubted her commitment even though she'd done everything he asked for months. "I reserved myself for you the moment I accepted your proposal."

His palm covered her hand, but he didn't meet her eyes.

"You believe that now. Opportunities will surface that you never knew existed. In four months, you altered your appearance and added friendships, enlarging your outlook on life." He paused, squeezing her fingers. Bringing their hands to his chest, he used them as a resting place for his chin. "Keep maturing. Continue to flourish, but let's shape our lives together, not apart."

Neka frowned. "That's what we've been doing."

"My life is the same as it's always been. Long hours and crawling into bed too tired to even make a phone call." He paused, narrowing his eyes. "You did a sea change. I just wanted to limit avenues of escape from me."

Neka fell back against the cushion. All this time she'd imagined he understood her hope for their future. She'd gone along with his decisions because of his contentious past. What could she have done differently to allay his fear?

"I attend the same prayer meetings and outreach centers weekly. In the evenings, I fill in time with others because you're busy." She shrugged. "What else should I do?"

His pupils took on an orange glow. "Read a good book lately?"

Neka laughed, then she sobered when he didn't join in. He really imagined she would walk away from him. Her choices considered their future and how it would impact their children.

Even with detailed planning, no individual could cover all the bases.

"Only God can manage every area in our lives. We hand the reigns over to Him in order to live the abundant life Jesus promised in His word."

James folded her into his arms. His hand brushed her neck as he combed his fingers through her hair. Remembering their numerous false starts, she was content to wait until he shared his thoughts.

"Will you accept me as I am?"

Now they were getting to the crux of the matter—dread of dismantling the coping mechanisms that propelled him through life. Removing the crutch allowed his whole beautiful personality full reign.

But they couldn't operate by separate rules.

"Do you accept me as I am?" She pulled away, placing a finger on his lips. "You prefer the idea of an amiable Neka that doesn't exist. I usually yield unless my beliefs are affected." Her eyes sparkled. "I admit to having several."

"I like your beliefs."

"Until they interfere with your agenda." She couldn't meet his eyes and instead focused on his collar. "Our ideas won't always match. Can we disagree without you turning me into an adversary?"

He grinned, trailing a finger across her cheeks. "A friend today might become an enemy by tomorrow."

"You wouldn't marry a woman capable of plotting against your welfare."

"Not on purpose."

"Try 'not ever,' because you wouldn't." Neka stood up, flexing her tired muscles. She understood James better than ever. Refusing people entry into his private sanctum failed to stem his disappointment, and it made his loved ones miserable. "Sometimes you mishandle disruptions to your plans."

"And you misjudge people's real intentions," he countered.

She shook her head.

"If I fail to perform to your liking, you doubt that I love you," he continued. "Unless a Celia hits you in a direct attack or a Jeff tips his hand, you gloss everything over." James tilted her face toward him. "Starting today, I vow to protect you from me." He paused when she smiled. "Give everyone a blank slate going forward. Take nothing at face value and don't pile on unearned kudos. It is better to accept the bitter truth than believe a sweet lie."

Neka sighed and laid her head on his shoulders. He pulled her into the crook of his arms. She smiled, nestling closer. "You must trust that there are good people."

"You told me we can only trust God." His eyes narrowed. "Why throw others into the mix? Problems are harder to solve than prevent."

Pondering the question, Neka caressed his fingers. Her sisters offered protection. His brothers sheltered him from everyone but themselves. Lifelong mindsets were hard to change. But it was unfair to punish someone until proven guilty.

"God works through people all the time." She hesitated, looking downward.

In his office Tuesday, neither of them was prepared to shift positions. Settling somewhere in the middle proved difficult. For both of them.

Father, show me how to compromise on a wedding that will either be this November or next. My fiancé has been through a lot, but so have I.

Neka leaned closer. "I feel confident enough to wait until next year. I have faith that you love me, that you meant it when you stated Jesus destined our lives to become one in Him."

James turned her face upward, then trailed a finger over her lips. "Those beliefs remain the same. I'll delay a year, because you're worth waiting for."

Tears sprung to her eyes as his declaration sealed their future. Without a doubt, God purposed to mold them into a vessel for His glory. James proved worthy of any discomfort she might endure along their journey.

He wasn't the only person growing in wisdom.

A rash decision made in June had jumpstarted events that she couldn't control. In the heat of the moment, she'd embarked on a pathway fraught with pain. It had disrupted lives of people she loved, along with those she'd never met. All ending well didn't absolve her responsibility.

"Though leaving Tulsa with you was a major blunder, God protected us." She smiled, biting her lip when James brushed tears from her cheeks. "I love you so much. Your willingness to meet me halfway makes me confident enough to marry you this November."

Joy lit up his face like she'd never seen. Walls were coming down, even while they talked. Gathering her into his arms, James buried his cheek against her neck.

Neka closed her eyes, knowing that this was the beginning of a whole new life for both of them. As her mom loved to say: a day of new beginnings, bright tomorrows, and endless promises in Christ.

Epilogue

Her dad placed his hand on the crook of her elbow. "You look beautiful, my dear."

Neka focused on the handsome man who strove to secure their future throughout the generations. Every day he worked hard to balance love, protection, and provision. "This morning I thanked God for the resilient man He set in our family," she told him.

Grinning, he kissed her cheek. The love in his eyes brought a smile to her face. She laid her head on his shoulder. Far from being perfect, her dad orchestrated events to his liking whenever possible. Unlike the old James, he never reinvented situations unless he was personally challenged. Over the years, he'd used wisdom and insight to deal with circumstances imposed on their family.

Movement caught her eye as the wedding party took their places. Marriage ceremonies in the Lacey and Singleton clans were family affairs. Two men from both sides of her family served as ushers. Cousins Bridgett and Sandy distributed baskets to flower girls. James's nieces—Marissa, Leanne, Amy, and Yancey—giggled in excitement. Once the ushers opened the double doors, the girls marched in step down the aisle, strewing flowers everywhere.

A few petals actually landed on the white runner.

Laughing, Neka scanned the crowd to seek the reaction of family and friends. Her smile broadened when attendees followed the girls' progress to the altar. She'd thought she only wanted her sisters' children in the ceremony, but she had grown to love these children. She dabbed her eyes at the sight.

God kept growing her up, despite her temper tantrums. She couldn't imagine not considering the groom might want his relatives in the event.

People definitely saw in others what they failed to realize within themselves.

During their trip to St. Louis she'd discovered James's traits of self-absorption, never considering she held selfish tendencies of her own. These days, instead of whining for easy living, she welcomed God simplifying her life. She wasn't always good at it, but she knew He loved her anyway and would grow her up in spite of herself.

Squinting, she tried sending vibes to Ryan's son Danny to make him hold the pillow straight. Her pulse quickened once Kelly and Ryan strolled down the aisle. Once they were halfway to the altar, Tammy and Matt started behind them, followed by Brandie and Blake.

The elegant Hazelle stood out of sight, ready to make an entrance in her vintage-inspired ensemble. Head held high, she glided across the white runner, capturing the admiration of the guests. Ushers used the distraction to close the double doors, signaling Neka and Lawrence into position.

The trembling eased when her dad kissed her cheek. "Don't be nervous, darling. I'm escorting you down the aisle to the man you love—a man who loves you. That assurance persuaded me to give you away."

His confidence soothed her nerves. "Thank you, Dad. We'll be happy together."

Hope softened his eyes as he smiled. "Those are among my daily prayers to the Father—security for my family."

Neka closed her eyes when the music started again, then she glanced at her dad. "We're up."

The ushers opened the doors, giving them a full view of the sanctuary. A hush spread throughout the room. All eyes turned to them.

As if glued to the spot, her feet refused to move. Lawrence placed her hand on his arm, taking the first step down the aisle.

Neka's gaze caught glimpses of people. Her mom sat on the front row. Granny and Granddad Singleton sat to her right, while her Grandmother and Grandfather Lacey sat on her left. The empty seat beside her mom was for her dad.

Supporters filled the sanctuary just as she'd envisioned in her dreams. Every person invited liked them and advocated their union. How befitting to marry in the church her Grandfather Singleton founded over forty-five years ago.

Only a few empty chairs existed on the groom's side of the aisle. A host of family and friends traveled to Tulsa for the nuptials, including fourteen members of Mimi's family. Also present were ten members of the Hodge family.

Her gaze alighted on James. Awaiting their arrival, he and David separated themselves from the others. Once they reached the altar, James stepped to the forefront, receiving her hand from Lawrence. Neka stared into his eyes without moving until soft laughter penetrated her thoughts.

Grinning, he led her up the steps to the altar.

When they stood before the pastor, Neka's Uncle Joe, David and Hazelle gathered closer. In fact, the entire wedding party closed in. Handing her bouquet and gloves to the waiting Hazelle, Neka smiled when James squeezed her hand.

In the background, someone coughed and a few sniffles sounded. Whimpering off and on, Michey got in on the show as well.

Still nervous, Neka fought the urge to massage her earlobe. Listening to her uncle's calm voice helped her to relax.

"Do you, James, take Nikhol to be your wife, to live together in the covenant of marriage? Will you love her, comfort her, honor and keep her, in sickness and in health, and forsaking all others, be faithful to her as long as you both shall live?"

Without hesitation, his strong voice rang out. "I do."

Uncle Joe turned to Neka and repeated those sacred words. She almost couldn't hear him through the sound of her own pounding heart, though she smiled at James and repeated the vow. "I do."

"We will now exchange rings."

James accepted the ring from David, then gazed into Neka's eyes without speaking. After a long pause, he held the ring poised at the tip of her finger. "Nikhol, I give you this ring as a sign of my love and commitment to you. From this day forward, we shall never be apart." He slid the ring onto her finger.

Only the wedding party heard her gasp, shocked he'd changed the words they were scripted to say. Her hands shook as Hazelle placed the ring in her palm. Tears formed as she repeated James's words as if she'd memorized them for days.

Clearing his throat, Uncle Joe spoke to the congregation. "Before I make God's declaration over this couple, the groom will share a few words."

Neka's eyes opened wide. Though none of this was rehearsed, her uncle was prepared beforehand.

271

Gaze locked with hers, James held her hands to his chest.

"Through the years I realized God had a special lady for me. A woman who desired to be cherished and loved by the man she waited to receive. Though drawn from the moment I saw you, I failed to recognize the love of my life. I thank Him for making your presence unforgettable. If not, I would've missed His second-greatest blessing after salvation."

He cleared his throat and paused.

"Neka, in front of those persons closest to both of us, I declare gratitude. Thank you for accepting me into your life."

Body trembling, tears streamed down her face onto her gown. In James's mind, Neka had never been more beautiful.

"Ahem ... sweets, my dear sweetie, I love you. Neka, I pledge my life to you this day and forever."

Dropping his hands, she wrapped her arms around his waist.

Head tilted back, Neka stared into his eyes. "From the moment you introduced yourself I've only had eyes for you."

There wasn't a dry eye in the place. Several people blew their noses. Tissues crinkled, and throats cleared.

And then peace descended on them.

The couple faced Uncle Joe when he moved closer. "Neka and James, you have both agreed to live together as husband and wife. By repeating vows and exchanging rings, you pledged your faith to this union and to one another. From this day forward, may your love be the centerpiece for your hearts and your home. May God bless you and your marriage today and forever. Now, by the authority vested in me by the state of Oklahoma and before God, I now pronounce you husband and wife. You may kiss your bride."

In one swift movement, James swept Neka against him. He gave her a chaste kiss. Then, smiling, he kissed the tip of her nose and both dimples, then snuggled her into the comfort of his arms.

The End

A Note From E. C. Jackson

"The Write Way: A Real Slice of Life" is the slogan on my website and Facebook author page. If every person reading my book feels connected to the characters, my job is done.

A Gateway to Hope is my first book and has been a labor of love. I hope you enjoyed Neka and James's story just as much as I enjoyed sharing it with you.

Though the journey continues, I will not say good-bye to old friends.

If you liked reading this novel, please leave a review on the site of the retailer of your choice.

Thank you for your time!

If you enjoyed reading *A Gateway to Hope*, please check out the second book in the standalone hope-themed series.

A Living Hope

It was a match made in heaven. Or so everyone thought. Sadie Mae Cummings is all set to marry her childhood sweetheart, Kyle, when she is assigned to tutor Lincoln, the new college football running back. This sophomore phenomenon has all the girls on campus knocking on his door. But Sadie isn't interested in his advances.

Lincoln's overblown ego doesn't take well to being shunned, and he resolves to make Sadie his own. He pursues her relentlessly, until finally Kyle finds himself shut out of Sadie's life, with their shared future crumbling around him.

After two years, Sadie's relationship with Lincoln ends, and she is left having to put the pieces of her life back together. She desires nothing more than to recapture her relationship with Kyle. He has stayed true to the dreams they had planned together, living the vision even without Sadie by his side.

When she moves back to her hometown, she labors to rekindle their love. But things have changed, and Kyle has moved on. Sadie quickly discovers how hard it is to rebuild burned bridges.

Follow Sadie's story as she fights for a chance to restore broken dreams. Will love endure?

This inspirational romance by E. C. Jackson is book two of the Hope series and is a standalone book.

Excerpt

Restless, twenty-one-year-old Sadie Cummings wiped down the counter space in her small kitchen nook. It was eleven o'clock. Five minutes had passed since the last time she'd checked. Sighing, she fretted about her boyfriend's visit that morning.

"Why does he agree to come over, then not show up?"

In no time, morning had slipped into early afternoon. The breakfast she'd hoped would receive raves from Lincoln congealed on the stovetop. So much for using her cooking skills to entice him. With several swift movements, she scraped the masterpiece into the garbage disposal, fighting to control the uneasiness she couldn't dismiss.

She was an expert at fooling herself and others, but today her mind refused to be pacified. One could only pretend for so long before the bottom dropped out completely. Truth had a bad habit of intruding into fairy tales. Especially when the make-believe stories were about real-life events.

The ringing cell phone grabbed Sadie's attention. That her mother was on the other end was a forgone conclusion. Except for an occasional chat with her younger sister and older brother, the cell phone never rang. These days only her mother contacted Sadie on a regular basis. She peeked at the caller ID.

A moment before the call transferred to voicemail, Sadie snatched up the cell phone, held it against her chest, then gave a cheery greeting. Minutes later, she sauntered through the studio apartment thinking up reasonable excuses to end the call early. Jeanette Cummings expected a good deal more than her middle child was able to give.

Still stumped about finding an excuse to satisfy her mother, Sadie walked around in circles.

"Mother, I'm not trying to hurry you off the phone. I recognize your concern for the Franklins. Our families have been friends for years. It's just ... look ... it's ... mother, I don't have time to talk now."

Sadie picked up twine from the counter and wove it between her fingers. Pulling it too tight, she winced, then unwound it from around her fingers and wrapped it around her thumb.

"I made plans for the day."

Lincoln could arrive any moment. Somehow, she had to quickly end this conversation without hurting the only person who regularly called. Friendships were difficult to maintain these days. And her brother and sister only gave duty calls, then ended the conversation in a snap.

Jeanette sighed loudly. "I would offer to call back at a better time, but there isn't one, is there, Sadie?"

"Mom ..."

Sadie slowly shook her head. Guilt surfaced each time she talked to her mother. Raised in an orphanage, her mother wasn't a clingy parent. She believed loneliness caused people to accept unhealthy conditions that a person who felt treasured might avoid.

"Of course, you're removed from the lives of the families in Shiatown," said Jeanette.

Blowing breath through her lips, Sadie laid her head on the cabinet with more force than intended. Wincing in pain, she rubbed the sore spot. The lull in the conversation helped gather her thoughts as her fingers massaged the painful area on her forehead. She parted her lips, then she shut them in hopes that her mother would continue speaking.

After a long pause, Jeanette spoke with a harsher tone than any she'd ever used with her daughter. "Listen to me. The Franklin family supported us through your father's illness and death. We are burying Pastor Franklin this afternoon. His wife deserves a phone call from you."

She paused before continuing. "Don't forget, Sarah treated you like a daughter. You and Pastor Franklin shared the same birthday. September twelfth is four days away. My friend is burying her husband four days before his fifty-eighth birthday. And ... what about Kyle? He lost his father and inherited a ton of responsibility on top of it. Honey, be the friend that I know you are. Time is slipping away. The funeral starts in two hours."

Sadie stretched her neck from side to side, hanging her head in despair. Lately, her mother had begun to accept her decisions without fussing. However, today she seemed determined for Sadie to send well wishes to a man she'd rather forget. Feeling faint, she squeezed her eyelids together, but all she could see was Kyle's sad gaze begging, pleading with her to choose him over the man Sadie picked.

Instantly, anger rose as Sadie justified that choice. She couldn't back down now. There was too much lost ground and no way to regain her footing. The future she'd hoped for was gone. Somehow the leftovers had to be salvaged into a win or, at least, a tolerable solution.

Eyes darting around the room, she braced against the wall. "Friend? Kyle and I didn't break up as friends. He acted like a judgmental pig; his last remarks were cruel."

Sadie fumed. With one look Kyle had made her feel like trash. Less than the muck beneath his shoes. Disposable at best, and at worse ...

"Sadie—"

"Don't excuse him, Mom. Kyle humiliated me in front of Lincoln." She glanced at her shoes.

And the truth is, I didn't deserve any better.

"Oh yes, Lincoln. The wonder man who is far from wonderful. I hate the way he treats you, honey. All women deserve respect." Jeanette continued when Sadie failed to respond. "So Kyle, the man we expected to welcome into our family, means nothing to you? You can just ignore the difficulties he's facing?"

Sadie rested her forehead in her palm. A magic wand could wave all her troubles away. Too bad real life didn't offer fantasy solutions. No one moved forward without blood, sweat, and tears. But where would she begin? Her mistakes had obscured her direction. She felt like a rudderless ship adrift on an endless sea.

Closing her eyes, Sadie brushed teardrops from her cheeks. "Mother, you don't understand."

"More than you can imagine my dear." She paused. "I admit life was difficult while your father was alive. For too many years, his illness handicapped the entire household. Nevertheless, we raised our children using godly values. Principles I'd hoped would follow you throughout your life."

Her mother's appeal fell on deaf ears. Reason came too late. Values? Sadie had surrendered those beliefs to the unpredictable man who could arrive any moment. Somehow Lincoln had worn down her defenses from the moment she met him. His mercurial personality had kept her off balance from the start. First, he'd downplayed her views, and then he stole her innocence, until finally her conscience hung in the balance.

Wavering, Sadie stared off into space, lowering her voice to a whisper. "No promises, but let me think about it, okay?"

"What more can I ask than for you to do the right thing? I love you, honey. We'll talk later."

Saying goodbye, Sadie made her way to the alcove she used as a bedroom. Her gaze went straight to the high school senior picture she'd once cherished. The one that showed a bright-eyed young adult bent on living out her dreams. The photographer had captured a smiling face that exuded hope for a happy future. The ecstatic senior had been on top of the world. About to embark on a new life, knowing the man she loved adored her in return.

Sadie sat on the floor, studying the photo. Her anticipation rose each time she recalled her life before college. Could it be possible? Might there be a second chance with her childhood sweetheart?

Remorse replaced her anger. Teardrops plopped over her neck and chest. In one regretful conversation two years ago, her relationship with Kyle had ended. Slowly, she shook her head at the self-created havoc. Her foolish decisions had destroyed the relationship with the man she'd never stopped loving.

Since then, multiple bad choices had taken her life in a different direction. But the obsession with Lincoln Miller increased in fervor. All Sadie knew was that she had to marry the man who'd single-handedly wrecked her life.

Her college graduation had offered a chance to walk away from the relationship that should've never begun. Instead of saying goodbye to Burgundy, Missouri, Sadie stayed on. She was determined to make a life for herself until Lincoln finished his senior year at the university. After that, who knew where a pro-football career might take them? Unable to find a job in her chosen profession, she was waiting tables at three restaurants to pay the bills.

But last June, Sadie had invited her mother and eighteen-year-old sister for a two-week visit. She'd had big plans for their arrival, revamping the space she rented from the Sloanes into a cozy home with a cottage feel. And after accepting the invitation, the duo drove three hundred fifty miles for a two-week visit.

Sadie had ticked off the hours until their arrival, happy for the first time in two years. But three days into the visit, they repacked their bags and left the following morning. And all because Lincoln's boorish behavior had finally pushed them beyond endurance.

At first, the surprised Sadie had been happy when he showed up to meet her family. However, ten minutes after arriving he'd revealed the real purpose for coming. Lincoln wanted her completely separated from everyone who loved her. He behaved horribly, sowing discord while smilingly shaking hands. He casually insulted her mother and sister whenever the opportunity rose.

So, Sadie had suggested touring the state to enjoy her family alone. But those plans ended once Lincoln invited himself along on the trip. In three days flat, he'd ruined the relationships she'd hope to rebuild, plus tarnished his reputation in her mother's and sister's eyes.

Although they had left her apartment in a rush, her mother and sister's spring vacation hadn't been an entire bust. After bailing out on Sadie, they took the scenic view home, spending eight days touring Missouri before driving back to Shiatown, Oklahoma.

Sadie remembered her sister's outburst as her mother climbed into the car to leave. Sadie had asked her why they were running out on her so quickly.

"No one's running out on you, Sadie," she said, frowning at her. "Trying to like your boyfriend is exhausting. You chose that piece of filth over Kyle; we didn't."

Sadie's spirit died as she observed the tears in her sister's eyes.

The younger woman grimaced in disgust. "How can you let him touch you?" Rolling her eyes, she stomped to the car, then spun around at the door. "Keep him," she whispered, "but don't inflict him on your family." And then, as if they'd just ended a pleasant discussion, her sister entered the car, swiveled in the passenger's seat, and waved goodbye.

Standing at the curb, Sadie had cried openly. Another lifeline had driven off, leaving her with Lincoln. Her family had brought the only happiness she'd experienced since breaking up with Kyle, and then they deserted her three days later. She was alone again, and it was her fault.

After her family drove off, Sadie saw less of Lincoln than ever before. His usual once-a-week stopover dwindled to the occasional Wednesday evening. Isolated from family and friends who had all stopped calling by now, Sadie depended on Lincoln's company more than ever.

Today, reliving the past depleted her energy. Sadie was already anxious before the conversation with her mother had begun, Jeanette's phone call had unsettled her even more. She walked to the bathroom and took a long look at herself in the vanity mirror, trying to bolster her flagging courage.

Moaning, Sadie tilted her head from side to side. Her sleepless nights had become quite noticeable in bright lighting. Troubled, dark-brown eyes, surrounded by blemish-free toffee skin, stared back at her. What did it matter anyway? Looking her best didn't count anymore. At least not to the man who was late showing up. Nowadays when he paid a rare visit, his gaze flickered across the room instead of centering on her.

Ever since she'd broken up with Kyle, she'd tried convincing herself that she was loved and appreciated. A persistent question hammered her mind day and night: Why had Lincoln stopped even pretending to care? The last time she saw him, her wonder man had smiled into her eyes, and then disappeared for three weeks.

While scouring the city, Sadie had realized he'd covered his tracks because no one knew his whereabouts. In fact, most people she'd contacted denied having seen him around at all. Refusing to search for Lincoln anywhere on campus, exploring off-campus hangouts had turned up nothing. Even his running buddy claimed that he hadn't seen Lincoln in weeks.

When things went wrong, the word lunatic surged through her mind as usual. Her hands trembled as she rested her face in her palms. An intense fear of hearing that word flung at herself always paralyzed Sadie. The fact that no one in her hometown had ever hurled that accusation at her father, at least not that Sadie heard, didn't matter. Young ears often heard words no one spoke out loud. *Sadie Cummings's father is a crazy man, and maybe his daughter is crazy too.*

Oh, Lincoln, please cooperate with me just this once.

She sank to her knees in front of the vanity cabinet. Could two years of servitude end with her prayers unanswered? Had she forfeited the man she loved only to lose the man she left him for as well?

Standing, her gaze darted around the room. She refused to give up. There must be a reasonable explanation for his three-week absence. At least one that she could live with.

Resting her chin on her chest, she considered her options. There was no easy way out of the mess she'd created. Following her heart meant facing Kyle, a man who might hate her. Anyway, her ex-fiancé had left Shiatown for California, moving himself light-years away from past burdens. Available females had flocked around Kyle since his thirteenth birthday. How much more would they swarm the man as he continued to live out his dreams?

God, I won't be able to rise above a rejection from him.

Mind made up, she took a deep breath. Call Kyle? The disgust in his eyes the last time she saw him still haunted her dreams at night. And Miss Sarah, the woman she'd always considered a second mother, must loathe her too. Gasping for breath, Sadie wiped a warm towel across her face. How could she contact the woman she'd ignored since breaking up with her son? It would be much better to express her regrets through a floral arrangement sent to their home.

She stared unblinkingly into space. Unless her suspicions concerning Lincoln were confirmed, she would forgive and forget as usual. How could she give him up? Too much had been lost. Her whole way of life had changed since their first introduction. No other viable avenue existed since she'd burned her bridges behind her.

Staring at her reflection, Sadie frowned at the shadows beneath her eyes. There must be a way to keep Lincoln. She snapped the lid shut on her makeup kit and squeezed her eyelids together. Why delude herself? Somehow, the man she lived for was slipping farther away.

But how do I fix a relationship I simply want to end?

She jumped when the doorbell rang. Should she ignore the person or shoo them away before Lincoln arrived? Walking slowly to the door, she peeked through the blinds.

"Lincoln?" Why hadn't he used the spare key he'd talked her into giving him?

Sadie took a deep breath. Mumbling to herself, "I won't be a pushover," she swung open the door and slammed into a brick wall of resistance from Lincoln.

You can buy *A Living Hope* from your favorite retailer.

More information: ecjacksonauthor.wordpress.com/books/a-living-hope/

About the Author

E. C. Jackson began her writing career with the full-length play *Pajama Party*. For three and a half years she published the *Confidence in Life* newsletter for Alpha Production Ministries, in addition to writing tracts and devotionals. Teaching a women's Bible study at her church for eleven years led naturally to her current endeavor of writing inspirational romance novels and teen and young adult fiction. Her mission: spiritual maturity in the body of Christ through fiction.

Made in the USA
Columbia, SC
17 December 2023

28797280R00163